EMERALD STAR

www.**randomhousechildrens**.co.uk

Jacqueline Wilson

EMERALD STAR

ILLUSTRATED BY NICK SHARRATT

Hetty's search for a happy ending

DOUBLEDAY

EMERALD STAR
A CORGI YEARLING BOOK 978 0 857 53105 6
TRADE PAPERBACK 978 0 857 53106 3

Published in Great Britain by Doubleday,
an imprint of Random House Children's Publishers UK
A Random House Group Company

This edition published 2012

1 3 5 7 9 10 8 6 4 2

Text copyright © Jacqueline Wilson, 2012
Illustrations copyright © Nick Sharratt, 2012

MIX
Paper from
responsible sources
C016897

Set in Century Schoolbook by Falcon Oast Graphic Art Ltd.

Random House Children's Publishers UK,
61–63 Uxbridge Road, London W5 5SA

www.**randomhousechildrens**.co.uk
www.**totallyrandombooks**.co.uk
www.**randomhouse**.co.uk

Addresses for companies within The Random House Group Limited can be found
at: www.randomhouse.co.uk/offices.htm

THE RANDOM HOUSE GROUP Limited Reg. No. 954009

A CIP catalogue record for this book is available from the British Library.

Printed and bound in Great Britain by Clays Ltd, Bungay, Suffolk.

For Naomi

*With many thanks
and lots of love.*

1

'What are you doing here, child? This is no place for a little lass like you. Come on, tell me your name.'

I drew myself up as tall as I could, standing on tiptoe in my clumpy boots.

'I'm not a child,' I said haughtily, though I knew I was so small and slight I did not look anywhere near fourteen. 'My name is . . .' But then I hesitated foolishly.

My name is Hetty Feather, but I had never felt it was my *real* name. It was a comical name chosen at random when Mama handed me to the matron at the Foundling Hospital when I was only a few days old. I had been christened Hetty Feather in the hospital chapel and people had been calling me that name in irritation and anger ever since. I was not a placid child and found it hard to stick to the rigid rules and regulations of the hospital. My hot temper and wild spirit made me stand out from all the other foundlings as clearly as my bright red hair.

I was plain, the smallest and slightest in my year, and cursed with my carrot hair – but I did have bright blue eyes, my one good feature. I fancied my mama might have called me Sapphire if she'd been able to keep me. When at last I found her, I discovered she really had wondered about naming me her little Sapphire.

I tried to call myself Sapphire Battersea when I left the hospital to go into service, proudly adopting Mama's distinctive surname. But they laughed at me in my new position and said Sapphire wasn't a servant's name. I did not *want* to be a servant. When I was dismissed in disgrace, I ran away to Mama, only to discover the dreadful truth – that she was dying of consumption. I had to earn my living all that sad summer by the sea, when I visited her daily. I could not find any respectable work at all so I chose a disreputable job instead. I fashioned my beautiful green velvet Sunday best dress into a mermaid costume and joined Mr Clarendon's Seaside Curiosities as a star attraction. I was Emerald the Amazing Pocket-Sized Mermaid. My new dear friend, Freda the Female Giant, called me Emerald every day.

'*Are you deaf or simple? What is your name?*' the innkeeper repeated.

I did not want to call myself Hetty Feather. I did not care for the name – and the governors at the

Foundling Hospital might well be trying to track me down. I longed to say that my name was Sapphire Battersea, but I had to be wary in this new strange village. This was where my dear mother had been brought up. Folk might recognize the name and run to tell my father. I wanted to seek him out myself and break my news gently.

The innkeeper tossed his head and turned to walk away.

'I am Emerald,' I blurted out.

The old men leaning on the sticky bar sniggered into their foaming pints.

'Emerald?' the innkeeper repeated. 'What sort of a name is that?'

'A fine distinctive name,' I said.

'What about a surname then?'

'I am Emerald ... Star,' I announced, giving birth to my new self right that moment.

'Emerald Star!' said the innkeeper.

This time the old men laughed openly.

'She's cracked in the head!' he said to them, and they guffawed and drank and spat contemptuously in the sawdust at their feet.

'I'll thank you not to mock,' I said. 'Emerald Star is my stage name. I am very well known in the south. In fact people pay to come and see me.'

'What do you do then, Emerald Star?' the innkeeper asked, an unpleasant tone to his voice.

'I perform upon the stage,' I said.

I wasn't exactly lying. When I exhibited myself as Emerald the Amazing Pocket-Sized Mermaid, it was upon a sturdy plinth, so that people did not have to bend down to see me reclining there, twitching my green velvet tail on a little pile of sand.

The word 'stage' made the men's heads rock. They set down their pints and stared at me as if I were about to perform then and there. Some looked smugly disapproving.

'So she's one of they actresses,' said one, and tutted with his two teeth.

'Are you a turn at the music hall then, lass?' asked another with interest. 'I go regular on a Saturday night over at Brackenly. I've seen them all – Simon Spangles, little Dolly Daydream, Georgie and His Talking Doll, the Romulus Brothers, Lily Lark . . . Great acts, all of them. But I've never seen you.'

'I'm not a travelling player. I perform on the *London* stage,' I insisted, telling a terrible lie.

'You don't look like one of them theatricals, all painted faces and high-pitched voices,' said the innkeeper.

'More's the pity,' said one of the old men. 'What sort of a costume's *that*?' He pointed to my drab grey dress. 'You're nothing but a little maid, spinning us all fairy stories. I don't believe a word of it.'

'Believe what you want. I don't care at all. My

business is not with you.' I turned to the innkeeper. 'My business is with *you*, sir.'

'She wants her pint of porter!' said the old man, chuckling.

'I simply want a bite to eat and a room for the night,' I said. 'I have adequate funds.' I patted my full pocket. 'And you advertise both on the sign outside.'

It was the only sign I'd seen. I'd tramped the length and breadth of this bleak little Yorkshire village searching for rooms. It was a seaside of sorts, but it did not seem to have hotels and hostelries. Beautiful Bignor on the south coast had these aplenty, and every second house had lodgings. It had bathing machines along the beach, and pierrots and hokey-pokey men and all manner of amusements. This bleak village of Monksby had a small harbour and a stinking fish market and a few streets of mean dwellings. Now it was past ten o'clock, the only place with any light and life was this Fisherman's Inn.

I was desperately tired. I had been travelling all day, cooped up in the third-class railway carriage, my heart beating wildly at the thought of finding my father. I was not sure quite how I would manage this. I did not even know his last name. Mama had simply called him Bobbie. I had not liked to ask her all the hundreds of questions humming in my head because she found it so painful talking about her past.

'Give the child a room, Tobias, and stop persecuting the poor little thing,' said the woman behind the bar. She was big and tough, with a great crooked nose like a picture of a witch in a storybook. She looked very frightening – but she was nodding at me kindly. 'Look at her – she's swaying on her feet with tiredness, and all you men can do is turn her into a little guy. You come with me, dear.'

'Thank you, ma'am,' I said meekly.

'Who are you to issue invitations, Lizzie? Do you own this inn?' said Tobias.

'No, but I own a human heart, and this girl needs food and drink and a bed for the night,' she said, and beckoned me behind the bar.

I ducked under the wooden top and Lizzie led me through a door into a gloomy kitchen at the back.

'You're shivering, child. I'd light a fire but old Tobias won't admit summer's over now. Here, put this on.' She took her own grey woollen shawl and wrapped it tight around my shoulders. I had proudly held my own when Tobias and the old men were baiting me, but Lizzie's simple little act of kindness made the tears start trickling down my face.

'There now,' she said, giving me a pat. She sat me at the table and bustled around the kitchen. She took a saucepan from the sink and tried to scrape it out. 'He had a fish stew for his supper but he's cleared the pot. I'll have to scratch around for something cold for you.'

She found a loaf in a crock and cut me two thick slices of bread and a generous chunk of cheese. They were both a little stale but I ate them gratefully enough. Instead of a cup of tea she fetched me a pint of ale from the bar.

'There now, this will warm you up,' she said.

I did not care for the taste at all, but I drank a few sips obediently. When Lizzie saw I was leaving most of it, she downed it herself, and wiped the froth off her lips appreciatively.

'Now, I'll show you the privy. I'm afraid it's not very nice – you know what men are like, and you sound like a London lass, used to fancy ways,' she said, lighting a candle and leading me by the hand.

The privy was unspeakably disgusting. Perhaps it was as well I couldn't see it properly in the dark. Still, I had no choice but to use it and then wash my hands thoroughly at the outside pump. Lizzie led me back inside and up the stairs. I was shivering now, and so tired I could barely carry my small suitcase.

'Let me give you a hand with that,' said Lizzie, taking it from me. 'Is this all your worldly belongings? You haven't run away, have you?'

'Not exactly. I – I am running *to* someone,' I said.

'Not a sweetheart, I hope?' said Lizzie. 'Never trust a man – a shilling's your best friend.'

'No, he's family, not a sweetheart,' I whispered.

'That's better. Though how come you're looking for family round here? You don't come from these parts, do you?'

'I think my mother did,' I said. I looked hard at Lizzie, trying to gauge her age. The lines on her face were set hard and deep and she looked many years older than my dear little mama – though in the last few desperate months of her life *she* had aged visibly too.

'She was called Ida,' I said, clutching hold of Lizzie, suddenly desperate, and deciding I could trust her. 'Ida Battersea.'

I willed Lizzie's face to soften, to say, *Oh my goodness, Ida Battersea! She was my dear friend.*

But she shook her head. 'Can't say I've ever heard of her, dear. Anyway, let's find you a room. Tobias has three or four guest rooms up here, though they're seldom in use. We'll find you the best one, eh?'

The rooms all looked the same to me – bare and basic, with a stripped narrow bed and striped ticking mattress, a washstand and a cupboard, and a rag rug on the cold lino. There were stern moral pictures on all the walls. Lizzie held the candle up to a representation of a woman in the gutter guzzling from a bottle and clutching a crying baby, while an uncouth man carrying a pint pot beat his poor dog in the background. It was clearly preaching against the demon drink – a strange choice for rooms in a public house.

'It's not exactly cosy up here, is it?' said Lizzie. 'Still, I promise you it's clean. I have a sweep and scrub every week or so, for Matty's sake. She was Tobias's wife and my dear friend – and now I try to keep the place decent for her. I trot up to the churchyard every Sunday, and when all the folk have gone away, their ears still ringing with the sermon, I go and sit by Matty and we have a little chat just like we did when she was alive.' She shot me a look, as if daring me to laugh. 'I know it sounds daft like.'

'It doesn't sound daft at all, it sounds lovely,' I said. 'I talk to Mama in my head and she talks back to me. Well, perhaps it's only my fancy, but it seems as if she does. She told me to come here, Lizzie.'

'Well, that's extraordinary, because this is a harsh, hard village without much comfort even for those born and bred here. Still, maybe she has her reasons. Now, I'll get you clean linen from the press and settle you down for the night.'

We made up the bed together, Lizzie nodding with approval when she saw me tucking the sheets in with precision. Years of hospital training had stood me in good stead in some ways.

'I'll come in early tomorrow and make sure you get a proper breakfast,' said Lizzie. 'Goodnight . . .

Emerald?' She gave a little snort. 'Though that's never your real name!'

'It is now,' I said.

Lizzie left me with the candle. She insisted on leaving her shawl with me too, and I certainly needed it. It was only early autumn but the north wind straight off the sea rattled the windows and I had only the thinnest of blankets. I wound the shawl tightly around me and laid out all my precious possessions on the bed: my little books of fairy tales, Mama's brush and comb and violet vase, a fairground dog, and the fat manuscript in which I'd recounted all my adventures so far. I turned the page, and put the date, *Friday September 29th 1891*, at the top of the page.

My name is Emerald Star, I wrote, in my best hospital-taught copperplate. *I am here in Monksby!!!* But in spite of the three exclamation marks I could not feel excited. Doubt made my heart thump, my stomach churn, and had me fidgeting from one side to the other in that narrow bed long after I had blown out the candle. Had Mama *really* said Monksby? Was it perhaps Monksford . . . Monkslawn . . . Monkton?

When we curled up together during those sweet stolen nights at the hospital, we had whispered the stories of our missing years. I had told Mama about the cottage in the country that had been my home

10

till I was five. I had told her about my dear foster brother Jem, though I found it painful talking about him then, because I thought he had forgotten me.

Mama wasn't so interested in any of my foster siblings but she asked endless questions about my foster mother Peg. I tried to give a truthful picture of that warm, work-worn woman but it was difficult remembering details. I just had an impression of her strong arms cuddling me close or giving me a royal paddling when I had been disobedient or overly fanciful. She frequently said I was more trouble than all her other children put together, but I knew she loved me dearly all the same. Mama could not see it that way when I told her tales of Peg. She sucked in her breath when I said I'd been paddled and became very agitated.

'How could any woman hit a tiny child, especially one as small and sensitive as you, Hetty,' she said fiercely, holding me close and rocking me as if the paddling had only just occurred. Poor Peg could do no right in her eyes. She asked what she'd given me to eat and poured scorn on my slices of bread and dripping.

'What sort of nourishment is there in chunks of bread and pig fat?' she said. 'No wonder you were such a little scrap of a girl with no flesh on your bones. And she was getting paid for your keep too! Didn't she ever give you any meat?'

'We had rabbit stew,' I said, licking my lips at the memory, but this didn't impress Mama either.

'Didn't she ever give you a decent plate of roast beef, or a proper chop or cutlet?'

This was unfair, because she knew they were simple country people and couldn't afford such splendid meals. Mama was totally unreasonable where I was concerned. She felt Peg had been a pretty poor mother to me – and frequently wept because she had lost the chance of mothering me herself for ten long years.

At first I had asked her many questions about her own past, but right from the start I could see she found it troubling to talk about.

She told me my father was called Bobbie and had bright red hair just like me and she'd loved him with all her heart – but he had left her to go to sea. I didn't know if he had left her because she was going to have his child, or whether he'd never known about me. It seemed cruel to question her because her voice always shook and her blue eyes filled with tears.

'He was a fine man, your father. All the girls in the village were after him, but he picked *me*,' Mama said proudly.

I wasn't so sure a truly fine man would get a young girl into trouble and then abandon her. Perhaps I wouldn't like this father at all if I ever found him – but I was sure Mama wanted us to meet.

'Go and find your father now!' she'd said to me, her dear voice clear in my head even though she had been dead for weeks.

I had no address – I didn't even have his last name – but I knew he'd grown up in the same village as Mama. She'd said it was called Monksby – or some such name. I hadn't quizzed her because her tears spilled again when she talked of it. I knew her mother and father had turned her out when they discovered she was having a baby – they could not stand the shame. I cried too at the thought of poor Mama, destitute and sick, making the long journey to London to leave me at the Foundling Hospital.

I fancied I heard her crying now, curled up beside me in the cold bed.

'I'm here, Mama,' I said, reaching out across the bare sheet and clasping thin air. 'You mustn't cry. I will be all right. I will find my father and I will love him almost as much as I love you, and we will live happily ever after – as happily as I can ever be without you.'

I squeezed tight, imagining the pressure of Mama's thin fingers squeezing back, and I fell asleep, our hands still clasped.

2

I woke early and lay tensely in the strange little room, not quite knowing what to do. I listened hard but could hear no bustling in the building. I wondered what time Lizzie started. I did not want to go downstairs without her and face surly Tobias alone.

There did not seem to be any maid attached to this place. No one brought me any fresh hot water, so I washed quickly in the cold suds from last night and pulled on my clothes. My dress was crumpled from the journey, the little white collar stained with smuts from the train. I looked a sorry sight to be meeting my father – if, of course, I could track him down.

I brushed my hair vigorously and tied it up in as neat a topknot as I could manage, pinning it into place. It seemed to have a will of its own and was forever trying to shake itself loose. Already little strands were curling down and gathering about my ears.

You have your father's hair, Mama whispered to me.

Perhaps it was going to be simple. I just had to take a quick turn about the village, see a red-haired man, and approach him. But then what? How was I to announce myself? *Hello, dear Father, I am your long-lost daughter. I am Hetty*. No, Sapphire. Emerald? Perhaps I wouldn't need to say a word. He would just catch a glimpse of me, stop short – and then open his arms. I would go running and he would hug me close, his red head bent to mine, holding me as if he could never bear to let me go.

I pictured it so vividly I had to wipe my eyes, overcome with emotion. Then I stepped out of my room and trod cautiously along the landing. Perhaps Tobias was snoring behind one of those closed doors? I hurried past and down the wooden staircase, carrying my clumpy boots in my hand so as not to waken him.

It was dark and still downstairs, the blinds drawn. I breathed shallowly, disliking the rich smell of beer and the stale reek of smoke. I picked my skirts up as I wandered around. I'd seen some of the old men spitting into the sawdust and was mindful of my hem. I went into the kitchen and found it empty. I peeped into the cupboard but it was bare, like Old Mother Hubbard's. I'd eaten the last of the bread and cheese. There was a jar of pickles, a tin of treacle, and pepper and salt – they would make a very sour breakfast. Still, at least I could make myself some tea, if I could get the ancient range working.

I went out to the privy – an even worse experience in daylight – and then started battling with the range. It was a complicated brute of a machine, but similar to the one in Mr Buchanan's kitchen, where I'd worked as a maid. Mrs Briskett the cook had taught me to master it – and with a little huff and puff I managed this one too. As the kettle slowly boiled, out of habit I seized a cloth and wiped down the greasy surfaces, and then took a broom and swept the floor.

I heard footsteps outside, and then Lizzie came in, her cheeks red from the wind, a basket hanging from her arm.

'My, my, you're up early!' She cast an eye around the room. 'And you might have spun Tobias a tale of being a theatrical, but it seems to me you've had a maid's training, judging by the state of this room. Thank you, dear. Now, let's get you breakfast – and I'll share some with you.'

'It's very kind of you, but I can't find anything to eat in the cupboard,' I said.

17

'See what I've brought in the basket!' said Lizzie, delving into it cheerfully. She unwrapped two strange orange fish and set them sizzling in the pan.

'What are they?' I asked.

She stared at me in surprise. 'Great Heavens, girl, haven't you ever tasted kippers? My family's smoked herrings for three generations. My, you're in for a treat. And I've a freshly baked loaf, a crock of best butter, a pot of my own raspberry jam, and a jug of full-cream milk.'

'You're giving me a breakfast fit for a queen!' I said.

'Well, you look as if you need feeding up. Look at you, thin as a pin!' said Lizzie, picking up my arm and circling my wrist with her large hand. 'You're not ill, are you, child?'

'No, I am naturally thin,' I said. The frying kippers were starting to smell wonderful. 'You will see I have an excellent appetite!'

'You need one. You're light as a little feather,' said Lizzie.

I gave a start, but it was clear she'd hit on my name inadvertently. I made the pot of tea, Lizzie buttered the bread, and we ate our kippers.

'They are delicious!' I said, taking a huge mouthful to show Lizzie that my appetite was healthy.

'Careful now! Eat cautiously, or you'll munch on

a mouthful of bones.' She shook her head at me in fond exasperation. 'Fancy you never trying a kipper till now. What did you have for Sunday breakfast at home?'

'Mostly porridge,' I said, truthfully enough. Then I thought of my fastidious employer Mr Buchanan, and his silver tureens of eggs and sausages and bacon. I could always count on scoffing a full plateful of his leavings. 'But sometimes a grand fry-up, if it was available.'

'Your mother never tried you with kippers even though she came from these parts?'

I swallowed. 'Mama and I could not always be together,' I said delicately.

'And what about your pa?' said Lizzie, wiping up kipper juice with a crust of bread.

I hesitated again. 'My father was away a lot,' I said. I took a deep breath. 'He came from these parts too, but he went away to sea.'

'Did he?' said Lizzie. 'My grandpa was away at sea when he was a lad, on the whaling ships. Most of our menfolk used to be whalers. My grandpa told me the stink was so bad when the ships came back you couldn't go near the harbour – running in blood and guts and blubber, it was. Sorry, dear.' She saw I'd stopped eating. 'I didn't mean to put you off your breakfast.'

19

'Perhaps – perhaps my father was a whaler too?' I said.

'No, no, there's no whaling nowadays, more's the pity. There's no steady job for any of the men round here. They fish with the tide and clutter up their houses during the day and drink themselves stupid here at the Fisherman's and are no real use to man nor beast – especially their womenfolk.'

'Do you have a husband, Lizzie?'

'More's the pity. I married him when I was a little lass not much older than yourself. Well, I was never as little as you, I was always a big strong girl even in my teens – but not strong enough. Before six months were gone he was beating me black and blue – for naught, just because he was in the mood. I should have left him then and there, but I was weak and there was already a baby on the way, so what could I do? If I ran away, folk would think I was having a child out of wedlock and shun me.'

I swallowed. 'I'm sure it's not always the woman's fault if she has a baby out of wedlock,' I said.

'I know that, dearie, but there's the shame of it all the same,' she said. 'And what would I have done once the child was born? How could I get work with a babbie at my breast?'

'Perhaps – perhaps you would have given the

baby to a foundling hospital?' I said, my voice wobbling.

'I couldn't have borne being separated from my firstborn,' said Lizzie, sipping her tea and sighing. 'I don't see how any woman could ever give away her own child.'

'Perhaps you'd have had no choice,' I said fiercely.

Lizzie looked at me. 'All these perhapses! Is this what happened to you, little Missy Emerald Star?'

I felt myself flushing as red as my hair. 'Perhaps it did – but I know my mama loved me with all her heart and soul,' I said, my eyes filling with tears.

'Oh dear, don't start crying now. I didn't mean to cause offence. Come on, finish up your kipper, don't let it go cold. Of course your mother loved you. Who am I to judge any different? And I might as well have given my Henry away, and Stewart and Andy, for all the good they do me now. They're all rough lads, the spit of their father, and they lead me a merry dance. I wash and clean and cook and care for them all, with never a word of thanks, and then I come here to earn an honest penny and I never get thanked for that either. That's men for you – especially Monksby men.'

I stared at Lizzie, perplexed. I had had little experience of family life. My foster parents had not been the sort of couple for open affection, but they had seemed very cosily settled together. During those long lonely years growing up in the Foundling Hospital I had thought all families living together were equally happy. When my dear friend Polly and I played picturing games, our favourite fantasy was playing Mothers and Fathers. We took turns being the parents and breathed life into the hospital bolsters so that they became our babies. We embellished our games with quaint dialogue: 'How are you today, dear Mother?' 'I am very well, dear Father. Pray come and kiss our pretty baby' – the very words bringing tears of longing to our eyes.

The turbulent experiences of the past six months had done nothing to alter my expectations of family bliss. Mr and Mrs Greenwood at Bignor had treated each other with great kindness and respect and loved their three children dearly. I felt a little pang remembering, because I had longed to be part of their family too. Most of all I'd wanted to be a family with Mama. Now that she had been so cruelly taken from me I felt my only hope was to try and find my father. I had pictured a strong, loving man welcoming me with outstretched arms and cherishing me for the rest of my life.

But now Lizzie was painting a far bleaker

picture. I saw my father turning from me with harsh words, I saw him reeling drunkenly, I saw him striking me . . .

I drooped over my kipper, unable to eat another mouthful. 'Are all Monksby men really like that?' I whispered.

As if on cue, Tobias came scuffling into the kitchen in his undervest and trousers, scratching himself and yawning. 'What's that smell? Have you been giving this girl kippers, Lizzie?'

'Yes, I have. The poor little mite would have gone hungry, left to your tender mercies,' she said. 'Go and stick your head under the pump, Tobias – you look a dreadful sight. I'll stick a kipper in the pan for you.'

'Who are you to order me about, Lizzie Hughes? I'm your gaffer, girl,' said Tobias, giving her a little push as he shuffled past.

'You're free to give me notice any time you want. You know you'll never get another woman to come and work for a surly, smelly old tyke like you,' said Lizzie with spirit.

Tobias swore at her but their dispute seemed reasonably amicable all the same. When he came back, marginally more kempt, Lizzie served him his kipper and he ate it with relish.

'You'd better start coming in this early every day,

Lizzie. I'm always partial to a cooked breakfast,' he said, smacking his lips. Then he turned to me. 'Right, lass. Are you staying on here or going on your way?'

'I – I'm not sure,' I said.

'Well, make up your mind – no shilly-shallying,' said Tobias.

'Could I settle up now but maybe leave my suitcase here for the day? And then stay another night if – if I can't finish my business today?' I asked.

'Very well. So that's half a crown, little miss,' said Tobias, holding out his hand.

'It says one shilling and sixpence on your board outside,' I said indignantly. 'I can't pay that much!'

'You showed me a whole purseful of money last night. I'm the landlord and I can charge what I like, whatever it says on that board. Half a crown, if you please!' said Tobias.

'You can't charge the poor girl half a crown! How can you possibly justify that?' exclaimed Lizzie.

'Simple! It's one and six for her bed, sixpence for a very fine breakfast, and another tanner for the storage of her goods,' said Tobias.

'*I* provided her breakfast – and I'll look after her suitcase,' said Lizzie. She reached for my purse and counted out a shilling and six pennies. 'There,

24

you're all paid up now,' she said, slamming the coins down in front of Tobias.

He swore again but seemed to accept the deal.

Lizzie followed me upstairs. 'Don't let that mean old skinflint upset you, dear,' she said. 'So what are you going to do today? Are you seriously looking for kinfolk? What was your mama's name again?'

'Ida Battersea.'

'There's no Battersea that I know of in these parts,' said Lizzie. 'But I suppose you could try over in Sandfleet or Rushmore – I don't know all the folk there. But you'll be tramping miles if you go there. Are you sure you're up to it?'

I stamped my feet. 'I have stout boots,' I said.

'And you're clearly not used to our fresh winds,' said Lizzie. 'You'd better keep my shawl for the day.'

'I couldn't possibly!'

'Go on, tie it tight about you. You need something to keep you warm. I'll get it back from you when you collect your case,' said Lizzie.

'Why are you being so very kind to me?' I asked, near tears.

'It's nothing, dearie. I'd happily swap a little lass like you for my great big lummoxing lads.'

I held that thought in my head when I set out to wander the village once more. Perhaps my father still ached for his long-lost daughter.

I had hoped there might be more to the village than I'd seen last night. I'd arrived after dark, exhausted after the long express train ride up north, and then the little local train that steamed up and down hills and set all its passengers shoogling in their seats. But no, even in daylight I could only find three or four uneven little cobbled lanes winding up and down the cliffside, with houses stuck on in clumps here and there, like barnacles.

I looked in vain for a post office where I might enquire. There were very few shops – a butcher's, a bakehouse, and a general provisions store. This latter was open, so I peeped inside timidly. A gaunt old woman in a bonnet sat knitting behind the counter. She gave a little start when she saw me, and her shaky hands dropped a few stitches.

'Oh, I'm sorry, I didn't mean to startle you, ma'am,' I said. Surely she *expected* customers to walk into her shop?

She sighed irritably, peering at her knitting. 'You're a stranger in these parts,' she said.

'Yes, ma'am.'

'Are you visiting?'

'Well . . . possibly. My mama lived here when she was a girl. Ida Battersea – did you know her?'

'There's no Battersea here,' she said, picking up stitches.

I decided to be bolder. 'And – and I'm looking for a gentleman. His name is Bobbie,' I said nervously.

'Bobbie what?'

'Well, I'm not sure. His Christian name was Robert. *Are* there any Roberts in this village? He may have gone away across the sea.'

'I know many a Robert. There's Bobbie Brown and Robbie Wright and old Robert Pegley and young Bob Pemberton and Bobbie Waters and Bobbie Donkeyman. Which one are you chasing?' she asked.

I hesitated helplessly. 'I'm not quite sure,' I said.

'Here's a girl wants a man by the name of Robert, and when I give her a choice of six she's still not satisfied,' said the old woman, her head bent over her needles. There was no one else in the shop so presumably she was addressing her knitting.

'Thank you for your help. I presume they all live locally? I – I shall do my best to seek them out,' I said.

'Well, off with you then, unless you'd care to make a purchase,' she said.

Lizzie's kipper was warm in my stomach but it had left an insistently fishy taste in my mouth. If one of these Roberts was my father and he swept me up in his arms in a paternal passion, I didn't want to breathe fish in his face.

'Might I have a quarter of peppermint balls?' I asked, fumbling in my purse.

The old crone took for ever setting down her knitting, getting to her feet, shuffling over to the shelf of sweetie jars, prising off the lid, shaking peppermints onto the scales ounce by ounce, tipping them into a little paper bag, and spinning it up and over so the corners were fastened. She was breathing heavily by the time she held her hand out for money. I gave her a penny and she put it into a cash drawer and then sat back down, exhausted.

She knuckled her rheumy old eyes and peered at me intently. 'Stand over by the door,' she said. 'I want to take a look at you in the daylight.'

I moved over to the door. She leaned forward on her counter, her eyes narrowed. 'You're a London lassie – but that shawl's knitted to a local pattern,' she said.

'Oh! Yes, it's Lizzie's, from the Fisherman's Inn,' I said.

'You stole it, you brazen hussy?'

'No, she lent it to me,' I said indignantly. 'She's been very kind to me – unlike *some* people. Don't you call me a brazen hussy, you silly old woman.'

'Oh, you've a sharp tongue in your head and a fiery nature, judging by your hair.' The old woman sucked her few remaining teeth. 'Tainted colour. Mmm! I reckon it's Bobbie Waters you're after, missy.'

I ran up to her. 'Do you really think so? Do I – do I look like him at all?' I asked eagerly, throwing caution to the wind.

'I'm just a silly old woman, so how would *I* know?' she said triumphantly, and bent her head over her knitting.

'Where would I find him?' I asked. 'Which house does he live in?'

She shrugged, stitching away.

'Oh please tell me – *please*,' I begged. 'I have to see him as soon as possible!'

She looked up at me, her eyes narrowed. 'If you really want to see him . . .'

'Yes? *Yes?*'

'Then go through the village, as far east as you can go—'

'East. Yes. And then?'

'And then gaze ahead and you'll be looking straight at him,' she said, and started cackling with laughter.

I plied her with further questions, but she rocked back and forth, still laughing, refusing to say another word. Then a couple of raggedy barefoot boys came scampering into her shop for two ounces of sherbet and I shut my mouth abruptly. I hadn't realized I'd be found out so quickly, and by a half-witted old woman too. I didn't want anyone else to work out whose red-haired child I might be before I had a chance to meet my father and tell him myself.

When I was outside the shop I unwound Lizzie's shawl from my chest and tied it tightly around my head instead, endeavouring to tuck in every wisp of hair. To my surprise and relief the women I saw in the narrow streets were mostly wearing their shawls tied about their heads in a similar fashion.

I was not sure whether I was walking eastwards or not, so I stopped one of the women and asked if she could kindly tell me which was east and which was west. She stared at me and then cupped her ear. I repeated my question.

'Aye, that's what I thought you said, lassie. And if I'd asked such a daft question not once but twice, I'd blush with shame. Are you simple, girl?'

'No, ma'am – and you're not the slightest bit civil. I'm a stranger in these parts. How do *I* know which way's east?' I said crossly.

'Well, follow that sharp little nose of yours. You'll soon find out,' she said, and hobbled on her way in her broken boots.

So I followed my nose. The street petered out. I saw the harbour wall, and a muddy beach with a few old boats in various states of decay mouldering on the sand. There were rocks where girls clambered with baskets, and a vast expanse of grey sea. I stepped onto the sand and gazed out to the faraway horizon.

3

What did the old shop woman mean? Where was my father? Mama had told me he'd run away to be a sailor. Was he still sailing now, far away in foreign climes? I remembered the old pink and yellow and green map in the classroom at the Foundling Hospital, and how I'd slid my finger around the edge of each land, imagining myself sailing the world. Perhaps Father was really living that dream. I saw him in sailor's navy, his face tanned deep brown, his body braced as his ship rode the big waves. Tropical seabirds flew over his head and marvellous dolphins frolicked in the wake as he sailed further and further away . . . away from me.

'Father!' I called into the wind, without quite meaning to. The girls on the rocks all stared at me, several giggling.

I felt a fool and tried looking round too, as if also wondering who had cried out. I walked up and down the beach for a few minutes, collecting shells in a desultory fashion. Then I spotted a strange grey stone with a coiled imprint and picked it up eagerly. I stared at it in my cupped hands. I was back in my classroom again, remembering the picture of fossils in the new set of science books donated by a rich governor. Our teacher had not taught from it. She considered it the work of the devil because it dealt with evolution, suggesting we were all descended from monkeys.

'Imagine! Do you want to think your great-great-grandmothers and -grandfathers had hideous furred faces and long tails?' she'd said.

None of us knew our great-great-grandparents. We had no knowledge of any relative whatsoever so could not take offence on their behalf. I did not mind the idea of simian ancestors, and pictured myself happily swinging through the trees and sharing their bananas. I wanted to read the science book if it contained such interesting, controversial ideas, particularly if it upset my teacher. I cordially hated her, especially as she'd once cruelly beaten my dear friend Polly. I sneaked into the classroom when we were meant to be outside taking the air and read eagerly, though the words were not as easy and inviting as a proper storybook. I learned about fossils – ancient small rocks with petrified little creatures trapped inside, turned to stone for ever like a spell in a fairy tale. I had pored over the illustration, tracing the whorls with my finger –

and here was a *real* fossil! I examined the stone carefully, turning it over and over in my hand. It really was a fossil, rare and wonderful. How much would it be worth? Perhaps I was holding a fortune in my hand?

One of the girls wandered towards me, dragging her pail. 'What's that you've got there?' she asked.

I put my hands behind my back, scared she might snatch my treasure away. I was still used to hospital ways. If you were ever lucky enough to be given a sweet by a gawping visitor you had to hide it straight away or one of the big girls would snatch it off you.

This girl was certainly bigger than me. She towered over me in fact, and she was sturdy too – but she was smiling at me in a friendly fashion.

'Go on, show us,' she said. 'Have you found a pretty shell?' She spoke to me kindly but as if I were about five years old.

'I have found something much more rare and valuable,' I said, with a proud nod of my head.

'Let's see, then.'

I reluctantly proffered my fossil. She stared at it.

'Oh . . . lovely,' she said. She looked as if she were trying not to laugh.

'You don't know what it is,' I said. 'It's thousands and thousands of years old. It might be worth a fortune.'

'It's a fossil,' said the girl matter-of-factly. 'It's not worth any kind of fortune, not that sort. Digger Jeffries in the gem shop might give you a halfpenny for it, but nothing more. You are funny.'

'No I'm not,' I said. 'I might start collecting fossils.' I looked in her bucket. 'So what are *you* collecting? Are they shells?'

'They're flithers,' she said.

'They're not pretty at all,' I said.

'Of course they're not pretty,' she said, giggling.

'So why are you collecting them?' I stared at them in disgust. I had seen cockles and whelks at Bignor. 'You don't eat them, do you?'

'They're bait, silly, for the fishermen. Don't you know *nothing*?' she said.

'I don't know these sorts of things,' I said. 'I'm a stranger here. I'm visiting from London.'

She stared at me, actually looking impressed. 'You come all the way from London town?' she said, as if it were Timbuktu.

'Yes, by myself, on two trains,' I said nonchalantly.

'My! I've never even been across the moors,' she said. 'What's London like, then? Have you ever met the old Queen?'

'I did once – well, nearly,' I said. 'On the day of her Golden Jubilee.'

'Did you see her palace? Folk say all the houses

36

in London are like palaces, built really big, with nine rooms, ten rooms, sometimes more,' she said.

'There were many more rooms than that in the place I grew up,' I said, truthfully enough.

'So what are you doing here then?' she asked.

'My mama came from this village. Did you ever hear of an Ida Battersea?' I asked eagerly – but the girl shook her head.

'I've never heard that name before,' she said.

'Then have you perhaps heard of Bobbie Waters?' I said.

She stared at me. 'Of course I have. We all know big Bobbie. What do you want with Bobbie Waters?'

I pulled Lizzie's shawl more firmly around my head. 'I – I just need to have a word with him. But I believe he's away on a sea voyage . . .'

'What? Oh yes, I'm with you. But he'll be back before noon,' she said.

'Really? Before noon *today*! You're sure?'

She looked at me queerly and then crossed herself. 'Please God, yes,' she said, and ran over to join her friends, prising more flithers from the rocks.

I couldn't believe the timeliness of my visit to Monksby. It seemed as if Fate itself had thrust a hand forward and propelled me like a chess piece into the right place at the right time. Of course, I did not know for sure that this Bobbie Waters was the right man. I only had that old shop woman's word for it. And it was so strange and depressing that not a soul in this small, tight-knit community remembered poor Mama. I felt her inside me, wound about my heart, and I could tell by the fierce beat that she was pleased I was back.

I peered out across the grey waves for the mast of a tall sailing ship. I stared until my eyes watered, but no vessel appeared on the horizon. I wandered up and down the beach, sand spreading in my boots at every step. There were no seaside amusements at all, not even a solitary bathing machine. A few very little boys were dashing in and out of the waves in their under-drawers – a couple were completely naked. They saw me watching, and jeered and gestured in a very rude and unfriendly fashion. I gestured back and stomped up the steeply sloping path to the clifftop. I had to sit on the tufty grass to recover, gasping for breath. It was windier than ever up there, and my eyes watered as I gazed over the sloping rooftops of the village.

It was a fine lookout spot. I wondered if Mama had ever sat up here with her Bobbie. Had she once clambered over the rocks and gathered flithers like the girls on the beach? They were all such stout, sturdy lasses. Mama was always so slight and slender. When she got ill she looked as if she could snap in two. My eyes were already watering, but now I shed a few real tears at the memory of Mama dying slowly of consumption during the summer. At least I had been able to pay for her to have a decent funeral, thanks to my dear friend Freda.

I decided to save again to pay for a beautiful carved headstone – no, a wonderful white marble angel to stand above her and keep her safe for ever.

There was a little church high up on the clifftop. I walked along to inspect the graves there, but I couldn't find any angels. There were just moss-covered old stones tipped to precarious angles by the fierce wind off the sea. I squinted at the names carved in the stone but I couldn't find any Batterseas.

I stepped inside the church and breathed in the quiet stillness, the dusty damp smell of old building, the fresh fragrance of flowers and candles and beeswax. There were rose petals scattered on the floor, curling and crushed. There must have been a wedding here recently.

I tiptoed up the aisle between the quaint pews, wondering if Mama had wished to be a bride here. How different our lives would have been if that wedding had taken place. I stood before the altar and wondered if I would ever marry. I'd rehearsed my wedding a hundred times over in the country meadows long ago, dressed up in a white sheet with daisies in my hair. In those days I was so sure I was going to marry Jem.

I felt a pang now as I remembered that tall figure in brown waiting for me the day I left the Foundling Hospital. He'd been the dearest person in all the world to me when I was a small girl. It seemed so sad that I'd stepped straight past without recognizing him when I was fourteen. I had written to him when I'd realized – and he had written back to me. I still had all his letters carefully folded and tied with ribbon, but when Mama became ill I had stopped writing. I couldn't think of Jem any more. I could only care for Mama.

I didn't write to my *other* sweetheart either – dear funny Bertie the butcher's boy, who had stepped out with me each week when I was in service at Mr Buchanan's. In some ways I'd grown even closer to him. I seemed to have lost touch with all the dearest people from my past. But I had to think of the future now.

I unlatched one of the boxed pews and knelt there, trembling. 'Please, please, please let me find my father,' I prayed. 'Let him be this Bobbie Waters. Make him realize I am his own true daughter, Ida's little girl. Have him welcome me with open arms and clasp me to his breast for ever. Oh *please* make this happen. If you do, I promise I will be a good obedient girl and know my place and never lose my temper ever again . . .' My voice tailed away. I knew I wasn't capable of keeping that promise, no matter how much I meant it.

I tried talking to Mama instead. 'I've done exactly what you told me to do, Mama. I'm here in Monksby. I think I'm going to see my father. His ship's expected at noon today! Can you make him like me, Mama – maybe even love me a little? I swear I will try to be a good daughter to him, even though I might be a little wild at times.'

I waited, my eyes shut, to hear Mama's voice.

You're a good daughter to me, Hetty.

'Oh, Mama – I am *Sapphire* now, Sapphire Battersea,' I whispered.

Make up your mind, girl – I heard you calling yourself Emerald Star last night!

'That was just to be cautious!'

Well, looks like you've thrown caution to the wind now, talking to old women and fisher-girls, bandying my name about.

'Why don't they *know* you, Mama?'

Oh, they know me all right – but not by that name.

I clutched the rail in front of me. 'They don't know you by that name?' I repeated, my voice sounding overly loud in the still church.

You're not the only girl who's needed to change her name.

'Hello? Were you calling me, child?' A parson in

41

a long robe had emerged from a side room and was shuffling towards me.

'Oh! I'm sorry. I was just . . . praying,' I said.

'Well, I'm sure God hears your prayers,' he said, giving my shoulder an awkward pat. He stood over me. 'If there's anything I can do . . .?'

All I wanted was for him to go away so I could carry on talking to Mama, but it seemed rude to tell him that in his own church. I bowed my head as if praying some more. He sat down near me and started praying himself, his head in his hands, mumbling holy words. I glared at him because Mama had gone silent now – and eventually crept away, leaving him praying alone.

Outside, cowering in the biting wind, I tried to speak to Mama again but she seemed to have finished her speech. She'd made her point.

You're not the only girl who's needed to change her name.

Of course! When Mama had taken me to the Foundling Hospital she had given them her real name. She'd have wanted it there on the records so that I could trace her one day. She lived in the workhouse for the next few years, got a job as a kitchen maid – and then had the wondrous idea of applying to the hospital for work so that she could watch me grow up. She couldn't apply under her own name. They'd have surely checked the records.

42

I'm sure many women had the same idea. So she gave them a new name – Ida Battersea. Of course, I had my new foundling name now, but Mama had no difficulty picking me out. I had been a tiny baby with bright blue eyes and flaming tufts of hair. She had only to look for the smallest, scrawniest five-year-old with sapphire eyes and red hair. She knew I was her daughter for five bittersweet years, but I didn't suspect a thing until I ran away when I was ten.

When I guessed the truth, I vowed that Mama and I would never be parted again. I suffered agonies when we were found out and Mama was sent away from the hospital in disgrace. I vowed that I would work hard and earn a fortune so that one day she and I could live together in our own house. But then Mama got ill – and all my dazzling dreams faded to grey mist.

I felt totally alone in the world until Mama spoke within my heart, reminding me that I didn't just have one parent. I had two.

I paced backwards and forwards across the clifftop as the church bell chimed the quarters through the morning. How could that girl on the rocks predict when Bobbie Waters would be sailing home so accurately?

I kept scanning the sea, and at last I saw a tiny blob on the horizon. Then another blob, and another and another. I wasn't looking at one big ship. I was seeing a little fleet . . . of fishing boats.

I breathed out, dizzy with disappointment. So my father wasn't a storybook sailor, coming home from a long voyage with an earring in his ear, a parrot on his shoulder, a purse of gold in his pocket. He was an ordinary fisherman, setting out to sea every eve, and coming home late morning with the night's catch.

I made my way down the winding path from the clifftop to the village below and stood waiting in the harbour. I wasn't alone. A little crowd gathered: men to help unload and sell the fish; women in big aprons with rolled-up sleeves, ready to clean and gut the fish; little children running about barefoot, watching the fishermen come home just for the fun of it. One very little boy wore a tiny fisherman's gansey and carried a toy boat.

'See Pa, see Pa!' he kept clamouring, tugging at his mother's apron insistently until she picked him up and swung him onto her shoulders.

I stood a little to one side, Lizzie's shawl pulled low on my head. People stared at me and murmured amongst themselves, wondering who I was. But I took no notice of them. I stared out to sea as the boats came nearer. Now I could make out dark figures working in them, sorting through the fish and throwing debris over the side as greedy gulls screamed and swooped.

The first boat drew nearer still, until I could see the fishermen clearly, burly in thick jerseys and coarse trousers, some with cork waistcoats strained about their chests. They all wore strange hats at jaunty angles. I narrowed my eyes, looking for the biggest man, the one with bright red hair.

I edged towards one of the waiting women. 'Excuse me, ma'am – is Bobbie Waters on that boat?'

She seemed confused by my London accent, or maybe she was a little deaf, because I had to repeat myself three times.

'Nay, lass, that's not *his* coble. Big Bobbie works the blue one yonder.' She pointed at the third boat. I had to wait impatiently as the first and then the second boat reached the harbour and the men started unloading their catch of cod. There were weird blue lobsters too, twitching their claws in their pots. I shuddered at the sight of them.

Everyone grew busy with barrels and baskets, but I only had eyes for the third boat. There was a man standing at the front, steering it into the harbour – and even before I could make out the wild red curls beneath his hat, I knew he was the one.

I watched, my mouth dry, my heart banging in

my chest. I was trembling all over, though the wind had dropped a little now. My legs were buckling beneath me and I had to take two steps backwards in case I fainted and toppled from the wall.

I waited until his crew's fish were all unloaded and he stepped along the harbour road, his boots ringing on the cobbles. Then I ran after him.

'Please, sir, might I ask ... are you Bobbie Waters?'

He looked at me, his eyes very blue in his weathered face. He was the most handsome of all the men, fine and upstanding, without a big belly filling his jersey. He was clean shaven and had good white teeth when he smiled. Oh, he had such a dazzling smile.

'Yes, I'm Bobbie. How can I help you?' he said pleasantly.

I swallowed, trying to think of the right words. I saw the woman I'd spoken to staring at us curiously. 'Could – could we perhaps go somewhere private?' I said.

He tilted his head to one side, frowning a little. 'Well, I'm needed here at the fish auction, but I suppose I can spare you two minutes, little lass.'

We walked along the street together until we got to the end. He yawned and stretched and then leaned against the wooden railings.

'Oh dear, it's been a long night. I shall be glad to get to my bed. So how can I help you? Who *are* you? What's your name?'

'I – I have several names. Folk used to call me Hetty, but I know my real name is Sapphire – though just of late I have been called Emerald.'

'My, my, you go in for some very fancy names! And what is your business with me, Hetty-Sapphire-Emerald?' He said the three names solemnly enough, but his eyes crinkled, his mouth twitched, and I knew he was laughing at me.

I took a deep breath. 'I – I think I might be kin of yours,' I said.

He stared at me. 'What, some long-lost cousin or something of that sort? Are you Hetty-Sapphire-Emerald *Waters*?'

'No, sir. I have taken the surname of Battersea, after my mother. She was Ida – but I don't think that was her real name.'

'My goodness, this is too much of a riddle for me. I'm not sure what you're saying, child.'

'I'm saying that you once knew my mother – more than fifteen years ago, when she was a young girl, little and slight like me, with blue eyes just like mine.'

He was looking straight at me now, standing very still.

'I don't know what she was called, but she was a

local girl and she loved you with all her heart. You and she were sweethearts.'

'Evie,' he said. 'Evie Edenshaw.' He grabbed hold of my shoulder. 'You know Evie? Will you tell me where she is? I would dearly love to see her again.'

Evie Edenshaw! Each syllable rang like a bell in my head. So this was Mama's real name!

'She's . . . not here. She passed away this summer. She died of the consumption,' I said, struggling not to cry.

His eyes filled too. 'Poor little Evie,' he murmured. Then he looked at me again – a long searching look. 'Are you telling me . . . ?' he murmured.

I unwound the shawl from my head and let my hair whip free in the wind. 'I am Evie's daughter,' I said. 'I think I am *your* daughter.'

'I wondered – dear God, how I wondered if that was the case. I went sailing halfway across the world, selfishly wanting adventure. At first I barely gave Evie a second thought. I had new sweethearts wherever the ship docked – but none proved as sweet and spirited as your mother. I sickened of them all, I sickened of life at sea. I came back two years later, wondering if she'd waited for me, if she'd maybe take me back – but she was gone, and no one knew what had happened to her. There was talk, of course. Some said her own folk had turned her out. I begged them to tell me where she was but they wouldn't even speak to me. So she was having a child – *my* child?'

'She couldn't keep me, so she gave me to the Foundling Hospital in London,' I said.

'My child, brought up a foundling?' he said, and now his tears spilled.

'But Mama came to work at the hospital and watched over me, and when I found out the truth we snatched precious moments together. We vowed that one day we would live together in our own little house, but then poor Mama got sick and – and now I am all alone,' I said.

'You are not alone any more,' he said. He reached out and drew me close, his strong arms around me. 'You are my child and you shall live in my house with me.'

4

I breathed in my father's strange smell of sea and wool and fish, and wept against his chest. He held me tightly. I think he was crying too. The sun suddenly came out between black clouds and the gulls screamed over the grey shoals of fish. I felt dazzled, deafened, unable to think clearly at all. I simply clung to my father as if I would never let him go. I had found him at last. My heart was beating so fast I felt faint, as if Mama herself were stirring within me . . .

Yes, Hetty, yes! We are a family at last.

I saw myself living cosily with my dear long-lost father. I would care for him and cook for him and clean for him. I would be the most dutiful daughter in the world, and he would love me and protect me and go out fishing every day. Oh, we would live so happily, just the two of us . . .

'Come, Hetty. I think you had better be Hetty here. Sapphire and Emerald sound a little too glittery and fancy for fisher-folk. Is that all right? Can I call you Hetty, child?'

I nodded. Even Mama had struggled to call me Sapphire. I did not care for Hetty now, but I didn't truly mind what my father called me – and there was such gruff affection in the way he said my homely name.

'And what shall I call you?' I asked.

'Why, Father, of course,' he said.

He pronounced it Feyther, so I said 'Yes, Feyther,' copying him as best I could.

He roared with laughter at me. 'That's right, we'll have you talking with a Monksby brogue before the week is out,' he said. 'Come then, Hetty. You must meet the rest of your family.'

I stared at him. 'My family?' I repeated.

'I have a wife, Hetty, and a son and a daughter.'

My chest tightened so I could scarcely breathe. 'They're *your* family,' I said, my dreams evaporating. 'They won't want me!'

'Of course they will. They will do as I say,' he said resolutely.

He rested his huge hand on my shoulder and steered me back to the crowd at the harbour edge. Women had set up crude fish stalls, large planks resting on two barrels, and were gutting the fish with startling speed, their sharp knives gleaming in the sunlight.

Father looked down and fingered Lizzie's shawl.

'Should I tie it round my head again?' I said.

'No, no – folk will put two and two together soon enough,' he said.

So we walked along the road side by side, a red-haired man and a small red-haired girl. Gradually all the fisher-folk stopped their busy work and stared at us. The women gutting the fish stared at us too – and then they looked over at the woman at the end, in a blue scarf and a dark green dress. She was tanned by the sun and wind, her cheeks naturally rosy. She went red all over as we approached.

'Can I have a word, Katherine?' Father said softly.

She looked up at him. 'What are you playing at, Bobbie?' she said. Her eyes flicked sideways. 'Who is *she*?'

I saw Father swallow nervously, the Adam's apple bobbing in his throat. 'This here is Hetty, Katherine. We need to talk. Could you come home with us?'

'What? What's all this nonsense? What are you doing with this girl? Of course I can't come home. I'm in the middle of gutting your fish, you fool,' she said.

Father's fists clenched. 'I'll thank you not to take that tone with me,' he said. 'Now come *home*, Katherine.'

She stood up, still clutching her sharp knife. It glistened with fish entrails. She looked as if she wanted to stick it straight in *me*.

'Could you call Mina from the shore? And where's Ezra? Is he playing truant from school again? Look for him on Long Beach. I need you all at home,' Father said. 'Come, Hetty.'

He spoke with calm authority, but I could feel him trembling as he turned me round and steered me onwards. I heard an excited babble behind us as folk repeated what he'd said. I peered round. Katherine was staring after me as she hurried down to the beach.

'Oh, Father, she hates me,' I said.

'Don't be silly, Hetty – she doesn't even know you yet,' he said.

I could not understand how he had made such a bad choice of wife. I thought of my pale little mama with her bright blue eyes and dainty ways. This woman was big and coarse and pink in the face – maybe a handsome woman, but certainly a hard one. The last woman in the world I wanted as a stepmother.

'How old are Mina and Ezra?' I asked.

'Mina is twelve and Ezra seven. Mina takes after her mother but Ezra is a chip off my block, with hair as red as mine – and yours. It will be a surprise for them to have a new ready-made sister. Mina has often said how much she longs for a sister, so she will surely be happy – and Ezra too. He's a fine lad, though he runs a little wild.'

I listened without commenting. I already admired and respected my tall strong father, but I couldn't help feeling he was soft in the head. I feared Mina and Ezra would hate me – and it was clear how their mother felt.

If only Father had stayed true to the memory of Mama. Why did he have to saddle himself with this new family? We walked along the cobbled lane together, Father asking me endless questions about Mama and my life in the Foundling Hospital. I was normally happy enough to tell stories of those bleak, loveless years, the strict rules and regulations, the meagre portions of food, the unkind matrons – but each hardship I touched on made Father wince and moan, as if he had personally inflicted these deprivations on me. I found myself downplaying my little dramas, doing my best to reassure him. The hospital might have been grim but they'd given me a decent education and taught me how to sew and scrub, and I could sing my way straight through the hymnbook. And above all I had had Mama near me, watching over me, sneaking me extra treats and titbits.

But mentioning Mama was torture for both of us, especially when I talked of her last few weeks in the sanatorium wing of the hospital at Bignor.

'If only I'd *known*,' Father groaned, actually hitting his head with his clenched fist.

'You mustn't take on so,' I said. 'I looked after her.'

'And I'll look after you, child, no matter what,' said Father.

No matter what was clearly Katherine.

We went down a winding lane – *Home* Lane, the very name a wonderful omen – to the very end cottage. It was weathered brick with a rust-tiled roof, two rooms upstairs and two down.

Father opened the green front door, looking bashful. 'It's not very grand, lass,' he said. 'There's nowt fancy in our home, but Katherine keeps it spotless.'

It seemed a little cheerless too. The meagre furniture stood at rigid angles, the clock ticked on an empty mantelpiece, the rug was limp with many beatings. There was only one picture on the white-washed walls, a painting of the sea with a tall ship on the horizon. I wondered if Father stared at it every day and wished he was sailing back around the world.

He shyly showed me the two rooms upstairs – a

double bed for him and Katherine, two little truckle beds for Mina and Ezra in the smaller room. I wondered where I would sleep. Father seemed to be pondering that too. The house seemed to be shrinking around us.

'It's not much to show for a life of hard work,' he said. 'I dare say the house where you were a servant was much grander, Hetty.'

I thought of Mr Buchanan's grand, tall house, each room crammed with fine furniture, ornaments crowded on every surface, and so many paintings on the walls you could barely make out the design of the wallpaper.

'I'd much rather be here with you . . . Father,' I said. It sounded so strange to call him by that name and it made us both blush.

We sat on the battered chairs and waited for Katherine to come home with the children.

I heard a boy's voice piping all the way down the lane. 'But *why*, Mam? Leave go of me, you're hurting me! Why are you so *cross*? I've not done nowt!'

Then the front door was flung open, and there was Katherine, striding in furiously, with a small red-haired boy in torn breeches and broken boots. A neater girl in an apron and headscarf edged her way into the house too, staring at me. She might well have been one of the girls picking flithers from the rocks.

Katherine slammed the front door shut and stood breathing heavily, arms akimbo. I wondered if her knife was still in her apron pocket.

'How dare you make a spectacle of this family!' she hissed at Father. 'Folks' tongues are wagging fit to drop out of their heads. What are you *doing*, parading around with this . . . this *girl*?'

'Calm down, Katherine,' said Father. 'Mina, Ezra, come here. This is Hetty. Say hello nicely to her. She's travelled a long way to find us.'

'Who is she, Pa?' said Ezra.

Mina said nothing, peering at me from behind her mother. She was tall for twelve, half a foot bigger than me, with broad shoulders and big arms. Stray fair curls peeped out from beneath her shawl – but there was nothing else soft and wispy about Mina. She looked as if she could flatten me with one blow.

'This is Hetty, children,' said Father. 'She is your sister.'

Katherine and Mina gasped, as if he'd said a swear word.

'My sister?' said Ezra, wrinkling his nose in simple puzzlement. 'How can that be?'

'Aye, how indeed!' said Katherine. 'What kind of

a fool are you, Bobbie? This girl bobs up out of nowhere and spins you a sorry tale, and you take her every word as gospel! She's no kin of mine – *or* yours.'

'Katherine, I told you once. Don't call me a fool, especially not under my own roof. I'll thank you to keep a civil tongue in your head, especially before the children. Mina, Ezra, this is your sister Hetty – and she's come to live with us.'

'Not in my house she's not,' said Katherine, folding her great arms. Mina folded hers too.

'It's *my* house and you'll do as I say. Did you not promise to *obey* me the day we were wed?' said Father.

'You never wed *this* girl's mother,' said Katherine. 'You can't palm her children off on me – though I still think she's playing a trick on you. She's down on her luck and needs protecting, so she's travelled as far as she can go and then cast her cap at the first man she's seen with red hair.'

This was in effect so near the truth that I felt myself flushing.

'See! Look at her!' said Katherine triumphantly. 'You've still got sea mist in your eyes, Bobbie. She's nothing *like* you, apart from the hair.'

'She's like . . . Evie,' said Father.

'*Evie!*' Katherine spat viciously on her own floor.

'I told you never to say that name to me again. I won't have you mooning after that girl. She left you, Bobbie.'

'No, she didn't! My father left *her* – he went away to sea,' I shouted. I saw Father hang his head. 'Perhaps he did not know about me. But he went, and Mama was left, and turned out of her own home.'

'And no wonder. She was a bad girl. We all knew she'd come to no good,' said Katherine.

'How *dare* you talk of Mama like that!' I said, and I rushed at Katherine and pushed her hard in the chest.

'I'll teach you, you little spitfire,' she said, and she slapped me so hard about the face I reeled back, staggering.

Father caught me and steadied me. Ezra burst out crying, but Mina clutched her mother protectively.

'I've never once been a violent man, but if you raise your hand to her again, I swear I'll floor you, Katherine,' said Father.

'That's right, take her side against me, when I've been your good true wife all these years and you've only just this moment met up with this sly little minx who's claiming you for a father. What proof do you have that she's Evie's child? Where's Evie then?'

'Hush, Katherine. Hetty's told me she passed away this summer.'

'Oh yes, very convenient. And she came toddling up to you and said, *Please, sir, I'm Evie's child and so that makes you my father.*'

'Well, not exactly. Hetty didn't know her mother was called Evie. Apparently she'd taken another name down south.'

'Oh my Lord! How can you be so gullible, Bobbie? The girl didn't know her own mother's name – and yet you're still sure you're her father?' Katherine cried.

'Yes I am,' said Father, but his voice wavered and he looked at me again, as if for further proof.

'I *am* yours, Father,' I said, saying the word again proudly. 'I knew you as soon as I set eyes on you – and I felt Mama in my heart telling me I was right.'

'I've never heard such claptrap in my life,' said Katherine. 'You've gone soft in the head, Bobbie, listening to such foolishness. Send the girl packing, back to where she belongs.'

'She doesn't belong anywhere else,' said Father. 'She belongs here.'

'And what of your own two proper children?' said Katherine, picking Ezra up with one strong arm and putting the other round Mina's shoulders. 'Do you want this girl living with us?'

61

'No, Mam. Send her away!' said Mina.

'I don't like her. She talks funny and she looks queer and I don't want her to have red hair. It's only me and Pa who have red hair,' Ezra sobbed, kicking his feet in fury against his mother's hips.

'Stop that baby nonsense, son,' said Father. 'I want you to act like a little man. And you, Mina, you're old enough to understand. Think how Hetty must feel. What sort of a welcome are we giving her? Look at her – she's shivering. Would you like a cup of tea, lass?' He patted me on the shoulder and looked at Katherine.

'Don't expect me to make it for her!' she said. 'I'm off back to my work. Someone's got to make some money if you're going to bring home every little stray slut that tells you a string of lies.' She pulled Mina by the arm. 'You come too, our Mina. You're having nothing to do with this girl, do you hear me?'

'I don't *want* nothing to do with her, Mam,' said Mina. She walked to the door with Katherine.

Ezra started kicking again. 'Put me down, Mam! I want Pa, I want *Pa*,' he said, struggling.

'Go to him then,' said Katherine, shrugging him off. She slammed out through the front door with Mina.

We were left in the dark little living room,

Father and Ezra and me, all of us staring wretchedly at each other.

'Pa?' said Ezra uncertainly.

'Come here, son. Never you mind your mam. She's had a shock, little laddie. Don't look so worried, you've done nowt wrong – for once! Come now, we'll fix a little meal for us, you, me and Hetty.'

'I can fix it, Father. I'm an excellent cook,' I said eagerly. 'I can make apple pies second to none. Shall I make us a pie?'

'A pie, eh? Well, maybe on Sunday – but I was thinking more in terms of soup, lass. I usually have a big bowl when I come back from fishing. It warms me up a treat. I expect Katherine has the makings of it in the pot.'

It turned out to be *fish* soup. The meals here seemed to consist of little else. It made my stomach turn over, seeing all the bits of head and tail simmering in the pan. It was like boiling up a bowl of goldfish.

When it was piping hot, Father poured out three bowls. He and Ezra started eating with gusto, Father with a spoon, Ezra picking his bowl up in two hands and slurping eagerly. I sipped a few mouthfuls of liquid cautiously, and nibbled at the odd chunk of carrot and potato.

'Eat up, Hetty! You need to get some meat on your bones – though Evie was always so little and light. I could pick her up one-handed, she was that dainty.'

I wondered if he were comparing my lovely little mama with his great surly lump Katherine. He certainly shook his head sadly.

'Did Evie speak of me much, Hetty?' he asked when he'd wiped round his soup bowl with a piece of bread.

'Not really – because I think it upset her.'

Father looked even sadder.

'I think it was because she'd clearly cared for you so much,' I said.

'But she told you of our courtship? We were such sweethearts all one spring,' said Father.

'You and Mam, Pa?' said Ezra, wiping his soupy mouth with his sleeve.

If any of us foundlings had done that we would have been smacked about the head, but polite manners didn't seem to be a priority in Monksby.

'Not your mam and me, son. That was later,' Father said awkwardly. 'I was meaning Hetty's mam and me when we were younger.'

Ezra screwed up his face and shook his head, not wanting to hear any more.

'So Evie never told you her true name?'

'She had to be so careful. When she applied for the position at the Foundling Hospital she would have had to choose a false name, Father, don't you see? If they'd checked the records and found she'd given up her own baby to them they'd never have allowed her to work there,' I said.

'Did she talk of her own kin folk here?'

'No, never. She just said she had to leave home,' I said.

I was starting to panic a little. Had Katherine made him start to doubt me? I also started to think properly.

'So – *do* I still have kinfolk here?' I said.

'Evie's mother died years ago – but her father's still alive.'

'My grandfather . . .' I said slowly. It was so strange realizing I had a proper family like normal folk.

'Do you have a father too, Father?'

'I lost mine long ago – he drowned. And two brothers along with him.'

'Oh, how terrible. They were fishing?'

'Out one night when a squall blew up,' Father said sadly.

'And couldn't they swim?'

Ezra spat out his crust of bread in contempt.

'Swimming's not much help when you're miles

offshore in a squall, Hetty,' said Father. 'Mother died six months later, with a bad chest. It was as if her heart was broken.'

'I'm so sorry, Father,' I said, blinking to have discovered four new relations and lost them in the space of thirty seconds. I paused. 'So my other grandfather – Evie's father – does he live near here?'

Father set down his bowl and spoon and set about making a pot of tea. 'He lives nearby,' he said shortly, his back to me. 'But I never see him.'

'You don't like him?'

'No. And he doesn't care for me either,' said Father.

'Then I won't bother trying to meet him,' I said quickly. 'I'm sure I would have detested him anyway because he sent Mama away.'

Father turned and nodded at me, as if to say, *That's my girl.* 'Eat some more soup – you've hardly touched it,' he said.

'Oh, it was delicious,' I lied. 'But I'm full right up now.'

Father shook his head and offered it to Ezra. The little boy stared at me as if I were mad and wolfed it down eagerly, smacking his lips. Father carried on with his tea-making but he seemed unused to the occupation. He spooned far too many times from the tea caddy to the pot.

'Shall I make the tea, Father? I think you'll find that will be a little too strong,' I said.

'We like our tea strong, dear,' he said.

He wasn't exaggerating. He had enough tea in the pot for ten men. I searched for crockery, looking for cups and saucers, but I could only find crude beakers. I found a jug of milk in the pantry and a bag of sugar, but no bowl, and no tea strainer either. Mrs Briskett had taught me how to set a tea tray but I was hampered by the lack of equipment here.

'Let me pour, Father,' I said, wanting to show him that I knew all the little niceties like holding the pot aloft and adding the milk last. I hoped to impress him, sticking my little finger out the way Mrs Briskett had done, but Ezra sniggered and Father shook his head.

'My, you've funny southern ways, lass. We just brew and pour and drink up here.'

The tea was as thick and black as treacle but Father drank it down thirstily, just as it was. Ezra had a little milk in his and drank it down likewise. I tried with my mugful, but the reek of tea made my head reel, and the few sips made me shudder.

'There's nothing like a warming cup of tea at the end of a long hard night at sea,' said Father. 'I usually smoke my pipe for a few minutes now, Hetty. Will it offend you?'

'No, please go ahead, Father,' I said.

He sat in the big chair in the living room, filling his pipe and then sucking it contemplatively. Ezra crawled onto his lap and laid his head on his chest, looking up at him possessively. I wondered what it would be like to clamber on Father like that with such casual adoration. Each time he took a puff of his pipe Ezra put a finger in his mouth and made little tutting noises as if he were smoking too.

Father ruffled his hair and smiled at me. 'You must tell me more about yourself, Hetty. Tell me where you've been since you left that wretched hospital.'

'Certainly, Father,' I said, and I embarked on the long tale of my travails. I decided to give him a highly edited version of my time displaying myself as Emerald the Amazing Pocket-Sized Mermaid. I was sure Father would disapprove. But I needn't have worried. I'd only said a few sentences when his head started to nod. His pipe went out but he still clenched it between his teeth as he slept. After a minute or so he started snoring.

I tried not to feel offended. He'd been out fishing all night long, poor man, and then he'd had a terrible shock. No wonder he was exhausted. Of course I didn't mind him sleeping – though I felt he might have made a *little* more effort to listen to his long-lost daughter.

Ezra stirred on his lap, gently rising up and down as Father's breathing grew deeper. I stretched my mouth in a sisterly smile. Ezra stuck his tongue out at me and waggled it violently. I forgot my manners and reciprocated, also crossing my eyes and waggling my hands from my ears. Ezra seemed startled, and slid off Father's lap. He dodged into the kitchen, took another hunk off the loaf of bread and then was off out of the door, chewing his crust.

I wondered if I should go after him, but decided he was probably old enough to look after himself. I sat on, staring at Father, scanning his visage for similarities. I ran my fingers over my own small snub and stared at Father's big straight nose. I fingered my little pointed chin and looked at Father's blunt jaw. I put my hands to my small ears and peered at Father's great lugs. I circled my slender neck and gazed at Father's short, strong neck as it disappeared into his navy knitted gansey. I saw his burly shoulders, his broad chest, his strong legs, his big wide feet bursting out of their old boots. I wondered if he really *was* my father. I fixed on his red hair, stroking my own as I stared at it. But mine was fine and flyaway, while Father's was coarse and curled about his head.

'Oh, Mama, if only you were here to tell me true,' I whispered.

Was Mama really Evie Edenshaw, the girl that

Father still cared for, the girl that Katherine still hated? How would I ever find out? I'd been there when she wrote her name in the mothers' book at the Foundling Hospital, but I'd been a newborn babe. If only I could see that book now and read the entry for myself. I couldn't go back there, not now I'd been dismissed in disgrace from Mr Buchanan's. Miss Smith had tried so hard to secure me a good position . . .

Miss Smith! She was a governor at the hospital. She would have access to the mothers' book. Would she look for me? She would be feeling very disappointed in me but she had frequently stuck up for me in the past. She had even collaborated with me in a tissue of outrageous lies to explain why I'd disappeared on the day of the Queen's Golden Jubilee.

She knew how much I loved Mama. She would be so sorry that she'd passed away. Perhaps, oh *perhaps* she would understand my need to find my father. She would see why I needed to prove that this tall red-headed fisherman was my own true parent.

I resolved to write to Miss Smith immediately. I quietly and systematically searched the kitchen drawers and the plain sideboard, but found no paper, no envelopes, no pens. But I had my own writing implements in the case I'd left in Lizzie's care at the Fisherman's Inn. I would go there immediately and retrieve them.

Father still slumbered deeply. I stood before him, hovering awkwardly. He was in such a sound sleep it seemed likely I could run over to the inn and back without him waking. But if he *did* wake up and find me gone, maybe he'd think I'd run for it, frightened away by Katherine. No, hopefully he would know I was made of sterner stuff. I wasn't going to let a jealous, mean-spirited battleaxe frighten me away. I'd been dealing with cruel, hateful matrons most of my life. I didn't care a fig if Katherine didn't want me. Father did – and that was all that mattered.

With sudden confidence I shook his arm, and said '*Father* . . .' aloud. He stirred, his eyes opened, he looked at me – and then he smiled, his whole face lighting up.

'Hetty,' he said. 'You're not a dream.'

'No, I'm absolutely real, and you may pinch me if you like to make certain sure,' I said, offering him my arm.

'I wouldn't pinch that skinny little arm for the world,' he said, giving it a pat instead.

'Father, I left my things at the Fisherman's Inn. Would you like me to stay lodging there, or – or shall I bring them here?'

'You must bring them here, Hetty, of course.

71

This is your home,' he said. 'You mustn't mind Katherine.'

'I don't mind Katherine – but she certainly minds me!' I said.

'She'll come round. It's simply such a shock to her. She's a good woman, Hetty, a kind mother to my two – but she's always been a little difficult if she catches me chatting to any of the village girls.'

'I'm not surprised!' I said.

'Not that I'd ever stray, Hetty. I'm a family man.' He caught hold of my hand. 'And you're part of my family now.'

I felt tears stinging my eyes. I squeezed his hand back and gave an immense sniff to stop myself blubbing.

'Then I will go and fetch my things, Father. You go back to sleep – I'm sure you need your rest. Let me make you a little more comfortable.' I knelt down, eased the laces on his old boots, and drew them off his feet. His socks were old and running to holes. There was a darn underneath, but it was inexpertly fashioned and must be harsh on his skin.

'I will darn your socks for you, Father,' I said. I'd suffered nine years of constant darning at the hospital so I was now an expert.

Father murmured sleepily and waggled his toes in a comical fashion. I gently took the pipe from his mouth and laid it on the mantelpiece, then crept upstairs and fetched the worn coverlet from his bed. I wrapped this round him, and as he seemed to be slumbering again, I bent forward so that my face was almost touching his. I did not dare to kiss his cheek. He was, after all, still quite a stranger. I simply pursed my lips and blew him a tiny silent kiss.

5

I found my way back to the Fisherman's Inn with no trouble at all. Monksby was such a small village – just three winding streets and the sea front. I avoided this, not wanting to encounter the rest of my new family.

The inn was open for business now. Tobias was behind the bar, chatting to a bunch of grizzled old men. I wasn't sure whether they were the *same* old men or a different set. They were all similarly wrinkled and weathered, with shaggy beards and whiskers. One small, sour-looking fellow sniffed at me contemptuously. I was pretty sure he was the one who'd commented so unkindly on my hair.

I sniffed back at him and asked Tobias if Lizzie was around. He couldn't be bothered to reply properly. He just jerked his head to indicate that she was in the back kitchen. I slipped behind the bar and through the door. There indeed was Lizzie, standing at the stone sink with her sleeves rolled up, washing out the beer tankards.

'Hello, little Emerald Star!' she said. 'My, our fresh Monksby air seems to suit you. You've got some colour in your cheeks now.'

'I think it's because I'm happy,' I said shyly. 'Oh, Lizzie, I have found my father!'

She stared at me. 'Who is he, dearie?'

There was no reason to keep it a secret now. 'It's Bobbie Waters,' I said.

'Never!' said Lizzie. 'My goodness me! Well, of course, you have his colouring. And – and have you spoken to him?'

'Yes, yes. He's welcomed me into his home,' I said proudly.

'Oh my! Does his missus know?'

I pulled a face. 'She doesn't seem to like me.'

'Well, she wouldn't, dear, would she? Katherine's a sterling sort in many ways – we were lassies together – but she keeps a tight watch on her Bobbie.'

'Were you perhaps ... lassies ... with my mother? I've found out her real name. Evie Edenshaw.'

'Little Evie! Oh my Lord, so you're her daughter! Well, I always knew she was sweet on Bobbie, but we all were, come to that. My, I can't get over it – he's your pa! So *that* was why poor Evie left home. They said she'd gone away down south to be in service. I must admit I couldn't see it at the time.

Evie was a fiery little girl, with her own way of doing things. I couldn't see her curtsying to a mistress and going *Yes, missus, no missus* all day long.'

I thought of Mama's years submitting to the strict regime of the Foundling Hospital. How she must have loved me to have stuck it for so long. Well, I could stick at things too. I wasn't fool enough to think that living with Bobbie Waters would be plain sailing. Katherine seemed fair set to make my life a misery, but perhaps I would find some way of winning her round. I hoped to make some headway with Mina and Ezra at least. It would all be worth it to be part of Father's family – wouldn't it?

If only he'd chosen Lizzie for a wife. She might seem big and tough, but she was as sweet as spun sugar.

'I know one thing about Evie. She might have struggled to be a good servant but she always had the makings to be a marvellous mother. She must have loved you dearly,' she said.

'Oh, she did, she did – and I miss her so,' I said croakily, knuckling my eyes. 'Folk say I'll get over her loss in time but it doesn't feel that way.'

'I don't think you'll ever get over it, Emerald. But you'll learn to live with it. You're clearly a girl with spirit, just like your mother.'

'You think I'm like Mama?' I asked eagerly.

'Now I look at you I can't see how I didn't guess before. You've surely got your father's bright hair, but your face and build are pure Evie. It's just like she's standing in front of me,' said Lizzie.

'Oh, you're such a dear friend already!' I said, and I couldn't stop myself giving her a big hug.

She didn't push me away, she didn't step back, she didn't shift in embarrassment. She not only hugged me right back, strong and hard – she actually whirled me round and round as if I were a baby.

'Look at you, light as a feather!' she said.

'That's my foundling name, Hetty Feather. That's what Father wants to call me. He thinks Emerald too fancy for these parts,' I said.

'Maybe it is – but maybe there's a fancy girl hiding under that demure print frock,' said Lizzie.

'Oh, I must give you back your shawl!'

'You keep it for a while. I'll show you how to knit one for yourself if you like,' said Lizzie.

'Would you really?'

'That'll impress Katherine. She can gut a crate of fish quick as a wink, but her hands are very clumsy when it comes to knitting. It's a wonder that man of hers doesn't catch a chill out at sea at night, there are so many dropped stitches in his gansey – and young Ezra used to look right comical in his baby woollens. She couldn't even knit the sleeves the same length, so he looked lopsided, poor little lamb.'

I felt a spiteful thrill that my very new step-mother was so cack-handed. 'She's certainly no great shakes at darning either. My father's toes are hanging out of his socks,' I said. 'But don't worry, I'll take them in hand. I'm an excellent darner.'

We looked at each other and grinned.

'I'm not sure you'll win her over that way,' said Lizzie. 'But don't feel too down if she's hard on you. Remember you've got a friend here, girl.'

'The best friend in Monksby,' I replied. 'And I'm right glad I've met you, Lizzie.'

'Hark at you! You're talking like a native already!' she said.

'Lizzie, what are you doing with those mugs? They're needed right this minute. Do you want the men to sup their ale from the chamber pots?' Tobias shouted from the bar.

'Half of them wouldn't notice the difference!' Lizzie whispered to me, and we both laughed.

She showed me where she'd stowed my suitcase, marvelling that I possessed such a fine leather object instead of an old tin box. I told her that it had once belonged to Sarah's mother. I felt a pang then, thinking of her and Mrs Briskett. I had hated my lowly position at Mr Buchanan's and I had hated

79

him with a vengeance too, but both women had been very kind and motherly to me – though of course no one could take the place of my own dearest mama.

I opened my case and showed Lizzie the fairytale books Mama had given me, and her precious hairbrush and comb, and her little violet vase, and her letters tied in neat bundles with satin ribbon. She admired each item reverently, as if they were holy relics, as indeed they were to me. I showed her the fat marbled manuscript book where I'd recorded my memoirs, and she seemed astonished to hear that I had written all the words myself.

However, Lizzie was most impressed with my nightgown! She marvelled at the fine cotton and the white embroidery, an S and a B embroidered on the yoke, entwined with daisies.

'It's beautiful, just like a real lady's! Where on earth did you get it, Emerald?' Lizzie said, looking at me uncertainly.

'I didn't steal it, if that's what you're thinking!' I said. 'I made it for myself, Lizzie.'

She peered at the stitches, one eyebrow raised.

'Truly,' I insisted. 'I told you, I'm good at sewing and darning.'

'I should just say so! They look like fairy stitches – and all so smooth!' she said, holding the fine linen to her reddened cheek.

'I had nine years of wearing harsh foundling uniform that scratched against my skin like sandpaper. This is my little luxury,' I said.

'Well, good for you, girl. This nightgown is fit for a princess,' said Lizzie.

I resolved then and there to make her a similar nightgown because she had been so kind to me. I bade her farewell and lugged my case the length of the street, all the way up to the clifftop. My arm felt as if it were being pulled from its socket, but it was worth it when I sat down on a tussock at the top. The very *grass* was rough at Monksby.

I looked down at the village below me, trying to work out which little slated roof was sheltering my father. I stared at the cluster of folk at the harbourside, trying to discern the burly shape of my new stepmother. I peered at the girls collecting flithers on the rocks, the little boys splashing in the sea. For one second I imagined a gigantic wave rising up and sucking Katherine, Mina and Ezra out to sea, so that I could live with Father in peace and comfort, just the two of us. I felt my face flushing, feeling as guilty as if I were truly Emerald Mermaid and had drowned them all deliberately.

I diverted myself from imaginary mass murder by opening my case and taking out my pad of writing paper, my precious pot of ink and my old chewed pen. It was very windy up on the cliff and I had to hang on tight to my possessions to stop them blowing away. It was a struggle to write coherently. I used my closed case as a desk, but it was a very bumpy one, and my writing wobbled this way and that, till I feared my letter was scarcely legible.

c/o Bobbie Waters' House,
End Cottage,
Home Lane,
Monksby,
Yorkshire

Dear Miss Smith,
   I should write OH dear, Miss Smith, because I have been a wilful and disobedient girl, and I am sure you are very vexed with me. You will have heard that I left Mr Buchanan's establishment. I did try hard there, I truly did, and I'm sure Mrs Briskett and Sarah will vouch for me – but Mr Buchanan did not help me with my writing as you had hoped. Indeed, he did not try to help me, he helped HIMSELF. He stole my memoir and attempted to rewrite it as his own work. When I discovered this and challenged him, he grew very angry. I suppose I grew angry too, and he dismissed me without a character.

I was tempted to write another page or two on

the same subject because I still burned with righteous indignation when I thought about it – but I'd already used up one piece of notepaper and it was very precious. I decided not to inform Miss Smith of my change of occupation. I could write persuasively, but I'd never convince her that displaying myself as a scantily dressed mermaid in a seaside freak show was a perfectly acceptable way of earning my living. I decided to cut to the chase.

I went to stay near dear Mama – and perhaps you are aware of the very sad fact that she became sick with consumption. I know you helped get her the position with that elderly lady at Bignor, and I'm sure you thought her a good kind Christian woman, but she was NOTHING OF THE SORT. She turned poor Mama out of her house.

I burned all over again with the injustice. It was so raw and painful writing about Mama that I couldn't go into detail.

Mama died at the end of the summer, so I resolved to find my father – and I have, Miss Smith, I'm sure I have! He is certain I am his daughter too, and we both have distinctive red hair – but for some difficult folk this is not proof enough.

I need to know Mama's true name. She must have used it when she registered me at the hospital. Could you please, please, please be an angel and look in the records for me and let me know Mama's birth name? Then I will be able to rest secure in my new house with my dear father – and other step relatives.

I know I am a sore disappointment to you but I do hope you still have a soft place in your heart for

Your own dear bad Hetty

I addressed the letter to Miss Sarah Smith, Board of Governors, Foundling Hospital, Guilford Street, London town, and stuck a stamp in the corner. I wrote STRICTLY PRIVATE in capitals across the flap of the envelope. I didn't want one of those nosy matrons prying! I walked back down into the village and posted the letter in the big scarlet box at the corner of two streets.

Then I walked along Home Lane to my new home. The door opened for me. Folk here did not seem to bother with locks and bolts. But Father was no longer lying slumbering in his armchair. He was gone – and Katherine was there in his place, with Mina sitting on the arm of the chair. Their heads were together and they were muttering furiously to each other, clearly plotting something dire.

I shivered but I stuck out my chin and faced them fair and square. 'Where's Father?' I said.

'He's not *your* father,' said Mina.

'Yes he is – and I hope to prove it to you shortly,' I said.

'Stop spluttering this nonsense,' said Katherine. 'Now be on your way. You're not wanted here.'

'My father wants me. He has invited me to stay,' I said. 'I went to fetch my possessions.'

Katherine sniffed at my fine suitcase. 'We're not a lodging house. We haven't got room for you. Look around! Do you see a spare bedroom? Do you see a spare bed for that matter?'

'I am looking around – and I see a highly ungracious, hard-hearted woman who wilfully refuses to do as her husband bids her,' I said. 'Do you want me to tell him that you're trying to send his own daughter on her way?'

'Pa's not here to tell, so you just push off,' said Mina fiercely. '*I'm* his daughter, not you.'

'So be off,' said Katherine, and she took up a broom as if she were literally going to sweep me out of the house.

My heart started thumping hard inside my chest. Katherine looked as strong as an ox and Mina was already bigger than me. If it came to a pushing match it was clear who would win.

I thought Father must have gone back to the

harbour to negotiate on last night's catch of fish –
but then I heard a snore from upstairs.

'If you lay a finger on me I'll shout my head off
and Father will come running,' I said. 'He wants me
to stay here, and I *shall*.'

Katherine stared at me. She was gripping the
broom so tightly she seemed ready to snap it in two.
'You're a curse on my house. I won't rest until I'm
rid of you,' she said, and she spat at me.

It didn't land on my dress, as I think she had
hoped. It landed short by several inches, falling on
the scrubbed floorboards, where it glistened like
venom.

'You truly are a fishwife,' I said, and I took my
suitcase and lugged it up the narrow staircase,
leaving them both.

I went into the smaller bedroom, divided into
two by a curtain. I snatched a pillow from one bed,
a quilt from the other. Then I went into the big
bedroom. Father lay flat on his back, still in his
trousers and socks, though he'd discarded
his gansey and lay there in his undershirt.

I stood quietly watching him for a while, and
then I set my suitcase down at the end of the bed. I
put the pillow on it, laid my head down, and covered
myself with the quilt. It was the middle of the day
and I was far too jangled for sleep anyway. I simply
lay there like a little dog at its master's feet.

I wondered if Katherine might seize hold of me and drag me away, but she let me lie there throughout that long afternoon. I tried to time my breaths to match Father's, thinking I would feel even closer to him if we could breathe in unison. Ezra crept in to peek at me once. He knelt close, peering right into my face. I could feel his breath on my cheek. I blew suddenly, right up his nostrils, making him jump and squeal and dash out of the room.

I lay there, head spinning, wondering what I was going to do. I was content with Father near me – but I knew he went out fishing every night. I did not want to be left to the far from tender mercies of his shrew wife. Might he take me fishing with him? I felt a surge of excitement at the thought. I saw myself in a small gansey and boy's breeks, with a battered hat set at a jaunty angle, sailing out to sea with Father. Oh, it would be glorious! I would stand shoulder to shoulder, riding the waves with him, the moonlight bright on the dark water. We would talk to each other night after night, catching up on our lost years, becoming even closer . . .

When Father woke at long last at the end of the afternoon, he sat up and called for me straight away. 'Hetty? Oh, my Hetty, have you come home?' he called loudly.

'I am here, Father,' I said, bobbing up from

87

below the bed. 'Would you like me to fetch you a cup of tea? I will make it very strong, the way you like it.'

'In a minute, my dear. Come and sit on the bed where I can see you. Were you lying on the *floor*? Have you not given yourself a crick neck?'

'I feel very well, thank you,' I said, though I was actually aching all over. I was used to hard beds, but Father's floor was the hardest yet.

'We will make you a proper bed for tonight, even so. I am sure you can share with Mina,' said Father.

I would have sooner shared a bed with a rattlesnake. 'I'm not sure she'd care for that, Father,' I said.

'Mina will do as she's told,' he said firmly. 'You two girls will soon become firm friends, I know it. She will take you over the rocks so you can go flither-picking for bait. She'll teach you all the girls' tricks, and I dare say Katherine will show you how to gut a fish. We'll soon have you trained up as a little fisher-girl, Hetty.'

'Could I not be a fisher-*boy*, Father?' I said eagerly. 'I want to go out fishing every night with you! Please let me. I will gather those flithers and gut haddock and cod with the womenfolk, but *please* let me fish with you too.'

I meant this seriously, but Father laughed as if I were cracking a good joke. When I persisted, he reached for me and put his arms around my shoulders.

'You're too little, Hetty. I wouldn't take you even if you were a lad. It's hard, cold, back-breaking work – and far too dangerous. I've lost my father and my brothers to the sea. I'm not risking the life of my brand-new daughter. I wouldn't take any woman aboard with me. It's bad luck to let a girl so much as touch a boat in the harbour.' Father spoke solemnly, as if he really believed this.

'Isn't that just superstition, Father?' I asked.

He frowned at me. 'I'll thank you not to question me, girl. If you are to live in Monksby you must learn Monksby ways. Custom is custom, and you must respect it, whether you think it superstitious or not, you pert little miss.'

'I'm sorry! Please don't be vexed with me, Father. I didn't mean any harm. I shall be right happy to learn Monksby customs,' I said earnestly, and he laughed and instantly forgave me.

6

I wanted to please my father, but I found I was not at all happy learning Monksby customs. Father sent me out to the beach each day with Mina. She met up with six or seven friends, all girls her own size and weight, scarcely distinguishable in their headscarves and shawls and aprons. I wore Lizzie's shawl and my own apron, yet I looked like a silly child beside them and they laughed at me. They gossiped together as they worked but it was hard making out what they said, they spoke so quick and so broad. It was clear from the way they nudged each other and looked at me that I was frequently the butt of their jokes.

I pressed my lips together grimly and resolved to ignore them. It was hard lonely work toiling on the rocks. I did not have the knack of picking off the limpets cleanly. Within an hour my nails were torn and bleeding. After a full day's work my hands were purple and swollen from the cold and wet. It took me much longer than the others to fill my bucket –

and then I could scarcely haul it, straining until I was sure my eyes would pop out of my head.

Mina set me to collecting driftwood instead – a job for the little children and a sad simple girl who could not speak. I did not mind so much. I quite liked the company of the little ones. They warmed themselves up by having vigorous 'sword' fights with the driftwood, and I joined in these battles too, telling them stories of knights and jousting and tournaments. They laughed at me because I seemed so strange and spoke with a queer accent – but they soon started clamouring for more stories. Big May, the simple girl, liked listening too, though I'm not sure she understood one tenth of what I was saying.

I recited poetry to the children too. One summer at the hospital I had learned the whole of *The Lady of Shalott*, and after a few verses I had them listening spellbound. I'm not sure Big May took in the sense, but she hummed the rhythm of each line, nodding happily.

I'd have been content to gather driftwood, but Father was indignant when he came sailing home and found out what I'd been doing.

'I'm not having my daughter set to work with babies and imbeciles,' he said.

'Well, Mina says she's right useless gathering flithers,' said Katherine.

'You take her under your wing, Katherine. She'll

learn to gut a fish in five minutes, she's got such nimble little fingers,' said Father.

Katherine didn't want me anywhere near her, but he insisted. I had to join my stepmother at the stalls with the other fishwives. In truth, the gutting was easy enough, but I never got used to plucking out those slimy entrails. I hated the very touch of the fat cod and haddocks, the pop of their eyes, the gawp of their mouths. The crabs were worse – and oh, those live blue lobsters with their terrible claws nip-nip-nipping! I couldn't help screaming at the sight. Katherine and her friends found this so amusing they were forever thrusting a lobster in my face to make me squeal.

I stomped off by myself, looking for Big May and the children on the seashore. The tide was out and I walked right round the rocks. I saw a raggle-taggle group of little boys running in and out of the waves. One rushed in boldly, mistimed the wave, and got absolutely soaked. They all shrieked with laughter and followed suit. They were all sodden in a matter of seconds. Then one pulled off his shirt and trousers and cavorted in the water stark naked. The others all squealed at him, and then stripped off too.

'Boys!' I said, shaking my head at them.

I walked nearer. Their hair was dark and dripping, but I was sure one of them was a redhead.

They saw me coming and swam away from me, yelling. Some of them could swim like little fishes, but some were clumsier, only able to paddle their arms doggy style.

'Be careful! Don't go out too far!' I called.

So of course they swam further out, some riding the waves like seagulls, some splashing and struggling. I looked for Ezra's bright head in the water. I spotted him and waved and he actually waved back, but then he got swamped by a sudden surge of water, choked, and went under.

'Ezra?' I shouted. I stared and stared but couldn't see him bob up. 'Where's Ezra?' I screamed at the little boys, but they simply gawped at me stupidly.

'Oh for pity's sake – Ezra!' I shouted. I kicked off my boots. I knew my skirts would pull me down as soon as they were drenched with water. This was no time for modesty. I pulled my dress up over my head, threw it on the sands, and plunged into the sea in my drawers and chemise.

The boys were shrieking all around me but I was only intent on saving Ezra. I dived down under the waves, opening my eyes wide in the salty water, trying to spot him. I surfaced, gasping, and then plunged back again. I did not like the child at all, but he was my half-brother and I had to save him from drowning. Poor Father had already lost his own father and brothers to the sea. I had to save his only son from the same fate.

Then I blundered right into something small and pale. I clasped it tight and pushed up out of the water. It was Ezra, choking and spluttering, water streaming from his nose and mouth like a veritable fountain.

'Oh thank God, Ezra!' I said, hugging him.

'Leave off! Don't you dare hug me in front of the others!' he spluttered, pushing and shoving me.

'You cheeky little varmint! I've just saved you from drowning. You might at least say thank you!' I said, and I ducked him back under the water.

Then he seized hold of me and tried to pull me under too, and soon we were bouncing around, play-fighting in the shallows. Some of his friends joined in, but I was used to rough-housing and could easily get the better of all these squirming little boys.

Now that I was soaking wet I decided I might as well enjoy a proper swim. I paddled along beside Ezra, keeping an eye on him, then glided up and down in the waves and practised the steady breast-stroke I'd learned during my summer at Bignor.

'Hey, Hetty, you're not a bad swimmer – for a girl,' said Ezra, which I knew was praise indeed.

When I got out of the water I felt a little foolish in my underclothes. I had no towel to dry myself. I had to put my dress on straight away, of course, for decency's sake. It was mighty cold and uncomfortable and I positively squelched as I walked, but I started up a running game on the sands with Ezra and some of the others, and I soon warmed up – in fact I started steaming. I combed my wet hair with my fingers and tied it in a topknot and stepped back into my boots and hoped no one would ever hear about my watery adventure – the boys and I still had the beach to ourselves.

But this was Monksby. It was impossible for anything to go unobserved. When I went back to Father's house at tea time, Katherine was red in the face with spite and fury.

'*There* you are, you little harlot!' she said, seizing me and shaking me.

'Katherine, Katherine, stop it now!' said Father, rushing to my side. 'And watch that tongue. Don't you dare call her names like that!'

'Wait till you hear what she's been up to! You're always so quick to defend her, always taking her side against mine. Well, just you listen – and you deny it if you dare, Hetty Feather! You were seen swimming in the sea this afternoon. Look, Bobbie, she can't deny it. You can smell the salt on her, see the damp stains on her frock!' said Katherine, poking me.

'Oh come! Can you truly swim, Hetty? How ever in the world did you learn to do that?' said Father.

'I'm certain sure they don't give swimming lessons to the foundlings at the hospital.'

'I learned this summer, Father, and I'm good at it too,' I said with spirit.

'Good at displaying yourself brazenly!' said Katherine. 'She took her dress off and cavorted almost naked!'

'I was in my undergarments – and I didn't *cavort*,' I said indignantly.

Father looked shocked all the same. 'Oh, Hetty, you're too old for such childish larks! Whatever possessed you?' he said, looking shamed.

'She went in the sea to rescue me!' said Ezra, peeping round the doorway. 'I went under and Hetty thought I was a-drowning. I wasn't, of course, but she thought it, and threw off her dress and came dashing in after me.'

I felt like hugging him again, though I knew he wouldn't like that! Father *did* hug him – and me too.

'I am so sorry, Hetty. I hadn't realized. You're my good brave girl and I'm proud of you,' he said, clapping me on the shoulders.

'Threw off her dress!' Katherine repeated. 'And what were you doing, frolicking about in the sea, Ezra? I've told you and told you not to go in the water. You could have drowned!' She clasped him tight, but then gave him a good shaking. 'Don't you *dare* disobey me again. Promise me never ever ever to go in the water again!'

'I promise, Mam!' Ezra gasped, his head nid-nodding wildly.

'Aren't you going to thank Hetty for saving her little brother?' said Father.

Katherine stiffened. 'He's *not* her brother,' she said. 'She might have fooled you, Bobbie, but she'll never pull the wool over *my* eyes. She's nothing to do with this family. She can call you Father this and Father that but she's not your true blood daughter. Are you *blind*? She's a London girl with flighty fancy ways. She's never a fisher-girl. For pity's sake, she's *afeared* of blooming fish!'

'I'm not afeared of anything, fish or foe,' I declared, lying a little. 'And I'll *prove* I'm Father's daughter, just you wait and see.'

I received a package the very next day! When the post boy knocked to deliver my parcel, there was a great flutter of interest from my kinfolk. Mina snatched the package and shook it curiously, while Ezra clamoured to have a hold of it too.

'It's mine, it's mine! It's my Christmas present come early!' he shouted.

'Give it here, Ezra. Careful – you'll drop it between you,' said Katherine. 'It'll be for me or Father, though I'm blessed if I know what it is.'

I had caught a glimpse of the neat brown copper-plate on the label. 'It's not for any of you. It's for *me*!' I said, trying to prise the package from Mina's hands.

'Don't be so stupid, Hetty Feather, you don't even live here,' she said.

'Look at the label. *You're* the one who's stupid. It's my package, can't you *read*?'

This was a low blow of mine, because I had discovered that Mina could barely spell out the simplest sentence. Katherine herself was scarcely more literate. She set great store by being religious and certainly knew a hundred hymns off by heart – I'd heard her singing them as she toiled about the house – but when she showed me her family Bible, stabbing at the names written on the front page, she had difficulty deciphering them.

'*This* is our family – and *you're* not written down here,' she said. 'These are *my* parents and Bobbie's parents, and these here are Mina and Ezra . . .' But I saw she had to squint hard before she could distinguish one from another.

Fisher-folk here had a casual attitude to schooling. Children attended the little dame school in the village when they had nothing better to do, and drifted away completely when they were old enough to make themselves useful collecting flithers or coiling ropes or mending nets.

But to my great delight Father was a man of learning. There were several battered volumes in the cabinet in the corner and I'd seen him read a few pages of *David Copperfield* while puffing away on his clay pipe. He had to point along under the words to keep his place, but he was reading all the same.

'I need Father to be watching when I open this package,' I declared, and I snatched it back from Mina and nursed it to my bosom until he sailed safely in with the night's catch.

I was skittering from one foot to the other – with excitement and fear in equal measure. 'Father, Father, please hurry!' I called, the moment he jumped up the harbour steps.

'Not now, Hetty. I've still business to attend to,' he said wearily – but I pestered him until he stepped aside with me.

Katherine and Mina and Ezra tagged along, lured by the promise of the parcel.

'Right! Please watch, all of you,' I said, breaking the red seal and sliding the paper open.

My fingers were trembling. I had no idea what Miss Smith had written. The package was fat but light, as if it contained an immensely long letter. Perhaps she had simply rebuked me at great length and ignored my question altogether. Perhaps she had looked up Mama's name in the mothers' register and found a different name entirely. It did not necessarily mean Mama was not Evie Edenshaw of Monksby – she could have used a false name all along. But perhaps – oh, perhaps Miss Smith had sent me written confirmation. If so, it was vital that Father and his disbelieving wife see me open the letter before their eyes so they could see there was no trickery.

I pulled not just one letter from the package – there were twenty at the very least. The first was from Miss Smith but all the others were in a clear round hand I also knew well. Letters from Jem, my dear foster brother and childhood sweetheart!

I was so startled I nearly dropped the package. I knew if I loosened my grip for a second the strong wind would make the letters fly far out to sea like gulls. I stuffed all his letters down the neck of my dress for safety and applied myself to Miss Smith's letter.

The Foundling Hospital,
Guilford Street,
London

My dear Hetty,
Oh child, it was such a relief to hear from you! I have been so worried about you. I was shocked to hear you left Mr Buchanan's establishment. I am disappointed in you, dear. I had hoped you would try hard in your position and gain from living in a house of culture and learning. I am sure you were mistaken in your assumptions. Mr Buchanan can surely not have wished to STEAL

your memoirs. I think he wanted to help you develop your writing style. But it's too late for me to intervene now. I have written to the gentleman and he has assured me in no uncertain terms that he will never take you back.

I do not know how you have been earning a living since. You know full well you should stay in touch with the hospital and accept guidance from your guardians. However, I will not be too hard on you, because you have clearly suffered sadly, losing your dear mother. I am so very sorry, Hetty. I know just how much she meant to you and it seems cruelly sad to lose her at this stage in your young life.

You asked me to ascertain Ida's real name. You must know this is totally against all hospital rules and regulations. Mothers' names must never ever be disclosed, no matter how pressing the circumstances. No governor could ever abuse his or her position in such a way.

However, I am not JUST a governor of the hospital, I am also your friend and mentor – and I am fully aware that it's vitally important to you to prove to your kinfolk that you are your mother's child. Therefore, simply as your friend, I glanced in the register, found your date of entry, and wrote down the name I found there. It is Evelyn Edenshaw.

I stopped reading. My eyes filled with tears. 'Look! Look!' I said, and I thrust Miss Smith's letter at Father. I stabbed at Mama's name. He gave a little gasp.

'See, Katherine!' I said triumphantly, waving the letter at her too, my finger underlining Mama's name.

'I see a piece of paper from a friend of yours,' said Katherine. 'It proves nothing, Hetty Feather. You've asked her to write to you to back up your lies and deception.'

'Oh Lord, how can you continue to be so *stupid*,' I said, wanting to scream. 'Can you not see the heading of this letter? It's official Foundling Hospital stationery. Miss Smith is a governor there – and she happens to be a very well-respected writer for the Religious Society too. Are you seriously accusing *her* of lying?'

'Don't you take that tone with me, missy, or I'll knock you flying over the harbour wall,' said Katherine.

'Oh, Mam, are you and Hetty going to have a fight?' said Ezra, sounding hopeful.

'Stop it, stop it, both of you!' said Father. He looked from one to the other of us, utterly perplexed. 'Katherine, you are my wife and I love you dearly. Hetty, you are undoubtedly my daughter, and I am that joyful to have found you. Can you not both make a little effort to get on?'

We could not. The best we could manage was a surly silence around each other. When Father was out at sea we frequently came to blows. I was scared of Katherine's burly fists – but I learned to lacerate her with my tongue.

Ezra was friendly enough out of his mother's sight. Sometimes we played childish games together, seeing who could skim a stone or spit the furthest. Sometimes I told him stories – gory tales of murder inspired by my long-ago reading of the *Police Gazette*. These stories made his eyes nearly pop out of his head but he always begged for more and he seemed to sleep sound in his bed at night.

I was not anywhere near as friendly with my new sister. Father said I had to share a bed with her whether I wanted to or not. We both hated this. Mina kept kicking and elbowing me to the very edge, and moaned and complained if I wanted to read or write by candlelight.

As she was such a poor reader and my writing was sophisticated copperplate, I had no fears about her reading my memoirs, which I updated nightly – but she was immensely curious when I read and reread Jem's letters. Oh, those letters! He had carried on writing to me long after I left Mr Buchanan's in disgrace. When I did not reply, he did not give up. He wrote to me care of the Foundling Hospital, hoping that someone there might know of my whereabouts. Miss Smith had kept each letter safe, and had now sent them on to me in her packet.

I read each one many times, finding such comfort in his sweet accounts of country life. If I shut my eyes tight I could picture myself back in that tumbledown cottage, tucked up in the feather bed, with the fresh honest smells of lavender and beeswax and bacon in my nostrils. I was not kin there, I was only a foster child, but I was accepted into the very bosom of the family and loved whole-heartedly. Jem himself had cherished me the most. He still seemed to care for me, writing me weekly letters long after I ceased to reply.

Well, I could reply now, and tell him my new circumstances.

My dear Jem [I wrote],
Thank you for all your very special letters. I am so sorry not to have been in touch sooner. You must not worry about me. Oh, Jem, I have found my own true father! I am living here in Monksby with my own kinfolk and I am so . . .

I paused, trying to think of the right word. I was happy, wasn't I? I had found Father and he was everything I had hoped for. Why could I not be content at last?

7

Mina might not have been able to read Jem's letters properly, but she seemed to ascertain their content by instinct.

'They're letters from your sweetheart, aren't they?' she said.

'No, no. They're from my foster brother,' I said.

Mina peered at the signature: *Ever your loving Jem.*

'Brothers don't write like that,' she said. 'He is your sweetheart, Hetty.'

'Perhaps he is – but don't tell,' I said.

I was more anxious about Father knowing than Katherine. I wasn't quite sure he would approve.

'I won't tell . . . if you give me the ribbon wrapped round the letters,' said Mina.

I gave her the ribbon. I gave her other treats and trinkets too – my own lace handkerchief, a small slither of scented soap, a pocket glass I found on the beach. At last I ran out of bribes, but Mina still didn't tell. When we were in bed together she begged me to tell her all about Jem and my feelings for him. I told her true tales of our rambles in the woods and wandering in the meadow, but omitted our ages, so she thought I was talking of a recent courtship.

'Did he ever hold your hand, Hetty?' she asked.

'Yes, he did,' I said, because Jem had always taken hold of my grubby little paw when he took me on walks.

'And – and did he ever *kiss* you?' Mina persisted.

'He kissed my cheek,' I said.

'But did he ever kiss you on the lips?'

I shook my head virtuously.

'Did you *want* him to?' she asked relentlessly.

'Why are you so curious about him?' I asked. I peered at Mina as best I could in the dark. 'I think *you* must have a secret sweetheart, Mina!'

'No, I haven't, of course I haven't. Mam would kill me,' she said, shrieking and giggling – but of course she then declared that *actually*, she did. I found this funny, as I still thought her a little girl, though she was certainly taller and more developed than me.

'So what's his name? Which boy is he? Is it Frank – or Peter – or Jonathan?' I said, naming the lads who manned Father's fishing boat each night.

'No! No – *Jonathan*?' Mina giggled, because Jonathan was particularly solid and slow and had an awful habit of letting his mouth hang open so that he looked truly simple. 'No, I can't possibly tell you, Hetty. I haven't told anyone, not even any of the other girls. I mustn't tell, no matter how you beg me.'

But of course she was desperate to tell me, even so. I didn't have to beg. She whispered his name right in my ear.

'It's Matthew. He's my sweetheart,' she said. 'Do you know Matthew, Hetty? He's the dark boy who wears his hat on the back of his head, the one with the wonderful dark eyes. He goes out every night in the Stevens boat.'

I knew Matthew Stevens – a cocky young lad about my own age, but already as bold and burly as a full-grown man. He winked at me whenever I walked by. The first couple of times I thought he suffered from a surprising nervous tic – but then he started making vulgar kissing noises after me. I tossed my head and walked on with my nose in the air. This made him laugh and call me 'Hoity-toity Hetty'.

'Matthew Stevens,' I said slowly. 'Oh, Mina, maybe he's not really a very good choice.'

'And why not?' said Mina, pushing me hard, so that I nearly fell out of bed. 'Is he not good looking? And he'll be head of the Stevens boat one day.'

'Yes, but – but he seems a little bold with *all* the

girls,' I said. *And me in particular*, I wanted to add, but knew she would not take kindly to learning that.

'Oh yes, I know he has a terrible weakness for the girls,' she said. 'But he says he wants me for a sweetheart, truly he does. He said I was the bonniest of all the lasses, and he held my hand and – oh, Hetty, you won't tell Mam, will you? – then he kissed me right upon the lips!'

'Mina! For goodness' sake, you're only a *girl*. He's no right to kiss you!'

'He says I'm already a lovely little lass,' said Mina, saying the words with sweet emphasis, as if they were poetry.

'Yes, a lovely little lass of *twelve*,' I said.

'I'm old for my age, everyone says that. I have a proper womanly shape already,' Mina said proudly. 'You should eat more, Hetty. It's a shame you're so underdeveloped.'

I felt it a shame too, and agonized when I peered at my flat chest and skinny hips in private, but I wasn't going to let Mina patronize me.

'All us London girls like to be slender,' I declared. 'And I dare say I'll fill out a bit later. But listen hard, Mina. If you start frolicking around with bold lads like Matthew Stevens you'll end up filling out a *lot*.'

Mina gasped and giggled. 'Oh, Hetty, hold your

tongue! What a thing to say. I'd never do *that*, never, not till I was married.' She paused. 'Do you know exactly what folk *do* do?' she whispered.

I had only the very vaguest idea. I had been brought up in the hospital after all, but I'd heard a lot of vulgar talk while appearing in Mr Clarendon's freak show, and that had given me a hazy idea of procreation.

'I know – and it sounds very comical and extremely uncomfortable,' I said. 'You stay a good girl, Mina. And stop all the sweetheart talk for now. Keep away from Matthew Stevens!'

'But some other girl will go after him then,' she said.

'Men don't like it if you're too forward,' I said, as if I had all the experience in the world. 'I have not written to Jem in many months, but see, it has made him even keener.'

'And are you really sweet on him, Hetty?' Mina asked.

I thought about it long after Mina had fallen asleep. *Was* I still sweet on Jem? I had felt a surge of joy when I saw those letters. I still liked to wear them tucked into my bodice against my heart. I felt comforted by their caring kindness, their strong sweet country air. I'd felt so *lonely* here in this harsh new Monksby world. Father seemed to love me, but most of the villagers actively disliked me –

and Katherine certainly hated me like poison. I had only made one true friend and that was Lizzie.

I took to visiting her every day, after I'd spent hours gutting the wretched fish. Oh Lord, the very smell of them made me retch now, and the arch of their slimy bodies against my hands made me shudder. I dreamed of those popping eyes and gaping mouths night after night. When I was finished, I'd wash my hands for a full five minutes under the pump, using my own cake of soap – but I still fancied I smelled fish whenever I held them to my nose. My hands grew so red raw I could scarcely sew at nights, and it hurt when I clicked my new knitting needles.

Lizzie was helping me make a shawl. I'd call at the inn mid afternoon, when all the fishermen were slumbering. Tobias himself often lumbered upstairs to take a nap after drinking several pints of his own ale at lunch time. Lizzie and I could hear him snoring above our heads as we sat together in the kitchen.

'Men! It's hard to distinguish them from pigs sometimes,' said Lizzie, helping me unpick two rows because I'd dropped a stitch.

I spluttered with laughter, but added loyally, 'Except my father.'

'Aye, Bobbie's a fine man, I'll grant you that. He used to be a wild one – but Katherine's kept him on a very tight rein since they were wed.'

112

'Was he *really* wild?' I asked anxiously.

'I'll say,' said Lizzie. 'He was always the boldest of lads, utterly fearless. He was the clear leader of all the boys – and as for the *girls* . . .'

I shifted uncomfortably in my seat. 'He didn't go after girls like – like Matthew Stevens?' I blurted out, tormented by the thought of Father winking and grinning and jumping on all the girls.

'No, no! Not at all! That Stevens lad is a menace – steer clear of him.'

'Mina says he's her sweetheart.'

'She's still a silly little girl, for all she's full grown. No, Bobbie wasn't remotely like the Stevens lad, chasing all the girls. The girls chased *him*. My goodness, Hetty, he was several years younger than me, but even *I'd* have chased after him. He was slimmer then, a whip of a lad, but hard muscled with work. His hair was brighter too, and he wore it curling on his neck, and his eyes were the clearest blue. No wonder Evie fell for him.'

'But he left her!' I said. 'He is my father and I think him very wonderful, but I cannot forgive him for leaving poor Mama.'

'That's men for you,' said Lizzie.

'If only he'd *stayed*. He should have married Mama. She'd have been a *much* better wife for him than Katherine!' I said fervently.

Lizzie laughed at me. 'Maybe, though Bobbie

seems happy enough with Katherine now,' she said. 'Well, he *was*, till you came along. You've not learned to get along with Katherine any better?'

'She won't try to get along with me! She hates me, Lizzie. And I hate her.' I clashed my knitting needles together and promptly dropped another stitch. 'Oh, look now! I *cannot* get the hang of this silly knitting.'

I was proud of my nimble fingers when I sewed and knew I could do very fine work – but those same hands fumbled helplessly when I tried to rib and purl and plain. It did not help that every girl child in the village past the age of five could knit beautifully. They carried their wool and needles around with them and knitted casually as they lolled on the rocks or sat on the harbour wall swinging their legs.

'Patience, patience,' said Lizzie, taking my knitting, deftly manipulating the needle and restoring the stitch to its rightful place.

'Even Big May knits beautifully. She's making a gansey for her pa and she carries the pattern in her head,' I wailed.

'She's had years of practice, Hetty. You want everything to be immediate. You want to knit like a native, you want to be able to gut a fish in seconds—'

'No I don't! I wouldn't care if I never saw a

single fish again in all my life,' I said, sniffing my fingers and wincing at the reek still there.

'Well, we'd all starve if there were no fish, so that's a silly way of talking,' said Lizzie. 'You'll get used to it soon. I'll lend you my special gutting knife. It's got a fair old blade on it – you'll get on well with that.'

'Lizzie, you're being so kind, but I don't *want* to gut fish. Or sell them on the stall or salt them in barrels or fry them in the pan. I don't want to pluck those flithers from the rocks or crack open mussels. I especially don't want to bake a crab or boil a lobster. Can't I – can't I work in the inn with you?'

'You can't have a slip of a girl working in an inn. It wouldn't be decent. And when those old men have sunk a pint or three you'd prefer talking to a shoal of fish, I'm telling you straight. Now stop your silly blathering. We'll have a cup of tea.'

'I suppose Mama could knit . . . I never saw her knit when we were at the hospital together.'

'I doubt there was any need for fisher-lassies' shawls and fishermen's ganseys in the heart of London,' said Lizzie.

'And we never ate fish at the hospital, so she didn't have to gut them,' I said. 'I'm sure she was right glad of it too.'

'She didn't work with fish when she lived in these parts,' said Lizzie. 'Her folk lived on

115

farmland, three or four miles away. Evie was a milkmaid.'

'Oh!' I said. 'So Mama was a country girl!'

I could have thrown my wretched knitting in the air, rejoicing. I'd been a city girl at the hospital, but I'd had five fine years with my foster family being a country girl myself.

'Tell me more about Mama, Lizzie,' I said, nestling up to her.

Lizzie took my knitting from me and started on a few rows herself, to help me out.

'Her folk were farm hands. Evie worked on the farm too as soon as she was in her teens. They have a fine herd of shorthorn cows on Benfleet Farm – they give very creamy milk.' Lizzie pinched my cheeks. 'You should drink more milk, Hetty, and make those cheeks rosy and plump.'

'Mama was always slender, yet I'm sure she drank milk every day,' I said.

'She was like a little elf girl beside us big lassies,' said Lizzie. 'But she was strong, mind. She'd haul great churns of milk about when she came to the village on market day in her little donkey cart.'

'She had a *donkey*!' I said. 'Oh, what did she call it?'

'I don't know!' said Lizzie, laughing at me. 'I don't think it was a pet. She just used it for work.' She put her head on one side. 'But of course she gave it the day off on Sundays and dressed it in a

116

bonnet and took it to church with her.'

'Oh, Lizzie! Don't tease. Tell me more about Mama. What else did she do on the farm? Did she plough the fields?' I remembered my foster father ploughing with the great shire horses. Jem probably ploughed those same fields now.

'I don't think lassies plough the fields – least-ways, not round here,' said Lizzie. 'I expect she fed the chickens.'

'Oh, chickens!'

'And helped with the harvest and went tattie-howking – there's always work to do on a farm.'

'I know, I know. I lived on farmland when *I* was little.' I was so excited I jumped up and whirled around the room. Mama had never been one of these dour women up to their elbows in fish. She was a farm girl and I had been a farm girl too. Oh, we were so alike!

I was filled with an intense desire to see this farm, to stand in the cow meadows and imagine Mama there.

'Will you take me to see the farm, Lizzie?' I asked eagerly.

'It's a little far for me now, Hetty. I have rheumatics in my knees. I doubt I could trek all the way there and back – and it's not really my place anyway. You had better ask your father, see if he'll take you.'

'Then I will,' I said.

I skipped nearly all the way back to Father's house, and when I was inside I busied myself darning his socks and a hole in his gansey.

'What are you fussing with his things for?' said Katherine, frowning. 'Give them here!'

'I'm *mending* them. Father said I could,' I insisted.

'I do the mending in this household,' she said.

'Yes, but you don't do it very well, do you?' I said, wriggling a finger through a big hole in Father's woolly sock.

'You mind your tongue, you cheeky upstart. Dear goodness, I rue the day I first set eyes on you. You're a little witch. You've cast a spell over my great lummock of a husband, you've made little Ezra look up to you, you're even starting to win over my Mina – but it won't wash with *me*.' She came rushing over to me, her fists clenched. I was sure she was going to strike me. She stuck her face so close to mine that she sprayed me with spittle as she spoke. 'I'll never accept you as a daughter – never never never.'

I forced myself not to flinch. I felt the blood beating behind my eyes. 'I don't *want* to be your daughter,' I declared. 'You'll never ever be my mother. I had the best mother in the whole world, the exact opposite of you. I'll miss her sorely till the day I die. But I have found my other parent. I can't help it if your husband is my father. He wants me here and there's nothing you can do about it. Oh, it's so sad for him to be stuck with you. He must wish he'd wed my mama when he had the chance.'

'Hold that wicked tongue!' she shouted, and she took hold of my hair and pulled it so hard my eyes watered. 'You might have the temper that goes with your red hair, but I'll not have you vent it on me!'

I reached up and yanked at her own dark curly hair, loosening half of it from its pins. It tumbled down past her shoulders in rich, shining brown waves. Her face was still red and ugly with rage, but I suddenly saw that she might have been considered a beauty when she was young. She could even have had a fine curving figure before childbirth and years of hard work made her stout and sturdy.

Father could have chosen Mama – but he had chosen Katherine. This made me hate her more. I pulled at her hair again and she slapped me so hard about the face that my knees buckled and I fell to the floor.

The noise of our scrap caused Mina to come rushing from the bedroom and Ezra to race from the privy, his trousers still round his ankles.

'A fight, a fight, a fight!' he squealed, in excitement and horror.

'There's to be no fighting in my house,' Father roared, coming straight from his bed, still in his nightshirt. He bent down and pulled me up with one hand, holding Katherine fast with the other. 'For pity's sake! Two women at each other's throats, and kinfolk too!'

'She's no kin of mine,' Katherine spat. 'Nor will I ever treat her as such.'

'Will you *stop* this. Look at both of you, scrapping like little boys. Even Ezra wouldn't demean himself like this.'

'Yes I would, Pa. I *love* scrapping,' said Ezra, but he was trembling, obviously disturbed by the sight of his mother fighting.

Katherine realized this. She took several deep breaths, quickly pinning her hair into place, and then pulled Ezra's trousers up almost to his armpits. 'Look at you, you naughty boy!' she said, trying to sound stern, but her voice broke. She picked Ezra up and buried her face in his chest so we wouldn't see she was crying.

I felt sudden shame, though she had started this new quarrel, had she not?

'Are you all right, Mam?' Mina asked, her voice high and frightened.

'Of course your mother's all right,' said Father. 'Come, Hetty. You and I will go for a little walk together and talk this over.'

'You're taking her side *again*?' said Katherine.

'I am trying not to take anyone's side,' he said. He went over to Katherine and circled her in his arms. Ezra was crushed between them for a moment, and then wriggled free. 'But you are my wife, Katherine, and this house is your domain. Hetty must learn to do as you say within these four walls.'

Katherine gave a little sniff, but as Father and I walked out of the house she nodded at me in triumph.

We set off up the lane towards the cliffs. I glanced at Father. He was staring straight ahead, his forehead puckered, dark circles under his blue eyes.

'You look so tired, Father,' I said timidly. 'Shouldn't you go back to bed? You've only been sleeping for an hour or two.'

'I'm tired all right – tired of all this strife between the two of you,' he said. He looked at me, shaking his head, and then peered at my arm distractedly. 'What's that on your hands, Hetty?'

I'd slipped his sock over my hand as I darned – and I found I was still wearing it now, in spite of my vigorous fight with Katherine. 'It is your sock, Father,' I said, taking it off hurriedly.

'My *sock*?' he repeated, sounding astonished.

It suddenly seemed so comical I burst out

laughing. Father frowned, but his mouth wobbled and soon he was roaring with laughter too. Every time our laughter died down I flapped the sock in the air and we convulsed again.

'Oh, Hetty, Hetty, you are such a puzzle to me,' he gasped weakly. 'Dare I ask *why* you are wearing my sock like a mitten?'

'I was darning it, Father, and making a good job of it too!' I said, showing him the patch. It was so neat it was scarcely visible and I'd made certain sure not to cobble the stitches because I'd suffered blisters half my life with poorly darned hospital stockings.

'It's not maidenly manners to praise your own work, but I have to agree with you. It's as good as new,' he said, thrusting the sock in his pocket.

'That was why Katherine was scolding me, Father,' I said.

'Scolding you for stitches as neat as ninepence?' he said.

'She feels *she* should be the one to mend your clothes, though I must say she doesn't seem to get round to it. All your socks are a total disgrace, more hole than wool. But don't worry, Father, I will mend them all for you, no matter how much she objects.'

'Oh, Hetty, I know you mean so well. You're simply trying to please me. But can't you see how this makes Katherine feel? She's been captain of my house the way I'm captain of my boat. She doesn't want some young whippersnapper coming along and showing her what to do – *especially* as you're clearly a champion at stitching. Can't you try to be a little more tactful, dear?'

'I don't think that is my forte, Father,' I said sadly.

'Well, I dare say it isn't usually mine, either,' he said.

We reached the clifftop and he threw back his head, drinking in great gulps of air as if it were water.

'There! No better way of clearing the head,' he said. 'Breathe deeply, Hetty.'

I breathed in and out in an exaggerated fashion, pulling Lizzie's shawl tightly around my shoulders. I stared out across the vast grey sea. I thought of all the fish swimming in the murky depths, all the fisher-folk falling from their frail little boats and wafting down, down, down, lying in grisly state upon the sandy bottom till their hair was twined with seaweed and their bones turned into coral.

I shivered, and Father put his arm round me.

'The sea's so splendid, isn't it, lass? It must be a strange sight for your eyes. It seems such a shame that you've been brought up in a great sooty town all these years.'

'I'm not a town girl, Father. I'm a country child,'

I said. 'For my first five years I lived in a cottage in a little country village. I used to run in the meadows and paddle in the stream with my foster brother. I rode on the horses as they ploughed the fields and I slid down all the haystacks and I tickled the great pink pig that lived in our back yard.'

'You can remember all that so clearly?' said Father.

'As clear as day. I used to think about it every single night when I was imprisoned in the hospital. I thought then that I was simply missing my foster family. I didn't realize that the countryside was in my blood.' I took a deep breath. 'Mama lived on a farm, didn't she?'

Father stiffened.

I slipped my hand into his. 'Will you take me and show it to me, Father?'

'I thought you said you did not want to meet your mama's kinfolk?'

'Yes, I know. That's still true enough. But I should so love to see where she lived and picture her there. Oh, Father, *please* take me. Take me there *now*?'

'I can't today, Hetty. It's too far and I have to snatch another couple of hours' sleep before going out to work.'

'Then I'll go myself,' I said, turning round and

staring out across the distant green and purple hills.

'Yes, and you'll likely get hopelessly lost and spend a night on the moors and be found gibbering like a loon days later,' said Father. 'You might fancy yourself a country child, but you'd get swallowed up by the moors in no time. I will take you – but not on a working day. I will take you on Sunday.'

'Oh, Father, you promise?'

'I promise, *if* you are a good girl meanwhile, and do your best to get on with your stepmother.'

'You strike a hard bargain,' I said. 'But I promise too. I will do my best.'

8

Father was as good as his word. When Katherine and Mina and Ezra set out for the little chapel on Sunday morning in their best bonnets, bib and tucker and polished boots, Father and I set out across the moors.

'The Lord will be watching you sorrowfully,' said Katherine, furious that he was not taking his usual place beside her in the narrow pew.

'The Lord will understand,' he said.

As we strode out, I kept looking up at the clouds in the sky, wondering if the Lord was indeed peering down at us. I pictured a very large eye like a second moon shining balefully from that mackerel-grey sky. I took care to keep my head lowered. But after twenty minutes' tramping, the clouds parted a little and a watery sun appeared. In half an hour the sky was blue and the sun shining so strongly I took off my shawl and trailed it along the grass and Father shrugged off his gansey and rolled up his shirtsleeves.

'The Lord seems to be smiling at us, Father,' I said.

Father did his best to frown at me, but his mouth crinkled and he was soon smiling too. It was indeed heavenly to be up on the moors in the bright sunshine, traipsing through the springy grass and purple heather. I breathed in the sweet honey smells and listened to the birds singing all around us. No smells of fish and seaweed, no constant *shush-shush-shush* of the sea upon the shore.

We passed several little hamlets, and I stared at the small cottages and pictured Father and me living there together, with roses round our door, a cabbage patch amongst a tangle of red and purple flowers, and a fat pig grunting in a sty.

I elaborated on this in my head, marrying Mina off to her horrible Stevens boy and grudgingly allowing Ezra to be brought up by us. I pondered over Katherine. I was in such a sunny mood to match the weather that I decided to be merciful. I wouldn't conjure up a horrible death for her. No, she could become more and more fervently religious and shut herself up in a convent, married to Jesus instead of my father.

I sighed happily and Father sighed back.

'It's lovely up here on the moors, isn't it, Father?' I said. 'Imagine if we lived in a little house like that one over there!'

'It must be so sad for these folk though,' he said. 'To live so near the sea and yet not even snatch a glimpse of it.'

'But the sea is so cruel, Father. Your own father drowned, and your brothers too. I hate it that you have to go fishing every night. It's so dangerous and cold and wet. People say I have a talent for writing. Perhaps one day I will come into my own and get my memoirs published, or some story, and make a fortune. Then you will never have to set out to sea again.'

Father laughed, clearly not taking me seriously. 'The sea is in my blood, Hetty!' he said.

'Well, the country is in mine,' I said firmly. I knew my blood was red but I pictured it running green as grass in my veins, pumped by a heather-purple heart.

I ran up and down, climbing little hills and jumping becks, while Father plodded on steadily.

'Don't use up all your energy, Hetty. We've a way to go yet, and then we have to turn round and trudge all the way home again,' he warned.

I would not heed him. I felt so buoyed up I could not control myself. I simply had to run and gambol and jump, until at last Father paused, his hand shading his eyes as he squinted into the sunlight.

'That's Benfleet Farm, over yonder,' he said.

I peered in the direction he pointed. I couldn't

see very much – a few fields in the midst of the moorland, a sprawl of ramshackle buildings, several tumbledown huts. Where was the farm-house, the cow meadows, the dairy, the donkey?

'Is this the farm where Mama lived?'

'That's right. Her folks didn't *own* the farm. Her father was a farm hand there and her mother worked in the dairy, same as Evie, churning the milk into butter and making cheese. Benfleet cheese used to win all the awards at the County Show.'

'But not any more?'

'There's only old Mrs Benfleet left now. Their only son was a simpleton, so there's no one to run the farm. I believe old Samuel, your mam's father – well, your grandfather – he does what he can, but he's crooked with arthritis and can't manage much.'

'Oh, poor Grandfather,' I said, picturing a frail, crippled old man limping his way to work. I imagined sitting him down in an easy chair, wrapping a shawl (knitted by me!) around his stooped shoulders, and then feeding gruel into his toothless old mouth . . . I could be such a comfort to him in his old age, a doting little nurse, a tender little helper. I sprang forward, eager to find him, even ready to forgive him for his terrible treatment of Mama. He must surely regret it now. He'd be haunted by the horror of casting his own daughter from his household. Surely he'd see me as a chance to make amends, to cherish his own flesh and blood.

I vaulted over the five-barred gate. It was half hanging from its hinges. There were old milk churns lying on their sides and a rusted plough. A few scrawny chickens picked their way around the putrid slurry heap, and a tethered calf in an old shed mooed piteously. Poor old Grandfather – it was clear he could no longer manage—

'Get off this land!'

A terrifying scarecrow of a man came stumbling out of the shed, a pitchfork in his hand. He glared at me, his weathered old face turning purple with rage. His stringy grey hair grew down to his shoulders and his beard hung greasily to his chest. He wore corduroy trousers and jacket that were so old, the colour was scarcely distinguishable, a filthy grey-brown, his trousers hitched up below the knee with string.

'Be off with you, you red-haired sprite of Satan!' he shouted, flecks of spittle flying, and he started jabbing at me with his pitchfork, tearing at my dress.

'Leave her be, Samuel! Stop that!' Father shouted, rushing over to me.

The old man spat in the mud at the sight of him. 'You get away too, Bob Waters, or I'll skewer you on this fork and roast you alive,' he yelled.

'Hold your breath, you mad old fool. You know

very well I could knock you over with one blow,' said Father, and he seized the pitchfork and threw it rattling across the yard. 'Now calm down and listen to me.'

'I'll not listen to a single word from your forked tongue – I'll tear it out first. You're a fiend from Hell. You ruined my girl, you turned her mother mad, you blighted my life,' the old man wheezed, shaking with fury.

'I know you feel that way. I don't blame you. I let poor Evie down, but I'm trying to make amends. See this girl, Samuel – she's my child. Evie's child. Your own granddaughter. She's come all the way from London to find us. Won't you calm down and greet her properly?'

Samuel stopped in his tracks. He stared at me, his mouth opening and shutting, though no sound came out. He blinked his rheumy old eyes and looked right into my face while I tried not to flinch. 'Evie's child?' he whispered.

'Yes, I am Evie's child. Hello, Grandfather,' I said, smoothing my torn skirt.

'Evie's child,' he repeated. He sucked in his breath – and then suddenly spat right in my face.

I sprang back, shuddering, wiping the spittle from my cheek.

'Don't you dare spit at my girl,' said Father.

'Get her out of my sight then! I don't want to

look at the red-haired brat. She's the cause of all our misery. She should never have been born,' he hissed.

'You are a cruel wicked man to say such a thing!' I shouted. 'And even more cruel and wicked to cast my poor mama out. I don't think you can have a heart inside that wheezing old chest. No wonder it rattles so. You don't have to worry. I wouldn't have you for my grandfather for all the world.'

I turned and ran. I was in such a hurry to get away that I lost my footing on the rickety gate and tumbled down, twisting my ankle most painfully. Father climbed after me and picked me up in his arms as easily as if I were a little babe.

'I'm not crying because of *him*,' I sobbed. 'I've hurt my leg!'

'I know, I know,' said Father, patting me comfortingly.

'You can put me down now. You will exhaust yourself, Father.'

'Silly girl, you're as light as a feather.'

'Well, I'm Hetty Feather, am I not?' I said, struggling to make a joke, though the tears were still pouring down my cheeks. 'I am Hetty Feather – or Sapphire Battersea – or Emerald Star – or perhaps Hetty Waters now. But I know one thing. I will never ever count myself an Edenshaw, kin of Samuel. He might be Mama's father but

I would not *deign* to claim him as kinfolk.'

'Well spoken, Hetty,' said Father. 'I should never have brought you here. I know Samuel has always hated me. But he has become sadly demented now. You must take no notice of the evil things he said. He has clearly lost his mind. Any other old man would welcome a lovely girl like you with open arms, Hetty, dear.'

'As you did, Father,' I said.

It was a very long trail home. Father was very strong, but it was clear he was struggling after ten or fifteen minutes. I insisted that he put me down, but my twisted ankle was already swelling, sore in my hard old boot, and I could scarcely put it to the ground. I limped along, Father supporting me under my arm, but it was such a painful effort I was damp with sweat, though the wind was blowing harshly now and the sun was hidden by clouds.

The direct route back to Monksby was straight over the moors, the way we had come, but Father steered us over to the west, where there was a cart track. I sat on the sandy stones, wiping my cheeks compulsively, because they still seemed to burn with Samuel's spittle. At long last we saw a horse and cart in the distance.

Father begged a lift and lifted me into the cart, where I sprawled uncomfortably amid grain sacks and cattle feed. I think I fainted, or perhaps I simply fell asleep with exhaustion. I was roused by the scream of seagulls overhead, and knew we were back in Monksby.

There was a clamour in the little house when Father carried me indoors and up the stairs. He laid me on Mina's bed and very gently eased my boot off, though it set my whole leg throbbing violently. I clamped my lips together so that I would not scream.

'You're a brave little lass, Hetty,' he said, and he gave my damp forehead a kiss.

I hoped he would cleanse and bind my ankle, but he sent Katherine to do it. I braced myself, certain she would hurt me – but she bathed it carefully and then bound it up with strips of clean linen, her hands deft and businesslike.

'Thank you, Katherine,' I said humbly.

'You don't listen, do you? Nagging on and on to go and see that evil old man, pushing yourself in where you're not wanted. You're lucky he didn't spear you with that pitchfork. He's certainly made a mess of your dress. Not that that will deter you, seeing as you're such a little genius at mending.'

'I think he *did* want to stick his pitchfork into me – and he spat at me – did Father tell you that?' I said, shuddering. 'He acted like he really hated me.'

'Well, I reckon he does,' said Katherine briskly, pinning the last strip of material into place.

'But it's so silly. It wasn't *my* fault. I couldn't help being born. Katherine, I can't *help* being Evie's daughter. Do you really hate me too?'

Katherine leaned back on her big haunches, clearly thinking it over. 'I'm not sure,' she said.

I felt the tears start dripping down my cheeks again.

'And you can turn off the waterworks. Crying won't work with me, Hetty Feather. Look, I don't suppose I truly hate *you*. I hate the fact that you're here. You don't *belong* here. Look at you – you stick out like a sore thumb. You're not a bit like any of the other lassies, you're so little and scrawny. You're useless at any kind of work and you can't even knit – a five-year-old drops fewer stitches than you. Why would you want to stay here? You're a London lass, with your clean fingernails and your snooty voice and your book-learning and your fancy airs and graces.'

'I'm not *fancy*. You know I'm a foundling. I only seem like a London girl because I was locked up in that hospital all those years. I'm a country girl at heart, like my mother.'

'I didn't know your mother very well, but from what I can remember she hated life on that farm with those strict Baptist parents. She couldn't wait to get away. She set her cap at Bobbie quick as a wink.'

'They were true sweethearts,' I said.

Katherine got to her feet, smoothing her coarse apron. 'For a matter of weeks, that's all. Maybe Evie fell for him, but I think he found her too intense. He panicked and ran away to sea.'

'He didn't know about me, I'm sure he didn't,' I protested.

'He didn't *want* to know. But whatever he knew, he didn't stay to marry your mother.'

'He loved her though. He loved her with all his heart, he's as good as told me that,' I said, crying hard.

'Stop that crying – you'll give yourself a sore head as well as a sore foot. Oh, Bobbie goes dreamy every now and then and thinks wistfully of what might have been – but that's the very nature of the man. He's a sentimental sap, for all he seems so tough and manly. That's why he's taken you in without a by-your-leave.'

'He's taken me in because I'm his daughter and he loves me,' I declared.

'Love! He's only known you five minutes. He's taken you in because he's sorry for you, and he feels bad about the past. It helps him feel good about himself now – but he's forgotten he's got a real daughter, and a son, and a wife who's stuck by him thirteen long years.'

'He loves me, I know he does. And I love him,' I said stoutly.

'You'd have loved any man in Monksby if you were told they were your father.'

'Well, blood is thicker than water, and Father is my kin.'

'So is mad old Samuel Edenshaw. Do you love him too?'

She had me there and I knew it. My ankle throbbed so badly that I had to stay in bed. Poor Mina had to sleep in Ezra's bed that night, because every movement made me gasp with pain. My leg swelled right up to the calf overnight and I developed a fever. I was terrified my ankle was broken and would never mend, so that I'd be left a cripple like my foster brother Saul. He was long dead but I always felt a guilty tremor when I remembered him. I knew I had not been a good sister to him – and alone in my bed during the day I cried for him. I cried for my whole foster family, especially Jem.

I read the letters he had written to me again and again. I even curled my hand and moved it along the lines, imagining Jem's strong brown hand executing each clear loop and flourish. I had not heard from him even though I had written more than a week ago. Perhaps he was vexed with me because I had not written to him throughout the long sad summer. Perhaps he had simply tired of me. This thought made me cry harder. I pulled the thin covers over my head and wept in fear and self-pity. Was Katherine right? Was Father simply sorry for me?

'Oh, no one loves me truly, no one at all,' I wailed.

Shush now, my sweet silly girl. I love you – and I always will.

Mama spoke inside my heart. I lay curled up small, my arms tight around myself, trying to clutch her close. Father came and sat awkwardly on the end of my bed. He tried hard to think of things to say to amuse me. He told me fishing tales, he told me about his own folk, he told me about his sea voyage – but his head kept nodding and I could see he was exhausted. He had had little sleep on Sunday and now he struggled to keep his eyes open.

'Go to bed, Father,' I begged, and at last he listened to me and dragged himself off to his own bedroom. Within a minute I heard his steady snores.

I lay listening to him, trying to puzzle out in my head our feelings for each other. I tried to write it down in my book of memoirs, but for once I could barely write a line.

I longed to read, but I had read my precious volumes of fairy tales so many times I could recite them without reference to the page. There was Father's set of Dickens, but it was downstairs and

I couldn't face hauling myself all the way down and then up again. I had my knitting beside me. Mina had given me my wool and needles, raising her eyebrows at the uneven rows. She could knit five times faster than me. She was in the midst of making Father a new gansey, coping with complicated cable patterning while I still struggled with plain and purl.

I longed to make something for Father myself. I sat up properly in bed and started knitting away, knowing that practice made perfect, but after a whole hour my neck and shoulders hurt, my elbows ached, and my poorly ankle was throbbing. I spotted a dropped stitch a good ten rows back and was so frustrated I threw the wretched wool across the room. All the stitches slid straight off the needle. I said something very rude and burst out crying again.

I heard footsteps downstairs, which came tapping up to my room. I clenched my fists, ready for another scolding from Katherine – but dear Lizzie put her head round my bedroom door.

'Hello, naughty girl! I heard that bad word!' she said.

'Oh, Lizzie, how lovely to see you. Have you come to see Father? I'm afraid he's sleeping – and Katherine's out at the fish stall,' I said.

'I know that, silly. I've come to see *you*! I hear

you've got a bad leg – and you've certainly got a bad temper!' said Lizzie, picking up my knitting. 'Oh dear, oh dear!'

'I just can't seem to get the knack, Lizzie, no matter how hard I try.'

'I can see it's going to be six years before I get my own shawl back,' she said, sitting down on the end of my bed and starting to unravel the rows back to the dropped stitches.

'You must take your own shawl back now, Lizzie!'

'No, no, I'm only teasing. Look, see what I'm wearing – I have this one. You can keep the grey shawl, dear. But with a little *patience*' – she deftly slid all the stitches back onto the needle – 'you can make your own shawl too!'

'I very much doubt it, Lizzie. I can't seem to do anything right here. I don't seem to belong at all,' I said, fighting not to break down in tears in front of her.

'There now, cheer up, my dear.'

'Oh, Lizzie,' I said, hurling myself at her, not even mindful of my painful ankle.

She held me close and rocked me while I howled all over again. When I reached the terrible snuffling, snorting stage, she gave me her own handkerchief and mopped me up tenderly.

'I'm so sorry. You must think me such a baby. I'm crying because you're so kind to me!'

'Well, I'll start being very unkind and unpleasant if it will make you stop crying,' said Lizzie. 'Don't fret, now, Emerald Star.'

'No one else will call me anything but plain Hetty, not even Father,' I said.

'Folk here don't see the need to reinvent themselves, that's all,' she said. 'We're all very set in our ways.'

'Yes, I know – and I can't seem to learn those ways no matter how hard I try,' I said mournfully.

'Give it time,' said Lizzie, but she sounded a little uncertain.

I pictured time passing. I saw myself knitting patterns, my hands flying across the wool. I saw myself gathering flithers, sorting driftwood, chatting with Big May and the children, week after week, month after month, year after year. I saw myself out courting with a lad like Matthew Stevens, settling down, rearing my own family. Would I ever feel like I really belonged here in Monksby? Did I *want* to belong? I didn't care for the cruel sea and the icy wind and the everlasting shoals of fish, dead or alive. I loved Father and Lizzie, I could tolerate Ezra and Mina, might even grow to like Katherine a little – but I didn't really care for Monksby folk.

Perhaps Mama would have left whether I existed or not. Perhaps she had taken against such a life.

She had never spoken of it – perhaps because she hated to think about it. She must certainly have hated that father of hers.

'I met my grandfather yesterday,' I said.

'Aye, I heard that – and I very much doubt he welcomed you with open arms. He's gone soft in the head, has he not?'

'He's not soft, he's very, very hard. He treated Mama dreadfully – and he called me a devil's child and spat on me and tore my dress,' I said. 'I shall give up any claim on *him* to be my relative.'

'Well, I'd certainly agree you're better off without *him*,' said Lizzie.

'Lizzie, do you think I'm better off here, with Father?' I asked earnestly.

'What do you mean?'

'I love him, and I know Mama loved him too, and I thought I should be truly happy if I could live with him as his daughter – but now I'm wondering.'

'Has Katherine been really hard on you?' said Lizzie sympathetically.

'Well, I think it's her nature to be hard on everyone,' I said. 'I know she doesn't want me here. But it's not just that. I don't really feel I *belong* here. I don't suppose you understand.'

'Oh I do, I do. I don't feel I belong here either. I don't think like the other women and yet I don't care to be in the company of men – leastways, not the men who prop up the bar of the Fisherman's Inn every night and drink themselves into a stupor. I've often thought of leaving, but I had my boys and I couldn't have lived with myself if I'd walked out on them. Or maybe I was using them as an excuse and I simply didn't have the courage . . . No matter. It's too late now to start a new life. I've nowhere to go, and I'm sure no one else would ever employ me.'

'What about me, Lizzie? Do you think *I* should start a new life?'

She set my knitting aside and put her arm round me. 'You're the only one who can make that decision,' she said. 'All I know is I shall miss you terribly if you move on from here.'

'And I would miss you too, Lizzie. You are my only friend in Monksby, apart from Father,' I said earnestly.

I lay awake half that night, my mind whirling, trying to think what to do with the rest of my life. I felt so bewildered, almost ashamed. I had so longed to find a family, but now that I had succeeded, I still wasn't happy.

I still think I would have stayed, in spite of my doubts and anxieties – but in the morning I received the letter from Jem that changed everything.

'Hetty has a letter from her sweetheart!' Mina crowed. 'Let me read it too, Hetty!'

'Certainly not, it's private,' I said, elbowing her away. This letter was stark and to the point.

My dear Hetty,

Please brace yourself. I have very sad news. Father's heart has failed and he passed away two days ago. Mother has taken it very bad and is not herself at all. We are burying Father on the nineteenth at twelve o'clock. Please say a prayer for him at noon. I am so sorry to have to be the one to tell you this.

I am very glad for your sake that you have found your father – but I wish you were here.

This scrap of letter is written with much love from your loving brother Jem.

P.S. I wish you could come home.

It was enough. I hobbled out of bed and limped to the window. I looked out at the gulls flying overhead, greedily waiting for the boats to come in. I squinted at the sunlight, and fancied I saw the first mast bobbing over the horizon.

'Keep safe, Father,' I whispered. 'And please understand. I love you, but I have to go. My first family needs me.'

9

It took me a matter of moments to pack my few possessions. I left my nightgown out, I took my sharp little scissors and carefully unpicked the swirly S and B embroidered on the yoke. Then I threaded my needle and quickly satin-stitched a fine big L for Lizzie. She was much larger than me, but my nightdress was suitably voluminous and should still cover her decently.

I suppose by rights I should have gifted my nightdress to Katherine, seeing as she was my stepmother and had kept me under her roof – but I couldn't find it in my heart to give her anything. I had a petticoat to give to Mina and a glass marble I'd found on the sands for Ezra. I wished with all my heart that I had something of value to give Father. In the end I snipped off a lock of my hair, tied it with green ribbon, and put it in a little envelope. I wrote carefully on the front:

To my dear father. Here is a lock of my red hair.
Please keep it twined about your heart. With the
greatest love and affection from your firstborn
daughter Hetty.

Father broke down when he carefully spelled out
the words. 'I want to keep *you*, Hetty,' he said. 'I'm
afraid that you will never come back. I cannot bear
to lose you already, not when I have only just found
you.'

'I will come back to visit you, Father, I promise,'
I said. 'But my other family need me now. Poor Jem
– he sounds distraught in his letter.'

'You are a good kind girl, Hetty. I'm proud of
you. But you're still only a little sprat. You can't
travel the length of the country all by yourself.'

'Yes I can! I travelled here, didn't I? I shall just
get on a train – a series of trains,' I said.

'Aren't you afraid to travel on one of those great
roaring monsters?' said Father.

'Oh, Father, of course not,' I lied, showing off a
little. 'I'm not a baby. And I've been on lots and lots
of train journeys.'

I had only been on four such journeys in my life,
and my heart still pounded whenever that great
puff of steam surged out of the chimney. Father
looked at me doubtfully. I realized that my great
brave father might be scared himself.

'You are so like your mother, Hetty,' he said softly. 'So fearless and independent. She must have been so proud of you.'

I felt the tears pricking my eyelids, but I was determined not to cry now. I wanted Father to think me brave as a lion.

He went over to his shelf of blue-bound Dickens, reaching over the top of the volumes. He picked out a small purse that had been hidden behind them. He opened it and started counting coins.

'No, Father! I don't want your money!'

'But the railway fare will cost a fortune!'

'I have money saved, truly I do – more than enough.'

I had earned a shamefully large amount showing myself as a mermaid at Mr Clarendon's Seaside Curiosities. I had spent less than half on my travel up to Monksby. I had prudently kept enough so that I could always return if I failed to find Father. And now I had found him and I suddenly wavered, wondering if I should stay after all.

'It means all the world to me that I have found you, Father,' I said, feeling my tears spill at last.

'It means the world to me too, Hetty,' said Father, and his own eyes were suspiciously bright. '*Please* take at least one of these sovereigns, even if you won't take the whole purse.'

'What would Katherine say if she thought you

were giving me your precious savings?' I said. 'Truly, Father, I can't possibly take even a penny from you.'

'Then . . . then take a book,' said Father, seizing hold of *David Copperfield*.

'No, I can't! That's the story you like to read yourself!'

'I can read another. I have the whole set.'

'But it will spoil your set if one volume is missing!'

'Yes, it will. So you must come back to Monksby and return it one day,' said Father, pressing *David Copperfield* into my hands.

'You are the dearest father in all the world – of course I will return it!' I said. 'And meanwhile I will read it and treasure it and think of you.'

We embraced, both of us clinging a little. Father stroked my hair, so that my pins scattered and my locks tumbled around my shoulders.

'My girl,' he whispered. Then his voice broke and he set me to one side abruptly and went out of the room so I should not see him crying.

He should have gone to bed after his long night at sea, but he walked me to the station instead. I said goodbye to Katherine at the fish stall. Her eyes bulged and her mouth opened like one of her own fishes when she saw I was really going, suitcase packed with all my possessions.

'Goodbye, Hetty,' she said. Perhaps because she was in front of all her friends, she took my hands and squeezed them hard. 'Take care, my dear,' she added.

Her own hands were slimy with fish guts and I had to fight not to wipe mine clean on my dress. For Father's sake I managed to parrot a few silly phrases: 'Thank you for having me – and thank you for tending my ankle – and for trying to teach me so many things.' I *wanted* to say, *Thank you for being the worst stepmother in the world and I hope I never see your ugly fish-face again* – but I managed to hold my tongue.

I said fond farewells to Mina and Ezra with more sincerity. Father waited with my case on the harbour wall while I limped over the rocks to Mina. I gave her a hug.

'You will have your bed to yourself now, Mina. Be a good girl – and don't go near Matthew Stevens for many years!' I gave her the petticoat and she admired its frills and popped it under her dress there and then.

Father had us stop at the dame school to see Ezra – but I knew it was a waste of time looking for him there. I didn't want to get him into trouble for truanting, but Father didn't seem too disturbed when we found him at last on the beach round the bay, playing pirates with his friends in the old wreck of a cobblestone boat. He was too busy and boisterous to calm down and say goodbye to me properly. He just snatched the marble and said, 'Shiver me timbers!' in a silly voice, while all the other little boys laughed. Then he put the marble in his eye and capered about, leering comically. Father remonstrated, but I made excuses for him.

'Let him be, Father. You know what boys are like.'

'I know only too well,' he said. 'Come on, then – we haven't got all day to wait for Ezra to calm down and recover his manners.'

We walked away, me hanging onto Father's arm because my ankle was starting to trouble me a lot. I turned as we climbed the stone steps up to the harbour. I saw Ezra far away take the marble out of his eye and wave it at me. He was shouting something, but I couldn't hear what it was.

'Goodbye, little brother,' I said, laughing a little.

We had one more stopping point before the station, and that was to see Lizzie at the Fisherman's Inn. She saw my suitcase and her whole face crumpled.

'Oh, Hetty, you're not really going, are you? Oh Lord, was it because of some of the things I said?' she cried, rushing to me.

'No, no, Lizzie – my foster father has died. I

want to go to the funeral and help the family a little,' I assured her. 'I have come to return your shawl. It has kept me so warm these past few weeks. You have been such a kind friend.'

'Please keep it, Hetty. Truly, it is a gift for you. I want you to have it,' she said.

'Well, we both know I'm never going to be able to make my own – or if I *do*, it will be all over holes from dropped stitches,' I said, laughing shakily. 'But very well, I will keep your shawl, Lizzie, and when I feel its warmth around my shoulders I shall pretend it's you, with your arms around me.'

'Oh, you're such a girl for saying sweet things. Stop it – you'll make me cry. I shall miss you so,' said Lizzie.

'You mustn't cry! Especially as I have a present for you! It's not new, I'm afraid, but I have fashioned it so that it can only belong to you now.'

I shyly took my nightgown out of my case and handed it to her.

'Oh, Hetty, I can't take your nightgown!'

'It's not *my* nightgown – look!' I showed her the large curling L I had fashioned on the yoke. 'There, you see? L for Lizzie.' I held it up against her anxiously. It trailed on the ground when I wore it but it barely reached Lizzie's calves. 'I am afraid it is a little short – and it might prove a little tight too. If it's truly uncomfortable you can always cut the yoke away and stitch it onto another nightgown. I was planning to make you one but I did not have the time,' I said.

'It's just beautiful, Hetty. I've never had such fine, lovely linen, not even on my wedding night.'

We kissed each other, and then Father called to me from outside, because he'd seen the first puff of smoke from the train. It was far away in the hills, but we had to run to the station, Father carrying my case. I was limping so badly now he was practically carrying me too. The train was already at the platform belching steam, ready to go, but Father shouted to the station master, begging him to wait for one more passenger.

I hastily paid for my fare to York, where I'd get the connecting train down to the south, and then ran along the platform to the third-class carriages. There was just time for Father to open the door and lift me in, thrusting my suitcase after me. The train started chugging away. We had not had time to embrace or even say goodbye. I struggled frenetically with the window, tugging at the leather strap, while Father ran alongside the train.

'I love you, Father!' I shouted. 'I'm so glad I found you!'

'Keep safe, Hetty. And stay in touch,' he panted. Then, when he was almost out of sight, he paused and called, 'I love you too!'

I flopped back onto the hard seat, sobbing. There were two old men sitting staring, sucking their pipes.

'My father and I are very fond of each other,' I said, with as much dignity as I could muster, settling my skirts about me and rubbing my throbbing ankle.

They sucked on silently, so I decided to ignore them. I extracted *David Copperfield* from my suitcase and opened the volume at the first page.

'This is a present from my father. He is a very well-read man,' I said proudly.

Father wasn't quite as well read as I thought. The first few pages were well-thumbed, and crumpled at the corners, but after Chapter Two the pages were all silky smooth, clearly untouched.

I felt a pang when I remembered how he said it was an excellent story, one he'd read many times. I felt sadder when I got to the Yarmouth passages and met Peggotty's family, who all lived in a fishing boat on the beach. Father would have *loved* Mr Peggotty and Ham, and sympathized with their travails at sea. Perhaps when I visited him again, I would bring the book and read him my favourite passages aloud?

When I arrived at York it was past lunch time, but I discovered I only had two minutes to leap from the little train and hurry across the platforms to the great big express train bound for London. My ankle was aching and my suitcase bulky and cumbersome, so I only just made it. I had no father to help open the carriage door and haul me up. I had to scramble up by myself, and slipped and banged my shins horribly on the step.

The carriage was very crowded and no one made room for me. I had to squeeze myself between two fat women who tutted and fussed and talked to each other over my head, complaining about *my* manners, simply because I had the effrontery to want to sit down. I sat there, thoroughly scolded, my stomach rumbling, but *David Copperfield* was a wonderful diversion and kept me totally entertained for countless uncomfortable hours.

I actually winced and whimpered out loud when Mr Murdstone beat young Davy – making the stout ladies start and look at me in alarm, clearly wondering if I were taken ill. Mr Murdstone's cruelty as a step-parent was so all-encompassing that Katherine seemed almost warm and welcoming by comparison. I could not help wondering if I should have tried harder to get along with her. Perhaps Father was right, and given time we'd have learned to tolerate each other, if not actually feel true affection. I pondered this, chin in my hands – but then smelled the still powerful fishy taint on my fingers and knew it was an impossibility.

When my eyes blurred after reading twelve chapters of very small print, I hunched down even smaller, drawing Lizzie's shawl tight around me, and, lulled by the regular judder of the train, tried to communicate with Mama. I could not will her to speak to me. Sometimes I could hear her voice, sometimes not. I badly wanted her approval for my sudden departure. I was afraid she might not think it a wise decision. Mama had fidgeted and sniffed disapproval when I'd told her tales of my foster family, convinced they had not given me the greatest start in life – but she would have criticized *any* family, for she felt nothing was good enough for me. She would surely have found fault with a nursery at Buckingham Palace.

Perhaps she was silent now because she felt I was making a grave mistake spending the last of my money on a journey clear across the country to attend the funeral of a man I scarcely remembered – a father figure to me, but not my real father. Mama might be wondering how I could bear to leave my own dear father when I had discovered him so very recently.

'*Speak* to me, Mama!' I looked up and saw the fat ladies staring at me, and realized I'd spoken aloud.

They did their level best to edge away from me, concerned that they were sitting next to a mad person. At least it gave me a little more room.

It was dark by the time we reached London at last. There was a great hustle and bustle in the vast station. I was caught up in it, and at first I was only concerned to find a ladies' room where I could relieve myself and wash my face. Then I purchased a meat pie and a cup of tea, and ate and drank with relish.

I looked around and wondered where to go next. I was worn out and my leg hurt and my head was spinning with all the noise and jostle and bright gaslight of the station. I knew I had to find my way to Waterloo to catch a train out to the Surrey countryside. I was not sure how to do this. I plucked up the courage to tug a kind-faced lady by the arm and asked her, but she advised taking a hansom cab.

I was not sure how much this would cost. Under cover of my skirts I fingered the money left in my purse. I still had to buy the ticket for this last train trip. I wasn't sure there would be enough for a cab as well. Perhaps I shouldn't have spent the money on the pie, though I had felt sick with hunger.

I decided I had better walk to Waterloo. I asked the direction outside Euston Station. First I was sent one way, and then the other. I was scared someone would try to snatch my suitcase away. I hung onto the handle so tightly that my fingers cramped. I tried to keep to the noisy main thoroughfare because I was frightened of what I might encounter in the dark alleyways.

My ankle was starting to swell alarmingly with all this unwonted exercise. I sat right on top of my suitcase for safety and rebound it as tightly as I could. I was so tired I was tempted to lie right down with the case as a pillow and sleep in a shop doorway. There were a few poor ragged souls doing just that, but they looked so vulnerable that it did not seem at all wise.

I gritted my teeth and limped onwards, dragging my case. I tried picturing in my head to divert myself from my pain and weariness. I imagined myself as a little girl again, playing with dear Jem in our squirrel tree. It had seemed a perfect fully furnished home when I was four or so. I remembered chairs and beds and tea sets, and a row of dear little squirrel babies tucked into their cots in their own snug nursery. I could see it all vividly, but perhaps we had just conjured them up from sticks and stones and mud and rags.

I was so tired now I seemed to be walking in a dream. I was not even surprised when I saw a familiar large bleak building coming into focus in front of me. I saw the entrance, the long path, the imposing door, the girls' wing on the right, the boys' wing on the left. I was looking at the Foundling Hospital.

I set my case down, stood still, and rubbed my eyes, thinking I had simply pictured it out of thin air. Surely it was simply an illusion. But no matter how hard I scrubbed at my eyes, the hospital stayed firmly in front of me, and as I watched, a dim light was suddenly extinguished upstairs, so that the whole hospital was in darkness. That must have been Matron Stinking Bottomly putting out her lamp after her final inspection of the dormitory. I pictured all those poor foundlings tossing and turning in their narrow beds.

It was hard to believe I'd been one of them scarcely six months ago. So much had happened to me in such a short time. I had lost my dearest mother and yet found a kindly father. I had toiled extremely hard in a conventional place of work and earned a pittance, and had idled through the days simply displaying myself in a bizarre costume and earned a relative fortune. I had lived in a variety of dwellings, large and small, but I had yet to find one that truly felt like my home. But I knew one thing. No matter how lost and lonely I felt right this minute, I would never wish myself back in the hospital. I was free now, and I was never, ever going back.

10

By the time I had limped all the way to Waterloo the last train had already gone. I bought another pie from a man just closing up his stall. He told me there were several cheap boarding houses in nearby streets, but I did not want to waste a penny more. I ate my meagre supper, then trailed round the vast station looking for a likely spot to settle. Eventually I wedged myself right in a corner, my back pressed against the hard wall so that no one could creep up on me.

The cold stone of the station made me shiver and I had no blanket, but I noticed that the sleepers in shop doorways had wrapped themselves in newspaper for warmth. There were any number of crumpled papers blowing around the platforms, so I gathered as many as possible and then set about making a newspaper nest in my corner.

I read *David Copperfield* for a while. David was away at school now, but I was free as a bird, so

I tried to console myself that my lot was far better than his.

Other homeless souls shuffled around the station. I shrank away from them if they came near me, clasping my case to my chest, but no one actually accosted me.

I heard one ragged old lady say to another, 'Poor little kiddie – she's new to this life. See how well-scrubbed she is?'

I was feeling especially grimy after my long journey, and my hands were blackened with newsprint, but I supposed I did look clean compared to them, with their grey-brown wrinkled faces and sour smells.

I wondered if I should offer them some of my newspapers, but they shuffled off, sharing several swigs from a brown bottle. They had other ways of keeping warm.

I did not think I would ever sleep in that great cold station, but after several chapters of David's adventures my head started nodding. I curled up small under my newspapers and dozed fitfully until at long last, at dawn, the first trains started hissing and puffing.

I cast off my newspaper nest and visited the ladies' room. When I emerged, my dress still needed a good iron, but I was scrubbed clean and my hair pinned up to make me feel older and in control.

I'd peered at my face closely in the looking glass, to see if all the emotional turmoil of the Monksby weeks had left any mark. I rather hoped for little lines and taut cheekbones and wan skin tones to give me a look of weary maturity – but my brow was smooth, my cheeks round, my skin clear, and I looked disappointingly childish. There seemed no danger of my foster family not recognizing me.

I went to the newly opened office and asked for a ticket to Gillford, the nearest town to our village. I had been right to be cautious with my money. I was left with only a few shillings. I was hungry and thirsty again, but I could not face yet another meat pie.

I stepped outside the station and found a baker's down the road. I bought two white rolls still fresh from the oven, and then, back in the station, a scalding cup of tea, and felt much better after I had breakfasted. I could not help feeling proud of myself. I had journeyed all the way from Monksby and spent the whole night in the station, and I had not cried or begged anyone for help.

Well done, Hetty! Mama's voice said within me. *I am proud of you.*

'I'm not Hetty any more. I do not seem to be Sapphire either. I am Emerald now,' I whispered. Mama didn't answer. I had a feeling she was laughing at me.

The train out into the country went a great deal more slowly than the big express train from York, and it stopped every five minutes at station after station. I peered eagerly at each sign, not daring to read *David Copperfield* in case I missed my station altogether.

The carriage grew uncomfortably full and was continuously a-jostle with people coming in and others getting off. They all had pale faces and sleepy eyes, and many smelled of the stale bed they had recently vacated. I sat primly in their midst, waiting and waiting to see the right station. I dimly remembered making the same journey in reverse with my foster mother, who took my brother Gideon and me to the Foundling Hospital when we were just five. We'd been such babies then, with no idea of the rude awakening from our carefree childhood that awaited us.

I wondered if Jem had also contacted Gideon, telling him about Father's funeral. And then there was my foster sister Martha, a year above me at the hospital, and Jem's own blood brother Nat, and Rosie and Eliza. I tried hard to picture them all in my mind, but apart from Gideon they were all a little hazy now, as if I were peering at them through a thick mist. I remembered the tall skinny young Jem with his tousled brown hair and bright eyes and ready smile. I remembered every detail of *that*

Jem – the knots of muscle in his thin arms when he lifted me up, his childish bitten nails, his jaunty walk. I could picture him laughing, his head thrown back, or yawning hard, mooing like a cow, at the end of a long day. I saw him running with a smooth steady pace – sometimes he would spot me watching and raise his legs and clop like a carthorse, neighing and shaking an imaginary mane, while I squealed with laughter. I saw him drawing with a stick in the dust, teaching me my ABC, I heard him reading aloud to me from our one tattered book, I felt him squeeze me tight when I crept into his arms.

I did not want to get his letters out of my case in front of everyone – but I could remember what they said. I repeated little phrases to myself. The very rhythm of the wheels beneath my feet seemed to judder *I wish you could come home.*

I had been mistaken to think my home could ever be with Father in Monksby, much as I loved him. Now that dear Mama was dead it was suddenly so sweetly clear to me. My home was with my first family.

At long, long last I saw the name of Gillford on the station platform. I rubbed my eyes twice, just to make sure, and then I grabbed my case, wrestled with the stiff door, and tumbled down the steps. My ankle seemed better for the rest during the train ride from Waterloo. It was still a little swollen, but if I unlaced my boot halfway down I found it reasonably comfortable. I was so eager to reach Havenford, so full of sudden surging energy, that I felt I could walk all the way.

I stopped an old couple outside the station and asked them if they knew the right road.

'You're intending to walk there, little missy?' said the old man doubtfully. 'It's seven or eight miles, all the way to Havenford.'

It was a lot further than I'd thought, but I refused to be deterred. 'I can walk that easily enough,' I said. 'If you would be so kind as to point me in the right direction I'll be on my way.'

'You're a spirited little lass,' said the old lady, fumbling in her bag of shopping. 'Here, take these to help you on your journey.'

She gave me two big rosy apples and I thanked her very gratefully. I put one in my pocket and bit into the other straight away. The crisp white flesh tasted wonderful and I set off freshly invigorated.

It was interesting walking through the town, seeing streets I dimly remembered from trips to market with my foster mother. I wandered up and down the stalls, and spent sixpence on a big bunch of Michaelmas daisies for Mother to show my sympathy. They were softly purple, an appropriate colour of mourning. I tied them in a tidy posy with a black velvet hair ribbon.

My spirits remained high until I reached the edge of town and saw the long, long lane in front of me, stretching as far as I could see. I stepped out determinedly, but my ankle was throbbing ominously now, my suitcase seemed to have doubled in weight, and even the bunch of flowers seemed an intolerable burden.

I tried to talk to Mama but she would not speak to me. I grew worried that she might not approve after all. She had urged me to find my father, so perhaps she felt that my place was still with him.

I sat down by the side of the lane, perching on my suitcase. I took my boot off and rubbed my poorly ankle, and ate my second apple to try to spur me onwards, but this time it didn't seem to work. When I stood up again, the pain shot right up my leg. I had a blister forming on the top of my foot where the loosened boot had rubbed it, and the sprain now felt doubly sharp, as if a wild animal were repeatedly gnawing at my ankle. I tried singing hymns to lift my spirits, but it was no use – I was practically sobbing with pain.

I felt myself grow hot and damp with effort in spite of the cold day. My dress was sticking to me and I was terrified I would sweat enough to stain the armpits. I felt the pins dropping one by one from my hair. I had tried so hard to look clean and neat and respectable, and now all my efforts were wasted. My bladder was clamouring too, so I dragged myself wearily off the road towards a distant clump of bushes. I was crouching there, whimpering, when I heard a rumbling, a clatter, getting nearer and nearer. I peeped round the bush and saw a man driving a horse and cart.

'Oh my Lord! Wait! Please sir, *wait*!' I screamed, very hastily pulling up my underwear. I grabbed my case and my flowers and stumbled back into view. 'Please, please, please wait!' I gabbled, lumbering desperately towards him.

The man stared at me, startled, and seemed about to urge his horse to trot on faster to escape the mad screaming girl hobbling from the bushes. Perhaps he saw the tears running down my face, because he pulled his horse up after all and sat placidly chewing his tobacco until I reached him.

'Oh thank you, thank you!' I said. 'Please, for pity's sake, could you give me a lift to Havenford?'

'I'm not a licensed carter, missy. I'm simply on my way home from market,' he said. 'I'm not going to Havenford anyway. I live on Carter's Bray.'

'Is that the big hill that overshadows the village? Well, could you at least take me there? I have hurt my foot and can't walk properly and it's vital that I get there. I am in mourning! I have to attend a funeral,' I said.

He peered at my tear-stained face and sniffed.

'Whose death are you mourning, then? You don't come from round these parts,' he said.

'I do, I do! I have come all the way from Yorkshire to attend the funeral of my father, John Cotton,' I declared.

The man sniffed again. 'What, big John the ploughman? *You're* one of his children?' he said doubtfully.

'He was my foster father when I was little,' I said.

'You're still a little squirt now,' he said, being one of the many who felt free to cast aspersions on my size.

In any other circumstances I would have marched past haughtily at such an insult. He did not seem a kind man at all, and his nose was running unpleasantly in spite of his sniffs. But I knew that he was my only chance of getting to Havenford today – otherwise I'd still be crawling along the lane when it got dark.

'Do you think you could possibly be kind enough to give me a lift to Carter's Bray?' I asked, opening my eyes wide and gazing at him imploringly. 'Please, please, please,' I added.

He chewed his tobacco thoughtfully and then spat a disgusting yellow wad over the edge of the cart. It sizzled in the sandy lane an inch from my foot. I drew my skirts up and struggled not to look disgusted.

'Well now, I *could* – but my horse is going lame. I don't want to put too much strain on the old nag, pulling two instead of one,' he said.

'Yes, but as you yourself remarked, I am very little,' I responded.

'And there's all your luggage.'

'My case is very light – and good gracious, my flowers don't weigh anything. Please let me up in your cart, sir.'

'Well, I don't want you travelling in the cart. I don't trust you at all. You'll be nibbling at all my provisions. You've got that hungry look in your eye. You *could* sit up here beside me . . .'

'Oh, thank you, sir!'

'But I think I deserve payment, don't you? A little compensation for my kindness.'

I took out my purse and tipped out the few coins I had left. 'This is all I have, sir, but you are welcome to it,' I said, making the theatrical gesture of turning my purse inside out.

'That's a very poor offering. I don't think that will do at all,' he said. His rheumy old eyes were brightening. He was clearly enjoying playing cat and mouse with me.

'It's all I have, sir,' I said. 'You can see that.'

'I'm not of that opinion. I think you could make more of an effort to please me. How about a kiss from those pretty little lips? Then I might consider taking you all the way to Havenford.'

I wanted to punch him. Kiss this creature with his tobacco-stained mouth and dripping nose? I'd have sooner kissed the backside of his poor old horse. But I forced myself to smile coyly, though it made my whole face ache.

'I think you are trying to take advantage of me, sir. If I kiss you now you can still drive off without me. How about you taking me to Havenford, and *then* I will kiss you gladly, several times.'

'Up you hop, then,' he said, leering at me. 'You drive a hard bargain, you saucy little baggage.'

I hauled myself up beside his horrible hulk, and he shook the reins and clicked to the horse to continue the journey.

Oh, what a torturous journey it was too! I tried to keep as far away from him as I could, clutching the seat to stop myself tumbling right down, but he kept trying to pull me closer. Every time he looked at me he made revolting smacking noises with his wet lips. I did my best to distract him by engaging in rapid conversation. I asked his name and age and livelihood, and pretended an interest in his unpleasant hobbies of ferreting and drinking. I knew his ferrets' names and habits and how many scores of rabbits each had killed by the time Carter's Bray loomed ahead.

He did not pause, carrying on driving round the

hill towards Havenford. I talked feverishly of types of ale and the charms of cider and the strength of spirits, until at long last I saw the village there before me, small as a child's toy model at the far end of the lane.

My heart started beating fast inside my bodice. The horrible man flicked the reins to make his tired old horse go faster – and smacked his lips. We drew nearer and nearer. We passed the first few cottages straggling on the outskirts of the hamlet – and then I saw *our* cottage! It wasn't quite as I'd remembered. It was smaller and more tumbledown, the thatch threadbare and mossy, the garden a tangle – but I knew that cottage come rain or shine, even though it was nearly ten years since I'd seen it.

The old man felt me start and gave me a very terrible grin. I could see shreds of tobacco stuck between the stumps of his teeth.

'That your cottage, missy?' he said.

'Oh no,' I said quickly. I didn't want him to know where I lived! 'No, my cottage is right at the other end of the village.'

So he drove us onwards and I sat staring at all the houses until my eyes watered. I remembered the big square one set back from the road, the village shop with the jars in the window and the rusting enamel sign by the door, the wreck of a cottage where Slovenly Nan lived with her ten children, the neat schoolhouse with the picket fence ... I had tried to jump over it once to run to Jem, and still had the scar where I'd tripped and cut my lip. I was in such a daze of reminiscence that I almost forgot my grim companion.

'Aren't we there yet?' he said. 'Are you sure we haven't passed it?'

'No, no ...' I spotted a woman hanging out her washing in the garden. I took a deep breath. 'Mother!' I shouted, and I grabbed my flowers and case and scrabbled down from the cart before he'd stopped.

'Hey, hey! Not so fast! What about our agreement? Come back here!' he yelled.

I ran fast, in spite of my pain – through the gate, full tilt towards the startled woman. 'Mother!' I shouted again. Then I whispered to her, 'Please, please, pretend you're my mother. I have to get away from that awful man!'

She stared at me, she glanced at him – and then, wonder of wonders, she clasped me in her arms. 'My little daughter!' she said, and she embraced me close, along with an armful of wet shirts and combinations.

'Come back here, you little vixen,' the man shouted. 'You owe me!'

'I gave him all the money I had for a lift to the

175

village but now he wants me to kiss him too,' I gabbled.

'Then he's a dirty old man,' said the woman, and she shook her big fist at him. 'Be off with you, you vile old fool,' she shouted. 'Trying to steal kisses from my girl! And you old enough to be her grandfather! Just wait till my menfolk get to hear of this! They'll poke you with their pitchforks till you look like a human colander. Be off with you!'

The old man waited a few seconds, his whole face contorted with rage. Then he shouted out a whole stream of rude and abusive words, spat furiously, urged his horse round, and went back down the village lane.

'Well, *he's* no gentleman!' said the washerwoman, laughing. 'Whatever were you doing, cosying up to a dirty old varmint like that!'

'It was needs must, missus,' I said. 'I'd never have got here otherwise. Thank you so very much.'

'So who are you, girl? It seems like you know the village, yet I'd have remembered that red hair of yours if you'd grown up in these parts.'

'I *did* grow up here, until I was five. I'm John and Peg Cotton's foster child,' I said.

'Oh my Lord! Then you're here for the funeral tomorrow? Such a shame – John was such a good man, and so gentle, even though he was so big. My, it'll be a hard job fitting that fine figure of a man into a coffin. And poor Peg's been taken bad too, I hear. It'll be a house of sorrow right enough. I don't know how they'll manage.'

'Well, I am going to do my best to care for everyone,' I said. 'Jem wrote and begged me to come.'

'Ah, Jem,' said the woman. 'He's a lovely lad, steady as they come. They're lucky to have a young man like that in the family.'

'I know,' I said proudly. 'Jem and I were always particularly close. Well, I had better go to them now. Thank you so much for rescuing me.' I twitched my skirt up and stepped round the little pool of spittle, and then hobbled on my way, leaving her to hang up her damp washing.

I walked back through the village. It already felt familiar to me. Whenever I saw someone in their garden or watching from a window, I gave them a merry wave, though they all seemed startled. I longed for someone to exclaim, *Why, it's Hetty! Dear little Hetty who used to skip about and play in the stream!* but I seemed a stranger to everyone.

I hurried onwards, in spite of my sore ankle, desperate to reach the cottage now. I turned down the pathway and made for the little door, half hidden by the tangle of honeysuckle and cluster roses, though none were flowering now. The only flowers in the November garden were Michaelmas daisies, a whole abundant purple bed of them. My floral posy seemed pointless now.

I could hear a hum of talk inside the cottage. I was suddenly too timid to march straight in. The door did not have a knocker, so I rapped on it with my knuckles. I waited, standing on my good leg. Then the door opened and a stout young woman stood there.

She stared at me. 'Yes?' she said, frowning.

'It's me, Hetty,' I said hoarsely.

To my horror she looked blank.

'You are . . . Rosie?' I said.

'Yes I am. But I'm afraid it's not a good time for

visiting. My father's to be buried tomorrow and the family's gathering.'

'*I'm* family. Surely you remember me, Rosie? Gideon and I came together when we were babies in a basket.'

She stared at me. 'Oh my Lord, you're one of the foundlings! What are you doing here? Have you run away from the hospital?'

'I left the hospital long ago,' I said. Though it was only last spring it certainly seemed long ago. 'I have been living with my own dear father. Did Jem not tell you? Where *is* Jem?'

'He's working on the farm,' said Rosie. 'He'll not be home till dark.'

'Dear Jem! He's always so conscientious. Imagine working at a time like this,' I said.

Rosie looked at me strangely, as if she thought it queer I should know anything about Jem.

'Well then, Hetty, you'd better come in,' she said. 'It's a good job you're so small. We can scarcely squeeze anyone else into the cottage.'

I followed her inside and saw that she was not exaggerating. A big circle of women were squashed together in the living room, sitting on an assortment of chairs and small bales of hay, all sewing, while little children played all about them, and twin baby boys toddled back and forth, grabbing at the shining needles.

180

'*Stop* that, you two! Naughty! You'll hurt your-selves,' said their mother, swiping at them. They dodged her, squealing with merry laughter. 'I'll give you a good caning before you're much older, you bad boys!' she said.

'Eliza!'

She turned and peered at me. When we were all little, Eliza had fancied herself a teacher. She'd made Jem and Gideon and Saul and Martha and me chant *The Good Child's ABC*, and if we stumbled, she'd caned us with a twig and sent us to stand in the corner.

'I'm Hetty,' I said, limping over to her. 'Don't you remember me either, Eliza?'

I was devastated. I had felt such a part of this family. How could Rosie have totally forgotten me – not even remember my name? But Eliza was nodding now.

'Ah, Hetty, you were the little naughty one!' she said. 'Always stamping your foot and screaming. Well, welcome home, dear, though it's a sad time for all of us.'

I looked around all the women in the sewing circle. There were several who were elderly, holding their sewing close up to their eyes, their fingers swollen at the knuckles, but none looked at all like Mother.

'Where's poor Mother?' I asked.

'Oh dear. She's upstairs in her bed. Bess is tending her. She's . . . she's not well, Hetty,' said Eliza.

A little ripple of sympathy went through all the women. They clucked and shook their heads and murmured.

'I will go to her,' I said. I limped over to the steep staircase.

Eliza watched me, looking puzzled. 'You're the one with the bad leg – yet I thought that was one of the boys,' she said.

'Yes, that was Saul,' I said. 'He had a bad leg from birth and limped all the time.'

'Oh, poor lamb,' said Eliza vaguely.

She didn't remember Saul either. Oh Lord, this was so terrible. We had all looked on this cottage as our true home and on these people as our family. Yet to these two Cotton sisters we were dim memories at best, pitiable little foundlings, interchangeable with each other.

Well, Jem remembered me vividly enough, didn't he? And my foster mother would surely remember me too. She had lavished such loving care on all of us. She had taken particular care with me. I was never her favourite (that was strange, shy Gideon, who always needed special protection), but she did her best to give me lots of cuddles – and lots of correction too. I had been paddled hard throughout my little girlhood, but I dare say I deserved it.

'Mother!' I called as I scrabbled up the shaky stairs.

The curtains were drawn as a mark of respect so her room was very dark and smelled mustily of dried lavender and rose petals. There was the large bed I remembered, with someone lying in it, and a figure on a chair by their side. But there seemed to be another bed too – thin and long. I stumbled nearer, and then gasped when I realized it was an open coffin.

I stared fearfully inside. There was just the flickering light of a candle on a wooden box beside the bed, but even so I could make out the stern features of my foster father. His hair was brushed and oiled back from his face in an unnaturally neat fashion. His white brow was exposed, so much paler than his brown, weather-beaten face. At first I thought his eyes were wide open and gave another gasp, but then I realized they were each covered with a round penny. His great square jaw was firmly tied up with a silk scarf so that his mouth should not sag in an ungainly fashion. Only his big beak of a nose seemed relatively normal. I remembered him snorting like a bull through it to amuse us little ones. It seemed so dreadful that he was now incapable of drawing breath in or out of those wide hairy nostrils.

Father lay eerily still in his Sunday best suit. It must have been such a trouble and trial fitting those great stiff limbs into trousers and slotting the still arms into the tight jacket. He had never felt comfortable in his Sunday clothes and was forever easing his starched collar and wriggling his legs. Why weren't they burying him in his everyday smock and soft cord trousers? And where were his big, honest boots with their knotted laces and mud-caked soles? Father had acquired a brand-new pair of patent leather shoes, their soles still as shiny as their uppers. I felt so sorry for him having to mince around in tight new shoes for all eternity.

I reached out, my hand shaking, and touched the very tip of his nose. It felt waxy and strange, and my hand flew up again as if I'd burned myself.

'He looks so peaceful, doesn't he?' said the plump woman sitting by the bed.

I peered at her as she sat there, her wild, curly hair scraped into a tight bun, her large chest forming a great cushion in the front of her print dress.

'Mother?' I whispered.

I approached her, slowly at first, and then rushed the last couple of steps and put my arm around her neck in the heedless way I'd done as a child. 'Oh, Mother!' I said, choked.

'What? *I'm* not Mother!' she said. 'I'm Bess, the eldest.'

'Oh! But you're *so* like Mother. Then . . . ?'

Bess drew back the sheets a little and held the candle up high. I saw the face in the bed. Was this poor sad twisted creature lying prone really *Mother*? She looked so old – far older than Father nearby in his coffin. She seemed like an ancient of old, her face furrowed and seamed with care – a face that had slipped sideways so one half of her mouth hung down alarmingly.

'Mother?' I said again.

She made a terrible strangled grunt. I could not tell if it was in pleased recognition or total distress.

'Oh, poor Mother,' I said, sitting down on the bed beside her and taking one of her hands in mine. I could feel her trying to clasp it back, but her fingers barely moved. 'Poor Mother! What has *happened* to you?' I whispered.

'It was when they told her Father had died. He was walking about the farm and then just dropped dead in his tracks. Felled like a great oak, that's what they said. The boys in the fields rushed to tell Mother, and the moment she heard the news she cried out and collapsed. She can barely move now, and Heaven knows what we're going to do. We're never going to be able to get her to the funeral tomorrow.'

'I shall help,' I said. 'Don't worry, Bess, that's why I've come home. Jem sent for me. I am Hetty.

I think you left home before I came to live here, but I love this family dearly. I have come to pay my respects to Father and I will happily help tend Mother, because I care for them as if they were my own flesh and blood.'

'Well, God bless you, Hetty,' said Bess. 'Would you mind sitting beside Mother right this minute? I need to go and see what my little girls are up to downstairs. They've been fretting to go and see the farm animals – the horses and the cows and all the chickens – and I should like to take them. They've been good little souls up till now.'

I would have liked to take the little children to see the animals rather than sit up here in the gloom with my dead father and my half-dead mother, but as I had offered my services so determinedly I could hardly back out now.

'Of course, Bess. You go. I will take my turn,' I said.

It seemed so much darker when she went. I hated the way the candlelight made such stark shadows, turning everyday items like the chest and wardrobe into malevolent demons, pressed against the wall, ready to pounce.

'It's all right, Mother. I am here to look after you,' I said.

I could see her eyes swivelling in the dark, looking at me.

'You know who I am, don't you?' I said shakily. 'I am bad little Hetty, remember? I'm sure I was more trouble to you than all the others put together, but I loved you so, Mother – almost as much as my own dear mama. I am sure Jem must have told you I found her – and I found my own father too. I tried to be a good daughter to him, but now I am here to be a good daughter to you. I had not realized you would have so many other daughters here to help you, but I will do whatever I can to cheer you up while you are poorly. It must be very sad for you to be lying here so helpless, but don't you worry, I'm sure you'll get better before too long.'

I wasn't sure at all, but I was desperate to re-assure Mother. She made a strange gargling noise, her mouth working hard.

'I'm sorry, Mother, I can't understand,' I said.

She tried again, but I had no idea what she meant. She sounded like a great sad baby, going 'Gi-gi-gi.' Did she mean *get up*?

'Yes, I'm sure you'll be able to get up soon,' I said. 'And tomorrow perhaps you will be able to ride to Father's funeral. They are all downstairs sewing black finery. I am sure they are making something special for you. I will sew too when I go down to join the others. I can sew very neatly now, Mother, and fashion my own clothes. I can also darn socks and stockings. You will see, I can be very useful. Are you just a little bit pleased that I have come back?'

I paused, and Mother gargled again. She could have been saying yes, she could have been saying no. She *could* have been saying *Who on earth are you? Get out of my bedroom and send me one of my real daughters*.

But I patted her poor heaving shoulders and gave her a kiss on her flushed cheeks. She smelled of sick old lady, but there was still a hint of the sweet Mother smell I remembered, which brought tears to my eyes.

Mother was crying a little too, tears seeping slowly down her cheeks.

'Poor Mother,' I said, very gently wiping them with the cuff of my sleeve. 'You must feel so sad to lose Father. He was a fine, hard-working man, a husband to be proud of.' It sounded strange to be using the past tense when he was here in the room with us, even if he was immobile. 'But you mustn't worry. Dear Jem will step forward as head of the household.'

Mother seemed slightly soothed at the mention of Jem's name, so I started reminiscing out loud about my childhood. I reminded her of how I'd tagged after Jem, following him everywhere like a shadow. I turned the little anecdotes into proper stories.

I had told tales in the darkness during bleak nights in the dormitory at the hospital – but they had been lurid tales of crime and murder. Now I told Mother sunlit stories of my country childhood with Jem. She stopped twitching and fretting and weeping, and lay very still. I wondered if she could be asleep, but her eyes were still open. Perhaps she was just listening intently.

I told stories until I grew hoarse, and then at last Bess came back upstairs.

'Ssh now, Hetty. You shouldn't really be talking so. You'll upset Mother because she can't respond, and it's disrespectful to Father,' she said.

'I was telling Mother stories about the past and she *liked* it, I could tell,' I said indignantly.

'All right, Miss Hoity-Toity! And keep your voice *down*. Now, they're having a luncheon break downstairs. You'd better go and get some. Off you go.'

It was a relief in some respects to leave that dark musty room and go down into the cramped living room, but it was hard trying to sort out who everyone was and whether they were related to me in any kind of way.

I tried to assemble my foster family in my head and then checked them off: Mother and Father were upstairs, with Bess, the eldest. I knew there was another sister, Nora, but Eliza said she was in service in a grand country house and they wouldn't give her leave to come home for the funeral.

'She's written to say she's that upset, but it's such a good position she's not going to argue and risk being dismissed,' said Eliza. She sighed. 'I think she's sweet on a footman there, but I doubt anything will come of it. She must feel it so, being the only one of us girls not spoken for.'

'*I'm* not spoken for,' I said.

'Don't be silly, Hetty. You're still a child – and you're not really a sister,' said Eliza, squashing me.

She saw she'd hurt my feelings and poured me a bowl of broth and gave me a hunk of bread. 'Here now, it's good chicken barley soup. Our Rosie made it, and she's a good cook. She'll be baking for tomorrow.'

'I can bake too. I could make apple pies. I've a very light hand with pastry,' I said, eager to be of use.

'No, dear, I think we've already got plenty of pies. Half the village have brought them,' said Eliza, gesturing around the room.

She told me who all the women were, but I found it hard to distinguish one from another. None seemed to remember me, though several said they knew that my mother Peg had had a spell fostering foundlings. It was a shock to hear Martha, Saul, Gideon, little Eliza and me talked of so casually and collectively, as if we were a flock of chickens.

'What about Nat?' I said, remembering the little wooden horse he'd whittled for me just before I was sent off to the hospital. 'Is he working on the farm with Jem?'

'No, he's gone to be a soldier. He can't get home either – his regiment won't give him leave.'

'Oh, Gideon is a soldier now. Do you think they might be together?'

'Gideon? He was the simple one that didn't talk, wasn't he?' said Eliza.

'He isn't *simple*, and he *did* talk – he talked to *me*,' I said.

'I'm surprised he could get a word in edgeways,' said Eliza drily, and some of the other women sniggered.

I felt myself flushing.

'Don't take offence, Hetty. It's just we couldn't help hearing you talking on and on to Mother upstairs,' said Eliza. 'You scarcely seemed to draw breath.'

'I was telling her *stories*,' I said. 'I just felt it must be terribly sad and lonely for her stuck up there in the dark, not being able to move. What must it be like for her, with Father in his coffin right beside her?'

'Don't start that talk in front of the children!' said Eliza. 'Consider their feelings!'

Her twin boys were busy playing duck ponds

with their broth, floating pieces of bread on the greasy waves, making them go *Quack-quack-quack*, far too absorbed to pay attention to me.

Some of the other women were nodding along with Eliza though, glancing anxiously at their children. They were so protective of their little ones – and yet no one seemed to think it odd that Martha and Saul and Gideon and little Eliza and I had been sent off to London when we were only five to be imprisoned in that dread hospital. No one had considered our feelings. I struggled to keep my temper.

A sweet-faced young woman with a long golden plait reached across the table and patted my hand sympathetically. 'I'm sure your mother loved your tales, Hetty,' she said earnestly. 'I remember Jem telling us all about your stories long ago!'

'Jem talked about me?' I said, swallowing hard.

'Oh, he was so proud of his little foster sister. He told us how you pictured until he felt he could actually *see* your castles and wild beasts and fairy lands,' she said, her face glowing. She was dressed like a girl but there was a womanly air about her. I struggled to remember her.

'Were you at school with our Jem?' I asked.

'Yes, I was. He was so kind to me too, always helping me with my lessons. I'm Janet.'

A little child in petticoats tripped as it ran past, and she caught it up and cuddled it close before it could draw breath to cry.

'And is that your baby?' I asked.

'Oh no! I'm not married,' said Janet, and her pale cheeks flushed pink.

'Not *yet*,' said one of the other women meaningfully.

'Come now,' said Rosie, starting to gather up the empty soup bowls. 'We've still so much stitching to do. Hetty, perhaps you could clean the pots for us, while we get on with our sewing?'

'Yes, I'll do that – but I'd like to sew too. I'm very good at it,' I said. 'I make all my own dresses and can follow any fashion.'

Some of the girls tittered.

'There's no need to boast,' said Rosie.

I hadn't *meant* to boast. I was just trying to make her proud of me and show her I could be useful. I could never seem to say the right thing in company. I hadn't known how to get along with Katherine and Mina and all the fisher-girls, and now I seemed just as inept with my own folk here.

Mrs Briskett and Sarah always said I didn't know my place. I didn't seem to *have* a place, even here, where I'd been brought up.

I attended to all the pots and bowls willingly

enough, though it seemed unfair that I should have to act like a servant to everyone else. Eliza then suggested I might take my turn amusing the children. It was easy enough to wriggle out of this task.

'Oh no, Eliza, I might be tempted to tell them a story,' I said. '*You* had better mind your little boys, while I take your place and sew.'

That settled *her* hash. I squeezed myself into the unwieldy sewing circle. It was good I had such a little behind because there was only a tiny three-legged stool to sit on. It made me much smaller than all the others, but I struggled not to feel at a disadvantage.

I could see we were sewing mourning for the whole family, but there was clearly not enough time or money for head-to-toe black dresses and suits. There was a black jacket to be stitched for Jem, now seemingly the head of the family, and chief mourner. Rosie was stitching one sleeve, Janet the other, while two girls fashioned a side each, and a stout woman called Norah hemmed the back. It was as if Jem himself were lying there in pieces, being lovingly handled by all these women.

I wanted to stitch Jem's jacket too, even if it was simply to sew on a few buttons, but there were too many workers already. I was told I could sew wide black bands onto the Sunday best jackets of the rest of the family, or fashion black velvet bows for the children.

'What about Mother's clothes?' I asked. 'Who is stitching them?'

The women shifted uncomfortably.

'I very much doubt Mother will be able to come to Father's funeral. She can't even rise from her bed yet,' Rosie said.

'Yes, I can see that, but surely we will carry her there, or take her in a cart?' I said.

'We don't want her to have another shock,' said Rosie. 'She's better off at home.'

'Is that what Jem thinks?' I said.

'Well, he's inclined to think we should get her there at all costs, but I think it's ridiculous – and it's Bess and Eliza and me that will have to manage her,' said Rosie.

'I'm here to manage her too,' I said. 'And I think we should do as Jem wishes. Shall I fashion a jacket for her? Oh, do please let me – I know I can do it.'

'There's not enough time to start from scratch, Hetty, don't be silly.'

'Then can I trim Mother's bonnet? She will need to wear it tomorrow, and she will want to show her respect and wear black,' I said.

'For goodness' sake, she's not *your* mother,' Eliza snapped as she tried to separate her twins. They had each seized a spare needle and were having a miniature fencing match.

I felt as if I'd been pricked all over by those very needles.

'I think it's a very good idea to cover your mother's bonnet in mourning black,' said Janet gently. 'It will be ready for her if she *is* able to attend tomorrow.'

Eliza and Rosie raised their eyebrows at each other and sighed, but they fetched me the old bonnet all the same. I cradled it as tenderly as if it were Mother's head. She had clearly not had a new bonnet for many years. The straw was limp and the material faded and threadbare. I pressed my lips together and reached for a length of black crape and a needle and thread. I was going to fashion Mother a mourning bonnet to be proud of.

I worked on it all afternoon. I was not content with covering it in crape. I took the black silk mourning-band material and completely lined it, so it would be smooth against Mother's head. I took the black velvet and made soft new ribbons from it. It was now finely finished, but still very plain and sombre.

I took another length of black velvet ribbon, cut it into little strips, then fashioned it into a rose. I held it against the bonnet. It looked extremely effective, but a little lonely. I fashioned another and then a third, to be a little black velvet bunch on one side.

'For pity's sake, Hetty, what are you doing?' Eliza snatched the bonnet and held it up. 'Mother's a sick old woman, not a fancy young girl. She doesn't need all this frippery. You're making a guy of her!'

'I am not! I just wanted to make her bonnet less plain. I think I've done it splendidly. I'm sure Mother will think so too,' I said defiantly.

'But Hetty, it's for a funeral. She can't wear velvet roses to her own husband's funeral,' said Rosie.

'I don't see why not. Don't you think it looks grand, like a whole new bonnet?' I said, my voice trembling.

'Well, it's all a little pointless anyway, as it's very unlikely that Mother will be able to go,' said Rosie.

I bent my head over the bonnet, cradling it on my lap. I didn't want them to see the childish tears in my eyes. I'd tried so hard and I'd been so sure they'd be impressed by my millinery skills.

'I think you made a simply *beautiful* job of the bonnet,' said a soft voice.

It was my new friend Janet. She stroked the silk of the lining and ran her finger gently round the whorl of a velvet rose. 'It's just like a bonnet you'd buy in an expensive shop,' she said. 'I'd love to have such a bonnet myself.'

I blinked hard and smiled at her. 'Well, perhaps I can make you one,' I said shakily. 'In soft greys with blue roses to match your lovely eyes.'

I was repaying her compliment, though I knew *my* eyes were far bluer. I liked Janet very much though. She was far more sisterly to me than my true sisters.

Eliza set me to sewing plain armbands, a repetitive and insultingly easy task that any five-year-old could master. She was treating me like the little girl I once was, bossing me around as if I were still that harum-scarum child in short skirts. I did not retort. I stared at my needle, and each time I poked it in the material I fancied I was pricking Eliza.

I had to keep on blinking to stop my tears. I had left my own father to come here. I had thought I was coming home – yet clearly I was not really welcome here in this cramped cottage. I had thought of my foster family with such longing. I had so wanted to help them and be a comfort to them in their hour of need, but my sisters seemed irritated and perplexed by my very presence. I was not even sure poor Mother had any idea who I was. I need not have made the long and troublesome journey. I was not wanted here.

Just then the cottage door opened – and a tall, broad-shouldered man strode in, smelling of fresh air and honest toil. He looked around the room and then stood still, looking stunned.

'Hetty – oh, my Hetty!' he cried.

'Jem!' I said. I leaped up from my stool and flew into his arms.

12

Jem swung me round and round until I was breathless.

'Oh, Hetty, I can't believe it's really you! How did you *get* here? I thought you were living right up on the north-east coast.'

'I *was* – but I caught the train – *three* trains – and then I hitched a ride from Gillford with a horrible old man with yellow teeth from Carter's Bray. Please hit him hard if you see him, Jem, because he wanted to kiss me!' I blurted out.

'*All* the old men from Carter's Bray have yellow teeth, and I shall hit each and every one for his impertinence!' said Jem, setting me down again.

I winced as I put my weight on my bad leg.

'Oh, Hetty, I haven't hurt you, have I?'

'No, no, I've just stupidly twisted my ankle. I did it days ago. I'm sure it will be better soon,' I said.

Jem knelt down and touched the swollen part very gently. 'Are you sure it's not broken?' he asked. 'Perhaps we should take you to a doctor . . .'

'No, it's fine, really.'

'How did you twist it?'

'I was jumping down from a high gate—'

'Oh, you're still the same Hetty!'

'It was to get away from *another* horrible old man.'

'They're pursuing you all over the country!'

'I think *this* one was my grandfather, but he did not want to own me – nor I him! But Jem, I have found my real father— Oh dear, I am so sorry!' In my joy at meeting Jem I had entirely forgotten the solemnity of the occasion. 'I am so sorry about *your* dear father, and your poor mother.'

He nodded sadly. Suddenly his square man's face seemed to soften and shrink, so he looked like a boy again, trying not to cry. 'It's such a blow, Hetty. Father still seemed so strong. And now Mother's taken so badly too. I don't know what we're going to do. It's clear she's going to be an invalid for the rest of her life. The girls are all quarrelling over where she will live – with Bess, Rosie or Eliza. I know Mother would want to stay in her own house and I'll do my best to keep her here, but I don't know how she will be looked after when I am out at work.'

'I do!' I said. '*I* will look after her, Jem!'

'But Hetty, you're far too young – and you have your life with your own folk in Yorkshire now.'

'*You're* my own folk, Jem. You always were when

202

I was little, and you always will be, no matter what,' I said.

'Well, we will talk it over later. Perhaps if you could just stay a week or two until I get everything sorted . . . Oh, what a weight off my mind! And how good it is to see you, looking prettier than ever too, with your big blue eyes and flaming hair.' He held me proudly by the shoulders. 'Isn't it wonderful to have our Hetty back?' he declared to the room.

There were general murmurs of assent, but I could tell they weren't necessarily sincere.

'I've no idea where Hetty is to sleep, Jem,' said Eliza. 'We are excessively cramped as it is. I can't see how we can possibly fit any more into the room upstairs, and all the menfolk will be squeezed down here on makeshift mattresses—'

'Hetty can come and stay at my house tonight. We would love to have her,' said Janet.

'Oh, Janet, thank you!' I said, very touched. I did not really want to sleep at her house, I wanted to be treated as part of the family in *this* house, but it was very kind of her all the same.

Jem seemed to think so too, because he squeezed her shoulder and said, 'Oh, Janet, you are such a dear friend.'

So I had to trail through the village with this new dear friend when the sewing was finished at last. When I was little, the village had seemed large and sprawling, but now it seemed so much smaller than I'd remembered. It was just as well, for I was limping badly now.

Janet insisted on carrying my suitcase and giving me her other arm to lean on. 'It's very fine leather, Hetty,' she said, admiring my case.

'It was given to me by the parlourmaid when I went into service,' I said.

'Oh my, so you're out at work already,' she said. 'You look too young to be in service, Hetty.'

'Well, I'm not any more. I couldn't bear being a servant,' I said vehemently.

'I do so agree. My mother wanted me to go into service at the big manor. Her cousin is a lady's maid there, and Mother thought I could get trained up to be one too – but I'm not really a girl for airs and graces, and I'm sure I'd never learn to arrange hair and care for fine silk and satins and style my lady,' said Janet.

'I think it's all such a silly set of rules. Why should all these rich ladies and gentlemen be treated like little children? Why can't they brush their own hair and dress themselves? They're useless layabouts, the lot of them,' I said firmly.

'You'd better not talk that way in front of Mother,' said Janet, giggling. 'So what did you do after you left service, Hetty?'

'Well, I – I worked a summer season at a seaside

show,' I said, deciding not to be too specific. 'And the last few weeks I've been working as a fisher-girl up north, but *that* is the worst job in the world. I am sure I am going to have nightmares of cod and haddock all my life.' I made a dead-fish face and Janet burst out laughing.

'Oh, Hetty, you're so funny. No wonder Jem's always loved you so!' she said.

'Really? Jem loves me?' I said.

'He was always boasting about you at school – Hetty this, Hetty that, telling us stories of what you'd done. It broke his heart when you went to the Foundling Hospital.'

'It broke mine too,' I said. 'But, oh, Janet, I am free of that place now. I found my dearest real mama but . . . but I've lost her now. I found my true father too, but I'm not sure he really needs me. I am needed *here*. I will keep house for Jem and tend poor Mother. That will prove the best work in the world.'

Janet was looking at me a little oddly, her sweet face suddenly clouded. 'You – you must not feel this is what you have to do, Hetty. You are so young, with your whole life ahead of you.'

'But it's what I want. Jem wants it too,' I declared.

'Well, you and Jem must decide together,' she said. 'I think he'd maybe want you to have some freedom and see a little bit of the world first after all those years at the Foundling Hospital.'

'I *have* seen a bit of the world! I've been to London, I've been to Bignor on the south coast, I've been all the way to Monksby in Yorkshire. Where have *you* been, Janet?' I said.

'I haven't been anywhere, Hetty,' she said, smiling wryly. 'I've simply stayed in the village. I teach the little ones at the school, which I suppose seems strange, because I struggled to learn to read when I was small, and the teacher used to get impatient and whip me, which made me even slower. But Jem helped me. He taught me so kindly, turning it into a game.'

'Oh, he taught me too! In just that way!'

'And now *that's* the way I teach the little five-year-olds. I never ever whip them and I like to think school is a happy place,' said Janet. 'Here we are, Hetty. This is my home.'

It was the largest house in the village, the one set back from the street. It was a proper country home, old and graceful, with timbered walls and a tiled roof, three whole storeys high. No wonder Janet's family had room for guests.

There was a large barn beside the house and Janet nodded towards it. 'Father's in there, but we won't disturb him now. You'll meet him at supper.'

I remembered playing in the hay in a big barn when I was little. I stared at this one. Was this the *farm* then? It seemed much too small – and yet the whole village had shrunk so maybe it was possible.

'Is this the farm where Jem works, Janet?' I asked.

She burst out laughing. 'No, Hetty! The farm is beyond the village, over there.' She gestured towards the meadows. 'But long ago, before any of the other cottages were built, this was a farmhouse, and Mother and Father like to keep it that way, plain and simple. Like me! Do come in.'

Janet's house was utterly unlike any others I knew. She might call it plain and simple, but it was much grander than the tumbledown cottage with its rough furniture and cramped rooms. There was a long solid oak table in the middle of the room, with elegant oak chairs arranged all around it. A big carved chest for linens stood at one side, and on the other loomed a huge dresser set with matching willow-pattern plates, enough to serve supper to the whole village. There was a proper rug with a swirly pattern on the polished wooden floorboards, two old paintings of the countryside on the walls, a big brass warming pan and a tall clock with a wooden case that ticked and tocked as if it were talking to me.

I'd only known simple cottages with sparse makeshift furniture and Mr Buchanan's over-stuffed modern villa, so full of gimcracks and whatnots that you sent half a dozen flying if you whirled past too quickly.

'I *love* your house, Janet!' I said, running my hand admiringly over the curved back of a chair.

'Oh, say that in front of Father and he will love *you*, because he's a joiner. He *made* that set of chairs to give to Mother as a wedding present. Come and meet Mother. She will be baking for tomorrow.'

We went into a fine airy kitchen with a proper range. Mrs Briskett would have loved to cook there. Mrs Maple, Janet's mother, was a dear, plain, earnest woman, very like her daughter. Her hair was plaited in a girlish braid, though it was now silver-grey. She wore a long white apron and her sleeves were rolled up as she beat eggs into a bowl of cake-mix.

'Mother, this is Hetty – do you recall, Jem's foster sister? She lived here until she was five, and then she had to go to the Foundling Hospital.'

'Oh yes, the little one with the bright red hair! I remember Peg carrying you around when you were a babe. You had a twin, did you not?'

'That would be Gideon. We're not related, but I always thought of him as my brother. He is gone to be a soldier now.'

'And are you here for poor John's funeral?'

'Yes, that's why I've brought her here, Mother, because there's no more room to bed down in Jem's cottage. I said Hetty could stay overnight with us. Is that all right?' asked Janet.

'Oh yes, dear, Hetty's more than welcome. Take her up to the guest room,' said Mrs Maple.

'Guest room' sounded very grand. A room just for me, their guest! It was right upstairs at the top of the house, a strange little room with iron ribs stretching across the ceiling and rows of hooks all around the walls. I fingered them curiously and Janet laughed.

'Whenever my sisters and I were naughty Mother always threatened to take us up here and hang us on the hooks,' she said. 'Oh, Hetty, your face! They're bacon hooks – this used to be a bacon loft long ago. They hung the smoked bacon here after it was cured.'

Now that she'd told me that, I fancied I smelled a slight whiff of salty bacon about the room, though the bed was fragrant with lavender sachets and there was a bowl of dried rose petals on the linen chest. The smell reminded me of the room where my poor foster father was lying in his coffin and I shivered again, pulling Lizzie's shawl tight around me.

I was glad when we went downstairs to the warm kitchen and sat chatting while Mrs Maple baked. She made a Victoria sponge which she spread with her own homemade strawberry jam, two dozen little custard tarts, and an elderflower madeira cake laced with her own home-brewed wine.

'Do you think that's enough, Hetty?' she asked me anxiously. 'I'll gladly make up another batch, for I know poor Peg isn't up to baking at the moment – but I reckoned your big sisters would be fixing the funeral feast themselves.'

'They have been baking, but not lovely cakes like these!' I said. I paused, looking at them hopefully.

'Perhaps you two had better try them for me, just to be sure they're up to standard,' said Mrs Maple, giving us each a warm custard tart and sprinkling it with sugar and nutmeg.

I had had only a small bowl of broth for my lunch. My custard tart disappeared in seconds. 'Oh my!' I said, with my mouth full.

'Mother's custard tarts are the best,' said Janet.

'I don't suppose you need to test your sponge or your madeira?' I asked.

'Absolutely not, you saucy girls,' said Mrs Maple. 'Now go into my pantry, you two, and pick a couple of jars of fruit. I dare say they will come in useful tomorrow too.'

I'd been in pantries before. I'd crept into the one at the hospital when I was in the kitchen helping Mama, and she'd slipped me a handful of raisins or a spoonful of sugar. I hadn't dared sneak morsels of food from Mrs Brisket's pantry. She might have chopped my fingers off if she'd found me with my hand in her sweetmeat jar. But those pantries were as nothing compared to Mrs Maple's. It was crammed with jars of fruit, preserves and pickles, arranged in glowing tones of colour, from the palest creamy-beige honey to the deepest purple damson. I stroked the shiny jars reverently, unable to choose.

'We'll have two jars of the yellow plums – Jem loves them so,' said Janet. 'Remember, Hetty? Jem always used to give himself a stomach ache. He'd pick them straight from the tree and eat two pounds at a time.'

I *didn't* remember. I couldn't help resenting the fact that Janet knew Jem so much better than me. I had only had five years with him, but she had had her whole life. But even so, Jem was *my* brother, not hers. I had 'married' him wearing a long night-gown with a daisy chain crowning my hair when I was four. He had been happy to call me his sweet-heart then.

I thought of Jem's letters. They weren't exactly *love* letters, but they were so fond, so dear, so full of affection. I would be living with Jem now, tending Mother, cooking and cleaning, washing his shirts and darning his socks. I would be acting like a little wife already. Perhaps, in the fullness of time . . .

I had my supper with the Maples – chicken and cabbage and potatoes, a simple enough meal, but beautifully cooked, with a rhubarb pie for pudding.

Mr Maple ate with us, but said very little. He was a tall, broad man wearing old corduroys, as plain and strong as his furniture. He sat at one end of the table, Mrs Maple at the other, while Janet and I sat at each side. Four of the chairs stood empty. Janet was the youngest of five, but all her sisters had left home to get married.

'But don't you worry, my petal, it will be your turn soon,' said Mrs Maple.

'Mother!' said Janet, going very pink.

'Don't you think it's likely, Hetty?' said her mother, turning to me.

'Oh yes, very likely,' I said politely, because Janet was a sweet kind girl, and if she'd been taught her mother's culinary skills she'd make any man a fine wife.

Mrs Maple was a magical healer too. She saw me limping, and after we had washed the supper dishes she bade me take off my boot and stocking so she could examine my ankle. 'Poor Hetty! It looks very angry and sore,' she said, touching it very gently.

'Yes, indeed it is,' I said.

At the hospital we had learned very quickly not to complain of our ailments. We never got any sympathy, and sometimes a complaint would actively aggravate a matron, and we'd get a slap on top of our sore throat or tummy ache. I had tried to bear pain stoically – but I'd had to be very brave all that very long day, and now my whole leg ached and throbbed, and the bruising was still deep purple.

'I will do my best to ease it,' said Mrs Maple. 'Janet, run to the cupboard and fetch me dried elderflower and chamomile.'

She bathed my ankle with vinegar and water, which felt very soothing, though I did not care for the smell. Then she made up a poultice, mixing the dried flowers with crumbled bread, and bandaged it into place. I don't know whether it was the vinegar bath, the herbal poultice, or Mrs Maple's kindness, but the throbbing calmed and my ankle felt almost as good as new.

'But you must rest it, Hetty. I don't know how you'll cope walking in the funeral procession tomorrow. Perhaps you'd better stay resting here . . .' she said.

'I shall go even if I have to hop all the way,' I said. 'And I will do my best to get Mother there too.'

The thought of her poor twisted face and her gargled speech made the tears spring to my eyes. I did not love her the way I loved my own dear mama, but she had cared for me like a true mother for five whole years and she meant a great deal to me.

I lay awake for hours that night in the bacon loft. The bed was very comfortable, with three feather mattresses as soft as thistledown, but I tossed and turned all the same. I thought of Mother lying immobile on her bed and Father even more stiff and straight in his coffin.

Then I thought of Mama in her coffin under the earth in faraway Bignor, and I turned on my front, put my head under the pillow, and sobbed hard, because I loved her so and missed her very much.

I am here in your heart, my Hetty.

I was a little comforted and slept at last.

Mrs Maple made us a fine platter of eggs and bacon and black pudding for our breakfast in the morning. I swallowed mine hastily, eager to get back to the cottage to see how they were faring.

'I will come with you, Hetty,' said Janet. 'I want to see if I can be of use too – and you need an arm to help you along the lane.'

'You're so kind to me, Janet,' I said, squeezing her hand. I felt my heart lifting. I had found a true friend here in my own home village.

I had made very few friends in my life so far. There was Polly, who had been my dear companion at the hospital, but she had been lucky enough to be adopted. There was Bertie the butcher's boy. We had walked out together and had great larks. I rather wished I had stayed in touch with him. Then there was Freda, my gentle giant friend at Bignor. I felt a pang remembering her. I had promised faithfully to write and tell her how I was faring, and yet

I hadn't penned a word. For a girl who fancied herself a writer I seemed to be a very poor correspondent. But at least I had written to Jem. I patted my chest reflectively. His letters were now in my suitcase, tied up with ribbon, but it still felt as if I were carrying them close to my heart.

Jem was standing in the garden outside the cottage, smoking a clay pipe, looking very smart and grave in his black funeral jacket.

'Oh, Jem!' I called, and I ran to him, forgetting all about my twisted ankle.

He swung me up in his arms again. 'Oh, Hetty, it's so good to have you here!' He looked over my shoulder at Janet. 'It's so kind of you to have her sleep at your house, Janet. I'm very grateful.'

'Think nothing of it, Jem. It's a real pleasure for us,' she said.

'You look very fine in your black jacket, Jem,' I said.

He wriggled uncomfortably. 'It feels very tight and strange. I'd much sooner be in my work clothes. But you two look very neat and trim too.'

We each had a black band wound about the sleeves of our print dresses, and I'd tied black velvet bows in our hair.

'There's such a to-do indoors, all the womenfolk tidying and cooking and cleaning and all the children forbidden to play out in case they get themselves grimy,' said Jem.

'What about Mother?' I asked.

Jem's face clouded. 'I sat with her before breakfast. She seems so agitated. She's trying to talk but she can't manage to make the right sounds. I feel so badly for her,' he said, his voice breaking. 'It seems so sad that she can't go to her own husband's funeral when they've been married so many years and rarely a cross word between the two of them.'

'She *shall* go, Jem! We can take her with us in a little cart, and then we can carry her into the church. She *needs* to go. I could not have borne it if I had been kept from Mama's funeral,' I said passionately. 'I will look after her in the church, Jem, and make sure she's tended and comfortable.'

'And I will too,' said Janet.

'You are such dear girls,' said Jem. 'Very well. I will ask old Molly if we can borrow her donkey and cart.'

Bess and Rosie and Eliza were appalled when we told them of our plan.

'Mother isn't fit!'

'The whole village will be gawping at her!'

'She can't go to a funeral in an old donkey cart, it's not seemly!'

They fussed and clucked like a lot of broody hens, but we would not be deterred.

'Mother shall go to the funeral in her newly trimmed bonnet – and I shall make the donkey and cart look *extremely* seemly,' I declared.

Old Molly's cart was clean, if a little rickety, and her even older donkey was a good, patient little creature with big brown eyes and long eyelashes.

'You'll pull Mother carefully, won't you, donkey?' I said, feeding him a carrot. He nodded his soft grey head and batted those beautiful eyelashes as if he understood every word.

'You'll be making a guy of Mother, taking her to church in a donkey cart,' said Eliza.

I had attended chapel weekly for nine long years. 'Didn't Jesus Christ himself enter Jerusalem riding on a donkey?' I said.

I took my drooping bunch of Michaelmas daisies and decorated the donkey, winding flowers around his bridle and fashioning them into a crown about his pointy ears. There was a little black material left over from the mourning bands. I draped the seat with this, and made black velvet streamers to hang at either side.

'For Lord's sake, Hetty, we'll look like a travelling circus,' said Eliza.

'Hush, Eliza. I think Hetty has dressed the donkey and cart wonderfully,' said Jem. 'Now Mother can go to the funeral in style.'

I went upstairs to tell Mother. Her eyes gleamed

in the darkened room. I was pretty sure she was thankful. She tried to clutch me with one poor hand and said, 'Gi-gi-gi . . .'

'Yes, Mother,' I said, to humour her. She nodded her head fervently, tears welling in her eyes.

'Now, Hetty, don't upset her so – I've just got her calmed down,' Bess snapped, dabbing at Mother's face with a handkerchief.

'Of course Mother's sad. It's her husband's funeral! I think she should weep all she wants. Now, help me lift her a little, so we can put on her dress and her new black bonnet.'

The girls had already bathed Mother and changed her into a clean white nightgown. It seemed an impossible task to squeeze her into her Sunday corsets and her petticoats and her stiff Sunday costume and her tight button boots.

'Surely she can stay in her nightgown. We'll simply put her jacket over the top. I will arrange my shawl over her lap like a blanket to keep her warm,' I said. 'She doesn't need her boots because she won't be walking anywhere.'

We had to get Father out of the bedroom first, to ride to church in his superior funeral carriage. The sexton came, wearing full black mourning from top to toe, with Mr Maple the joiner to nail the coffin shut. I was in the bedroom adjusting Mother's bonnet when Eliza suddenly darted forward and unlaced the shoes from Father's feet.

'Eliza!' I gasped as she removed first one shiny shoe, then the other.

'They are my husband's new shoes. He hasn't even worn them yet. We just lent them to Father so he looked grand in his coffin,' she hissed. 'There's no point wasting them.'

Father's feet looked very bare and vulnerable without shoes. One of his waxy toes was sticking straight through his sock, but it was too late for me to attempt to darn it. Mr Maple nailed the coffin lid in place, and then they summoned two strong farm lads and Jem, and together they slowly, carefully and laboriously carried the coffin downstairs. It was a tricky business, because the coffin was long and unbending and had to be handled very reverently, and yet it had somehow to be poked down the narrow stairwell and twisted and turned in the right direction. There was nothing to grab onto but a thin rope rail, and at one point halfway down the youngest farm hand lost his grip and buckled at the knees. It looked as if Father's coffin would toboggan down the rest of the stairs unaided.

There was a united gasp from all the women and children down below in the living room, but Jem stood stout and firm, bearing the weight until the young lad recovered.

The coffin was safely stowed in the shiny black

funeral carriage. The funeral horse was equally shiny and black, with a black plume on his head. He looked very grand and impressive, but I thought the donkey tethered behind decked in daisies looked equally decorative.

We brought Mother down next. Bess and Rosie tried supporting her, one on each arm, but her feet would not work at all, though it was clear from her face that she was making a huge effort. Jem came to the rescue again. He tried cradling Mother in his arms, but she was a large woman and he couldn't quite manage it. He had to hoist her over his shoulder and carry her down in that fashion, though it looked a little undignified.

Eliza twitched beside me, but when Mother was settled on the black silken seat in the donkey carriage, my shawl spread around her white night-gown, there was a murmur of tender approval. Her bonnet looked particularly fine, though Eliza had set it at an odd angle to try to hide Mother's newly twisted mouth.

Now that Father and Mother were in their rightful places the funeral procession could commence. Bess lined the family up in order of importance, which meant that she was first, walking alongside Jem. There was a whole tangle of husbands and children before I could get a look in, at the tail end. I found this upsetting but I struggled not to show my feelings, knowing it was not the occasion to have a squabble.

Jem saw my face and came forward, looking incredibly tall and gentlemanly in his black stovepipe hat. 'Hetty, I think you should ride in the cart with Mother in case she slips sideways,' he said.

'No, I shall sit with Mother, Jem,' said Eliza.

'I think you had better take Claude and Frederick by the hands and walk with them,' he said. 'Hetty needs to ride anyway, because she is lame.' Before she could object further, he lifted me up onto the donkey cart. I sat down triumphantly and put my arm round Mother.

'There now, Mother, it's all right. I'm here to look after you,' I said.

Her eyes swivelled past me, and she started her 'Gi-gi-gi'-ing.

'Ssh now, Mother,' I said, patting her and tucking the shawl more securely round her, but she kept up her agitated murmuring for the remainder of the journey.

It was a struggle getting her into the church. It would have been simple if we could have driven the donkey cart right inside, but even I could see this wasn't quite appropriate, and it would prove disastrous if the donkey answered a call of nature. So we had to lift Mother down from the cart – Jem and a cluster of clucking sisters – and then haul her inside. People stared, and Eliza became particularly agitated, but it was only for a few moments. Then Mother was propped up in the front pew between Jem and me, and everyone else could file through in an orderly manner.

Someone played the harmonium and I started to cry, because I'd heard the same doleful tune at Mama's funeral. There was always a sadness about me now because I missed her so much, but the solemn music made the sadness spread until I wanted to cast myself down on the stone floor and sob despairingly. However, I knew what Eliza would say if I did, and so I remained upright and decorous, though I couldn't stop the tears splashing down my face.

Mother leaned against me and stabbed awkwardly at my knee with her hand. She seemed to be trying to comfort me, in spite of her own grief and affliction. I was so moved that I hugged her hard, without caring a jot whether I was making a spectacle of myself or not.

Jem flashed a ghostly smile, but he too was struggling to stay composed. He had been so strong and manly before, but now, in church, with Father in his coffin in front and Mother keening beside us, Jem seemed to be losing all his mature authority.

His shoulders slumped and his chin started shaking. He closed his eyes as if desperate to keep them in place inside his lids. He was holding a piece of paper covered in his own clear round handwriting. He looked at it again and again, his hands shaking.

We had to sing the first hymn, 'Praise My Soul the King of Heaven'. We had sung it regularly at the hospital chapel, so I was word perfect and didn't need a hymn book. I did not have a very fine voice. It was a little shrill – but I sang loudly even so because Mother could not sing herself and Jem was so troubled that not a sound came out, though he was mouthing the words.

Then the parson read from the Bible and we said a prayer. We seemed to be rattling through the service without mishap. But then the parson paused and looked directly at Jem in the front pew. 'Now we will have the eulogy,' he said.

Jem clutched his piece of paper convulsively and got to his feet. He was very pale and shaking more than ever. He looked at Father's coffin, he looked at Mother in the pew. He had to screw up his face to prevent himself from sobbing aloud.

'Oh, Jem,' I said, and as he brushed past I clasped his clammy hand and squeezed it hard.

Jem barely seemed aware of my touch. He

groped his way to the front and stood squarely in front of the congregation, legs braced to stop them trembling. He held his piece of paper out in front of him and tried to speak, though his head was jerking hard in an effort to control his sobs.

We all waited, our hearts beating fast. Even Mother sat still as a statue, her eyes fixed on Jem.

He still said nothing, though we could see he was trying desperately – but he didn't dare risk it. If he started talking about Father, he'd lose all self-control and start weeping like a baby in front of everyone. I might not have seen Jem for nine long years, but I knew him through and through. I'd seen him struggling not to cry as a child. I'd seen his shame when he lost the battle.

I looked around desperately, but everyone was stuck to their seats, not a soul coming to his rescue. Then *I* would!

I stood up, leaned Mother against Eliza, and shot out of the pew to stand beside Jem.

'Sit down,' I said to him imploringly, but he seemed unable to move. Then I coughed and stood as tall as I could manage, my hands clasped behind my back.

'My name is Hetty Feather,' I said, for it was pointless trying to be Sapphire Battersea or Emerald Star in this village where I'd spent my little girlhood. 'Perhaps you remember me. I am so pleased and proud to be part of the Cotton family, though they are not my blood relatives. Dear Mother brought up many of us foundling babes.'

There was a little intake of breath from the congregation. People still said the very word 'foundling' in hushed tones, with a raise of the eyebrows, as if it were synonymous with 'child of sin'. Well, even if I was exactly that, I would show them that I could do my Christian duty and give Father a eulogy to be proud of.

'I have my own dear mama, but very sadly she has passed away. I have my own dear father too and have recently got to know him well. But I've been doubly fortunate to have two sets of parents. Though Peg and John Cotton were only my foster parents, they brought me up with the abundant love and care they gave to their own children.

'As you know, Father worked hard upon the farm. His strength and stamina were legendary and he toiled willingly all day long, a giant among men. When he came home at the end of each long day, you would expect him to call for his supper and then demand a little well-deserved peace – but no, he spent his evenings happy to chat and play with us children. He'd sit me on his knee and play "This is the way the ladies ride", and then he'd trot me up and down. When he got to the exciting "gallopy-gallopy-gallopy" part I'd shriek with excitement, feeling as if he and I were truly galloping across the countryside together. When I'd been a bad girl – and I'm sure the family will vouch for the fact that this was frequently – Father would take me to one side and be a little stern with me, so that I'd hang my head in shame, but he never struck any of us, though I'm sure I certainly deserved it.

'When I was tired each night I would curl up on Father's lap and he would tell me a story. He would gather us all around his knee and tell us tales of the lark he'd heard singing that morning, the baby foal out in the fields, the first pink blossoms on the cherry trees.

'Father's body is there in the coffin in front of us, but I like to think he is already in Heaven, singing along with the lark, petting that foal and walking under the flowering cherry trees.'

I stopped speaking and looked at the listening congregation a little anxiously. I expected them to be frowning and shaking their heads at my impromptu speech, but to my immense surprise and gratification they were all staring at me, rapt, with tears in their eyes. Even Eliza was dabbing away with a handkerchief, overcome. I looked at Jem. Thank goodness he was now totally comp-osed. He put his arm round me, squeezed my shoulder tightly, and then led me back to the front pew.

No one clapped because this was a funeral in a church and of course it wouldn't be seemly – but I could see that if we were in any other venue they'd be cheering me to the rafters.

13

The funeral feast back in the cottage was an absolute triumph. It seems dreadful to describe it thus. Of course we were all very sad. Father was much mourned and Mother totally pitied. Most of the mourners were in tears when Father was taken out into the graveyard and buried in the newly dug grave. All his true kin children threw specially ordered hothouse roses – from the gardener up at the manor – onto the coffin as a mark of respect.

There was no rose left over for me, so I scattered a handful of Michaelmas daisies instead. Yes, that was a time of great weeping – but within an hour we had all had a glass or two of cowslip wine and felt considerably cheered. It was the first time I'd ever tried wine. I didn't care for the taste at all. It was much too syrupy, with a dark flavour that made me shudder – but I liked the *effect* it had. The tight clench in my chest eased and I felt as good and welcome as anyone under that thatched roof – more so, in fact, because folk gathered round me in little clusters and praised my eulogy, saying how much it had moved them.

'You said it all so perfectly, Hetty. It was truly poetic,' said dear kind Janet. 'And you spoke out so clearly too, in front of everyone. I could never have done such a thing. Jem was clearly grateful to you, when he was so choked with emotion he couldn't get the words out.'

Jem was recovered enough to speak up for himself now. 'You said such splendid things, Hetty, simple yet so true, picturing it all so beautifully. I am glad now I couldn't read out my own words. They weren't a patch on yours, even though I had days to write down all my thoughts. You're a little star.'

'Oh, Jem, remember! Madame Adeline called me that the day the circus came,' I said.

'Because I'd bought you a gingerbread and stuck the star to your forehead,' said Jem.

'Oh, you *do* remember!'

'I remember everything about you, Hetty. You're my own dear sister,' he said, so warmly.

Jem's real sisters were perhaps a little put out that everyone was making such a fuss of me. They whispered amongst themselves, looking at me meaningfully, but they did not say anything unkind aloud. I was careful to make myself useful, taking my turn watching over Mother, who was now resting upstairs. She was calmer, but still murmuring 'Gi-gi-gi' as she fell soundly asleep. When my foster sisters took their turn with Mother, I handed round the wine and food downstairs.

I'd never seen such a display of food in all my life. It would have fed every child in the Foundling Hospital for an entire month. Every woman in the village had brought several platefuls, not just dear Mrs Maple. There were rabbit pies and chicken pies, and egg and bacon lattice tarts, and little pork pies, and slices of pink ham. The sweet cakes were a picture: Mrs Maple's Victoria sponge and elderflower cake and custard tarts, a fruit cake, a cherry cake, a jam roll, a Battenberg, apricot and apple and gooseberry pies, and a huge bowl of pink blancmange that set every child clamouring.

I ate and drank determinedly until I was truly stuffed. I felt myself flushing as pink as the blancmange. I stepped out of the stifling cottage and stood in the cold early evening air, looking up at the violet sky.

'I shall stay here, Mama,' I whispered. 'I have made the right choice, haven't I? I love Father, but I don't belong in Monksby. I don't believe you did either. Oh, Mama, we belonged together. Why were you so cruelly taken from me? I miss you so much. If only you were here.'

I knew Mama was in my heart, but I couldn't hear her tonight. I tried to imagine her in her own Heaven, rephrasing my eulogy for Father, but now my much-praised words seemed cheap and hollow. Mama would never be happy listening to larks and walking under cherry blossom. She'd want to listen to *me*, to walk side by side with *me*. She would be missing me unbearably too.

I started sobbing, covering my face with my hands, leaning despairingly against the cottage wall.

'Hetty? Oh, Hetty, are you crying?' It was Jem, come to find me. 'You poor little girl. You loved Father like a true daughter, didn't you,' he said, and he took me in his arms.

He seemed so moved I did not like to tell him I was crying for my own mama.

'I shall miss him so too,' Jem whispered in my ear.

We clasped each other for comfort.

'I shall have to be the man of the home now,' Jem said.

'And I shall be the woman of the home,' I declared. I meant it seriously, but Jem gave a great hiccup and then laughed.

'Oh, Hetty, you're such a dear funny child,' he said, hugging me.

'I shall show you. I shall look after you, Jem, and look after Mother, and we will all get along splendidly together,' I promised.

I was fired up and ready to start immediately, but all three of my foster sisters and their families were spending another night at the cottage, so again I had to avail myself of the Maple hospitality.

It was a struggle walking back to their fine old house. My ankle had started aching again and I was feeling unaccountably dizzy. When I lay down on the feather mattresses in the bacon loft, the little room seemed to whirl about me, the hooks performing a circular dance. I had to clutch the sides of my bed because I feared I might fall out altogether.

I felt very ill – but oh dear, that was as nothing compared with the way I felt in the morning. It was as if my head were crammed into a hard helmet. If I even lifted it from the pillow, pain throbbed in my temples. It even hurt to open my eyes. My stomach was affected too. Just the thought of the cakes and pies I'd golloped down so eagerly yesterday made me heave. When I tried to stand up, I felt so weak I had to flop back into bed again. I knew I could not possibly eat any breakfast. I had no desire for food ever again, although I was immensely thirsty and drained the glass of water on the little bedside table.

When Janet came to fetch me, I whispered to her that I was very ill. 'I am so sorry, but I am suffering from some terrible fever,' I murmured. 'Don't come too near lest it's contagious. I have never felt this ill in all my life, not even when I had pneumonia.'

Janet put her hand on my forehead and peered into my eyes. 'Oh, poor Hetty, don't worry! You aren't truly ill,' she said cheerfully.

'I *am*, indeed I am,' I said indignantly, and then winced at the sound of my own loud voice. 'I feel utterly wretched.'

'Yes, dear, I don't doubt it, but it's only because you drank too much cowslip wine yesterday,' Janet said gently.

'What? Then . . . am I *drunk*?' I said in horror.

'You were just a little bit last night. And now you will have a sore head and a dry mouth and feel very weak,' said Janet.

'Yes! *Very* sore and *very* dry and *very* weak,' I said. 'But oh, how terrible, to have been drunk!'

I had seen drunken men on the streets of London. I had watched poor Sissy's father bellow and rant in a drunken rage. I had seen cocksure lads quaff their ale and then stagger into the sideshow to sneer at poor Freda, my dear female giant friend. I associated drunkenness with all that was cruel and loud and base. Oh dear Lord, had I behaved in a similar fashion? I pulled the bedclothes over my head in shame, unable to look kind Janet in the eye.

'That's it, sleep it off, Hetty,' she said, patting my shoulder gently.

'I feel so ashamed,' I said.

'It was an emotional day yesterday – and you probably didn't realize how potent cowslip wine can be,' she said.

'I shall never ever drink another drop again,' I vowed.

I felt I should drag myself up and make amends to the Maple family as best I could, but the smell of breakfast cooking downstairs made me feel so nauseous that I knew it was much safer to stay in my bed. I tossed and turned uneasily until lunch time, taking care to breathe shallowly. I fancied I could still smell long-ago smoked bacon in the tiny room and its odour was now immensely offensive.

Janet came up to my room at midday, with a bowl of chicken soup, a crust of bread – and a large glass of yellow liquid.

I gazed at it in alarm. 'I cannot drink any more wine!' I said wretchedly.

'No, it's not *wine*, Hetty. It's Mother's lemon cordial. It will make you feel better, I promise. Take a few sips and see,' said Janet.

I tried, very gingerly, and after a few minutes I agreed that she was right, though I only felt *minutely* better. 'How is it you don't feel as terrible as me, Janet? I'm sure you drank the cowslip wine too,' I said, rubbing my head and groaning.

'I only had one glass,' she said.

'Oh dear! I was so thirsty I kept gulping it down. I am so stupid,' I said, shame-faced.

'You're not the slightest bit stupid. You're just a little inexperienced. You haven't had a very normal life,' said Janet.

'Sometimes I don't think I'll ever catch up and learn to be like other girls,' I said.

'I think you should just be yourself,' said Janet.

By mid afternoon I really was starting to feel quite a lot better. I got up and washed and dressed and went downstairs, hanging my head, to apologize to Mrs Maple.

I thought she would scold me but she was as sweet as her daughter, and just gently laughed at me. The Maples wanted me to stay another night under their roof, and in any other circumstances I would have loved to accept their hospitality – but I knew some of my sisters were journeying back to their own homes today.

'I need to be at the cottage with Mother,' I said.

'Well, we will help you all we can, child,' said Mrs

Maple. 'But it will be a great burden for any young girl, caring for a helpless invalid and running the household. Do you know how to cook at all?'

'Oh yes! Well, I can't bake the way you can, but I can make simple meals – and I'm very good at apple pie. I will make one soon and invite you round to sample it,' I said.

I gathered my things together, and Mrs Maple made me one more poultice for my sore ankle, though it was nearly better now. I kissed her and Janet goodbye, thanked them many times, called farewell to Mr Maple in his workshop, and then set off down the road to the cottage.

It was strangely silent inside now. Bess and Eliza and their families were departed – only Rosie had stayed on. While I was flopping around in my bed she had washed and dried all the many dishes, packed up the makeshift spare beds, swept the cottage throughout, prepared a stew that was now bubbling in its pot, and had tended to Mother throughout.

'Oh, Rosie, you're like the good fairies!' I declared. 'I feel so terrible that I wasn't here to help you, but I felt so poorly I couldn't get out of bed.'

'Well, you'll *have* to get out of bed tomorrow, for I must go back to my work. Those children will be running riot without me, plaguing their poor mother to pieces.'

Rosie was a nurserymaid in a large house ten miles away, looking after four unruly children and a babe in arms.

'I'll be leaving them anyway next spring to get married,' she said. 'But I've been thinking I should give up my position now and care for Mother – and then she can live with us when I am married.'

'No, Rosie! *I* will look after Mother. She'll want to be *here*, in her own cottage. I will look after Jem too. He needs me now,' I said stoutly.

'Hetty, you're still a child – and you're not even a relative, you're just a foundling,' said Rosie.

'Don't be so horrible!' I said, stung.

'I'm sorry. I didn't mean to hurt your feelings. I'm just speaking the truth. You say you want to look after Mother, but where were you today?'

'I told you, I was ill,' I mumbled.

'Yes, I know you *felt* ill. I'm sure we all did after the funeral feast. But *we* all got ourselves up and got on with it. Jem was up before dawn to start work on the farm. And what would poor Mother have done if we daughters had kept to our beds all day long? She's as helpless as a baby, Hetty. She needs to be washed and changed and spoon-fed, don't you realize?'

'Yes, yes, I know – and I'll do all those things gladly, because she did them all for me when I was a babe. She's *like* a mother to me, even if she's not my own. And I love Jem like a brother, and in future *I* will get up at dawn to send him on his way with a good breakfast inside him – and whenever you or Bess or Eliza or any others come to visit I will cook and clean for you and make you as welcome as I can because I think of you as sisters, even though you point out so painfully we are nothing of the kind,' I said, standing facing her with my hands on my hips.

'Oh, Hetty,' she said. 'We all know you're full of fine fancy words – but it's *deeds* we're worried about. But very well, we'll try it for a little while, for I don't think we have any alternative just at present.'

'It would not kill you to sound a little *grateful*,' I said, and I turned my back on her and climbed the narrow stairs to go and see Mother.

She was lying looking at the wall, her face screwed up. No doubt she had heard us squabbling downstairs. She must feel such a helpless burden now, this kind, hard-working woman who had reared us all and done her level best for us.

'Oh, Mother, I am so sorry,' I said, and I curled up beside her on the bed and stroked her hair. Rosie had combed it up into a neat topknot but the sparseness made her look very severe, and I thought the long pins must be digging into her scalp. I pulled them out and let her hair down loose around her shoulders.

'There, that feels better, doesn't it?' I said, giving her scalp a massage.

Mother made a little appreciative murmur.

'Yes, you like that, don't you? And you like me just a little too? I know I wasn't your favourite, but you were always so good and fair to me, even though you paddled me royally at times. I'm sure I deserved it, because I could be a very bad little girl, but I'm going to be good from now on, I promise. I shall care for you as if you were the Queen herself.'

I cuddled into her and stroked her gently. She lay still, and after a short while started snoring. There! I'd comforted her and soothed her to sleep. I could look after Mother as well as any of my foster sisters – probably *better*. I just wished I'd been able to nurse dear Mama properly. I closed my eyes so I would not start weeping all over again, and hung onto this big helpless hulk of a woman because she was the only mother I had left now.

When I heard Jem come home, I gave Mother a kiss and then flew downstairs so quickly I lost my footing on the narrow steps, failed to grab the piece of rope that served as a handrail and tumbled into the living room in a heap.

'Oh my Lord, I hope I haven't bust my *other* ankle now!' I gasped – but when Jem helped me up I found I was fine, just a little shaken.

'Poor Hetty! I hope you're not too bruised in the morning,' he said.

'*Silly* Hetty, flinging herself around so wildly,' Rosie sniffed. 'You're worse than Eliza's boys.'

'I *slipped*,' I said indignantly.

Jem bent down to examine my clumpers. 'No wonder! The soles are coming away from your boots, and they're worn so thin there's hardly any tread,' he said. 'I will try to cobble you new soles, Hetty.'

'Hateful things. I've had them for years. They were much too big to start with, and rubbed great ridges on my feet,' I said. 'They're *still* too big, even though I'm fully grown.'

'You'll never be fully grown, Hetty, you're just a little pint pot,' said Jem. He drew in a deep breath. 'My, something smells good. Have you girls been making me a stew?'

'*One* of us girls,' said Rosie. 'The other lay ailing in her bed with a thick head.'

'Why do you have to tell tales on me?' I said. 'You wouldn't have lasted a week at the hospital, Rosie.

If you told tales there, all the other girls would take against you and torment you.'

'Was it really dreadful there, Hetty?' asked Jem. 'I used to worry about you so much. It seemed so terrible to send you off so young.'

I started telling Jem all about my time at the hospital. I described Matron Pigface and Matron Stinking Bottomly with relish, exaggerating their punishments a little for extra effect. Even Rosie listened open-mouthed.

I broke off to feed Mother her meat broth. She could not seem to chew any more and could only sip pathetically, but her mouth opened like a little bird for every mouthful. Then Rosie and I washed and changed her for the night, tucking her up in a clean nightgown.

'Dear Lord, every day is going to have to be washing day, never mind Mondays,' said Rosie, sighing. 'Have you ever tackled a proper wash, Hetty?'

'I've taken my turn in the hospital laundry and had to deal with a hundred nightgowns at a time, plus all the sets of caps and cuffs and tippets. Mother's nightgowns won't worry *me*. And I shall make her new gowns so she always has plenty. I shall decorate them specially. I do very fine embroidery.'

'Clearly you were allowed to boast at this

hospital, even if you couldn't tell tales,' said Rosie, doing her best to squash me.

But when we'd settled Mother for the night and returned to the warmth of the kitchen downstairs, she was eager enough to hear more tales of the hospital. Jem took his pipe down from the rack on the chimneybreast and puffed away as I spoke. I think he felt his pipe-smoking was a manly occupation, but he wasn't very practised at it and kept having to relight the tobacco.

I told how I'd had my hair shorn the day I arrived, and my clothes and my precious rag baby had been taken from me and burned.

'What about the silver sixpence I gave you for luck, Hetty? Did they take that too?' Jem asked.

'No, I hid it under my tongue – and then for years I kept it inside the knob on the end of my bed. But somebody stole it eventually. It was so hard to hang onto any possessions. We were all so starved of love and punished so hatefully.'

When I told them that I'd once been locked in the dark garret all night long, Jem reached out for my hand and pulled on it tightly, as if he were trying to rescue me. Even Rosie clucked with her tongue and shook her head. This spurred me on to new and possibly fictional revelations, inventing novel punishments and humiliations for my child self.

'This is so terrible,' said Jem. 'And little Eliza is still there! We must rescue her somehow.'

'I wish we could,' I said. 'But I don't see how. We'd never be allowed to adopt her. Even if her own birth mother tried to take her back she'd have to be very rich indeed. The governors would want to be repaid for the entire cost of her board and education. I've only known one girl who was adopted. She was my friend Polly. She was bought by a couple who had lost their own little girl. I was *so* close to Polly. I wrote to her but she only wrote back once.'

'You stopped writing to me,' said Jem.

'I know. I'm sorry – very, very sorry,' I said. I felt so bad that I told a little lie. 'We weren't allowed to write home after a while. The matrons said it was a waste of good pens and ink and paper.'

'Eliza still writes,' said Jem gently but reproachfully. 'And Gideon wrote weekly to Mother.'

'Well, I – I was being punished,' I said. 'I wrote to you when I went into service, didn't I? And I wrote again when Miss Smith forwarded your letters. Oh Lord, Miss Smith . . . I owe *her* a letter too. And I must write to Father to tell him I've arrived here safely and he mustn't worry about me. And I promised to stay in touch with my dear friend Freda. Oh, let me tell you about Freda, a lovely sweet gentle lady, but a very unusual one . . .'

We sat up for hours while I told my tales, one of us checking on Mother every half-hour or so.

'Come, we must all go to bed, it's nearly midnight!' Rosie said at last.

'Do you think we will all be turned into pumpkins?' I said.

'Poor Jem has to be up at dawn, Hetty. So do I, to journey back to work. And you will have to get up to tend to Mother,' she said.

'Yes, yes, I will do that, I promise,' I said.

14

I kept my promise too, but I had no idea how very hard it was going to be. That first day I was on my own with Mother seemed very long and strange. I did not particularly care for my foster sister Rosie – or Bess or Eliza for that matter – but I would have given anything for them to be with me helping to cope with poor Mother. She was so heavy and so helpless. It was hard work hauling her to one side or another as I changed her bedding. She knew I was trying my best to make her comfortable but she groaned in an alarming fashion or started up her agitated cry of 'Gi-gi-gi.'

As soon as I'd fed or changed her and felt I could leave her for ten minutes so I could steep the sheets in the washtub or prepare vegetables for the evening meal or start a little sweeping to make the cottage spick and span, Mother would call out and I'd have to go running to her.

When eventually she slept after her lunch, I slept too, stretched out on the bed beside her, utterly worn out. I woke with a start because I'd heard knocking. For several moments in that dark room I did not know where I was. Could I be back in the hospital, in the scullery at Mr Buchanan's, in the boarding house at Bignor, in Father's Monksby cottage? I'd slept in such a bewildering number of beds over the last six months – but I wasn't in a strange bed now. This was the very bed I'd often slept in as a little child.

The knocking carried on – and then I heard the door latch creak downstairs. 'Hetty? Are you there?'

It was Janet! She'd come straight from her school-teaching to see how I was coping.

I called her upstairs and she sat with Mother and me for a little while. She talked so pleasantly and naturally to Mother. I knew my sisters loved Mother dearly, but they raised their voices and talked to her as if she'd turned into a baby. I was sure the real Mother was still there inside her head. She just couldn't make herself understood. She certainly seemed to enjoy Janet's talk of the little children at school, and her mother's planting of bulbs, and her father's work on twelve fine rush-bottomed chairs for the manor-house kitchen.

Then I took Janet downstairs and made her a cup of tea and we ate a slice of cake. I had enough food left over from the funeral to feed the whole village.

Jem found us chatting together by the fireside when he got home. His face brightened as he came in the front door. 'My two dear girls,' he said, smiling at us.

'I must go home soon. You'll be wanting your supper, Jem,' said Janet. 'See, Hetty has it all bubbling ready for you.'

I had only made a simple vegetable stew. I'd thought we could eat it with leftover pie, and I could mash the vegetables and spoon-feed it to Mother. Any fool could toss a few potatoes and carrots and parsnips into a pot with a little seasoning, but Jem acted as if I were Mrs Beeton herself.

'It smells delicious, Hetty – and you made it all yourself! You're a real little housewife already,' he said. 'And how is Mother?'

'Hetty's looked after her like a good little nurse,' said Janet.

'I'm so proud of you, Hetty,' said Jem.

I felt my cheeks glowing. It felt so good to be praised. We sat together a while, my new good friend Janet and my dearest old friend Jem. I felt content at last, in spite of the sad turmoil of Father's death and Mother's illness.

Jem and I were polite to Janet and insisted she stay a while. She chatted to Jem while I went upstairs and fed Mother her mashed vegetables. Much as I liked Janet, the best time of all was when she'd gone home, and Jem and I were together at last. I served him his supper and he complimented me again, smacking his lips appreciatively. Then he smoked his pipe by the fire while I cleared the table and washed the pots.

It was so strange to be with him, and yet it seemed familiar too. I found I could chatter on about the first thing that came into my head, while Jem laughed appreciatively and showed interest.

We went upstairs to check on Mother again. Jem was especially tender with her, giving her all the messages of sympathy from the lads on the farm.

'They all say just how much their John Cotton will be missed. They all remarked on his strength and kindness. *A great ox of a man, but as gentle as they come*, said one. It made me feel so proud, Mother. He's set me a great example. I'll never be able to take Father's place, but I'll try hard to be as fine a man as he was,' he said, taking Mother's hand.

Mother murmured softly. It was as clear as day that she was telling him he was already a fine man and she was proud to have him as her son.

I settled her for the night, then sat downstairs with Jem again while he had another smoke of his pipe.

'This is so strange, Hetty,' he said. 'How can I be so sad and yet so happy at one and the same time?'

'It's more than strange,' I said. 'When I was sent

to the hospital I'd lie in bed every night picturing myself back here with you. It was so vivid it came as a terrible shock to raise my head and peer around that awful dormitory. I keep feeling that's what's going to happen now.'

'No, Hetty, you're here with me. You can stay here for as long as you want, if you're quite sure it's what you *do* want,' said Jem.

'I'm quite sure, I said firmly.

I so hoped it was what Mama would want for me too. I was a little worried on that score. She had never enjoyed hearing tales of my foster family, resenting them bitterly. She had taken a particular dislike to my foster mother, scoffing at the simple food she'd fed me and shaking indignantly when I said I'd frequently been paddled. It would seem especially hard that I was here nursing that mother when I hadn't been able to nurse my own mama the way I wanted through her last terrible illness.

When I went out to the privy, I stayed outside for a few minutes, in spite of the cold. I stared up at the huge black sky spangled with stars.

'Are you there, Mama? Do you mind that I am here? I have come home again, where I truly belong. I love my true father, but I don't think I can ever be happy there. You do understand, don't you, Mama? Please give me your blessing!'

I waited, shivering. Mama was silent.

'Mama?' I whispered aloud.

'You'll be freezing, Hetty,' said Jem, coming to stand beside me. He took my shawl and wrapped it tightly round my shoulders. Then he stood beside me, staring up at the stars too.

'There are so many of them shining up there,' I said. 'I'd forgotten how beautiful country nights are. When you look up at the sky in London it's so murky you can't see the stars properly at all. Look at that huge one right above us!'

'That's the Pole Star. That's always the biggest and the brightest. And there's the Great Bear, see – and the Plough.'

He pointed and named them while I leaned against him, listening and learning. It was another step straight back into childhood, Jem gently teaching me.

'I *know* I'm right to come here, Mama,' I said inside my head.

'*Yes, Hetty, of course you're right, my child,*' I replied, but I was acting like a ventriloquist, saying Mama's words for her.

I went to bed happily even so, but I had a very disturbed night. Mother cried out repeatedly, and I had to keep stumbling out of my own little bed to go to her. Eventually I lay down beside her and it seemed to settle her.

I'd resolved to get up when Jem did and make

him a proper breakfast, but I was so exhausted I didn't hear him stirring. When I opened my eyes, Mother herself was awake and looking at me reproachfully.

The day slid downhill after that. I scrubbed at the sheets in the old redware tub but could not get them as clean as I wanted. Then it rained so I couldn't hang them on the rope outside. They dripped dismally downstairs instead, so that I could barely move for the damp dreary things. I started ironing yesterday's sheets, but first the iron wasn't hot enough to smooth the wrinkles, and then I heated it too much and scorched a brown triangle on the white linen.

Then I tried my hand at baking because we'd run out of bread and couldn't very well eat leftover cake with our broths and stews. I kneaded the flour in a satisfactory manner. I rather enjoyed letting off steam by pummelling it, but something upset it in the oven, for it refused to rise and stayed at the bottom of the bread pan in a surly lump.

Mrs Maple came calling and saw all these failures but tactfully ignored them. She had a cup of tea with me and we ate the excellent fresh muffins she'd brought with her. Then she went upstairs to visit Mother.

'Your Hetty's doing a grand job, Peg,' she said, which was a total lie but kindly meant.

Mrs Maple offered to sit with Mother for an hour or so to give me a little rest. I thanked her very much and set off to buy a few provisions from the general stores with some money Jem had left for me. I walked sedately enough into the village, but it was such a relief to be out of the damp dark cottage that once I'd bought some fresh eggs and sugar and tea I could not help wandering off across the meadows in spite of the rain, exploring my childhood haunts. I was soaked through by this time but I didn't care. My ankle was completely better now and it felt so good to stride out. In fact when I was out of sight of the last cottage, I actually ran.

I reached the meadow where Mr Tanglefield's circus had once performed and pranced crazily round and round in a ring, like one of Madame Adeline's rosin-backed horses. Then I slipped on an especially muddy patch and my bag went flying and half my precious eggs were broken.

I sat on the soggy grass in the pouring rain and wept, feeling such a failure, but eventually I trudged back home, hanging my head. Mrs Maple was kind enough not to comment on my muddy skirts and went on her way. Mother seemed to miss her company and did not settle after she went. She kept crying out, and set up her 'Gi-gi-gi' call until I felt like screaming.

I wanted to have the cottage clean and tidy for

Jem's homecoming, but he was early and caught me in a turmoil, with the sheets still flapping, scrubbing my own muddy footsteps off the floor in my petticoat to save dirtying my other dress.

'Oh, Jem, what must you think of me?' I said miserably.

'I think you're a sweet, hard-working girl who's doing her best,' he said.

I think I'd almost sooner he'd scolded me. He went to change out of his sodden work clothes and then sat with Mother while I struggled to set myself and the cottage to rights. I served him up a cheese omelette with the salvaged eggs, plus Mrs Maple's muffins and yet more cake. It was a scrappy meat-less meal for a man who'd been labouring hard in the rain all day, but Jem ate it with relish.

'That was so good, Hetty. I've never tasted better,' he said, licking his lips.

It was as if we were back in our long-ago squirrel tree and he was pretending to eat one of my mud pies.

'Is the squirrel tree still there?' I asked.

'Of course it is! We've been working nearby copse-cutting to make hoops – but I'd never ever let anyone chop down our squirrel tree,' he said.

'So Eliza liked to play there too?' I said, still meanly minding that he'd shared our games with my little foster sister.

'I taught her how to keep house there. She enjoyed the game very much. But she couldn't seem to make it come real the way you did, Hetty. Sometimes when I was with you, it seemed as if we truly lived in that old tree. You had such a way of picturing it.'

I smiled at him, thrilled.

'Perhaps – perhaps you can picture things for poor Mother. It must be so wretched for her, stuck up there in that dark room all the time. When she's a little stronger, I'll see if I can carry her downstairs so she can sit in her chair during the day. But meanwhile, if you could tell her a story or two, it might make such a difference to her, Hetty,' Jem said earnestly.

I started picturing for Mother the next day. I washed the sheets and did some cooking, but in between times I sat with her and pictured for both of us. I could not imagine into the future, because I was still not sure what would happen to me, and poor Mother did not seem to have a future. Her present was severely limited, so I pictured the past, constructing Mother's days when she was young and tireless, Father was bold and strong, and there were little children tumbling around the cottage. I could not help putting myself to the forefront of these tales, elaborating on the day when Gideon and I arrived in a basket, two foundlings for the price of one, ready to join the family for five years.

'Gideon was the good little baby who seldom cried. I was the bad little babe with red hair who yelled her head off,' I said.

Mother tried to smile with her poor lopsided face, and started her chant again, trying to join in.

I pictured for us day after day. When I ran out of memories, I consulted the fat memoir book I'd started keeping when I was ten. I winced at my babyish tone and blushed when I remembered showing my rambling jottings to Miss Smith, sure they were good enough to be published.

Jem came home unexpectedly with a basket of butter and cheese from the farmer's wife, and heard me reading aloud. He begged me to carry on, declaring my childish tale a masterpiece. I knew it was nothing of the sort. Still, the story of my life was unusual, to say the least. My former employer, Mr Buchanan, had poured scorn upon my memoir, and yet he had copied it out himself, scarcely changing my words, clearly trying to pass it off as his own work.

Perhaps I could rewrite the weaker parts myself and try to get it published, in spite of Miss Smith's forebodings. I was not sure how much money you made out of publishing books, but I thought Mr Charles Dickens had certainly made a fortune. I was reading *David Copperfield* with enormous enjoyment, but Mother's attention wandered when I tried it out on her. She preferred my own story because she could relate to those first few chapters.

Perhaps I would have enough money to keep house in style. Maybe we could even move to *another* house and live like the Maples. But meanwhile I had no money at all and no means of earning any.

Jem gave me money to buy necessities – and when I'd stayed a whole month he gave me two shillings from his savings. 'I'd like you to go to Gillford today. It's market day and I want you to buy something special. I'll ask old Molly to sit with Mother and fix for Peter to take you there on the carrier cart,' he said.

'What have I to buy?' I said, fingering the two silver coins.

'You must buy a present for yourself, Hetty!' said Jem. 'You've been so good and kind and uncomplaining. You deserve a special treat.'

'Oh, Jem!' I said, and I flung my arms around his neck. '*You're* the one who's good and kind and uncomplaining, not me!'

I knew I wasn't good, and although I tried very hard to be kind to Mother, there were times when I was so tired that I simply lost patience with her and spoke abruptly. And I was far from uncomplaining. When I saw Janet, I frequently moaned about the sheer hard work and monotony of my daily life.

I did not feel I deserved a present, but I was

excited all the same. I was up very early on market day, in time to make Jem a proper breakfast for once. It was a cold frosty morning so I made a big pot of porridge, and set a rabbit stew to cook slowly all day long, plus an onion soup for Molly and Mother.

'You're turning into a fine little housewife,' said Jem, eating his porridge appreciatively. I'd sprinkled sugar on it, with a spoonful of cream.

'No I'm not,' I said at once, though I felt myself blushing.

'In two or three years' time you'll be ready to be a real wife,' Jem said softly.

Molly came knocking early, so I could leave the cottage with Jem and walk through the village with him. I tucked my hand in his arm and skipped along beside him in my slipshod boots. Jem had carefully patched the soles for me, but he still shook his head at them.

'I don't suppose two shillings is enough for a new pair of boots,' he said wistfully.

'My clumpers are fine, Jem. You've mended them beautifully,' I said.

'I'm going to work so hard, Hetty. Farmer Woodrow's been very kind, hinting that come the spring he might put me in Father's place as head hand, even though I'm not yet twenty. That'll mean more money – and I've plans to make a little more for ourselves on top. We'll rear another pig, and I reckon there's room for a few chickens if I build a little run for them, and bees too. Soon you'll be going to market to sell our own eggs and honey, and we'll have enough profit to buy you a pair of pretty shoes as well as stout boots, and we'll find you a dressmaker and order a fine frilly dress for you into the bargain.'

'You're so sweet, Jem, but I can make my own dresses, you'll see,' I said.

There was a little queue of women waiting at the crossroads for the carrier's cart, all intent on going to market. Jem knew most of them and bade them good day.

'You'll keep an eye out for my little sister Hetty, won't you?' he said earnestly. 'You'll make sure she doesn't get lost and knows where to wait for the cart home?'

'Oh, Jem, don't treat me like a little girl!' I said.

'Well, you *are* my little girl,' he said sweetly. He'd said it several times already. It had pleased me greatly the first time he said it.

He kissed me on both cheeks to say goodbye and then hurried off to the farm. I was glad enough of the women's company at first because I was afraid the carrier might be the awful man from the hill – but he was a kindly, ruddy-cheeked old man who treated us all like ladies, helping us up into his cart as if it were a royal carriage, and apologizing for the squash.

The women all knew I'd come to keep house and care for Mother, helping my brother cope. They clucked amongst themselves at my sisterly sweetness, which was very agreeable, though the tartest of the womenfolk raised her eyebrows and said, 'I'm not so sure young Jem thinks of her like a sister. He seems mightily smitten, if you ask me.'

The others hushed her and clucked some more, while I pretended I hadn't heard, though my heart was beating hard.

'If that's the case, then *someone*'s nose will be put out of joint,' said another woman, before she was hushed too.

Someone? Did she mean Jem had a sweetheart? But I'd been living at the cottage for weeks now and he hadn't gone out courting anyone. I thought momentarily of Bertie and our days out together when I was in service at Mr Buchanan's. Dear Bertie, he had been such fun to be with. He'd be amazed to see me now, turning into a real country girl. I wondered if he ever thought of me.

When we got to Gillford at last, I jumped down from the cart, ran away from all the kindly mother hens and circled the fruit and vegetable and dairy stalls. I petted the rabbits and kittens and puppies in their cages, and then hovered at a stationery stall, fingering the notebooks and quill pens. There were marbled manuscript books with leather spines and corners, very similar to the beautiful red book Miss Smith had bought me, but they were much too expensive so I didn't trouble looking at them. I opened up each threepenny notebook instead, flipping through the blank pages.

'They're all the same inside, missy. You don't have to examine them,' said the man at the stall, brushing my hands away as if they were flies.

'I am *choosing*,' I said with dignity. 'I'm going to make a considerable purchase.' I rattled the shillings together in my pocket to give the illusion I had enough money to buy up the entire contents of his stall.

I touched the scarlet notebook, stroked the grass green, but settled eventually on bright blue to match my eyes. I might have reverted to Hetty back in the village, but in my heart I was still Sapphire. I still had one shilling and sixpence left. I looked around the stalls again, wanting to buy Jem and Mother a little present, and maybe Janet too, because she'd been such a kind friend to me.

At the edge of the market I found a whole lane of material stalls with bolts of fine muslin and lawn and silk and lace. I wandered up and down this fairyland, while fine gowns danced in my head, but I knew this was a fantasy. I walked the stalls a second time, delving in and out of the remnants baskets.

There was a piece of deep blue velvet that could make a beautiful little bodice, and a cheap sky-blue floaty muslin would make the sleeves and skirts, with a velvet trim. Oh, I saw it, down to the last hook and eye and ribbon edging. I knew such a dress would truly suit me. I ached for that dress. I could afford it too, because the velvet was only threepence and it was such a small piece. I could get away with just three yards of blue muslin at fivepence a yard. It was the one advantage of being so small. But then I would have nothing left for presents.

'I can see you're taken with the blue velvet. It's a bargain at that price,' said the stallholder, grinning. My dress seemed to be swirling in his head too, because he added, 'It would go lovely with your colouring. You'd be the belle of any ball.'

I so *wanted* to be the belle of the ball. I saw myself swishing my skirts, Jem's hands circling my blue velvet waist – but common sense prevailed. Jem might be persuaded to dance a quick jig on the village green come May Day, but he'd never be taking me to any proper ball. I was Cinderella without a fairy godmother or a handsome prince.

I put the velvet back in the remnant basket with a sigh and left the bolt of blue muslin untouched.

I looked at plain white lawn instead. I figured it up in my head: a nightdress for Mother, a shirt for Jem, a pocket handkerchief . . . Seven yards, eight yards, at threepence a yard. I didn't have enough.

I'd have to content myself with four yards for Mother's nightdress. But what about the fine shirt for Jem, with a proper collar? He only had his rough work shirts. He'd look so handsome in a crisp white shirt.

'You're clutching that bolt of lawn as if it were a dolly!' said the stallholder. 'How many yards do you want?'

'I'd really like eight, but I can't quite afford that many,' I said.

'Well, that's a pity, but this ain't a charity, dear. I'm not giving it away,' he said, shaking his head at me.

It was cold and draughty at the end of the stalls and he kept clapping his mittened hands over his elbows to warm himself.

I took a deep breath. 'You must be very chilly,' I said. 'I'm sure you'd like to go to the market alehouse and warm yourself up with a pint.'

'Well, that's very perceptive of you, dear – but there's not much chance of that when I've got a stall to run,' he said. 'Now, how many yards is it?'

'I've got one and sixpence. Look, that's all I have,' I said, turning my purse inside out.

'Then that's six yards. Let me measure them,' he said, taking the bolt from me.

'There won't be much left on the roll – two yards, maybe three at the most. You'll have to sell it as a remnant, reduced price. Tell you what, if you let me have that extra couple of yards, I'll watch your stall for you while you warm up in the alehouse.'

The stallholder burst out laughing. 'You've got a cheek! You want me to give you a whole lot extra for nothing *and* you'll steal all my day's takings into the bargain!' he said. 'You must think I'm simple if I'm falling for that trick. You can bat those pretty blue eyes at me as much as you like, but I'm not budging.'

'You take your money with you! As if I'd steal! I'm a good Christian girl who knows her ten commandments,' I said.

'Yeah, and I do too. Don't it say you mustn't covet your neighbour's ox? Well, don't you go coveting my material what you can't afford,' he said, nodding his head at me.

'In the New Testament Jesus says "Suffer the little children to come unto me" – so couldn't you suffer me and let me have that extra couple of yards so I can make my poor sick mother a nightgown and my dear hard-working brother a good shirt for Sundays?' I said.

'You could make them with six yards,' he said, laughing.

'Yes, but I don't want to skimp. Poor Mother's a big lady and a helpless invalid. She doesn't want a tight nightgown riding up round her knees. And my dear brother—'

'Oh, save us your dear brother! You've got the gift of the gab, little girl, I'll say that.'

'Then think how I'll talk lots of customers into wanting lengths of materials for fine dresses while you're sitting toasting your toes at the alehouse fire,' I said.

'I must be crazy – but all right, I'll take the opportunity,' the stallholder said, tying his takings purse around his waist. He took my one and sixpence and dropped them in the purse too.

'You'll give me the extra lengths in return?' I said.

'Well, let's see how you do. If you've sold to three satisfied customers while I'm gone, then I'll give the extra to you gladly,' he said.

'That wasn't quite the bargain!' I said. 'But all right, it's a deal, so let's shake on it.'

He shook my hand, still chuckling, and called to the man at the neighbouring stall to keep an eye on me. 'Make sure she doesn't run off with a couple of bolts of material under each arm,' he said.

'The very idea!' I said indignantly. 'I'm an

honest God-fearing girl – and I'll get you three customers, you just wait and see.'

So I was left in charge of his stall, though he kept looking back at me doubtfully. Even when he went into the alehouse I saw him peeping back through the door at me.

I decided I'd truly show him. His stall was in the worst place possible. Folk wanting material had eleven others to look at before they reached this one. Most stopped and made their purchases before they were halfway down. Women drifted by, of course, but always seemed intent on visiting the shops further on.

I had to attract attention. I had seen the effectiveness of Mr Clarendon's pitch.

'Roll up, roll up, ladies,' I shouted at the top of my voice, startling everyone. 'Come and see the bargains on my stall! Look at this fine muslin all the way from India!' I shook out a bolt and held the material up to my face. 'There, isn't it pretty! Look, madam – imagine wearing a beautiful dress as blue as the sky come the spring. Who's got blue eyes among all you beautiful ladies? Just think how lovely you'd look. All the gentlemen would come running. Buy ten yards for a wide skirt to flounce and frill and I'll throw in this netting for an under-skirt half price. Who's going to snatch up this bargain and be the envy of all her friends?'

A crowd started to gather, but they were all just staring, some of them open-mouthed. *Come on, just one of you buy, and the others will follow like sheep*, I thought.

Several lads were gathering too, acting a little rowdy at the back, passing comments on me.

'You, sir!' I said, picking on the biggest and boldest. 'I reckon you must have a pretty sweetheart. Does she have a birthday coming up? How about presenting her with a lovely length of patterned muslin? I'll tie it up with a satin ribbon and make it look like a gift fit for a queen. Oh my, won't she look a beauty in this blue? Won't she love you so for giving her such a splendid present? Won't you feel proud, walking out with her in her pretty dress?'

The lad looked as if he might be wavering, but his mates were still joshing.

'His Susie can't sew to save her life,' said one.

'Well, of course not, if she's a lady,' I said quickly. 'She'll go to a good dressmaker, and have her frock made up in the very latest fashion.'

'Yes, she'll do just that,' said the big lad, pulling a handful of coins out of his pocket. 'How much will it be?'

'Half a crown – and that's a very fair price!' I said.

I expected him to object, so I was all set to come down gradually to two shillings, but perhaps he didn't want to look cheap in front of his friends.

'A fair price for a very fair girl,' he said, and he pushed forward through the crowd and gave me his half-crown piece.

I measured out his muslin while everyone clapped.

'Any other gentlemen sweet enough to treat his lady?' I asked hopefully. 'Or if you don't have a gentleman, why don't you treat yourselves, ladies? You get yourself up in my fine muslins and silks on a Sunday, and then you'll have gentlemen aplenty. Or what about decking out your little girls, all you mothers? Look at this cream silk, just longing to make your little darlings look lovely. You there with the beautiful baby, madam! Buy this length of fine silk for her and I'll come and nurse her for you.'

The crowd laughed again – but the mother *got out her purse*. By the time the stallholder came back from the alehouse I'd shifted practically a *mile* of material and created such a buzz around his stall that the other end of the market was empty.

'Have I earned my bolt of linen, sir?' I sang out loudly, giving him handfuls of coins so that everyone could see. I didn't want him to cheat me out of it, pretending he'd never struck a bargain.

He handed over the material happily, with a flourish – and he let me have the blue velvet remnant too. 'You're a funny little lass, but you're brilliant for trade. I've never seen anyone drum up a crowd like that. Do you want a job, by any chance?'

I wasn't sure if he was joking or not, but I took him seriously. 'I wish I could work with you, sir, but I'm needed at home,' I said. 'I can't travel around with the market, much as I'd like to. But could we strike another bargain? Every time the market comes here, could I come and sell from your stall while you have your lunch break, in exchange for more material?'

'You sell like you did today and you can have the pick of my stall,' he said, doffing his cap to me.

I swaggered off with my bolt of material, happy as a lark. I didn't have any money left for my lunch but it was easy enough to find good food in the market. I searched the gutter and found an apple and a pear that had rolled off a fruit stall, and someone else had dropped a big penny bun with only one bite taken out of it. I wiped them all carefully with my skirts and then had an excellent lunch.

I was a little hampered by my large bolt of material, but I cradled it like a baby and took a turn around the town. It was still an enormous thrill to wander up and down the shopping streets. I spent a very long time at the window of the draper's shop. I was pleased to see that my market stall purchase really *was* a bargain. I took note of the fashion patterns for future reference, and sighed wistfully at the satin ribbons and flower trimmings – but I had enough sense to know that the dour-looking assistants inside would not be prepared to barter them for my selling spiel.

I ran in and out of the grocery store, delighting in the fact that I was no longer in service, sent by the cook Mrs Briskett to buy half a pound of raisins or a sugar loaf. I was almost mistress of my own house now.

I went past a butcher's shop too, its doors decked with hanging chickens, its windows a rosy pattern of joints and chops coiled round with sausages. I was reminded painfully of Bertie. I'd promised I would keep in touch with him and let him know if I found my father, but I'd been so bowled over by doing just that I'd somehow had no time or inclination to write about it, not even to my dearest friends. Perhaps it wasn't simple laziness. I'd been reluctant to write down my feelings about my father, even for myself in my own memoirs. I loved him dearly. He was a fine upstanding man. In many ways he was everything I could wish for, and yet somehow . . . he didn't feel like a parent. I'd loved Mama with my whole heart and soul, but it was too strange meeting up with Father after such a long time. It was almost as if I'd pictured him out of my imagination. He didn't seem *real*.

I still cared about him though. I would write to him, maybe visit again when I'd saved up enough money, but I didn't think I could ever feel part of his home – especially not with Katherine there too!

My home was with Jem and Mother now. I could not wait to tell them of my triumph at the market.

Mother seemed pleased enough when I told her. She nodded, her eyes bright, though she could no longer smile.

Molly roared with laughter and clapped me on the back. 'You're a character, you are, young Hetty. Good for you! Well, you feel free to go off and strike similar bargains any market day you like. I'm happy to sit with Mother Cotton here. We get along fine and dandy, don't we, Peg?' she said, and Mother gargled agreement.

But Jem seemed curiously disappointed when I thrust my bolt of material at him and told him the tale of my triumph all over again. 'I wanted you to spend those shillings on something you really wanted, Hetty,' he said.

'I *did*! Lord knows I wanted those extra yards or I'd never have risked making such a fool of myself.'

'But it's plain linen.'

'It might *look* plain, but you wait till I've em- broidered a yoke and cuffs. Mother will look as grand as a bride, I promise you. And with the extra yards

I shall make you the finest shirt you've ever worn. You'll be quite the dandy, you'll see. All the village girls will be dancing round you,' I said, reaching up and ruffling his hair to try to make him smile.

'I wanted you to buy something pretty for yourself. Why didn't you buy something fine and frilly to be made into a dress? Or ribbons for your hair, or glass beads, or a little toy or trinket? I wanted you to have a special treat, because you've worked so hard and been so good to Mother and me. The shillings were for *you*, Hetty.'

'Then when you've saved up two more I shall gladly spend them for you, Jem! But meanwhile, Mother will have a new nightgown and Janet will have an embroidered pocket handkerchief because she's been so good to me. You've been best of all, so you will get a shirt, and I promise I won't get too carried away. I know how much you'd hate frills or fancy collars – but inside, where no one can see, I'll find space to embroider *love from Hetty*. Whenever you wear your shirt you'll see it and remember just how much I love my dear brother.'

I thought at first he might cry. His face crumpled the way it had done at Father's funeral. But then he smiled and hugged me hard.

'And I love you too, my dear little Hetty,' he said. 'Oh, I do so hope you are happy here.'

'Of course I am,' I said. 'I have come home.'

15

I tried so hard to be happy. I settled into a routine. I couldn't help it. I rose early, I lit the fire, I made Jem porridge for his breakfast to warm him before he spent his day toiling on the farm. I washed and changed Mother and fed her too, then tackled the washing, the ironing, the sweeping, the baking, the stewing. I had to make the same simple meals day after day with the same ingredients – pork, rabbit, cabbage, carrots, turnip, onions, and endless bread and dripping, bread and cheese, bread and blackberry jam.

Long ago Mr Maple had carved a wooden toy for Janet. She still kept it on the windowsill in her bedroom. It was a little wooden girl in a cap and clogs alongside a line of tiny wooden chickens. When you turned a wheel, she threw out her wooden arm as if feeding them, and every chicken opened its beak wide. It was a clever toy, and when you saw it you simply had to pick it up and turn that wheel, so the little wooden girl fed her chickens again and again.

I couldn't help feeling like that wooden girl, repeating my daily tasks again and again until sometimes I felt I could scream. I did not know what was the matter with me. I was surely *used* to routine. I'd had nine years at the Foundling Hospital when we did exactly the same things every single weekday, with chapel and public dinner on Sundays.

I tried my hardest to vary things a little, especially for Mother. Her life was far more restricted than mine, confined to her bed in that stuffy little room. I asked Molly if we might take Mother for a little trip out in her donkey cart, but it was a very cold winter and Jem worried that she might get a chill.

He tried lifting her up in his arms in the early morning and carrying her down the stairs so that she could sit in her old chair for a change of scenery. She seemed to like that a lot, especially when I chatted to her as I did my household tasks. It was impossible for me to move her from the kitchen to the living room and back because I simply could not carry her, try as I might. I stared at the legs of her chair, wishing they could walk for her. Then I thought of the wheels on Molly's cart!

I went to have a word with Mr Maple the joiner. He came along and fixed four wheels to Mother's chair, one on each leg. What a difference it made!

I could lean on the stout back and bowl Mother along, choosing a different spot for her each day. She liked to look out of the window most, though it often started her up on her 'Gi-gi-gi' chant.

She was recovered enough to start speaking a little. Her first word was Jem, clear as a bell. She couldn't seem to manage Hetty. When I told her my real name, Sapphire, and my performance name, Emerald, she glanced at me sideways with her old Mother look. It was obvious she was never going to attempt such frivolous names. She called me 'Goo-gir' instead. I think she meant good girl, and I truly tried to be a good girl for her.

I worked very hard on her nightgown. I knew Mother would have been perfectly content with a plain gown, straight up and down, with no frills or furbelows. She wouldn't even have minded if the stitching was big so long as the seams held fast. But I sewed fancy stitches all the same, and finished the gown with three ruffles instead of an ordinary hem, and I embroidered an entire flower garden on the yoke: red roses, yellow daffodils, purple pansies and blue cornflowers, with a little green trail of ivy twining round all of them.

'Oh, Hetty, it's a work of art, not a nightgown!' said Janet when I showed it to her.

She had started to come calling every day after school. I made the three of us a cup of tea, and

Janet talked slowly and sweetly to Mother, telling her about all the children's funny ways and little escapades. Mother loved Janet's company, but usually tired after ten minutes and nodded off to sleep, and then we girls could chat more naturally.

I made Janet her handkerchief. I think she was expecting floral embroidery, but I chose little child motifs instead. I stitched infants skipping right round the handkerchief in a circle, curly-haired girls in lilac dresses, mischievous boys in pale blue, with tiny babies in cream frocks crawling in each corner.

'Oh, Hetty! Well, I can't possibly use my handkerchief. I couldn't wipe my nose on these dear little children,' said Janet. She had her father make a special wooden frame for the handkerchief and hung it in her bedroom like a picture.

Jem grew a little nervous when I started making him a shirt. 'It's so good of you, Hetty. You do such fine embroidery, but I'd really sooner you didn't sew flowers or babies or suchlike on my shirt,' he said.

'Don't worry, Jem. I have a different design in my head for you. I thought a farmyard theme would look well – chickens around the collar and cuff, a row of fat pink pigs trotting across the chest and a big plough horse plodding along your back,' I said – and then I burst out laughing when I saw his face.

'I'm *joking*, Jem! I won't do any embroidery, I promise.'

I kept my word. The shirt was perfectly plain, no flowers, no frills, no fripperies of any sort – though I stitched the promised *love from Hetty* inside the collar where it didn't show.

'It's the most beautiful shirt in all the world,' said Jem. He wore it very proudly every Sunday, easing his collar and airing his cuffs in church to show it off to the whole village.

I made more shirts, handkerchiefs and night-gowns throughout the winter. The villagers started giving me orders and paying handsomely for my stitch work.

I had a fine supply of materials because I went to market most Thursdays. Jim the stallholder let me drum up trade for him each time. It was my little lunchtime show and I enjoyed myself enormously. I was almost too successful, so that Jim grew a little resentful, even though his Thursday takings increased dramatically. The other stallholders hated me royally. They seemed anxious that I might set up my own stall and put them all out of business, but I did not *want* to be a professional market girl. I did not even want to be a seamstress, though I enjoyed sewing, and loved fashioning new outfits for folk.

I wanted to be a writer. Every day now I worked

at my memoirs, recording my current thoughts and feelings and rewriting my earlier childish jottings in my new market notebook. I used up every scrap of paper in the notebook and had to buy myself a new one. I bought one for Janet too. She had seen me scribbling away, page after page, and had watched in wonder.

'How can you write so quickly, Hetty? You never seem to pause to think what to say!'

'I don't have to think, I just write it!' I said. 'Haven't you ever kept a journal, Janet?'

'Well, I did start one once when I was little. I began each entry with *I got up* and finished with *I went to bed*, and there was scarcely anything in between,' she said, laughing. 'It was the silliest record ever.'

'Perhaps mine is silly too, but it's a great comfort and joy to me,' I said.

Janet peeped over my shoulder and glanced at my page. 'Is that *Jem* you've written there?' she said.

I snapped my book shut. 'You should never read anyone else's journals!' I said.

'It *was* about Jem!' said Janet.

'It might have been. I write about everyone. I write about you!' I said.

'Do you really? What do you say? Do you say *I know a girl called Janet and she is very dull?*'

'I write lovely things about you because you're such a good kind friend,' I said.

'No you don't!' said Janet.

I flipped back through my memoir until I found the passage where we first met and let her read a paragraph.

'Oh, Hetty, that's such a sweet passage! You make it all come alive as if it's a real story,' she said.

'It *is* a story – the story of my life,' I said. 'Anyone can write one.'

The next market day I bought a pretty new notebook in green and white check, and wrote very carefully on the first page: *Janet Maple – The Story of Her Life*.

Janet was so pleased. She gave me a kiss on both cheeks and declared I was the kindest girl ever.

'It's for your thoughts and feelings, remember. If I peek at it and find an entry starting *I got up*, I shall score it out,' I said.

'You said yourself, you should never ever read anyone's journal,' Janet laughed.

I loved Janet's company so much, though I was happiest of all with Jem, of course. He came home every night at dusk, when I liked to have supper ready, Mother fresh, and the house clean and welcoming. I couldn't pick flowers for the table because it was winter, but sometimes I arranged little branches in a jar in a decorative fashion, tying tiny scraps of painted paper to each stem to look like flowers. I tried to be as imaginative as possible with food too, though the ingredients for our meals were so limited. I put each portion on the plate in a particular pattern, or spelled out the initials of our names with thick gravy or sauce.

I varied Mother's dress too. One day I played Lady's Maid and dressed her up in her newly trimmed bonnet and mantle, with a string of beads around her neck. I styled my long red hair a dozen different ways, even though it usually came tumbling down by the time I was halfway through my meal.

'I never know what I'm going to find next!' said Jem. 'Oh, Hetty, it's a delight to come home to you and Mother now.'

He was so sweetly appreciative of the simplest little thing. He ate his meals as if they were royal banquets. He had fine table manners for a man, cutting things carefully with his knife and fork and chewing with his mouth closed. He didn't bolt his meal, he took his time, and he often helped give Mother hers, gently feeding her each spoonful and skilfully wiping her lips and chin so she stayed clean and dainty.

It was so much nicer now she could join us at the table in her chair. Although she couldn't join in our conversation properly, she nodded and took it all in.

Jem fed her snippets of gossip as well as food, telling her about all the different farm lads and their wives and children.

But the best times of all were when Jem and I had put Mother to bed and could sit together by the fire. Jem had used up all his stories over supper, so I did most of the talking, spinning him tales of this and that. There was nothing different to tell about my daily life, so I generally went off into a world of fancy. I tried to get him to join in with my games. 'Jem, if a fairy flew right in that window and landed on your head and spun round and round and awarded you three wishes, what would you ask for?' – or 'Suppose you could travel anywhere in the world, where would you go and what would you do?' – or 'If you were digging in the potato patch and suddenly came across a crock of gold, what would you spend it on?'

Jem always smiled fondly at my silly questions but never gave satisfactory answers. 'I'd wish we were as happy as this every day. I'd wish it three times over. I don't want to travel anywhere else. I like it here with you, by my own fireside. I don't need a crock of gold. I don't want for anything.'

'Oh, *Jem*,' I'd say, wishing he'd join in my games.

He seemed happy enough for me to chatter on, but he didn't often join in with ideas of his own. I kept thinking back to our childhood. Jem was always the one telling me things, pretending, helping me picture . . . Why wouldn't he do it now?

Then I remembered how young I had been. When you're four, your big nine-year-old brother knows so much more than you, and whenever he tells you something it's new and fresh and exciting. But when you're fourteen you're not so very different to a nineteen-year-old, especially if you've had a bleak upbringing and nine chaotic months trying to get on in the world. Jem only knew this village life.

'Don't you ever long to travel, Jem? To see a little bit of the world?' I asked.

'I saw London the day you left the hospital and I didn't think much of it,' he said.

'I'm so sorry I walked straight past you. I was just in such a daze. I never thought you'd be there, waiting for me at the gate,' I said.

'I said I would come for you. Surely you didn't doubt me?'

'But that was when we were both little. I thought you were just telling me stories.'

'I'll always keep my word to you, Hetty. I thought you'd know that,' said Jem, a little stiffly.

'Don't make me feel bad, Jem,' I begged.

'I won't do that either,' he said, smiling at me. 'It doesn't matter now anyway. You're here. I wrote to you and you came. It means the world to me.'

'To me too,' I said solemnly, though I felt a little

awkward. There was something so sweetly sincere about Jem. I knew he truly meant every word he said. I had often used words to make people like me or to get my own way. They'd flood out of my mouth in a colourful torrent, but I wasn't quite sure whether I was only acting for effect.

Jem sometimes gazed at me with such intensity as we sat by the fire together in the evening. His brown eyes were so big, so shiny, so earnest. I was pleased that he looked at me like that – and yet I couldn't help thinking of Farmer Woodrow's docile cows with their moist eyes and strangely long lashes.

I felt uncomfortable whenever our conversation petered out, though Jem didn't seem to mind. I suggested we read aloud to each other.

'You read to me, Hetty. My eyes are too tired for deciphering small print by rush light,' he said.

So I read aloud from my precious copy of *David Copperfield*. At first Jem took a great interest, and laughed and commented, but gradually he stopped talking and closed his eyes.

'Oh, Jem! Wake up!' I said.

'I'm not asleep. I'm simply resting my eyes. Go on, Hetty – it's a wonderful story and you read it so well,' he said – but in two minutes he was snoring.

I stared at his nodding head, trying to make excuses for him. The poor man was up before dawn, doing hard physical labour all day long. Of course he was bone tired. He couldn't *help* falling asleep. I knew this, but I couldn't help feeling lonely and disappointed.

It was almost as if we were an old married couple already. I'd sunk into the cosy routine of a woman twice my age, and it frightened me. I started longing for change – any change at all in our daily life.

I got very excited and enthusiastic about Christmas. It had never been an extraordinary occasion at the hospital. We'd each been given a penny and an orange – that was the extent of our Christmas gifts. There had been no lessons, no hours of darning, but there had been a punishingly long session in the chapel that gave us all aching backs and pins and needles in our dangling legs.

I had read about Christmas though, and was convinced that all other folk sat down to huge tables groaning with capons and figgy puddings galore, with a Christmas tree and coloured lanterns and many presents.

I looked around our small, dimly lit cottage, saw our big stewing pot, and sighed at the few coins rattling in my purse. 'How can we make Christmas *special*, Jem?' I wailed.

'We don't really set so much store by Christmas,' he said. 'Perhaps we can have a bit of stewing beef. That'll make a nice change.'

'It should be a *roast*,' I wailed. 'And I need to decorate the house to make it pretty. But what are we going to do about presents? I want to give *real* gifts. Folk will be getting tired of me stitching them silly clothes.'

'Oh, Hetty, you stitch *beautiful* clothes. We don't really give elaborate gifts – but I do have a tiny present for you.'

'Really? What is it?'

'You'll have to wait until Christmas Day! And listen – perhaps one of the girls will invite us to her house. Both Bess and Eliza have big ovens, so we could share their roast. We could bundle Mother up and drive her over in Molly's donkey cart,' said Jem, a little doubtfully, because both sisters lived miles away.

There were certainly a flurry of letters inviting us over for Christmas, and Mother seemed excited by the idea. But when Jem and I talked it over together, it didn't seem at all practical. It was getting so cold. Mother would freeze to death on the journey, even if we wrapped her up in twenty blankets. We couldn't take her special wheeled chair too, so she would be trapped in a corner – and would there be room enough for her in any spare bed?

It was dear Janet who solved our problem. 'You must come to our house for Christmas Day,' she said. 'I'm sure Jem and Father could give Peg a chairlift to our house. We have a big oven, and you know how much my mother loves cooking. Please say you'll come, Jem and Hetty.'

I think we were both torn. I wanted to have a wonderful Christmas in *our* house, and that was what Jem seemed to want too. If only our walls could expand so *I* could invite the Maples and many other guests besides. Perhaps not my foster sisters. I'd seen a little too much of them at the funeral.

I'd have liked to invite my father for Christmas. Katherine and Mina and Ezra could have smokies and baked cod and fishy pudding back where they belonged. I'd have liked my dear friend Freda the Female Giant to come too, though we might have to raise the ceiling specially. I'd have liked to see my pal Bertie the butcher's boy too, and he would surely bring us a fine turkey or a side of beef, but I wasn't so sure Jem would enjoy his company. And oh, most of all I'd have liked to send an invitation up to Heaven and have Mama pop down for the day. I'd make her a feast even better than manna, whatever that was. I just knew it was the only food they seemed to eat in Heaven. I paused, trying to decide what Mama would most like to eat during her visit.

'Hetty?' said Jem. He gave me a little nudge. 'I'm sorry,' he said to Janet. 'She's got that look in her eye. I think she's picturing again.'

'Don't tease me, you two,' I said, coming back to my senses. 'It's so kind of you and your family to invite us for Christmas, Janet. We'd love to come, wouldn't we, Jem?'

So that's what we did. It was all very jolly and we ate like kings. Mother particularly enjoyed herself. Mrs Maple was so kind to her. She'd made up a special chair like a throne, with extra cushions and blankets and shawls, and gave her a special Christmas meal tactfully cut into tiny pieces.

Mother was learning how to feed herself again now, though her hands were very shaky and she sometimes lost concentration halfway to her mouth. She couldn't help making a mess on the tablecloth and looked upset, but Mrs Maple patted her shoulder and said calmly, 'Don't fret, Peg dear, you're doing splendidly.'

We ate turkey, the very first time I'd tasted it. I didn't care for the live birds at all, with their weird worm-pink heads and fat feathery bodies and yellow claws. I always skirted round the turkey shed, keeping my distance. I'd had no idea that such a grotesque creature could taste so sweet and succulent. We had roast potatoes too, crisp and golden, and parsnips and carrots and small green sprouts like baby cabbages.

We ate until we were nearly bursting, but when we were offered a second serving we said yes please, and Mother nodded enthusiastically. There were puddings too – a rich figgy pudding with a custard, a pink blancmange like a fairy castle, and a treacle tart with whipped cream. I could not choose which pudding I wanted because they all looked so wonderful, so I had a portion of each.

This was a serious mistake, as I was wearing my first proper grown-up corset for the occasion. I'd bought it in the hope that squeezing my stomach in with its strong whalebone might help a little bust to pop out at the top, but I remained disappointingly flat-chested – and unable to breathe properly into the bargain.

I was glad I hadn't tried to encase Mother in her own corsets. She spread comfortably underneath her loose gown. She usually fell fast asleep after a big meal, but she stayed wide awake for the present giving. The Maples gave her a specially wrapped little package. I helped her unwrap it. Mr Maple had carved her special cutlery, cleverly designed to help her manage more efficiently. The spoon had a deep bowl to prevent spillage, the fork had clever prongs for easy spearing, and the knife had a curved handle so that Mother could grip it.

She seized hold of her spoon and fork, wanting to try them out immediately, so Mrs Maple gave her another bowl of figgy pudding, even though she was already full to the brim.

Of course, Mother had no presents to give the Maples in return, but Jem and I had done our best. Jem gave me several shillings from his farm wages and I bought them an ornament at the market – a little china model of a house, not unlike their own, with a little lumpy extra bacon room beside the chimney. There was a message written carefully across the plinth: *Bless This House*.

I'd wanted to find something special for Janet too, because she had been such a dear friend, so I bought her a special pen. It was a fine one, with a green mottled casing, and I rather wanted it for myself, but I decided to be generous.

The Maples were very satisfyingly pleased with their presents. Janet hugged me hard and said she would use her beautiful pen every day and think of me.

'Then at least your journal will have variety,' I said. 'You can write *Today I got up – and I love my friend Hetty!*'

Jem and Mother and I had kept our presents to give to each other at the Maples. I didn't want to fob Mother off with yet another nightgown. I bought her a new china washing jug and bowl, white with pink babies playing all around the inside. There was also a matching chamber pot, though it seemed a shame to piddle on the little children. I kept the pot at home because it might have been embarrassing unwrapping it in company.

I couldn't wait for Jem to open his present from me. Market Jim had let me have an end roll of scarlet worsted because it had a flaw running through the weave. I cut it out carefully on the slant and avoided the flaw altogether. I'd made it into a waistcoat with pockets and brass buttons.

'Oh I say!' said Jem, going as red as the cloth when he unwrapped the waistcoat. 'I shall look a right robin redbreast! Oh, Hetty, it's the finest waistcoat I've ever seen. I shall wear it every Sunday.'

'You don't think it's too bright?' I asked anxiously.

'Not at all – the brighter the better,' said Jem, though I'm not entirely sure he was being truthful.

'Try your waistcoat on, Jem!' said Janet.

'Yes, do – I need to see if it fits properly,' I said.

'I probably won't be able to get the buttons done up because I've had so much Christmas dinner,' said Jem – but they slid easily into place. Although it sounds dreadfully like boasting, his waistcoat looked magnificent. Even taciturn Mr Maple murmured that it was a tremendous fit.

'But I wish I knew what the time was,' I said excitedly.

They all stared at me. The Maples' brass clock was ticking steadily on the mantelpiece.

'I'd like to *check* the time,' I said. 'Doesn't anyone else have a timepiece, Jem? Don't gentlemen keep a pocket watch about their person?'

'You know very well I don't have a pocket watch, Hetty,' said Jem.

'Not even in your fine new waistcoat?' I said. 'Why don't you check the pockets?'

Jem stared at me, and then slid his fingers into the slim pocket at the front. His hand felt something. His mouth fell open as he drew out a gold fob watch. It wasn't real gold, it was pinchbeck, and it wasn't brand new. I'd seen it on a curiosity stall in the market and I'd bargained hard for it. It was truly a pretty ordinary watch and it didn't even have a chain, but Jem cradled it in his hand as if it were part of the crown jewels.

'Oh, Hetty,' he whispered. 'Oh, Hetty!'

'Do you like it? I thought it was time you had a watch. Now you haven't any excuse to be late home and keep supper waiting,' I joked.

'I've never had such a splendid present,' said Jem. 'Thank you so much. Thank you so very, very much. Oh dear, I wish I'd got you something as special.' He handed me a tiny parcel apologetically.

I felt it carefully. 'Is it . . . jewellery?' I asked, my heart beating fast.

Janet gave a little gasp. 'Oh, Hetty, *open* it!'

I picked the paper open and saw a little necklace.

It was a silver sixpence with a hole bored into it so that it could hang on a dainty silver chain. 'Oh, Jem, it's lovely!' I whispered, putting it round my neck and fumbling with the clasp.

'Here, let me,' he said. 'It's an odd plain thing, I know – but you lost your last sixpence, the one I gave you as a token when you had to go off to the hospital. I thought you could keep this one hanging safe around your neck.' He fastened it in place for me. 'Perhaps it's just a silly whim. It's not very fancy like a real necklace,' he said uncertainly.

'It's perfectly lovely, Jem. I shall treasure it for ever,' I said.

I felt dangerously near tears and I could scarcely breathe for the wretched corset. I plucked at the terrible whalebones constricting my stomach. 'Oh dear Lord,' I said, gasping.

Janet drew me to one side. 'Why don't you slip up to my bedroom and loosen the ties, Hetty?' she whispered.

'I think that's a good idea,' I said.

I ran out of the hot living room, up the stairs to Janet's quiet pale bedroom. I shut the door for privacy, pulled off my frock, and struggled with the wretched laces until suddenly they gave and I could breathe deeply again. It was such a relief I pulled the corset off altogether and had a good stretch and scratch, delighting in my freedom.

Janet had a looking glass, so I peered at myself, though I looked a figure of fun in my chemise and drawers. The sixpence was cold against my chest. I fingered it lovingly. It was such a sweet kind thought of Jem's, and it looked so pretty too. I knew I should feel delighted. I was delighted – and yet I rather wished he hadn't given it to me even so. It would have meant the world to me once . . . when I was back in the Foundling Hospital. But somehow, now that I was grown up, the touching little keepsake worried me. Well, I wasn't quite grown up yet, I knew that, but I seemed to be growing *differently* now.

I glared at myself in the looking glass. 'What's the matter with you, girl?' I said to myself. 'All your dreams have come true. You live in your own home with Jem, the kindest man in the world, and he loves you dearly. This is what you longed for, year after year, in that wretched hospital. You've got what you wanted, Hetty Feather, Sapphire Battersea, Emerald Star. You can't live with Mama, you won't live with Father. You want to live with Jem, don't you? You want to be part of this village and look after Mother, and when you're a little older, Janet's age maybe, you and Jem will marry and you'll live happily ever after, like your precious fairy tales . . .'

I put my hot forehead against the cold glass,

wondering why I couldn't feel properly happy. Then I looked over my shoulder in the glass and saw Janet's checked journal on her little bedside table.

I wondered if she'd started writing out all her thoughts and feelings. It was her private diary. It would be terribly bad even to glance inside. But somehow my feet were tiptoeing across the rug, and my hands were reaching out for the check cover.

No, Hetty, I told myself sternly, but I opened it. *Well, perhaps just one peep!*

There were dozens of closely written pages in Janet's neat schoolteacher hand. My goodness, she was writing down *copious* thoughts and feelings. I smiled down at the neat lines, not properly focusing – and then I saw my name and Jem's. I couldn't help reading it then.

Oh dear, it's so hard spending time with Jem and Hetty now. Jem is clearly utterly devoted to her. He can't stop looking at her whenever she is in the room, and when she says something his eyes shine and he smiles so proudly. I do not blame him. Hetty is so lively, so witty, so enchanting, forever saying something droll or fanciful. I wish I didn't like her so myself. It would be much easier to hate and resent her. Before she came I was beginning to hope that Jem might be starting to think of me romantically – but now she is here I can see I have no chance whatsoever. Jem thinks of me as a good friend and companion, but that is all. It is Hetty he loves. He only has eyes for her. It is so hard to bear when I love him so myself. Oh, Jem, Jem, Jem. I love you, I love you.

16

It was so dreadfully difficult to roll up my corset, put on my dress and go back downstairs again.

'Are you all right, Hetty?' Janet asked, seeing my stricken face.

'Yes, yes – just a little queasy because I've been so greedy,' I said.

I certainly felt sick at heart for the rest of the evening. Carol-singing children came calling from another village, standing earnestly on the doorstep with their turnip lanterns, singing 'Here We Come A-wassailing' and 'God Rest You Merry, Gentlemen' and 'Hark! The Herald Angels Sing'. Several were Janet's pupils. They clustered around her, wishing her a special merry Christmas.

'Is that your mister, miss?' one asked, pointing at Jem.

'No, no!' Janet said, blushing, while the Maples and Jem himself laughed heartily.

Yet when I looked at them together, they really

did look as if they belonged to each other. They were both tall and handsome and kindly and gentle. I watched them talking to Mother, clearing the table, setting my china ornament on the mantel-piece. They could be a couple already. They *would* have been a couple, if I hadn't come along.

Janet had been so sweet to me too. She had tried her hardest to befriend me and make me feel welcome, when all along she knew I was unwittingly stealing her chances of happiness.

Jem loved me. I didn't need Janet's journal to tell me that. I knew it was true. And I loved him, didn't I?

It was a great palaver getting Mother home again and settled back in her bed. She had clearly enjoyed her day but she grew agitated now, turning her head restlessly, calling 'Gi-gi-gi' again. I had to sit with her for a long time, holding her hand and talking gentle nonsense to her before she would quieten.

I was bone tired now and ready for my own bed. I thought Jem might have retired, but he was down by the fire, although it hadn't been lit all day and the empty grate was cold and cheerless.

'Jem? Aren't you going to bed? It's so late.'

'I'd like to sit a little while and think over today, Hetty,' he said. 'Come and keep me company.'

'But it's so cold!'

'I'll warm you up a little,' he said cheerfully, holding out his arms.

We had hugged each other a hundred times, but now I felt a shrinking self-consciousness as I sat beside him. He pulled me close, so that my head rested on his shoulder.

'It's been a splendid day, hasn't it?' he said. He pulled out his pocket watch. 'Nearly midnight! Oh, Hetty, it's such a beautiful watch. I shall treasure it for ever.' He paused. I knew I should say something about my sixpence necklace.

'And thank you so much for my lovely necklace, Jem. It was so thoughtful of you. I shall treasure it too.'

'I'll keep it polished for you,' he said.

He reached up and plucked a handful of ivy from the mantelpiece. I'd decorated it with holly and ivy to make the cottage look festive. He started fashioning it this way and that.

'What are you doing? You're spoiling my decoration!'

'I'm making a kissing bow,' said Jem.

My heart skipped a beat. 'Isn't that meant to be mistletoe?' I said.

'We haven't *got* any mistletoe, so ivy will have to do for now,' he said. 'Here, Hetty, you do it. Your fingers are more nimble than mine.'

'Oh, Jem, don't be silly. Let's go to bed.'

'Wait!' Jem fashioned the ivy into the clumsiest of bows and then held it above our heads. 'We must have a Christmas kiss.'

I heard the church clock at the end of the village starting to chime. 'No, sorry! It isn't Christmas any more,' I said, and made a bolt for it up the stairs.

Jem didn't try to follow me or call after me. When I went downstairs the next morning, the ivy kissing bow had been unravelled and threaded back into the greenery on the mantelpiece.

He didn't mention trying to kiss me when he came home. He couldn't expect it either, because he'd been carting manure to the wintry fields and reeked of it, even though he stripped off and washed himself thoroughly.

I felt so sorry for him having to work in the bleak fields all day long. He was put to digging ditches for most of January – really hard labour as the ground was frozen.

He caught a chill and yet refused to take time off, going to work even though he had a fever and his nose was streaming. I made him thick soups and wrapped Lizzie's shawl around him for extra warmth when he came home – simple little gestures, but he was heartbreakingly grateful.

'You're so good to me, Hetty,' he said thickly.

Mother caught the chill too, though I struggled hard to keep her warm and comfortable. She had a fever, and for a few days frightened me because she seemed so ill.

'I reckon we'd better get the doctor to her,' said Jem.

The doctor's visit cost a great deal, and was a total waste of money, because he told me to make sure Mother was well covered and had plenty of fluids. What did he *think* I was doing with her – sitting her out in the frosty fields and refusing her a drop to drink?

He also said something so dreadful that Jem and I were dumbfounded.

'It might be better for the poor soul if her lungs gave out altogether. She's no use to man nor beast in that state,' he said, wiping his boots on our mat and marching out.

I felt as if he'd wiped his boots on me, and given me a good kicking into the bargain. 'How dare he say such a wicked thing!' I said furiously. 'I've a good mind to go after him and give him a good slapping.'

'Hey, Hetty, hold onto your temper. I don't want you had up for assault!' said Jem. He put his arms round me.

This time I clung to him in the old easy, natural way. 'How *could* he say such a thing about Mother – and him a doctor too!' I said.

'I know, I know. It's wonderful that you love Mother just the way I do, and want to keep her here as long as possible. On her last visit even Eliza seemed to think that it would be a blessing to us when Mother goes.'

'I don't care for Eliza too much – I never did. But I *do* care for Mother. I tried so hard to keep my own mama alive, but I couldn't manage it. I shall always have a huge ache in my heart for her. But I will try and keep *our* mother as long as I possibly can,' I said stoutly.

'The ache will lessen one day, Hetty,' said Jem, cuddling me close.

I knew he was simply trying to comfort me, but I pulled away from him. 'How can you talk such nonsense?' I said. 'You can't possibly understand how I feel about Mama.'

'I'm sorry, Hetty. I didn't mean to upset you. Please don't be offended,' said Jem.

He'd always been so used to telling me things that I'd accepted without question. It was painful for both of us when I argued back – but I couldn't seem to help it now.

At least we were united in our attempts to nurse

Mother back to reasonable health, though of course she would never be well again. Mrs Maple made her various herbal tisanes that seemed to ease her lungs and stop her coughing, and we rubbed goose grease on her chest, binding it with flannel.

Mother was still very poorly for weeks, which was a strain on all of us. I did not feel I could go to market on a Thursday and leave her with Molly. I felt very guilty but I missed those market days so *much*. The only material I had left was the red worsted and I didn't want to make anyone else a waistcoat like Jem's, so it stayed untouched. Instead, during those long anxious hours sitting beside Mother while she took such painful breaths, I rewrote my memoirs. I kept to the truth but arranged them like the three-decker novels Janet lent me, with lots of conversation and a proper story structure.

The first volume dealt with my time at the hospital. I carefully did not give it its full name now. I finished that volume with my bolt for freedom the day of Queen Victoria's Golden Jubilee. There was a lot of repetitious material thereafter about the hardship and injustice of my hospital life during the next four years, so I discarded those pages and started the second volume when I was just fourteen and leaving the hospital. I wrote about my life in service, my jaunts with Bertie, and then that sad summer at the seaside, watching over Mama. I ended with her telling me I should go and find Father.

Now I was writing the *third* volume, keeping my writing as small as I could to cram all my story onto the pages. The first part of this volume dealt with finding Father. I felt the wind in my hair and tasted fish on my tongue as I wrote. When I described my return to the village and my meeting with dear Jem, my pen slowed down and I did not know how to continue. I'd caught myself up. I wasn't sure how my story was going to end.

All Janet's three-decker novels ended identically – with the heroine marrying the hero and then hopefully living happily ever after. I was clearly the heroine, because this was my life, my story – and the hero was probably Jem.

Why did I write *probably*? Of course he was my hero, the boy who had looked after me so sweetly when we were both children, who had continued to care for me, and had now taken me happily into his home. He was waiting patiently for me to grow up. Then my story would finish traditionally, with a wedding.

I put my notebooks away, feeling troubled. I loved Jem dearly as a big brother, but I wasn't at all sure I could love him as a husband. I hated realizing this now, when it had always been my childhood dream. It seemed particularly perverse when poor Janet was silently suffering, longing to marry Jem herself.

I grew oddly subdued and withdrawn. Jem worried about me, wondering if I was going down with the chill myself. He asked Mrs Maple for a tonic for me, which I drank obediently every day, but all the herbs in the world could not lighten my heavy heart.

I was very tired all the time and yet I couldn't sleep properly. I tossed and turned all night, wondering what I should do. 'Oh, Mama, why can't you still be here?' I said, starting to cry. 'I need you so!'

I'm always with you, Hetty, you know that, Mama said in my heart.

'What am I going to do about Jem?'

Wait and see, she said. *You don't know what's going to happen next.*

'But I *do* know, Mama. It's always the same here in the village. It's only the seasons that change. I do the same thing every single day, and every night Jem and I say the same things. It's as if we're little wind-up dolls and can't do anything else. It's not what I *want*, Mama.'

So what do you want?

'I don't know! I want . . . I want . . .' I stretched out in my bed as if I were literally trying to grow.

It's a long winter, said Mama. *Wait for the spring.*

It seemed as if spring would never come. January and February were so cold and bleak – but then in early March the sun started shining, so warmly that I didn't need to huddle inside Lizzie's shawl.

'It's a lovely day, Mother. Shall we sit you in your chair on the doorstep, so you can feel the sun on your face?' I said. 'You'd like that, wouldn't you?'

Mother nodded yes, making it clear that she would like that very much. I kept her wrapped up in all her own shawls and blankets because she still coughed a little and wheezed when she drew breath. She had lost a lot of weight during her illness and I found I could push her quite easily. I left her there on the doorstep like a great sweet baby while I set about the familiar chores inside the cottage.

I was on my knees scrubbing the floor when I heard Mother give a startled cry. Then she started calling – her old frantic 'Gi-gi-gi-gi!'

I jumped up, and in my haste kicked my bucket of water over, soaking my skirts. It took me a minute to wring myself out, all the time shouting to Mother that I was coming, but she took no notice.

'Gi-gi-gi-gi!' she shouted, and then gave a great gasp.

'Oh my Lord! Have you hurt yourself? Hang on, Mother, I'm coming!' I cried, and shot out of the door.

There was Mother, gasping in her chair. A tall man was bending over her, a terrifying stranger with a great black patch over his eye. He took hold of her – and I seized my broom and waved it above my head.

'Leave my mother *alone*!' I screamed, beating at him.

'No – no!' Mother shouted. 'Gi-Gi-Gi-*Gideon*!'

I stopped, dumbfounded, my broom waving in mid air.

'Gideon,' Mother repeated, enunciating each syllable perfectly, tears of joy streaming down her face.

I couldn't believe it. This wounded stranger was my foster brother Gideon, who had served his strict nine years at the hospital too? He'd been sent off to be a soldier. What on earth had happened to him?

'Gideon!' I said. 'Oh, Gideon, your face! Your poor face! Were you in a battle? Oh my Lord, when did it happen?'

Gideon put his hand up over the right side of his face, covering the patch and his badly scarred cheek. I could have bitten my tongue off for my total lack of tact.

'But never mind!' I said, wildly and stupidly. 'It's wonderful that you've come home! See how glad Mother is to see you. She said your name as clear as anything. She's been so ill since Father died, but now look at her, saying your name! She must have been missing you so much!' I was just burbling in my embarrassment, but as I spoke the words, I realized they were absolutely true. All this time Mother, with her 'Gi-gi-gi', had been calling for Gideon. Why hadn't we realized before? Gideon had always been her favourite, the odd little boy forever creeping onto her lap. I think Mother loved him even more than her own birth children. They had always been so close. Now, seeing them hugging each other, I felt tears stinging my own eyes.

'It's wonderful to see you, Gideon! You will act like a tonic for Mother. Oh my, wait till Jem sees you! In fact we *won't* wait.' I called the biggest of the little boys playing hopscotch in the dust – too young for school, but still old enough to run errands. 'You – Phil, is it? You know my brother Jem, big strong Jem, who works over at the farm? He'll be in the field by Magpie Wood, sowing barley with the horses. Think you could find him? Tell him Gideon's come home. Got that? His brother Gideon! See if he can come as soon as possible.'

I made a cup of tea for Gideon, gave Mother hers in a beaker and then rushed upstairs to change into a clean dry dress. When I got back, they were hand in hand, Gideon perching on the arm of Mother's chair. The sunshine was still so warm that I brought two chairs out from the kitchen and we all sat on the porch.

'How long are you here for, Gideon?' I asked. 'Have they given you an extended leave because of . . . of your injury?'

Gideon lowered his head, his hand hovering in the air, as if he wanted to hide his face again. He made a little grunting noise which could have meant anything.

'Is it a recent injury, Gideon?' I asked.

He gave another grunt.

'What was the battle? Did it happen abroad? Are we at *war*?' I enquired.

Gideon grunted yet again.

He was so silent that I began to wonder if he was seriously mute. When he was a little boy he had stopped talking altogether after a fright. I guiltily remembered that I'd been partly responsible. He would not say a word to anyone. It wasn't till we were sent off to the Foundling Hospital together that he had found his tongue again, but he was always a taciturn boy.

His injury was clearly extensive. Perhaps it had also affected his mouth and he couldn't, rather than wouldn't, speak. I put my hand over my own mouth, horrified that I'd been plaguing him with questions, wondering if I should run and fetch pen and paper to help him communicate more easily. Then I wondered if his *brain* had been affected too, because he seemed to be behaving so oddly, silently sitting there beside Mother, holding her hand. He'd made little or no acknowledgement of me. Perhaps he didn't know who I was any more.

'I am Hetty,' I said, tapping my chest.

He stared at me with his good eye as if I were very strange. He nodded, clearly thinking me a fool. I laughed nervously, wondering what to do next. I wished Jem would come, but I knew he couldn't leave his three-horse team to do the work by themselves. It would be lunch time at the earliest before he could come home, and only if there was another farm hand free to take over.

We sat on in silence for several minutes, my flesh crawling uneasily. I found any kind of silence hard to bear. When I was alone with Mother, I chatted to her all day long, the way a little girl does with her doll: 'Now, Mother, let's get you out of that night-gown. There now, bend your arms and let me get these silly old sleeves off. It's a lovely sunny day today, Mother. Oh, we're going to sit you out in the sunshine and make you completely better, yes we are . . .' I'd carry on like that for hours, never quite knowing if Mother was taking it all in, but it seemed to make the day easier for both of us.

I couldn't talk like that with Gideon here. I was getting nowhere asking him questions about himself, so I started a long rambling monologue about my own life.

I told him about being in service, I told him about Mama's illness, I even told him about Mr Clarendon's freak show and my starring role as Emerald the Amazing Pocket-Sized Mermaid. Both Gideon and Mother stared at me then, looking shocked, so I cut short my account of life as a showgirl and talked of my father in Monksby.

'Did you ever try to find out who your parents were, Gideon?' I asked instead. 'I wrote to Miss Smith to ask the true name of my mother. You could write to her and ask after *your* mother.'

Gideon's look was withering now. He picked up Mother's hand and held it against his good cheek. It was obvious he was declaring that she was the only mother he could ever want. Mother herself seemed a changed woman. She was sitting up straight in her chair, looking intently at Gideon's face. She seemed disconcerted by his patch and scarring, shaking her head in sympathy, but there was still such happiness shining out of her old eyes that she seemed to be smiling all over, even though her poor lips could not make the right smiling shape any more.

I could not believe I'd been so stupid and not realized how badly she was pining for Gideon. She had tried again and again to ask for him, and we had been so slow on the uptake. I was glad she was so happy now, but I couldn't help being a little jealous too. I had tried so hard to please Mother and had looked after her lovingly for months, but she had never once looked at me the way she was looking at Gideon.

Little Phil came running back and jabbered, 'Jem says welcome and he'll come as soon as he's able and can I have my penny now?'

I gave it to him, my heart sinking at the thought of the whole day trying to cope with my un-communicative brother.

After what seemed like endless hours I stole away to continue with the household chores. Several times I thought I heard low murmurings and Mother's excited cries, but whenever I came out of the house they were silent. I gave them both broth and bread for lunch. Gideon supervised Mother's feeding, guiding her shaking hand, gently holding the spoon to her lips. I seemed redundant now.

Mother fell soundly asleep after her lunch.

'I think I should get her indoors where she can stretch out more comfortably,' I said, but when I gently tried to detach Mother's hand from Gideon's to wheel her away, she woke and clung on determinedly.

It was a major relief when Janet came calling. She was clearly taken aback when she saw this tall young man with an alarmingly wounded face sitting close to Mother on the doorstep, but her manners were always impeccable no matter what the circumstances.

'Oh, Janet, this is my foster brother, Gideon. Do you remember him? We were at the Foundling Hospital together and then he went away to be a soldier.'

'Oh yes, Gideon, I *do* remember you! And clearly dear Mrs Cotton is very glad to have you back just now. Look at her face! What a happy day for you both.' She talked naturally and sweetly, never once referring to Gideon's patch or his wounds, and looked him in his one eye fearlessly. I felt ashamed that I had exclaimed at his injury straight away and questioned him clumsily.

At last she helped me to wheel Mother away and tend to her in the privy, and over Mother's head we had a whispered conversation.

'It was such a shock to see him, Janet! His poor face! How do you think it happened – and why won't he talk about it?' he said.

'I think he's still suffering from shock, Hetty. Perhaps he needs time. The poor boy – he was such a good-looking little chap too,' she said. 'But clearly he's a true hero now.'

I wasn't so sure. I knew my brother Gideon. He had never been remotely heroic before. 'I don't quite know how to cope with him, Janet,' I said.

'Wait till Jem comes home. He will do the coping,' she said.

She was right. Jem managed to leave his work an hour or so early and came rushing home. Mother and Gideon were inside now, in the living room.

'Gideon! Oh, brother, it's so good to see you!' said Jem, giving him a huge bear hug. 'Welcome home!'

Gideon stiffened when he said this, and then burst out crying. It seemed somehow to release his voice too. 'Oh please . . . can I . . . really stay?' he sobbed.

'Of course you can, for as long as you want. For ever, if you like!' said Jem.

Mother was making sad crooning noises, trying to hold out her arms.

'There now,' said Jem, patting Gideon on the back and then gently propelling him towards Mother, so that they could comfort each other.

I pulled Jem into the kitchen. 'He hasn't spoken a word up till now, though I've asked him all sorts,' I whispered. 'His face is so badly hurt. Janet thinks he's still in shock, as well as wounded. She came by and was such a help.'

'Dear Janet,' said Jem. 'And dear, dear Hetty too.'

'He hasn't answered a single one of my questions!' I said.

'He doesn't need to, does he? Perhaps he truly can't talk about it. We don't want to upset him further, do we?'

'I – I suppose not,' I said, though I was burning with curiosity. I knew Jem was right though. For once it felt good for him to be putting me gently in my place and telling me what to do.

It wasn't long before Gideon told us of his own accord. We had supper together, and then he spent ten minutes upstairs alone with Mother after I'd put her to bed. We wondered if he was going to bed himself. I'd put an extra pillow on Jem's bed, as they would have to share again, just as they had done as children – but he came back down the stairs.

'Mother's asleep,' he said.

'You've made her so happy,' said Jem.

'I wanted to come when you wrote to me about Father dying,' said Gideon. 'But . . . I couldn't.'

'They wouldn't give Nat leave either. The army won't bend its rules,' said Jem. 'But I don't suppose I need to tell you that, Gideon. Would you care for a glass of ale, lad? Or there's a bottle of cowslip wine, though we won't let Hetty get her hands on it or she'll be drunk as a skunk in no time.'

'I will not! Don't tease, Jem,' I said, though I knew he was only joshing me to make it easier for all of us.

We all had a small glass of wine sitting by the fire. Jem offered Gideon his pipe too, treating him like a man. Gideon was still very tense and hesitant in his speech, and he often held his hand protectively in front of his face.

The sips of wine loosened my tongue again. 'Does it still hurt, Gideon?' I asked.

He ducked his head. 'Yes, it does,' he mumbled.

'How . . . how did it happen?'

'Hetty,' said Jem warningly. 'I don't think Gideon wants to talk about it.'

He sat between us, opening and closing his

mouth, clearly not able to find the words.

'You were in a battle?' I asked again, though Jem nudged me.

'No. No, I was still a cadet. We don't go to war, we just . . . train,' said Gideon. 'Oh, I hated it so much there.' A tear fell from his good eye.

'Was it as bad as the Foundling Hospital?' I asked softly.

'It was much, much worse. Oh, Hetty, why didn't I ever listen to you? I had my chances to escape. I could have run off with you that day in Hyde Park, when we were ten. I could have run away when you left the hospital to go into service. But I never had your spirit. I was too scared, and so I let them parcel me off to the barracks and . . . it was so dreadful.'

'Did the sergeants treat you badly, Gideon?' said Jem, taking his hand and squeezing it.

'They weren't the worst. It was the other boys. There's something about me. I'm always the one that gets picked on. I'm so different. I knew nothing because of being in the hospital, so they teased and tormented me. I was their sport, night after night.'

'You have to learn to fight *back*, Gideon,' I said, my own fists clenched.

'How can I, when it's not in my nature?' he said. 'But I don't have to fight any more. I have been discharged because of my . . . my injuries.'

'Was it a gunshot wound? Oh, Gid, those boys didn't *shoot* you, did they?' I asked, starting to cry myself.

'All the cadets were sent off with the proper soldiers one night. There was an emergency – there'd been a breakout at a prison. We were sent to round up the escaped convicts. We were told they were dangerous – robbers, murderers – and we had to protect the public. We were each given guns, though we'd barely handled them before. It was a terrible night, very stormy, and the men had got out on the commons, where it was so dark you couldn't see anything, only hear the rustling of bushes in the wind. One of the escaped convicts crept up on a lad and tried to strangle him to get his gun – and after that we were told to fire on sight.

'We were all spread out in the dark. I somehow lost the others, and I didn't dare call out. I was stumbling around, half mad with fear, scarcely able to keep hold of my rifle because my hands were so slippery with sweat – and then I suddenly walked straight into someone. It was one of the convicts, right in front of me. He was just standing there, breathing hard. I knew what I had to do. Without really thinking, I just lifted my rifle and aimed and fired—'

Gideon broke down altogether, sobbing. 'I hit him, I know I did, but he didn't go down. He tried to run, though his legs were shackled. He hobbled, and he called out, "Don't shoot again, sir, please don't shoot." Perhaps I would have let him go, but then the others came running at the sound of my shot and they all rounded on him, and fired. He didn't have a chance. He wouldn't die straight away though, no matter how they fired. He writhed and screamed.' Gideon put his hands over his ears as if he could still hear the screaming now. The cottage was very still as we waited for him to continue.

'And after that night . . .' He couldn't manage to go on.

'Don't, Gid. Please. It's so awful for you,' I said, wishing now I hadn't asked him any questions at all.

Jem poured Gideon another drink and quietly passed him his handkerchief.

Gideon struggled to compose himself. 'After that night I kept seeing the convict. No matter how I rubbed my eyes he was still there in front of me – even when my eyes were shut. He was there all the time, standing before me, breathing hard, while I stared down the barrel of my gun with my right eye. I shot him, over and over again, while he begged for his life. I thought I was going mad. No, I *knew* I was mad – or else I was the only sane one in the barracks. It was so bizarre. I'd suddenly turned into a queer sort of hero overnight, because I'd shot the convict first. I was congratulated, told I was starting to shape up, patted on the back. The other boys stopped tormenting me. But I was in a worse torment, seeing the convict there all the time, right before my eye. One day, out on a run on those commons, I couldn't bear seeing him any more. I took my rifle and tried to put my eye out.'

'Oh, Gideon,' I said, standing up and throwing my arms around him. 'Oh, Gideon!'

'I thought I would die. To be truthful I *hoped* to die – but a few days after my accident the letter came from Jem to tell me that Father had died and Mother was taken ill. A nurse read it out to me. Somehow that gave me a little strength. I was anxious about Mother. I decided to try to live for her sake. I developed a very bad infection around the wound and was in a fever for weeks. My mind was still in a torment. I found it hard to speak. I couldn't explain to anyone. There was talk of my being charged with attempted suicide, but the doctor argued that I was in a state of nervous prostration, prone to fits of lunacy – and who was I to argue with that?

'So here I am, a free man, but I'm no use to anyone. I cannot think what job I can do now.

They've warned me I might well lose the sight of my good eye too. But don't worry, Jem, I'm not going to be a burden on you. If I can stay for a week or so and see Mother, then that is all I ask.'

'You must stay for ever, Gideon. This is your home, and we will make you as well and strong as possible, won't we, Hetty?' said Jem.

'Of course we will,' I said, embracing both my brothers.

17

It was so strange being a family of four. In many ways it was a lot easier for me, as Gideon did more than his fair share of the work. He had done his nine years at the hospital too. He knew how to make himself useful. He'd never done laundry work or cooking, but after watching me carefully for a couple of days, he started shyly offering to take a turn himself. He was a little clumsy at first, and grew very upset when he scorched the sheets with an over-heated flat iron, but he soon got the knack – and he quickly became a champion cook. He didn't just stick to my basic soups and stews. He chatted to Mrs Maple and experimented with herbs and spices. Soon he was taking a turn in her kitchen and baking scones and barm cakes and fruity slices that rivalled her own.

She took Gideon to her heart and loved having him around. In fact, all the village women made a pet of him. Jem and I didn't breathe a word about how he'd lost his eye. I don't know whether the village folk thought him a hero or a coward. Perhaps they didn't care. They simply saw that Gideon was a poor gentle chap who meant no harm and were kind to him.

The village children were a different matter. Some of the boys were cruel enough to jeer at him and call him the one-eyed monster-man. They didn't do it twice. I rushed out and smacked them hard about the head to teach them a lesson. Gideon's black patch and red scars frightened the little girls, making them shrink from him, covering their own faces. I think this upset him more than the boys' jeering. But gradually they grew used to him, and when he shyly offered them little iced cakes as a peace offering, he grew to be a favourite friend.

He was Mother's favourite too, of course. They were inseparable now. He tended her like the gentlest of nurses and knew how to coax her if she was in a contrary mood. Sometimes she wasn't hungry and deliberately knocked her spoon to spill it. I'd struggle for half an hour to feed her, practically ramming the spoon into her mouth, but Gideon would cluck his tongue at her, jolly her into a good mood in two minutes, and have her scraping her bowl clean.

I was pleased for both of them but I couldn't help feeling a little put out too. I'd wanted to be king pin in the house, and yet Gideon had bobbed up out of nowhere and taken my place.

'How do you feel about Gideon living here, Hetty?' Jem asked one evening when Gideon was upstairs settling Mother.

'It's good to see him gradually relaxing, and he's lovely company for Mother,' I said.

'Yes he is. But what about for you?' Jem asked. 'You seem a little . . . dispirited, Hetty.'

'I'm fine, Jem, really,' I said, forcing a smile.

He reached out and took hold of my hand. 'Come for a little walk with me, Hetty,' he said. 'Mother will be fine with Gideon. Let's go to one of our old haunts. Shall we seek out the squirrel house?'

I hesitated. Jem was being so sweet and considerate. What was the matter with me? I'd always loved our squirrel tree. Why did I feel so reluctant to see it now? Jem looked so eager I didn't want to hurt his feelings.

'Yes, what a lovely idea,' I said, and we slipped out of the cottage together.

It was twilight, the sun still faintly staining the sky, the trees turning into dark silhouettes. We walked demurely side by side down the village lane, but when we got to the woods Jem took hold of my hand.

'In case we get lost,' he said.

'Silly! You must remember the way. You took

little Eliza here enough times,' I said tartly.

'Don't, Hetty. I feel bad now, when it was *our* special place. I should have let her play house in another tree.'

'Yes, maybe you should,' I said, because it still rankled – but when we found the squirrel tree it seemed ridiculous to be harbouring such a grudge.

I'd remembered it as such a special place. The tree had seemed hundreds of feet tall, a hard and hazardous climb until we reached the hollow hideaway. We'd furnished our house with chairs and beds and a fire with a cooking pot. They weren't real of course – just rags and rubbish, sticks and mud pies – but we pictured them so vividly it seemed like we were really sitting and sleeping and eating in our house.

It was incredibly disappointing to see that the tree was really quite small and spindly. I climbed up to our little house in seconds. There were still a few sticks littering the floor, and a scrap of blanket, but that was all.

'Oh dear,' I said, feeling desperately disappointed.

'We could make it grand for you again, Hetty,' said Jem. 'I could fashion you a real little chair and we could buy some proper cups and plates.' He was trying so hard he made me want to cry.

'It's so kind of you, Jem, but it's all right, really.

328

It's not the way I remembered it. It's just a tree,' I said.

'Perhaps I could build you a proper treehouse in the summer,' he offered. 'Would you like our own private little hideaway, Hetty?'

'Oh, Jem, we're not children any more,' I said gently.

'I'd still like to hide away with you,' he said, and he pulled me close.

I knew he was going to try to kiss me again. I wriggled away, climbed rapidly down the tree and started running through the woods.

'Hetty? Hetty, wait for me! Don't run off. It's getting dark. You'll get lost,' Jem called anxiously.

I pretended not to hear. I urgently wanted to get away, though I wasn't sure why. I wasn't running from a frightening stranger, a cruel man, a hateful one. This was my dearest brother Jem, the man I loved most in the world. Somehow that made me run harder – and then I tripped over some brambles and fell.

'Hetty! Hetty, it's all right, I'm coming!' Jem shouted. He was by my side in an instant, gently helping me up.

'Oh no, I haven't twisted my ankle *again*, have I?' I wailed. 'How could I have been so stupid?'

'It's all right. Lean on me. I'll help you. I'll carry you if you like,' said Jem. 'Yes, I'll carry you!'

'You can't carry me all the way home,' I said, putting my foot down gingerly. I took several little steps. 'It's all right, I think it's fine. Yes, really, I can walk perfectly, thank you, Jem.'

My ankles were intact, but I could feel blood trickling down my shins and knew I'd gashed both knees. It didn't show in the dark under my dress and I didn't say a word about it. I felt I deserved some sort of punishment.

Jem held my arm tightly, doing his best to support me, murmuring encouragement. 'There now, Hetty. Good girl. Nearly there,' he kept saying, urging me on. I couldn't help thinking it was exactly the tone he used to the animals on the farm.

'I'm not a little horse, Jem!' I declared.

'No, of course not,' he said. 'And – and you're not a grown woman either, even though you keep telling me you're not a child any more. Don't worry, darling Hetty. I will try to remember you're only a girl and not . . . not frighten you. I will wait, my sweetheart.'

I thought of Jem waiting patiently year after year until he thought I was old enough. It made me long to run again, in spite of my sore knees.

I was filled with this new restlessness now, and it wouldn't go away. I tried hard to tire myself out with housework, but no matter how much I swept and pummelled, I never settled happily in my chair at the end of the day. I slept fitfully, and in my dreams I started to run. I ran through woods, meadows, streams. I ran across moors and along cliffs and sandy beaches. I ran on hard pavements through dark crowded towns.

I grew thinner than ever, as if I really *had* been running miles every night. I had no trouble now lacing my corset. It was pointless wearing it, because it hung off me, and would not produce any kind of chest.

Mrs Maple grew concerned and baked me pies and cakes, and dosed me with herbal remedies, though nothing seemed to have any effect.

'What's the matter, Hetty?' Janet asked quietly when we were up in her bedroom one day. I was fashioning her a new summer dress, a white muslin to wear on May Day. I was supposed to be making one for myself too, but I could not get interested in the project.

'Nothing's the matter,' I said quickly, turning her round and pinning the hem of her dress. 'Nothing of any consequence.'

'Aren't you looking forward to May Day?' she said.

All of us girls were going through the village in a great procession, and then we would dance on the green and have a picnic on the grass. One of us would be crowned the May Queen.

I shrugged. 'Yes, I suppose so. I think you'll be

chosen as May Queen, Janet. You're by far the prettiest girl in the village.'

'Nonsense, nonsense!' she said, blushing. 'No, I think they'll pick *you*, Hetty, because – because . . .'

That made me laugh. 'Because I'm the ugliest, with my bright red hair and scrawny body.'

'No, because you're the youngest – and the lightest – and the brightest – and definitely the most loved.'

'Oh, Janet, you're always so incredibly kind to me. But not truthful! You love me, and I think your sweet mother does too, and my mother – but most of the villagers think me a very odd fish indeed.'

'Jem loves you,' Janet said.

We both went pink now.

'Jem's my foster brother, and very kind, so of course he loves me. And Gideon too. But they're not . . . like sweethearts,' I said hastily.

'But they could be when you're a little older,' said Janet, a little shakily.

'I don't think so,' I said as firmly as I could. 'They could just as easily be your sweetheart, Janet.'

We both knew I wasn't talking about Gideon.

Janet shook her head. 'I know I'm right, Hetty,' she said.

'No, *I* know *I'm* right,' I insisted.

'Well, you'll simply have to get up at dawn on

May Day and bathe your face in fresh dew and then go and peer in the looking glass,' said Janet, in a lighter tone.

'Why? Will I suddenly become beautiful?'

'No, silly. You're meant to see the face of your true love standing behind you,' she said.

'Well, my looking glass will be blank, because I haven't got a true love,' I said.

'When you're older you'll change your mind,' said Janet.

'I don't think so,' I said. I went and knelt beside her. 'Janet, I love Jem so very much, but not in that way. He won't ever be my sweetheart. I'm not right for him. But it's clear as day who is.' I took hold of her by the shoulders. '*You* are!'

'*I* might want that, but Jem doesn't,' said Janet. 'He only has eyes for you.'

'Then – then I will go away,' I said.

'Don't be silly, Hetty. This is your home now. Jem would be devastated.'

'Only for a little while – and you could comfort him.'

'You could never leave home! What about your mother?'

'Gideon is much closer to her than I am. He's wonderful at nursing her, and old Molly could always help out.'

'You sound as if you're serious. Have you been planning this?' asked Janet, looking shocked.

'No, I've only just this minute realized – but I think it's what I have to do,' I said.

'But where will you go? Back to your father?'

I thought about Father in Monksby. I still felt great affection for him but I knew I would never make a fisher-girl – and would certainly never get on with Katherine. I might go back on a visit, but not to stay.

I had to earn my own living. I had my memoir almost finished, apart from its ending, but in my heart I knew it was highly unlikely that it would ever be published, let alone make my fortune.

I couldn't go back into service because I didn't have a character reference. I could set myself up as a seamstress, but I needed somewhere to live.

I clutched my head, feeling as if it might burst with all the thoughts buzzing around inside. Then I heard shouts from the street – the cries of excited children.

'What's that?' asked Janet. 'I hope it's not my little class misbehaving! I wonder why they're making such a noise? Should I go out and make a fierce teacher face at them, Hetty?'

I listened and then heard the strangest sound – an odd, high-pitched, strangled roar that was somehow familiar.

'What on earth's that?' said Janet. 'Are they playing some kind of musical instrument?'

'No – no, it's an elephant!' I said.

'*What?*' said Janet, laughing, thinking I was fooling.

'It *is*. Oh, Janet, I think it's the circus!' I said, running to the window. I threw back the sash and leaned out as far as I could go.

'Careful, Hetty!' she said, hanging onto me by my petticoats. 'Oh my goodness, it *is* a circus!'

'It's *my* circus!' I breathed as I peered down at a great wagon painted scarlet and emerald and canary yellow. It was hard making out the curly writing on the side from this angle, but I could see enough.

'It's the great Tanglefield Travelling Circus,' I whispered, barely able to talk. 'And there's Elijah the elephant – look!'

'You're right, Hetty! It comes every year. Do you remember it from when you were little?' said Janet.

'Oh yes, I remember it,' I said. 'I think that's Mr Tanglefield in the great coat and boots, leading Elijah, the largest elephant in the entire world.'

That's how he was billed, but Elijah seemed to have shrunk a little, and was even more wrinkled about the face and belly – but still extraordinarily exotic to be plodding down our little village street. All the children ran along beside him, shrieking with excitement. A lion roared from another wagon and they all screamed, clutching each other.

'Oh, there are the silver boys in their tights, though they've grown so, they're not boys any more. But look, look, there's a new tiny one . . .'

A little girl skipped along behind them, only about five or six, in a short white dress and silver ballet slippers. She looked just like a little fairy. She had a small silver tiara sparkling in her blonde hair and carried a wand with a star on the end.

'Oh, the little lamb!' said Janet, leaning right out of the window too. 'Surely she can't be part of a circus act, she's much too tiny.'

'I'd have given anything to be part of the circus when I was that age,' I said. 'And so would Gideon. I do hope he's watching. He loved those silver acrobats. And I loved . . . Oh please, please, let her still be part of the circus!'

I waited impatiently while Chino the clown capered past in his ridiculous clothes, deliberately tripping over his own feet, with his sidekick Beppo scampering after him, red mouth agape. I saw a woman in a fancy dress and gasped, but it was only Flora the tightrope walker, plumper than ever, but gamely marching along twirling hoops about her wrists, making a fine show herself.

Then, right at the end of the procession – oh, glory! – there was a woman in a short pink spangled skirt. She was riding on the back of a sprightly black horse which set off her pale pink costume and

336

white limbs a treat. It was Madame Adeline herself, bravely powdered all over to give off a pearly gleam of youth, her long legs still shapely in her shining white tights, her bright red wig gleaming in the sunlight. She was my Madame Adeline in all her valiant glory, somehow managing to look glamorously beautiful even in the harsh daylight.

'Madame Adeline!' I called.

My voice was too hoarse to make much noise and she urged her black horse onwards.

'Madame Adeline, Madame Adeline – oh *please* look, Madame Adeline!' I screamed.

She paused and turned and looked up. I waved to her frantically. She could not really have recognized me. She probably did not even remember our two encounters – or so I thought. But she hesitated, then smiled, her crimson lips beautiful against her white teeth, and then she tapped the star decoration on the bodice of her dress.

Little Star! She had once called me her Little Star. My heart beat so fast I felt it would burst. 'Oh, Madame Adeline!' I called, tears rolling down my cheeks.

'Hetty, Hetty, what is it? Who is she? Do you know her?' Janet asked in concern.

'Yes, I know her. I know her very well! And she knows *me*!' I said.

Madame Adeline urged the horse onwards to

catch up with the rest of the Tanglefield parade –
but she turned and waved again, looking straight
at me.

'How do you know her? You can't have seen her
since you were four or five,' said Janet, putting
her arms around me.

'I met up with her when I was ten,' I said, still
crying.

'There now, Hetty. How you're trembling! Did
she come to perform at the Foundling Hospital?'

I stopped crying and burst out laughing at this
preposterous thought. Janet still had no inkling of
the harsh regime at the hospital.

'No, no, it was when I ran away, when Queen
Victoria had her Jubilee. I found Tanglefield's
circus up on Hampstead Heath, and Madame
Adeline was so kind to me. She invited me into her
caravan and made me tea and listened to my story.
I begged her to let me travel with the circus and be
part of her performing act. I loved her so. I wished
she was my mother.'

'Well, I dare say you can go and see her perform
tomorrow. If Jem and Gideon want to go too, I will
come and sit with your mother. Oh, I'm so glad the
circus has come. It's brought the roses to your
cheeks at last. You look a different girl!'

I *felt* different. I could not wait until tomorrow. I
flew home and told Gideon. I described the three

acrobat brothers in their sparkly suits, and just for a moment fire flickered in his one good eye as he remembered.

'Isn't it wonderful, Gideon? We'll go tonight – and tomorrow – and the day after! Wait till you see the tiny girl who seems to be in the troupe. She's so *little* it's hard to believe she's part of the circus. Wouldn't *we* have loved to be in the show and perform like that! Oh to be a circus child!'

Gideon's mouth formed an *Oh* too. But then he looked at Mother, he looked around the cottage, and he shook his head. 'I'd sooner live here, safe and sound,' he said.

Mother made a soft gurgling sound in her throat. 'Good boy, Gideon!' she said. She spoke slowly, her voice a little slurred, but it was clear enough. Gideon had been encouraging her day by day, and it was as if she was slowly coming back to herself, inhabiting her old body properly. It was so good and noble of Gideon – but it truly seemed to be what he liked to do most.

I wanted to talk on and on about the circus, though Mother shook her head and tutted.

'Hush, Hetty. Mother doesn't approve of circuses, you know that. She didn't want us to go when we were little children,' said Gideon.

'But I still went. Jem took me!' I said, making Mother tut more. 'You never got to go that time,

Gid. You must go now!'

Mother mumbled something.

'Not if Mother doesn't want us to,' said Gideon.

I stared at him. 'Are you mad?' I mouthed, over Mother's head. 'She can hardly stop us now!'

'I don't want to upset her,' he said.

I felt like shaking him. 'Then you'll miss out on all the excitement,' I said.

'I think I've had enough excitement in my life, thank you!'

Gideon wouldn't speak any more that day. He just sat holding Mother's hands, gazing into the middle distance.

I could not fathom my brother. He seemed so strange now that I sometimes wondered if his accident had interfered with his intellect. But then he had always been an odd little boy, given to strange fears and fancies, retreating into silence whenever he was shocked.

It made me sad to see such a tall young man sitting holding onto Mother like a toddling child. All those grim lonely years in the hospital had stunted him. I remembered his one shining moment playing the Angel Gabriel in the tableau one Christmas. He'd looked so glorious, gracefully stretching out his arms and legs, as if his paper wings could truly fly.

Poor Gideon might now be a willing prisoner in

the tiny cottage – but I wasn't. I prepared our supper stew, tossing in carrots and onions willy-nilly, and paced about the cottage in a fever of impatience. When I heard Jem's footsteps, I flew to meet him, running so fast my sixpence bounced on its chain and hit my teeth. I spat it out, laughing.

'Oh, Jem, Jem, wait till you hear!' I said.

'Wait till *you* hear, Hetty,' said Jem, seizing me and swinging me round and round the way he used to when I was little. 'Farmer Woodrow came and worked with me today, watching me with the horses. He's making me chief farm hand in Father's place!'

'Oh, that's lovely for you, Jem, and much deserved – but *listen*—'

'Don't you see what that means, Hetty? My wages go up by five shillings a week! We'll have so much more money to spare – isn't that marvellous?'

I knew how worried Jem had been about money, with three dependents to support now, though I had done my best to earn my keep with my sewing.

'It *is* marvellous, Jem! I shall buy a side of beef every Sunday now and cook you a meal fit for a king,' I said.

'That would be good for just *one* Sunday, Hetty, but I'm going to want to save a lot more too – for the future.' Jem set me down on my feet. 'Our future,' he whispered.

The room stayed spinning round and round, even though I was standing still.

'Now, Hetty, what's *your* great news?' Jem asked, steadying me.

'The circus has come!' I said.

'Oh yes, I thought it was due. It always comes in the spring,' he said casually, as if he were talking about May blossom. 'Remember when I took you to the circus when you were little?' He laughed. 'We sneaked in under the tent flap. It's a wonder we didn't get whacked for it. You loved that circus, Hetty.'

'I remember,' I said.

'There was one lady who had a whole troupe of horses—'

'Madame Adeline.'

'What? Yes, I think that *was* her name. Fancy you remembering after all this time! And she gave you a ride around the ring on one of her horses. You were only tiny and I was terrified you'd take a tumble, but you rode that horse like a little star.'

'That was what she called me. She said I was her Little Star,' I said. 'Because you'd stuck a ginger-bread star on my forehead.'

'Did I? Well, anyway, I was that proud of you, Hetty. I'll take you back to the circus tomorrow night if you like, but I think you'll be too big for circus tricks now,' Jem said, still laughing, ruffling my hair.

I dodged away from him. 'Tomorrow? I must go tonight!' I said.

'Tonight?' he said. 'Don't be silly, Hetty.'

'I'm *not* being silly. I *have* to go,' I said wildly.

'There won't be a show tonight. They'll still be setting up, putting up the big tent and exercising the animals after the journey. There's never a show the first night they get here. I'll take you tomorrow, Hetty, I promise.'

I knew Jem was talking sense. He was being kind, as always. Why did I find it so irritating?

'I'm going tonight. I'm going right now,' I said, pulling my shawl around my shoulders.

'What? *Now?*'

'Yes! Why do you have to keep repeating everything I say?' I said.

'But you haven't even had your supper yet.'

'I don't want my supper. I want to go to the circus.'

'Then wait. Wait for me, Hetty,' Jem said as I made for the door. 'I'll come with you.'

'No. You eat *your* supper. I want to go on my own,' I said, and I ran off as fast as I could.

I felt very bad, knowing I was treating Jem appallingly, especially when he was so excited and wanted to celebrate his promotion – but I simply couldn't help it. I couldn't wait any longer. I *had* to go to the circus.

18

Jem was right. There was no show tonight. Men were still circling the bright canvas of the tent, hauling on ropes to raise it up, cursing and shouting to each other. Great Elijah trumpeted in frustration, tethered to a big oak at the edge of the field. The horses were being led round and round, the glossy black one too, but I could see no sign of Madame Adeline. Lions roared, bears growled from their cages and sea lions splashed in a pool of water. It sounded like a strange jungle, yet the scene seemed cosily domestic as folk sat on their wagon steps and cooked their suppers over small fires.

I stood in the shadows, scared they would see me and send me away. I was suddenly conscious of soft snuffles coming from the nearest wagon – from *under* it, I realized. They were very slight sounds but I knew instantly what they were. You can't spend nine years at a foundling hospital without instantly recognizing the sound of a small child crying.

I bent down and peeped under the wagon. I saw a little girl lying there, sobbing into her hands, stifling the noise as best she could. Her hair was dishevelled and she wore a tattered petticoat with a grubby grey shawl draped round her thin shoulders – but I still recognized the little fairy acrobat.

I knelt right down to see her properly. She gasped when she saw me looming there, and tried to cover her head.

'It's all right. I'm not going to hurt you,' I whispered.

She looked up, trying to peer past me.

'And I won't let anyone else hurt you either,' I said. 'See my red hair? I am so fierce that everyone is scared of me. Even the biggest, ugliest ogre quakes when he sees me coming. Evil giants tremble and whimper at my approach.'

She made a little noise that could have been a chuckle.

'But I never ever hurt little fairy girls,' I said. 'And *you're* a little fairy, aren't you?'

'Please, miss, I'm the Acrobatic Child Wonder,' she said dolefully, scrubbing at her eyes. Her nose needed attention too.

'Here, I have a handkerchief,' I said, thrusting it under the wagon.

She stared at it, obviously not used to the concept. 'There's a picture and letters!' she said, touching the embroidery.

'They're flowers – and the letters are an S and a B, the initials of my name, Sapphire Battersea. Although no one calls me that now. All the folk here call me Hetty. What do they call you? Acrobatic Child Wonder is a bit of a mouthful!'

'They call me Diamond, but I *used* to be Ellen-Jane,' she said, still sniffing.

'Oh, Diamond is a most beautiful name,' I said. 'Do wipe your nose on the handkerchief!'

'It's too pretty. I don't want to smear the picture,' said Diamond, and she pulled up her petticoat and used the ragged hem instead. She handed the handkerchief back to me reluctantly.

'You can keep it if you like it so much,' I said.

'Really? For my very own?' said Diamond, and she quickly stuffed it down her bodice in case I changed my mind.

'Won't you roll out so we can have a proper conversation?' I said. 'It's not very comfortable kneeling down like this.'

'I'm scared to come out, because Mister will get me,' she said.

'Mister?'

'He's my master and I hate him because he beats me,' said Diamond, starting to sob again.

'I'm sure he's not allowed to beat you! You're too little!' I said indignantly.

'He *is* allowed, because I am stupid and can't learn,' she sobbed.

'Is he your *teacher*?'

'I think so. He teaches me how to tumble and do tricks, but it hurts and I'm afraid and I won't, so he beats me.'

'Can you tell your father?'

'No, miss – he sold me to Mister, and now Mister can do what he wants.'

'Isn't there anyone kind who will look after you?' I asked, reaching further so I could pat her little shaking shoulders.

'Madame Addie is kind,' said Diamond. 'She sits me on her lap and rubs my sore arms and legs and gives me cake.'

'Oh, Madame Adeline! Yes, I am sure she is very kind. I have come looking for her. Will you show me her wagon, Diamond?'

'I will take you, but don't let Mister get me!' she said.

'I will look after you,' I said, though this Mister sounded terrifying.

Diamond wriggled out from under the wagon, giving her face another wipe with her petticoats. She patted the slight bulge in her bodice where she was hiding the handkerchief. 'Can I really keep it for my very own?' she asked.

'Of course you can,' I said, taking her hand.

She led me along the back of the wagons, cautiously peeping through the gap at the end of each van. She didn't need to tell me when we were passing Mister's wagon. She clung tighter, her whole body shaking. I peered through the gap too. I was expecting a great cruel monster of a man with a whip in his hand, but saw instead a small skinny creature in combinations and baggy trousers sipping tea before his fire. He wore an odd little bowler hat on the back of his head. It looked as if it was glued to his sparse hair.

'Is that *him*?' I whispered.

Diamond nodded, shuddering.

'Is he one of the clowns?' I asked, noticing traces of bright red on the tip of his nose.

'Yes, he is Mister Beppo,' Diamond whispered. 'He manages the act, with his three sons.'

'The silver boys?'

'He was a silver boy once, but he fell and hurt his back so he has to be Beppo instead,' said Diamond.

'Does he beat his boys too?' I asked.

'Sometimes, especially the youngest. The others are big and strong now, much bigger than him – but they're scared of him too,' she replied.

'Well, don't you worry. I'm looking after you now, Diamond,' I said.

'I know, though I am still a little bit worried,' she said.

'We'll creep away then. We'll find Madame Adeline.'

Her wagon was right at the end, painted green, with green velvet curtains at the little window. It was my turn to tremble now.

'This one's hers, Madame Addie's,' said Diamond.

'I know,' I said, remembering how I'd sought it out five years ago, when I'd run away from the hospital.

We sidled round the side of the wagon – and there was Madame Adeline herself sitting on the steps before her fire. I'd braced myself, knowing she was quite an elderly lady without her red wig and make-up, but she looked wonderful, her red hair still in place, her make-up giving her cheeks a pink glow. She was wearing a silky dark green tea gown and a royal blue woollen shawl, and wore two feathers, a green and a blue, in a sparkly clasp on her head. They gave her a regal air, as if she were a queen with an exotic crown. We stood timidly at the foot of her steps, peering up at her.

'Hello,' she said, gazing at us with interest. 'Oh dear, Diamond, I think you've been crying again. Come here, darling.' She held out her arms and Diamond rushed to her, hiding her face in the green tea gown. 'I think I know you too, my dear,' Madame Adeline said softly, looking at me.

'I'm not sure you really *do* know me, Madame Adeline – though *I* certainly know *you*,' I said fervently. 'We met five years ago – and five years before that too.'

'My goodness, I'm right. It's Little Star,' said Madame Adeline, smiling at me.

I burst into tears.

'Whatever's the matter?' she said, reaching out so that I was tucked within her embrace too, along with Diamond.

'Nothing's the matter. It's just so wonderful that you remember me!' I sobbed.

'Of course I remember you. I was very worried about you when we last met – on the Heath, wasn't it? You were a naughty girl and ran away.'

'Only because you were going to take me back to the hospital.'

'But you *did* go back, I checked,' said Madame Adeline. 'I felt so bad. I wished I'd weakened and let you stay with me. I *wanted* you to stay for my sake, though the circus is a harsh home for children. Look at this poor little soul.' She stroked Diamond's hair out of her eyes.

'She says that clown, Beppo, *beats* her,' I said.

'Yes, he does,' said Madame Adeline sadly. 'He is a warped little man who thinks the only way to teach is through fear. It was the way he learned. It's the only way he knows. But I try hard to look after little Diamond, don't I, darling?'

'Yes,' said Diamond, climbing properly onto Madame Adeline's lap and twining her skinny little arms round her neck.

'I can't always protect her. Beppo is cruellest when we're rehearsing and I have to take Midnight through his paces then.'

'Midnight! That's your new black horse!' I said eagerly. 'He's beautiful.'

'Isn't he! He's given me a whole new lease of life. I thought I was finished when Firelight and Sugar grew too old for the ring, but then I saw this young colt at a gypsy fair. He was supposed to be too wild to ride, but I tamed him – with kindness.' She kissed Diamond's hair. 'Beppo should train you with mint balls and apples, they work wonders.' Madame Adeline looked at me. 'Someone's been training you too, Little Star. You look such a pale, peaky girl. Look at those sharp cheekbones and dark circles under your eyes. Who's been working you so hard?'

'I'm *not* worked hard. I'm back here in the village, and I'm very much loved and cared for, but somehow I'm still not happy.'

'What would make you happy, dear?' said Madame Adeline.

'I – I don't know,' I said.

She held me close. 'Did you ever find your real mother?' she asked softly.

'I did! Oh, dear lovely Mama! She was there at the hospital all the time, working as a kitchen maid to be near me. But then last summer she was very ill and . . . and I lost her.' I felt my eyes welling with tears again.

'I'm so sorry. Oh dear. Now I will weep too.'

'Is your mother dead too, Hetty?' said Diamond. 'Mine went to live with the angels.'

'My mama lives there too. I'm sure she has wonderful white feathery wings and a dress as blue as the sky. Maybe they fly from cloud to cloud together. But my mama flies down to see me every now and then. She creeps inside my heart and speaks to me. She is a great comfort. Perhaps your mama will do the same.'

I hoped Diamond's mother had been a kindly

soul. Her father certainly sounded a callous villain, selling his own daughter to that cruel little clown.

'Now, my girls, I'm going to have a cup of tea. Would you like one too?' said Madame Adeline.

'And cake?' said Diamond hopefully.

'I expect we can find a cake if we search hard,' said Madame Adeline, laughing.

'Can Hetty have some cake too?' Diamond asked.

'Of course she can. Let us go and look for it.'

Madame Adeline went up the steps and opened the green door painted with silver stars. We followed. I held my breath. There was the green velvet chair with the lace antimacassar and the little table with the fringed chenille cloth; there was the cabinet of dainty china shepherdesses, each with her own little white sheep; there was the bed with the patchwork quilt let down like a shelf from the wagon wall. It was all quite perfect, exactly as I remembered.

Madame Adeline set her silver kettle on top of the spirit stove and fetched three willow-pattern cups and saucers. 'Now, where can that cake be?' she said. She looked under the table. 'No cake here!'

Diamond gave a timid chuckle.

Madame Adeline looked in her armchair. 'No cake here!'

Diamond laughed properly.

Madame Adeline went over to her bed. 'Perhaps it's curled up and gone to sleep?' she said, searching under the sheets.

Diamond laughed so much she had to sit down on the rug.

'Where do you think that naughty cake is hiding?' said Madame Adeline.

'In the tin, in the *tin*!' Diamond shouted, pointing to the big Queen Victoria cake tin on the shelf.

'Ah!' said Madame Adeline, lifting down the cake tin, prising off the lid and peering inside. 'Yes, Diamond, you are absolutely right, you clever girl.'

I was all agog too. When I saw the pink and yellow chequered cake with the thick marzipan, I cried out, 'That's the *same* cake! The very same kind of cake you gave me five years ago. Oh, I love that cake.'

Madame Adeline made the tea and we sat down together. She sat in the chair, I took the little velvet stool, and Diamond sat cross-legged on the rug. We sipped our tea and ate the soft moist cake. Diamond peeled the marzipan off hers, wrapped it round her finger, and then licked and nibbled as if it were a hokey-pokey ice cream. Madame

Adeline shook her head and raised her eyebrows, but didn't scold her.

We were like a cosy little family, the three of us. I felt as if I were in a wonderful dream – but then I heard men shouting outside, and dogs barking.

'That's Mister!' said Diamond, sticking the rest of the marzipan in her mouth quickly.

'It's not just Beppo. It sounds like there's a stranger in the camp,' said Madame Adeline.

Then I heard someone calling my name.

'Hetty? Hetty, are you there?'

'Oh my Lord, it's Jem. He must have followed me,' I said, sighing. I opened the door and went down the steps.

There was Jem in the midst of a group of angry circus hands. They had tried to seize him but he shook them off furiously, prepared to fight. 'Where have you hidden my Hetty?' he said, his fists clenched.

'They haven't hidden me, Jem! I'm here! I'm perfectly fine!' I said, running down the steps.

They started shouting at *me* now, but Madame Adeline put her arm round my shoulders.

'Hey, hey, lay off, boys! This girl is an old friend. She's here as my guest, to take tea with me,' she announced imperiously. She nodded at Jem. 'And you, sir, are very welcome too.'

Jem looked astonished, his mouth agape. The men still muttered amongst themselves, but let him go free. They went about their business, even Beppo. I heard Diamond let out a little sigh of relief from the depths of Madame Adeline's wagon.

'Well, Hetty, are you going to introduce us?' said Madame Adeline.

'Madame Adeline, this is my foster brother Jem,' I said.

She held out her hand in a refined gesture. I think Jem was meant to kiss her fingers but he shook her hand heartily instead.

'Pleased to meet you, ma'am,' he said. 'And thank you for your kind offer of tea, but I've my supper at home. I'd better be getting back – and so had you, Hetty.' He took hold of my arm in a proprietorial fashion.

I wriggled free. 'I want to stay here with Madame Adeline,' I said.

But she smiled at me sweetly and shook her head. 'Perhaps you had better run along with your brother just now, Little Star. But will you come and see the show tomorrow?'

'I would not miss it for the world,' I said, giving her pink cheek a shy kiss. 'Goodbye. And goodbye, Diamond! I shall look out for you in the ring tomorrow and give you a big cheer.'

I let Jem propel me away from the semicircle of wagons and the big top.

'There, Hetty, I *told* you there wouldn't be a show tonight,' he said. 'And how did you make friends with that painted woman?'

'Don't talk about her in that way!' I said. 'What are you *doing*, rushing after me and telling me what to do?'

'I was concerned about you, Hetty. Those circus folk are like gypsies, not to be trusted,' said Jem. 'The men are all very rough, and the women scarcely decent.'

'You don't know anything about them! Madame Adeline is my dear friend, and a highly respectable lady. She came to my rescue long ago, when I ran away from the hospital. It's wonderful to see her again! I was having such a lovely time. Why did you have to come interfering and spoil everything?' I hissed.

'I have to look out for you, Hetty. You're so head-strong. You think you know it all but you're still a child. You don't know the ways of the world,' said Jem.

'I've got far more experience of the world than you have, Jem Cotton. You've simply stayed in the same village all your life long. You're just a country boy,' I shouted, marching off across the meadow.

'Yes, I am – and proud of it too,' said Jem. He

took hold of me by the elbow. 'Hetty, why are we quarrelling? I just want to look after you.' He looked so stricken that I felt very guilty.

'I know. You're so kind to me, Jem. But I don't *need* you to look after me all the time, can't you see that?'

'I love you, Hetty, so I want to look after you,' he said. He put his arm round my shoulder and pulled me close.

I knew how much it would hurt him if I pulled away again, so I let us walk all the way back home entwined like sweethearts. It was very uncomfortable, because he was so tall and had such long legs, so his gait was very different to mine.

Gideon had served Mother her supper. Mine was still in the pot, but I didn't want to eat rabbit stew tonight. I wanted to keep the sweet taste of Madame Adeline's cake in my mouth, so I went to bed hungry.

I scarcely slept – and when I did I dreamed I was in that circus procession, dancing along with little Diamond, while Madame Adeline pranced before us on Midnight.

I got up very early the next morning to make Jem a proper breakfast – I was still feeling guilty. He thanked me very earnestly and ate with great relish, as if his simple egg and bacon were a true feast.

'I'll take you to see the circus tonight, Hetty,' he said, patting my hand.

I couldn't wait for the evening. I did my chores. I worked with extreme thoroughness, sweeping and scrubbing every inch of the cottage, and pounding the sheets in the tub until they flapped white as clouds on the washing line.

I was extra patient with Mother and Gideon. I made them a set of cards, drawing a simple figure on each – a cat, a rabbit, a broom, a bed, a whole set of everyday objects. Then I got Gideon to hold them up for Mother and encourage her to try to say the appropriate word. It was a game they both enjoyed. Mother especially liked the cat card and amused Gideon greatly by stroking the little creature with one shaking finger.

This gave me an idea. The Maples' tabby cat had recently had four kittens. I went and begged one off Mrs Maple and brought it home as a surprise. The kitten was a cute little creature, very perky and self-assured. She scampered all over the cottage, sniffing here and there, investigating corners delicately with her front paw. She ran right up Gideon's long length and crouched on his shoulder, not at all perplexed by his patch and scars. When she felt tired, she scrabbled up Mother's skirts and settled down cosily on her lap.

'Kitty,' Mother murmured. 'Kitty, Kitty, Kitty,' until she fell asleep too.

Gideon seemed content just to sit beside her, but I lent him my precious copy of *David Copperfield*.

'It's a wonderful story, Gideon. I know you'll enjoy it,' I said, giving him a hug.

'Won't you read it to me, Hetty?' he said.

'You can see perfectly well with your one eye. It will be good practice for you,' I said gently. 'I can't read to you just now, Gid. I have to go out.'

Gideon stared at me with that one good eye. 'You're going to the circus, aren't you?' he said quietly. 'I thought Jem was taking you tonight?'

'He is. But I want to go to this afternoon's performance too. Do you mind? I could see if Molly could sit with Mother if you wanted to come too,' I said, a little reluctantly.

'No, no, you go,' said Gideon, opening up my book. 'I shall read.'

I checked the stew, bubbling on the stove, and then ran. The circus was putting on a special early show at four o'clock and so the fields were seething with children scurrying along from school. I saw Janet hurrying with them, a child hanging from either hand, her long plait flying. I could have sat with her, but I wanted to hug this experience all to myself.

I sat right at the back, my heart thumping hard, as if I were about to perform myself. The small band struck up, playing a jaunty tune. Then there was a roll of drums and in strutted Mr Tanglefield himself, circus owner, ringmaster and elephant trainer.

'Ladies and gentlemen, welcome to Tanglefield's Travelling Circus,' he said, and then he made a series of announcements, but it was very hard to make out what he was saying. He had a thin reedy voice, and although he spoke through a loudhailer it seemed to distort it further. The children were too restless to listen properly. They just wanted the show to get started.

They laughed when Chino the Clown and his sidekick, sinister Mister Beppo, came capering into the ring in their outsize trousers and flipper shoes. They fooled around with Mr Tanglefield, creeping up on him and pulling his coat tails. He kept threatening them, to no avail, until he went stomping off and brought back Elijah the elephant.

The children screamed and shouted at the great creature as he plodded his way through the same old tricks. I wondered if Elijah ever felt restless too, and wanted to jerk his chain from Mr Tanglefield's fist, throw up his great head and charge out of the ring. I hated to see him made such a clown, laboriously balancing on different tubs, waving one leg in the air to the beat of the orchestra. If *I* had charge of Elijah I'd adorn his back in fine silks and brocade and paint his face and treat him royally, with respect.

Mr Tanglefield led him out of the ring at last and then hastened back to announce Flora the tightrope walker. She was so plump now that every seam in her costume was at bursting point. As she advanced along the tightrope with her balancing pole in her little pink hands, every child in the audience breathed hard, hoping that her bodice might pop right open before their eyes.

I grew tired of poor Flora as she trekked backwards and forwards – but I clapped hard when Mr Tanglefield announced in his tired tones that the Silver Tumblers were next.

In came the three boys in their sparkly silver suits, two young men with broad shoulders and muscled legs, one still a slender stripling, and there, skipping in their wake, was little Diamond in her fairy frock. She twirled about the boys as they somersaulted and stood on each other's shoulders. Then she climbed right up them like a little spangled monkey and stood high in the air, arms outstretched, a smile on her face, as the audience applauded. I marvelled, but I could hardly bear to watch her. One little slip and she'd smash to the ground and break her neck.

She climbed down again with seeming confidence, and ran about the ring turning cartwheels, her lips still stretched wide in a smile – but I saw her eyes keep swivelling to the corner where Beppo was hunched, watching her like a hawk. I cheered her very loudly indeed, encouraging everyone around me to clap and call out too.

The lions were next, leaping out of their cage and jumping through golden hoops. I wished they'd leap a little further and mistake Beppo for a side of prime beef.

Mr Tanglefield's voice grew shrill as he shouted the name of each act through his loudhailer. I grew impatient as I watched them. I saw a man throw daggers at his wife and then eat fire, I saw sea lions bark in unison and wave their flippers and play trumpets, I saw a new and fabulous monkey act where the little creatures tumbled about playing a bizarre game of happy families. I especially loved seeing a baby monkey dressed like a tiny Diamond in a fairy frock, but I even tired of these endearing little furry people. I was waiting for one act only.

At long last Mr Tanglefield mumbled Madame Adeline's name, and in she came on Midnight, looking glorious in her pink spangles.

She stood upon Midnight's glossy back, pointing her toes, one elegant arm in the air. She galloped bareback to wild music and then slowed down almost to a halt while Midnight did a complicated little dance, picking up his hooves and sashaying daintily to the left and right.

Madame Adeline asked if there were any children celebrating their birthdays in the audience. Young Phil went dashing into the ring, bursting with pride. Madame Adeline produced a birthday cake and a handful of candles. She looked at Midnight and asked him to guess Phil's age. Midnight tapped one-two-three-four-five times with his hoof, while Phil jumped up and down and clapped. Madame Adeline stuck five candles in his cake and lit them. She told Phil to take a deep breath and then try to blow them all out in one go, but as he was puckering his lips Midnight got there first and blew out mightily through his nostrils, extinguishing every candle.

Then Madame Adeline gave Phil a ride on Midnight's back while everyone cheered. I remembered riding with her when I was Phil's age. Oh, how I wanted to join in now and ride with her again, but I knew I would look a fool if I ran forward with all the little children.

I so admired Madame Adeline. She was no longer youthful so she couldn't perform particularly athletic or daring tricks. She didn't have a troupe of six fine rosin-backed horses any more, just the one.

She had overcome all these disadvantages and refined and renewed her act to make it work just as well.

I cheered her until my throat hurt, and clapped and clapped at the grand finale, when all the acts paraded round the circus ring. I'd have liked to stay and congratulate Madame Adeline and Diamond, but I knew I had better go home.

I ran all the way, but Jem was home before me even so, and already washed and brushed, wearing his red waistcoat.

'You're home early, Jem,' I said, stirring the stew and warming the plates.

'I slipped away specially, to take you to the circus,' he said. 'But you've already seen it for yourself, haven't you, Hetty?'

There was no point trying to deny it. 'Yes, I have, and it was *wonderful*. Oh, wait till you see it, Jem! Madame Adeline is still by far the best act, but this little girl Diamond is very sweet and entertaining, though I wish she wasn't part of that tumbling act. Gideon, are you *sure* you don't want to see the circus. I know you'd absolutely love it.'

'No, Hetty, you know it would upset Mother. She's never approved of circuses,' said Gideon, irritatingly pious.

'Well, *I* approve one hundred per cent!' I said.

'Come, Jem, let's eat quickly and then go and get a good seat.'

'You want to go *again*? You've only just this minute seen the show!' he said.

'I want to go again and again and *again*,' I said. I tugged on his arm. 'I especially want to go with *you*, Jem.' I was just saying it to make him feel good, but his whole face lit up with happiness.

I wished he didn't care about me so much. I was just making it worse for him, living under his roof. He'd never stop languishing after me if I was always there. If I disappeared, I was sure he'd soon get over me and realize that one sweet Janet was worth ten tempestuous Hettys.

We went to the circus together, sitting right at the front this time. Jem bought me gingerbread and stuck the gold paper star on my forehead again, as if I were five years old. I smiled back, but when the lights were down and Mr Tanglefield came strutting into the ring to announce the forthcoming attractions in his reedy tones, I quickly unpicked the star and folded it up in my hand.

I found myself feverishly irritated by Jem's reactions all through the show. He laughed uproariously at Chino and Beppo, especially when they clowned with great Elijah. Everyone else laughed too. I didn't mind that they were laughing at a sad old man, an evil little bully and a huge dignified animal, but I wanted my Jem to have finer feelings.

'Don't you find them funny, Hetty?' he said.

I nodded and tried to laugh to please him.

'You *are* enjoying yourself, aren't you?' Jem asked, not quite fooled.

'Yes, yes, but Jem, wait till you see the Silver Tumblers with little Diamond. And of course Madame Adeline is the true star,' I said.

'Of course,' said Jem.

But somehow he wasn't enthusiastic *enough*. Diamond was a little hesitant this time, and very nearly slipped when she stood up precariously on the biggest boy's shoulders. She was still so young and clearly tired out after the first performance. She was wearing pink greasepaint to disguise her pallor, but there were dark circles under her eyes. I wanted to rush into the ring and hug her reassuringly, the poor little mite.

'She looks so sad. I just can't bear it,' I said to Jem.

'She looks happy enough to me,' he said, taken in by Diamond's strained smile. 'You've got such a soft heart, Hetty.'

I waited impatiently for Madame Adeline and felt a tingling all over as she rode into the ring, looking regal and splendid on glossy black

Midnight. 'Isn't she wonderful!' I breathed.

'Well, she's certainly a game old girl,' said Jem.

I think he was trying to be nice, but I was so offended I withdrew my hand and hunched away from him in the seat, horrified that he could talk about dear Madame Adeline in such disparaging tones.

When she finished her act, I stood and clapped and cheered. Madame Adeline saw me and swept me a deep curtsy.

'There, Hetty, she's curtsying to you,' said Jem. 'Fancy, you knowing all these circus folk. I don't think you should come over here again though, especially by yourself. Some of those men are really rough.'

'They were rough with you, Jem, not with me,' I said. 'Of course I am coming here again! I have to see Madame Adeline. She is my dear friend.'

'Oh, you and your dear friends!' said Jem.

'What do you mean by *that*?' I said.

'Nothing! Calm down, Hetty! What's the matter with you? You're so touchy tonight. I can't seem to say anything right,' said Jem. 'Now listen to me. I don't want you running back here to the circus, not by yourself. It's not the place for a young girl like you. I don't want you mixing with all sorts.'

'All sorts?' I said.

Jem sighed. 'I know you've taken a shine to this

madame and I'm sure she's very nice in her own way, but she's hardly a lady, is she?'

'I'm sure it's not gentlemanly to make that point,' I said sharply, making him blush. 'You're utterly mistaken anyway. Madame Adeline is very refined and kindly and has the most perfect manners.'

'I dare say, but she parades about in a short skirt up to here. It's not decent to dress like that in front of folk,' said Jem.

I wondered what he would have said if he'd seen me dressed as Emerald the Amazing Pocket-Sized Mermaid, and felt myself blushing too.

'There! You know I'm right,' said Jem triumphantly.

'I know you're wrong, wrong, wrong,' I said. 'And I shall do as I please.'

'Oh, Hetty, I know why you got paddled so often as a child,' said Jem. 'Why must you be so wilful? I don't understand you at all.'

I suddenly stopped feeling angry and felt desperately sad. Jem really didn't understand me any more. When I was little he'd been my big, all-powerful brother and I ran around worshipping him. I might still be very small in stature, but I felt I had grown up in so many ways.

Jem was a fine strong man now, but his mind was essentially the same. He was like one of his own plough horses – dear and steady and faithful and very hard-working, content to trudge up and down the same fields year after year, shying if anything strange stepped into their path.

'Oh, Jem, don't let's quarrel,' I said, taking his hand.

He kissed my fingers joyfully. 'I don't *want* to quarrel, dear Hetty,' he said.

I think he felt I was capitulating – but I was even more determined to visit the circus at every opportunity.

19

I went back the very next day. I did not wait for the afternoon performance. I went straight after lunch, when I'd settled Mother for her nap. Gideon was out in the garden, on his knees, weeding. He had taken it over now that Mother could not tend it and had proved to have green fingers. He had planted out rows of vegetables as well as flowers, and we now had new raspberry and loganberry canes and a strawberry patch.

I tapped him affectionately on the top of his faded straw hat as I passed.

'Where are you going, Hetty?' he asked.

'Where do you think?' I sang out, and hurried down the path and out of the gate before he could say any more.

I ran all the way to the circus meadow. I knew they were staying in the village until the end of the week. It said so on all the bills. Yet I couldn't help fearing they had collapsed the big top and stolen away in the night.

It was an immense relief to spot the bright red and yellow tent, see for myself Elijah's great grey head high above the bushes, hear the babble of strange voices, smell the lunchtime frying onions and stewing meat.

I walked quickly across to the wagons, making for Madame Adeline's green van at the end of the semicircle – but this time Beppo caught me.

'Where do you think *you're* going?' he said, speaking softly in a way that sent a shiver down my spine.

He was almost as small as me, a bent little man with crooked teeth, his collarbone sticking right out of his open shirt – yet I could see why Diamond and the silver tumbling boys feared him so much.

I faced him boldly, not wanting him to see I was frightened. 'I am visiting my friend Madame Adeline,' I said. 'May I congratulate you on your performance last night, Mr Beppo. I thought you were very droll indeed.'

He stared at me suspiciously. 'Don't think you can come smarming round me, missy. I'm wise to your tricks.'

'And I'm wise to yours, Mister,' I said. 'Now excuse me. I wish to pay a visit to my friend.'

'She's no business inviting stray girls to come here. This is private, off-limits to all outsiders,' said

Beppo. 'Don't you go poking your nose around where it's not wanted.'

'Oh my, you're not quite as cheery out of the ring as in it,' I said, and I marched past, with my head held high – though my heart was thudding hard in my chest.

'Hetty! Oh, Hetty!' Diamond was lurking behind Madame Adeline's wagon, clutching an old rag doll to her chest. 'Oh, Hetty, I saw you talking to Mister! You really aren't afeared of him!'

'That's right. *He's* the one that's afeared of *me*. I told you. He'll be quaking in his bed tonight, wondering if that red-haired girl will be coming to get him. Most likely he'll wet his sheets in terror,' I said.

Diamond burst out laughing and then smothered her face in her old doll.

'Is that your baby, Diamond?' I asked.

'Yes, she's called Maybelle and I love her very much,' she said.

'She's very beautiful,' I said, pretending to shake Maybelle's limp hand. 'But perhaps she is a little chilly,' I went on, as the doll wore a pair of ragged drawers and nothing else. 'Doesn't she have a pretty dress to keep her warm?'

'She did have a dress once but Mister Marvel took it off me to dress his monkey in,' said Diamond mournfully.

'Well, never you mind. I am very good at stitching tiny dolly dresses. I think Maybelle has a chance of a whole new wardrobe by the end of the week,' I said. 'Now, shall we call on Madame Adeline together?'

I was a little worried that Madame Adeline might sigh at my intrusion, even tell me to run away, but she held out her arms and hugged me close, so that I could smell her beautiful perfume, like roses and honeysuckle.

'Dear Hetty, what a treat!' she said. 'And little Diamond too, plus Maybelle! Come along in, girls, and we'll have a little tea party.'

'I think I had better not have cake,' said Diamond sadly as Madame Adeline fetched down her Queen Victoria tin. 'Mister says I must stay as small as I can – and you can't do back-flips on a full stomach.'

'You're like a little elfin child already, Diamond. A small slice of cake won't make you fat,' I said indignantly. 'And what's a back-flip?'

Diamond took me outside, behind the wagon. '*This* is a back-flip,' she said, suddenly leaping up in the air and flipping over backwards. She did it again and again while I clapped.

'Oh, show *me* how to do it!' I said. No one could see us behind the wagons, so I tucked my dress into my drawers and tried to copy her, but try as I might

I simply tumbled flat on my back. I lay there, laughing. 'Oh dear, I'm hopeless,' I giggled.

'Mister could teach you, but it hurts and hurts. You have to have your bones cricked till they nearly snap in two,' said Diamond. 'Then you get extra bendy like me – watch!' She bent right over backwards and walked across the grass like a little crab.

'You're brilliant, Diamond!' I said.

'Maybelle can do it too,' she said, folding her old doll in half and making her prance along bent over. 'But it doesn't hurt her one bit.'

When we were back in the wagon having tea and cake, I asked Madame Adeline if she thought I could ever learn a few acrobatic skills.

'I rather doubt it now, Hetty,' she said. 'You would need to have practised since you were tiny.'

'Then . . . could I ever be an equestrian like you? I would so love to dance bareback on a fine horse. You don't need to have your bones cricked for that, do you? I think I could well be a natural rider, Madame Adeline. Do you remember you let me ride Pirate in the ring with you when I was five?'

'Well, we'll have to see, my dear. I shall put Midnight through his paces this afternoon. You can have a try then.'

Madame Adeline lent me a pair of her white tights for decency when I tucked my dress up anew. She led Midnight up to me and I stroked his black velvety head and patted his glossy flanks until we seemed to be friends. Then Madame Adeline helped me up onto his back. I wanted to shine so badly. I had ridden bareback with ease before. I had even stood up on Pirate's back while everyone clapped. But now I seemed to have lost all ability. I could not even sit upright. I slumped forward, clutching Midnight's mane, slipping and sliding alarmingly.

'Grip with your knees, Hetty,' said Madame Adeline as she led Midnight along.

I could not grip with any part of my anatomy and tumbled ignominiously onto the sawdust. 'Oh dear, I think I'm going to have a lot of bruises,' I said. I picked myself up, dusted myself down, and tried to remount.

I fell again. And again. And again.

'Oh, darling, I think that's enough for today,' said Madame Adeline. 'I admire your spirit, but you truly will be black and blue.'

'Maybe if I practised hard every single day I would start to get the hang of it. Then maybe one day I would be good enough to be part of your act?' I said breathlessly, examining my knees. 'I'm so sorry, but I've torn a hole in your tights!'

'It doesn't matter, child. They're only my old practice skins.'

'I shall take them home and wash and darn them for you,' I said. 'Wait till you see how neatly I can darn. Madame Adeline, *do* you think my riding will improve, given time?'

'Of course it will improve, Hetty,' she said, but she didn't sound very positive.

'You can be truthful with me,' I said, bracing myself.

'I don't think you are a natural, my dear,' said Madame Adeline. 'Oh goodness, please, don't be so upset!'

I am sure my face had crumpled, for I was trying hard not to burst out crying. 'I *was* good at it when I was small. You called me your Little Star,' I said miserably.

'And you're *still* my Little Star, dear. I'm a very lucky soul to have such a delightful visitor. But I don't see why you're so keen to learn my sad old circus skills.'

'Because I want – oh, I want to be part of the circus,' I said, all in a rush. 'You wouldn't let me stay with you when I was ten, and I can understand that now. I was still a child and had to return to the Foundling Hospital, Lord help me. But I am an adult now – well, very nearly – and can live wherever I wish . . . and dear Madame Adeline, I want to live with you.'

'Oh, Hetty,' she said, embracing me. 'You're such a sweet child, but can't you see, it's still not possible.'

'*Why* isn't it?'

'The circus is no life for a young girl, surely you can see that. Look at poor Diamond.'

'But I am bigger and fiercer than Diamond. If I travel with the circus I can look after her – and Mister Beppo can go hang. I can look after you too, Madame Adeline. I can cook and clean for you and mend your costumes and help tend Midnight. I can make myself extremely useful. I'll try to learn *some* kind of circus skills so that Mr Tanglefield will take me on in an official capacity. I so want to be one of his performing troupe.'

'It's a hard life, Hetty, far harder than you realize – and humiliating too. Most folk look down on us and feel we're not respectable. You could not stand to be gawped at and commented on by ugly louts.'

'Oh yes I could! I know exactly what it feels like – and I know I can cope very well,' I said. 'I have learned a sizeable amount by being Emerald the Amazing Pocket-Sized Mermaid in a seaside carnival show. Oh, could I be a mermaid here? Perhaps I could be part of the sea-lion act?'

Madame Adeline burst out laughing, but I was serious – until she took me to the tank where the sea lions were kept. They were alarming creatures close up, great blubbery beasts with fierce whiskers, swimming in murky grey water that smelled very bad.

Madame Adeline introduced me to Neptune, King of the sea lions. He was rather grey and blubbery himself, with his own full set of whiskers.

'I think little Hetty hankers to be part of your act,' said Madame Adeline.

'Does she now? Well, it's hard work, very hard work, training these beasts. If you don't put them through their paces regular, they forget all their tricks, and there's times they go sulking on you out of sheer cussedness. They don't take to just anyone, you know, even if you feed them right. Here, girlie, this is how you do it to make 'em willing to leap right up.' He reached for a bucket brimming with dead fish, eyes all popping and mouths agape. I swallowed hard, not sure I could ever thrust my hand into that bucket now. I had developed a real phobia of fish since living in Monksby.

Then I gasped as Neptune ran up the steps to the top of the tank, leaned out over the water, opened his mouth wide, and *put the fish between his own lips!*

The sea lions all started barking, swam rapidly towards him and then leaped up with one accord to snatch their supper.

'See! That's the way to do it,' said Neptune, grinning. 'Want to give it a try?'

'No thank you, Mr Neptune. I'm not sure I've got the stomach for it after all,' I said weakly.

I begged Madame Adeline to show me round the animal cages, but the lions all roared at me, their golden eyes narrowing as they contemplated a tempting snack of girl-meat. The bears looked less savage, poor tethered creatures, and for a few moments I saw myself as Goldilocks while my three bears lumbered about me. However, Bruno, their trainer, snarled contemptuously at me, looking as if he'd happily use his cruel whip on me as well as his unfortunate animals.

I was charmed by the monkeys. When I talked to them through the bars of their cage, they stuck their little hands out, trying to take hold of me, and chattered excitedly.

'Oh look, Madame Adeline, the monkeys like me!'

'They're just hoping you're going to feed them, dear,' she said.

'Yes, you can give them a bite to eat if you want,' said Marvel, the monkey man, smiling at me.

'What do they like to eat?' I asked, a little nervously.

'I give them a little handful of fruit and nuts just now. I don't want them too full or they won't perform proper,' said Marvel, chopping oranges and apples into several dishes.

'Oh, monkey food is delicious – and they're so *sweet*,' I said.

Marvel unlocked their cage door. 'In you go, then, missy,' he said, giving me the bowls.

'Careful, Hetty,' said Madame Adeline. She looked at Marvel anxiously. 'They won't bite her, will they?'

'They're not carnivores. They might just give her a little nibble, but she'll come to no harm,' he said.

They swarmed around me eagerly as I crawled into the cage. I hoped they'd sit down neatly in a row and take it in turns to eat, but they scrabbled here and there and fought each other for titbits and mistook me for a tree and climbed all over me. I wasn't sure if I liked all these little paws clinging here and there to me.

I squealed a little when the baby monkey squirmed out of my arms and scrabbled up my body, stepping on my nose, and then squatted right on the top of my head. He seemingly mistook me for a privy while I shrieked my head off!

Madame Adeline was very kind (though she laughed a little) and let me wash my hair in her wagon. She rubbed it dry with a towel and then gently brushed it for a hundred strokes to make it gleam. I lay back against her knees, feeling such a deep sense of peace, wishing I could stay there for ever. The only other person who had ever treated me so tenderly was Mama, and it made me miss her terribly. I cried a little and told Madame Adeline some of the very sad things that happened last summer. She bent forward and put her arms around me and held me close. I knew she could never *replace* Mama – but I also knew she was incredibly dear to me. I had longed to live with her when I was five and when I was ten. I couldn't bear to wait another five years to see her again.

'*Could* I join the circus and live with you, Madame Adeline?' I whispered. 'I know you keep telling me it's a hard life, but I don't mind at all, just so long as I'm with you.'

'You have a proper home now, Hetty, and your brother clearly thinks the world of you,' she said.

'I know, and I love dear Jem – but not in quite the way he wants. I love Mother too, but she's far happier with Gideon. He's clearly her favourite. I'm fond of Gideon too, for all he's so strange, and I'm very attached to my friend Janet, but I don't feel I *belong* with them. My days are so ... restricted. I cook the same meals, wash the same sheets, see the same folk, even talk the very same talk, over and over again. I can't stay because I know I'm starting to make Jem unhappy – and I'm unhappy too.'

'You might be making yourself unhappier still if you run away,' said Madame Adeline.

'But at least I will be experiencing new things,

living an exciting life, going to a new village every week. Oh, Madame Adeline, please don't be so discouraging! Don't you *want* me to join the circus? Please be truthful!'

'Of course I want you to travel with me. I've met thousands of eager girls in my time but you're the only one I've wanted to be with. You seem like a daughter to me already, Hetty. But I want to do what's best for you.'

'Then that's easy!'

'You're not necessarily the best judge of that. Besides, as you rightly perceive, you would have to earn your keep or Tanglefield won't let you stay.'

'I'll find a way! I certainly can't be a monkey trainer – or work with the sea lions. I'm no good at tumbling, and we both agree I'll never make a bareback rider, but there must be *something* I can do. If I find it – and *if* Mr Tanglefield says yes – *may* I live with you in your wagon?'

'These are very big ifs, Hetty, but yes, of course you can live with me. I can't think of anything I'd like better.'

I watched the circus performance that afternoon with beady eyes. I went home and strung the washing line low down between two trees, pulling it taut, and then balanced along it, clutching Mother's old broom handle as a balancing pole. I tried to dance along in my stockinged feet – and fell.

Little Phil was playing nearby with a couple of grubby friends. They all screamed with laughter to see me sprawling. Then Phil infuriated me by jumping up onto the washing line and managing several steady steps before losing his balance. It was hopeless. Even a four-year-old had better circus skills than me.

I'd hurt my ankle again too. If I carried on like this it would soon snap right off.

Jem saw my long face when he came home from work. 'Cheer up, Hetty,' he said.

'I don't *feel* cheerful,' I muttered.

'Look, I tell you what, I'll take you to your precious circus again tonight,' said Jem.

'I thought you disapproved of the circus and all its performers,' I said sulkily.

'I do, but I'd do anything to put a smile back on that little face,' said Jem, cupping my chin and trying to make my lips curve with his other hand.

'Oh stop it!' I protested ungratefully, but I accepted his offer all the same.

Mr Tanglefield stepped into the ring and announced the first act in his shrill tones.

'Who *is* that chap – and what's he saying?' said Jem.

'He's Mr Tanglefield himself, and he's a terrible ringmaster,' I said. Then a thrill went through me. I watched the entire show in a fever of excitement, concentrating so hard I barely answered when Jem spoke to me, though I clapped hard for little Diamond and Madame Adeline.

'There, did you enjoy that?' said Jem as all the performers paraded around the ring.

'Oh, Jem, yes I did!' I said, and I threw my arms around his neck. 'You are a dear kind brother. I'm so sorry I've been so scowly and sharp. I don't deserve your kindness.' The thought of what I was planning to do practically overwhelmed me. 'I am a very bad girl, Jem,' I muttered. 'Please know that I love you dearly and always will.'

'I know that, Hetty, and I love you too,' said Jem. He clasped my hand. I feared he was going to become too affectionate.

'Let's race each other home. I'm sure I could beat you now,' I said.

It was a ridiculous suggestion. Jem's legs were far longer and stronger than mine, and I had a sore ankle too. Jem raced ahead, but then waited for me, and when he saw I was struggling, he picked me up and carried me all the way home piggyback style.

I tried hard to make a fuss of him and show him I was grateful, but it was a huge relief when he started yawning and went to bed. I waited impatiently until I could hear snoring. Mother seemed fast asleep too, so I gathered material and sewing things as quickly as I could and then stole downstairs. It was hard seeing clearly by candle-light, but I was too impatient to wait till morning, and I needed to fashion my outfit in secret.

I spread out my old print frock on the table as a guideline, and then cut out a newspaper pattern, narrow and snug across the shoulders and bust, but sweeping down as far as my knees at the back. It was a strange shape, but it was very clear in my head. Then I spread out my material, the fine red worsted left over from Jem's waistcoat, pinned the pattern into place, and started cutting, opening and shutting my own mouth to the rasp of the scissors.

I was wrapped in an old blanket, sitting cross-legged on the floor, when I heard footsteps on the stairs. My heart started beating fast, but it wasn't Jem's firm tread. It obviously wasn't Mother.

'Gideon?' I whispered up into the darkness.

I could just make him out halfway down the stairs in his nightgown. He wasn't wearing his patch, and when I said his name he gasped and I saw him clutching his face, hiding his wound.

'It's all right, I can't see you properly,' I said, lying a little. I had seen his unmasked face several times already. If truth be told I had once crept into his bedroom at night and hovered over him to take a peek. I had been very shocked at first to see the empty eye socket and purple scars – but after that first look I started to get used to it, and now it didn't seem quite so bad. After all, it was still my dear brother Gideon underneath.

But he went running back to his room, groaning softly, and then returned with the patch in place. He said nothing, just stumbled outside to the privy. I listened, and thought I heard the sounds of vomiting. I had a glass of water from the jug ready for him when he came back.

'Here, Gideon, drink this. Oh dear Lord, is it my cooking? Have I poisoned you?' I asked anxiously.

'No, no,' said Gideon, sipping cautiously. 'I – I had a nightmare about – about the incident. It often happens. And when it is very vivid I wake with my stomach churning and sometimes I am sick.'

'Oh, poor boy,' I said, and I went over and cradled his poor head. 'But it's all over now and you are safe at home with Mother and Jem, and they will look after you – and you indeed will look after them. You've made such a difference to Mother, Gideon. You've given her a life back.'

'I know you're just trying to be kind, Hetty, but thank you,' he said, giving me a quick hug. Then he peered at the garment I was stitching. 'Is that for Jem?' he asked uncertainly.

'No. He has his red waistcoat,' I said.

'Then . . . is it for me? It's very kind of you, but I'm not sure . . . It's such a bright red, isn't it?'

'Yes, but it's not for you, Gideon,' I said quickly.

'Then who *is* it for?' he asked.

I didn't answer. I went on stitching steadily. Gideon came and sat down beside me. He tried to cross his legs too, but they were too long and unwieldy. He drew his knees up under his nightgown instead and clasped his hands around them. It was exactly the way he'd sat at night when he was a little boy. I suddenly felt so fond of him.

'It's not for *you*, is it, Hetty?' he whispered.

'It could be,' I said.

'But it's a man's jacket, isn't it? Though you could wear it with style. Remember when you dressed up as a boy to come and see me in the boys' wing at the hospital? That was an amazing day. The boys talked about you for years!'

'It was such an awful place, that hospital, wasn't it? Why were we all so cowed and frightened?'

'Because we got whipped!'

'Yes, but there weren't enough matrons to whip us *all*. We should have rebelled. We should have pulled their silly caps over their eyes and locked them up in their own punishment attics. Imagine! Then we could have slid down the banisters and danced around the big table and played with all the new babies and eaten all the food in the cupboards,' I said, laughing.

'And then what?' said Gideon.

'And then we could have run out of those big doors and down the long path and right out the gate and been *free*,' I said.

Gideon thought for a few minutes. It was very quiet in the cottage. We could just hear the *pluck-pluck-pluck* of my needle as it darted in and out up my seam, and a soft steady snoring from upstairs – either Jem or Mother.

It seemed very dark and still outside too, everyone in the village asleep in their beds. Then, from far away, I heard the strange strangled sound of an elephant trumpeting.

Gideon heard it too. He crept a little nearer to me. 'You're going to run away with the circus, aren't you, Hetty?' he whispered, right in my ear.

I was startled. I was used to thinking Gideon was as simple as a child. No one else seemed to suspect my plans, not even Jem.

'I – I don't know,' I said. 'They might not take me anyway. But if I do go, I promise I'll come back to visit. You'll be fine, Gideon.'

'I know I will,' he said. 'But it will break Jem's heart.'

'No, no, it won't. Jem will miss me a little, of course, but then he will realize that Janet is his true love. She loves him dearly, Gid, I know it,' I said.

'But he doesn't love her, Hetty. He loves you,' said Gideon relentlessly.

'Oh don't! You'll make me feel so bad I won't be able to go,' I said.

'You'll go whatever anyone says,' said Gideon. 'You won't be able to help it.'

'Gideon, don't tell Jem. Not yet.'

'Don't worry, I never tell,' he said. Then he leaned closer and kissed my forehead. I was astonished, because Gideon and I never touched. 'I shall miss you, Hetty,' he whispered, and then he went back to bed.

Now that Gideon knew, I could sew during the daytime in front of him – and in front of Mother too. She could say a little now, but not enough to question me. She seemed to have lost all her old assertiveness. She sat in her adapted chair placidly watching me sew. I stitched on, picturing each circus act in my mind, thinking how I would describe each one. I was in such a fever of excitement my hands shook, and it was difficult to stitch neatly.

I finished an hour or so before the afternoon show began. I washed my face and hands, unpinned my hair and brushed it out until it shone, then put on Madame Adeline's mended white tights beneath my dress. I folded up the new red garment and took Jem's funeral stovepipe hat from the peg in his room. Then I marched out of the cottage towards the circus meadow.

Diamond was in her fairy outfit, practising her tumbles in the grass, with Maybelle propped against a tree, watching.

'Hey, Hetty, did you see me do three back-flips in a row?' she called.

'Yes, bravo!' I said, clapping her.

'Have you come to play with me?'

'I would *love* to play with you, Diamond, but I'm afraid I have other business just right now,' I said, striding onwards.

'Are you going calling on Madame Adeline? I shall come too!' said Diamond.

'I'm not intending to visit Madame Adeline either, not just now. I am here to see Mr Tanglefield,' I said.

'Oh!' said Diamond, looking shocked. 'Did he send for you, Hetty? He is very stern! If Mister is very cross with me he threatens to send me to Mr Tanglefield for a good whipping.'

That halted me in my tracks. 'Does he really *whip* you, Diamond?' I asked.

'No, but I'm always afeared he might,' she said. 'He has a very *big* whip, Hetty, and every time he cracks it in the ring it makes me shiver.'

'Well, I'm not afraid of Mr Tanglefield or his whip,' I lied. 'Please can you point out his wagon, Diamond?'

She pointed to the largest wagon in the semi-circle, the grandly decorated crimson, canary and emerald vehicle.

'Thank you,' I said, striding towards it hastily before I lost my resolve and ran for it.

'I don't think you had better disturb him right this minute. He'll be getting ready for the show,' Diamond wailed.

'I can't wait,' I said, and I hurried towards the wagon.

'Hey, girl, what are you doing here? Get out!' called a circus hand, running towards me.

'I have business with Mr Tanglefield,' I said fiercely. 'I'll thank you to let me pass. I need to keep my appointment with him.'

I ran up the steps before he could stop me and tapped smartly on the door. Someone grunted in a surly manner from within the wagon, telling me to go away.

'I need to speak with you, Mr Tanglefield. It is extremely urgent,' I said.

Mr Tanglefield opened his door. He was in his shirt and breeches, his braces looping about his hips. I had caught him in the act of putting shoe blacking on his hair and moustache, so he had an oddly chequered appearance, half grey, half shiny black.

'What the hell do you want?' he said, glaring at me. He had his riding whip in one hand, which seemed very ominous. I still wanted to run but I forced myself to stand my ground, my head held high. I made myself smile.

'Good afternoon, Mr Tanglefield. Might I have a few private words with you? I feel it will be greatly to your benefit,' I said.

20

Mr Tanglefield stared at me as if I were talking a foreign language. He took a small step backwards. I accepted this as an invitation and darted into his wagon.

Mr Tanglefield's wagon was twice the size of Madame Adeline's, but it seemed more cramped inside. He had any number of chairs and sofas and tables and desks, all strewn with handbills and receipts and account books. There were unwashed cups and glasses on every surface, and ashtrays brimming with cigar ash and stubs. The smell of smoke was thick and stale, and his paintwork had acquired a dingy brown-yellow sheen.

It was an effort not to start scurrying round like a housemaid putting the wagon to rights. I looked around for an empty chair, and eventually stayed standing, clutching my new garment and borrowed hat.

'Well?' said Mr Tanglefield.

'Please, sir, I'd like to join your circus,' I said, deciding to come straight out with it.

He stared at me and then laughed. It was not a merry sound. 'Get out. You're wasting my time,' he said. 'You're a country girl. You have to be brought up in the circus to be truly skilled.'

'Oh, I totally agree, sir. I cannot tumble or walk the tightrope or ride bareback and I don't have a knack with animals. But I have other skills that could be immensely useful to you. I am a professional seamstress, for a start. I can work magic with a few scraps of material. Your star turns are magnificent, sir, but I couldn't help noticing that their costumes are a little shabby. I could sew fine new frocks for the ladies and fashion the prettiest little outfits for your child star Diamond. I would not confine myself to costumes for your human stars. I feel the animals would benefit too.'

'You're going to put jackets and breeches on my lions and bears?' said Mr Tanglefield, going to his mirror and continuing with his blacking.

'Oh, very droll, sir,' I said. 'No, of course not, but I feel the troupe of performing monkeys could indeed sport little costumes. The smallest one already wears a doll's dress in the ring, but it's a little bedraggled. Think how charming it would look in baby clothes, with the rest of the troupe dressed in style, the males in jackets, pinstripe

trousers and miniature bowler hats and the little
furry ladies in long frocks and mantles and dainty
bonnets. They would look adorable. Children would
love them and beg to come back again and again to
see the little monkey people.'

Mr Tanglefield paused in his blacking. He stared
at me in his mirror.

'And then there's Elijah,' I said. 'I'm not sure if
you have any idea how exciting it is for country
children to see such a fabulous beast. I remember
simply encountering Elijah as one of the most
amazing incidents of my childhood – spotting his
great head high above the hedges as he plodded
along to the meadows. But I think you could make
him look even more exotic and extraordinary!'

'Now I know you're mad,' said Mr Tanglefield.
'What kind of apparel do you have in mind for my
elephant? A frock coat, and gaiters on each foot?'

'You're quick with your quips, sir – but I beg you
to take me seriously. It's sad to see Elijah act the
clown in the ring. It takes away his dignity. Why not
be true to his Indian origins? Deck him in jewelled
cloth and paint his great head. Attire your good self
in the robes of an eastern prince, in rich hues of
scarlet and gold and purple. Then when you ride
into the ring, everyone will gasp at the spectacle.'

Mr Tanglefield turned round, taking me
seriously at last. He held out an arm as if imagining

it clothed in scarlet silk. 'You could fashion such a garment?' he said.

'Sir, strange garments are my speciality. I fashioned the costumes for the world-famous Clarendon's Seaside Curiosities. Once you've dressed a female giant and clothed a mermaid, tail and all, you know you can tackle any project.' I paused, then lowered my voice to what I hoped was a beguiling whisper. 'You would cut a fine figure in such a costume, sir – and your hair would be entirely hidden beneath your turban, rendering all cosmetic disguises unnecessary.' I gave a discreet little nod at the shoe blacking.

'But I can hardly stay in eastern costume while I am ringmaster,' said Mr Tanglefield.

'I think it is a little beneath you, sir, to have to act as ringmaster when you own the entire circus *and* the most exotic act. After you have taken Elijah through his paces you should recline elegantly on a little gold throne in front of the band, presiding over the circus. When every turn comes tumbling into the ring, they should bow to you first before commencing their act. It would give you such regal authority, don't you think?'

I swept him a low bow myself so he could see what I meant. He couldn't help smirking and standing straighter, snapping his braces into place. But then he frowned again.

'But someone needs to announce each act properly,' he said.

'Exactly, sir!' I said triumphantly. 'Allow me to show you who I have in mind!'

I shook out my red garment and put it on. It made a fine riding coat. I had worked golden frogging across the chest. I tucked up my skirts until they were invisible. Mr Tanglefield gasped when I exposed my legs, but they were decently covered in Madame Adeline's white tights, which made them look very shapely. I stuck the black stovepipe hat on my head and stood with one hand on my hip, my chin in the air.

'Allow me to present my very own self. I am Emerald Star, ringmaster supreme,' I said. 'Once funds permit I will sport a proper top hat and riding boots. Meanwhile you will have to picture them in place. I shall present all your acts, Mr Tanglefield, in the following manner.'

I took a deep breath, filling my lungs. 'Ladies and gentlemen!' I bellowed, making Mr Tanglefield blink and step backwards. I had no need of his tinny loudhailer. My voice was loud enough to circle any tent. 'Ladies and gentlemen, girls and boys, little children and babes in arms – take heed! You are about to see sights that will dazzle your eyes and delight your hearts. Here is the amazing, magnificent and ultra-marvellous Tanglefield's

Travelling Circus, come trekking cross-country to perform twice daily in your very own village. May I present to you Mr Tanglefield himself, in the guise of an Indian sultan. Gaze at him in awe and wonder on his extraordinary exotic beast, Elijah the performing elephant. Wave your long trunk at all the children, Elijah – and they will give you a loud cheer.' I paused momentarily, and then continued, 'Oh, prepare to hold your sides and squeal with laughter at the comical antics of our two clowning gentlemen, Mr Chino and Mr Beppo. Better duck now, ladies and gentlemen in the front row. You're in danger of getting a bucket of water thrown all over you. Do you want to see Mama and Papa having a public wash, little children? Shout now if the answer's yes!'

I worked my way through every single act. I waxed particularly enthusiastic over our child acrobat, the tiny sparkly Diamond, little more than a baby, yet already the star of our show. I saved my greatest praise for Madame Adeline, the empress of the equine world, magnificent on her glossy stallion Midnight, here to delight you with her grace, her agility and her dancing.

Then I summoned all the acts to parade around the ring, instructing my imaginary audience to applaud until their palms stung. I led the clapping myself, stamping my feet too, while Mr

Tanglefield slumped back in his chair, his mouth open.

'There!' I said, twirling round. 'Do you see, Mr Tanglefield, sir?'

'Yes, I see,' he said, blinking as if dazzled. 'What did you say your name was, girl?'

'I am Emerald Star,' I said. 'A name you won't forget again.'

'That's true enough,' said Mr Tanglefield. 'Well, run along and let me prepare for tonight's performance.'

'What? But – but, sir, I entreat you, give me another chance. I know I can drum up trade for you and encourage the audience into fervent appreciation. My tongue is my circus skill and I will wag it for you tirelessly.'

'I can well believe it, Emerald Star. But keep it shut up in your mouth inside my wagon. I'm still reeling from the noise.'

'But won't you let me persuade you—'

'You've *already* persuaded me. You're hired.'

I stared at him, dazed.

'Ah, cat got your tongue at last!' he said, breaking into a wheezy little laugh. 'Report here first thing in the morning. We're travelling tomorrow. You can help break up the ring.'

'Yes, sir,' I said. Then, 'What about my wages?'

'Wages! You're just a child. You'll be getting free

board, and lodging too. I'll be acting like your parent,' he said. 'You don't pay your children.'

'I'm not a child any more, I'm fifteen – and I've already *got* a parent,' I said. 'I have a tall strong father who'd hate to see his daughter exploited. I'll be sewing for the company as well, remember. I want at least ten shillings a week.'

'Ten shillings! A chit of a girl like you is barely worth ten pennies.'

'Then I'll find another circus, sir, with an owner who'll appreciate my skills and pay accordingly,' I said, my head held high. I was taking an immense risk, but I wasn't going to be cheated out of a proper wage.

We argued – but Mr Tanglefield didn't tell me to be on my way. He grudgingly offered me five shillings. I poured scorn on that suggestion. I actually turned on my heel and opened the door of his wagon.

'Wait!' he said. 'Seven shillings and sixpence a week, and that's my final offer.'

'Accepted – for a three-month trial,' I said. 'And then I will claim my ten shillings, and you will happily pay me every penny because you will see I am worth it. Is it a deal, sir?' I stuck out my hand.

He stared at me. His arms stayed resolutely by his sides for at least a minute, while we both breathed heavily. Then, very slowly, his arm lifted and we shook hands.

'Where are you going to bed down?' he said. I wasn't sure I liked the way he was staring at my exposed legs. I untucked my skirts quickly. 'I've got the biggest wagon. I suppose you'd better bunk down in here with me.'

'Oh no, sir, that's definitely not part of the bargain,' I said quickly.

'I meant in your own bed, of course,' said Mr Tanglefield.

'Well, that's very kind of you, sir, but don't worry, I won't need to cramp you. I shall be sharing with Madame Adeline,' I said.

I got myself out of his wagon while the going was good and ran towards Madame Adeline's.

'Hey, girl, where are you going?' called mean Mister Beppo, doing his best to look menacing. 'No strangers allowed here.'

I saw Diamond's anxious face peeping out from under one of the wagons.

'I'm not a stranger here, Mr Beppo, sir. I'm the new star act,' I said. 'Just ask Mr Tanglefield if you don't believe me.'

He stared at me while I swept him a bow, flourishing my stovepipe hat. His face creased in contempt, but he didn't say another word. I heard Diamond gasp and giggle beneath the wagon, but I didn't react to her because I didn't want her hateful Mister to discover her favourite hiding place. I was going to look after Diamond properly when I was part of this circus. Mr Beppo beware: I was going to be like a second mother to her.

I rushed up to the green wagon and tapped on Madame Adeline's door. 'It's me, Hetty, your Little Star. Guess what, I'm going to be a *big* star now, really, truly!' I declared.

For a full five minutes dear Madame Adeline thought it was all just fancy. I had to demonstrate my skills as a little ringmaster before she truly believed me – but then she threw her arms round me and hugged me close. I think she wept a little, because my cheeks grew wet, yet I knew I wasn't crying.

'Mr Tanglefield even offered me a bed in his wagon!' I said.

'No, you absolutely mustn't do that!' Madame Adeline gasped.

'Of course not. I want to share *your* wagon, if that's all right with you. I can make do with a little mattress on the floor and I'll hide it away neatly in the morning. I'll keep everything truly spick and span, and I'll buy all the food out of my new wages and do all the cooking. I'm very practised at soups and stews, and given an oven I can make an excellent apple pie.'

'Oh, Hetty, of *course* you can share with me. It will be my total pleasure,' said Madame Adeline. 'But I still feel you're making a very reckless decision. You know the circus can be a harsh and ugly place. The men are hard and often brutal. The women are sometimes treated badly. Folk might flock to see us and gawp, but they look down on us too.'

'I'm used to that! Try being a foundling child.'

'But you're not a child now, you're a young woman. You need protecting from all those stares and sniggers,' said Madame Adeline.

'If I can survive the stares and sniggers at Mr Clarendon's Seaside Curiosities, I can take a few country whispers,' I said determinedly. 'And if I am the new ringmaster I shall get myself a whip. They'll see I can take care of myself. And I shall take care of you, Madame Adeline, and little Diamond too.'

'That will be wonderful, Hetty – but what about the people you care for now? Won't they miss you terribly?'

'They will want me to be happy,' I said, though my stomach clenched. 'I must go and say my goodbyes.'

I felt sick at heart as I walked back to the village. I went to the Maples' house first. Janet was home from school, and greeted me warmly.

'You look very flushed, Hetty! Have you been to the circus again?' she asked, smiling at me.

'Yes I have,' I said.

'You are so sweet. I think you like it even more than the children,' said Janet. 'Oh, they have talked of nothing else. They play at being clowns or try to turn somersaults like that scrap of a child – and you should see their chalk portraits of the elephant!'

'Janet – Janet, I have to tell you something,' I said softly, scarcely able to speak.

She looked at me anxiously, seeing I was very serious. 'Hetty? Come up to my room. We'll talk there,' she said.

She led me up to her neat little room. I saw her green and white checked notebook on her bedside table and glanced away guiltily.

'I still keep my journal every day,' said Janet. 'Though try as I might, each day is pretty much the same as the one before.'

'That's true. But – but *my* journal will be different, because . . . Oh, Janet, I'm leaving,' I said.

She stared at me, clearly perplexed. 'Leaving? You're going back to your father after all?'

'No, I'm going to join the circus.'

Janet stared at me. She could not have looked more astonished if I'd said I was off to join the

Foreign Legion. 'You are joking, aren't you?' she said.

'No, I am very serious. I am leaving in the morning. Don't look at me like that, Janet. I know it might seem a very foolish thing to do—'

'Yes, it is!'

'But it's what's I *want*. I know the circus life is hard, but I still want to be part of it. I am going to be the ringmaster! Do you want to hear what I'll be like? Ladies and gentleman, boys and girls, little children, babes in arms—'

But she wasn't listening. Tears were running down her cheeks.

'Why are you crying, Janet?' I asked, perplexed.

'Because this is terrible news!' she sobbed.

'Oh, Janet, don't cry! You've been such a dear friend to me. I will miss you so,' I said, putting my arms around her.

'But what about your family?' she said.

I swallowed hard. 'I feel bad about leaving poor Mother, but Gideon is so gentle and good with her she doesn't really need me any more – and I dare say Molly will come calling every day too.'

'What about *Jem*?' said Janet. 'What does he say?'

'I – I haven't told him yet,' I said. 'I dare say it will come as a shock to him, though he knows just how much the circus means to me. I know he will miss me a little at first—'

'Hetty, you're not a fool. You know it will break his heart,' said Janet.

'Oh don't, please. All right, he will be very unhappy at first, but he will eventually forget all about me. You will be his kind friend and eventually he will realize you are worth ten of me.'

'I think I know Jem better than you do, Hetty. You are the only girl for him. Oh please stay, for his sake,' Janet begged.

I marvelled at her unselfishness. This was her chance to claim Jem for herself, but she was only concerned for him.

'I think if I stay I might only hurt him more,' I said. 'I love him so much, Janet, but not in the way he wants.'

'Then you must tell him,' she said. 'Don't think you can run off and just leave him a letter.'

I flushed. I had thought of doing just that, and had hoped that Janet herself might even help break the news to him.

'I'm not sure I *can* tell him,' I said, hiding my face on her shoulder.

She shook me off and made me look at her. 'You're many things, Hetty Feather, but you're not a coward. You have to tell Jem to his face. You surely owe him that,' she said steadfastly.

I knew she was right. I kissed her, and then went on my way home. I had left a good thick stew bubbling on the stove. I started serving it as Jem came through the door.

'My, that smells so good!' he said. 'You're an excellent little cook, Hetty. What would we do without you?'

'Oh, I am sure you would manage splendidly,' I said, trying not to panic. 'Gideon can cook much better than me, we all know that.'

Gideon looked at me. 'Yes, I like to cook,' he said, trying hard to help me.

'I know you do, Gideon, and you're brilliant at it,' said Jem warmly. 'But you're a young man – and try as you might, you can't quite manage that woman's touch. Look at the way Hetty serves each meal. It's a work of art in itself.'

'Oh, any fool can play around with a bit of food and make a picture,' I said quickly, serving the meal, my hands shaking. It was rabbit with onions, parsnips, potatoes and carrots, sprinkled with a handful of Mrs Maple's herbs. I'm sure it really *was* tasty, but I felt as if I were munching rat and toadstools. I could only get one mouthful down and even then I had to force myself to swallow.

'No appetite, Hetty?' said Jem, ever watchful of me.

'I ate at Janet's house,' I lied.

'It's good that you two have become such firm friends,' said Jem.

'Janet is the sweetest girl in the world,' I said.

'No, she isn't!' said Jem, laughing. 'That title's already taken – by you, Miss Hetty Feather. And as a reward for winning the aforesaid title on a daily basis, would you like me to take you to your wretched circus just one more time? I hear they're leaving tomorrow.'

'I – I don't think so. Not tonight,' I said.

I was very conscious of Gideon's one eye staring at me. Mother was peering at me intently too. It was hard to tell what she was thinking, because her face was always strangely immobile now, but I didn't care for the look in her eyes.

I couldn't blurt it out in front of them – for Jem's sake, if not for mine.

'Shall we go for a little walk after supper?' I said to him. 'It's a lovely evening.'

'Why, Hetty, yes!' he said.

He sounded so eager that I felt worse than ever. He even went to smarten himself up, coming back downstairs wearing his Sunday best and his red worsted waistcoat.

'Oh, Jem,' I said, nearly in tears.

'I've got to look my best when I go out walking with my girl,' he said. He took my hand and we left the cottage. 'Which way, Hetty?'

'Let's go to our squirrel tree,' I mumbled.

We walked silently to the woods. I knew Jem was

looking at my face, trying to gauge my mood. I couldn't make myself look up at him. We threaded our way through the trees, still hand in hand.

'We're like those children in the fairy tale. Was it *Hansel and Gretel*? Shall we lie down and cover ourselves with leaves?' said Jem, making an effort to be fanciful because he thought it would please me.

'It would be a bit muddy, I think,' I said, walking with care along the track, my boots slipping.

'Here, let me carry you over this bit,' said Jem, picking me up before I could protest.

'No, no, Jem, I'm fine,' I said.

'I can't have my girl getting her shoes and stockings all messed up. Oh my goodness, you're as light as a feather. My Hetty Feather. Hetty Feather, Hetty Feather, Hetty Feather.'

'Oh, Jem, do stop it. I've grown to detest my silly name,' I said.

'One day you might have a different name,' said Jem, galloping on through the wood until we got to the squirrel tree.

'I have different names already. I am Sapphire Battersea and Emerald Star,' I said.

'I mean a different *real* name,' said Jem, lifting me into the tree and climbing up beside me. 'I hope that one day you will be Hetty Cotton.'

'Oh, Jem,' I whispered, ducking my head. 'Please don't say any more.'

'It's all right, Hetty. Don't be worried. I'm not going to press you any further just now. You're far too young. But we both know we've had an understanding for the last ten years—'

'We played at being married when I was *five*, Jem. It was only a child's game.'

'I think we both meant those vows even then,' he said.

'Yes, but I didn't *understand*. I loved you so much – I still love you dearly – but, Jem, you are my *brother*.'

'I'm not a blood brother. We are not related in any way, Hetty. We were simply brought up together for a few years. It is perfectly right and respectable for us to marry one day.' Jem blushed a little. 'I asked the parson privately and he reassured me on that point.'

'I know you're not my blood brother, Jem, but I love you as if you were my brother. I can't love you as a sweetheart.' It felt so terrible saying it. I hardly dared look at his face.

'It's because you're still too young, Hetty,' he said.

'No, it's not. It's the way I feel, and I don't think I can ever change.'

Jem took hold of me, pulling me closer by the elbows. 'I shall *make* you change,' he said.

'You can't make me, Jem.'

He let me go then. 'That's true. No one can make you do anything, Hetty,' he said wretchedly. He swallowed. 'Is there some other sweetheart you've not told me about?'

'No, no, no one,' I said, though I thought guiltily of Bertie. But we had only been friends, not proper sweethearts, and anyway, that seemed so long ago. I would probably never see Bertie ever again.

'You've not fallen in love with anyone at the circus?' said Jem.

'*No!* But – oh, Jem, please don't be angry, don't mind too much, but I am going away with them tomorrow,' I blurted out.

'What? Are you *mad*, Hetty?'

'I think perhaps I am. I know I'm doing a truly crazy thing, but I can't help it. I have to go with them.'

'But they're dreadful folk, vulgar and rough.'

'They're not all like that. Madame Adeline's a true lady,' I said fiercely.

'Hetty, have you *looked* at her? She's a sad old woman with a painted face, still brazen enough to show her legs to everyone who wants to pay their sixpence.'

'Don't you *dare* talk about her like that! She's like a mother to me,' I said, hitting him hard in the chest.

'You're thinking of leaving your own poor

415

afflicted mother for that painted charlatan?' said Jem.

'Mother will be happy with Gideon, Jem, you know that.'

'And what about me?' he said bitterly.

'Oh, Jem, I don't want to leave you, of course I don't. I shall miss you terribly. Maybe you can come and see me perform . . . I am going to be a young ringmaster in a red coat. In many ways it is the star part of the circus show! Please can't you be just a little bit happy for me? You *know* how much the circus means to me. It was *you* who took me there when I was five.'

'And I wish to God I hadn't,' said Jem. 'You're completely crazy, Hetty. You're besotted with this dreadful woman and yet you don't even know her! You saw her once when you were five years old!'

'I met her again when I was ten and I begged her to let me travel with her then. I *have* to go, Jem. I feel it is my destiny.'

'I thought *I* was your destiny,' he said. 'Didn't we always plan to live together? It's all I've ever wanted. I thought it was what you wanted as well.'

'I thought so too, but it's not meant to be, Jem. If I go away, you'll realize who your true love really is. Everyone else knows but you! You'll be so happy once you forget all about me.'

'I shall never forget you, Hetty. You are my

whole life,' said Jem, and then he turned away from me, and started sobbing.

'Don't, Jem, please don't!' I begged. 'I can't bear it when you cry. All right, I won't go, not if it hurts you so terribly.'

I put my arms right round him and held him close. I stroked his thick hair and his sunburned neck and murmured little words of comfort. I tried to wipe the tears from his eyes with my fingers. I kissed his forehead and his wet cheeks – and then I was kissing his mouth. He kissed me back, clinging to me. I couldn't help pulling away instinctively. We both broke apart.

'It's all right, Hetty. You *can't* make yourself care for me the way I want,' said Jem. 'I'm not going to try to keep you here. You'll only grow to hate me.'

'I'll never hate you, Jem. I love you more than anyone else anywhere, even my own father – but do you mean it? You'll let me go?'

He nodded and I hugged him close again.

'You promise you will write regularly this time?' he said.

'Yes, yes!'

'And you will stay away from all those rough men – and all the lads who will flock to see you? You will stay a good girl?'

'I shall act like a little nun, Jem, I promise.

Madame Adeline will look after me, and I will look after her, and little Diamond too.'

'And if you're at all unhappy you will come running back home to me, do you promise?' said Jem.

'I promise,' I said.

We climbed down out of our tree and walked slowly back through the woods, still hand in hand. I looked at all the cottages, softened in the milky moonlight, and wondered if I was a fool to run from the only real home I'd ever known.

I went to bed wondering if I might really stay after all. I lay wide awake in my childhood bed, my whole life flickering before my eyes. I had been so carefree and happy here in the country as a little girl. I thought of my bleak hospital life, my servant cot, the seaside boarding house, Father's cold cottage – none had been true homes for me.

'What am I to do, Mama?' I whispered into the darkness.

You must follow your heart, Hetty.

I heard her voice so clearly, as if she were whispering in my ear. I lay very still, fancying Mama curled beside me on the bed, her arm round me protectively.

When the first silvery grey light shone through the thin curtains, I got up very quietly and gathered my things together – my makeshift ringmaster outfit, my few clothes, Lizzie's warm shawl, my little fairground dog, Mama's brush and comb and violet vase, my fairy tales and *David Copperfield*. I wore my silver sixpence round my neck. I sat flicking through my memoir books, wondering if there were any point in taking them too. I decided I couldn't relinquish them. I wrote *Hetty Feather* on the first, *Sapphire Battersea* on the second, and *Emerald Star* on the third. I packed them away carefully, wondering if they might ever be properly published. Then I did up the clasp of my case, and hauled it out of the room.

I kissed Mother goodbye and she stirred a little, but didn't wake. I left both my dear brothers alone because I'd already said my goodbyes. I crept down the little staircase and paused at the picture of the two children in nightgowns with their tall white guardian angel spreading his wings over them. Well, I had Mama as my guardian angel now.

I unlatched the door and stepped out into the dawn. My case was weighed down with my note-books, but I walked quickly and steadily towards the meadows, ready to start my new life.

Reading Notes for the
HETTY FEATHER series:

1. The Foundling Hospital was a real place for orphans and abandoned children in the nineteenth century. How different would Hetty's life have been if she had been born in the twenty-first century? Think about what has changed since then. Here are some key words to start you off:

MONEY SERVANTS ILLNESS CIRCUS
EDUCATION GIRLS MARRIAGE PARENTS

2. What are the key things that make Hetty's life so very different to yours? Are there any aspects of Victorian life that you wish were part of your own?

3. During the Victorian era, very different things were expected of boys and girls. Is Hetty's life more difficult because she is a girl? Compare Hetty's experiences with Gideon's.

4. As a foundling with no money of her own, Hetty has to find work as a servant to survive. Do you think the idea of people having servants is ever fair, both in Victorian times and today? If Mr Buchanan had been a kind and generous employer in SAPPHIRE BATTERSEA, might Hetty have stayed there?

5. Hetty narrates all three books, so we always see events through her eyes, and hear her side of the story! Is she a fair narrator? How do her emotions and moods influence the story? Do you think she always does the right thing, or would you have ever behaved differently?

6. In EMERALD STAR, Hetty finds her real father. Do you think Bobbie lived up to her expectations? Would he have made a good parent to Hetty?

7. Bobbie's wife Katherine is upset and angry that her husband has another daughter, and is rather unwelcoming towards Hetty. Do you think her reaction is fair? Imagine you discovered that you had a long-lost brother or sister. How would you feel?

8. In HETTY FEATHER, Madame Adeline is described as being very young and beautiful. Several years later, when Hetty meets her again, she is described quite differently. Compare the two descriptions. Why do you think this is? Think about how much older Hetty is in EMERALD STAR.

9. In EMERALD STAR, Hetty must choose her future, and is faced with several different paths: life with her father in Monksby, marriage to Jem, or a future with Madame Adeline at the circus. What did you think of her final choice?

10. Writing has been an important part of Hetty's life throughout the series. At the end of EMERALD STAR, is she still determined to be a writer? Do you think joining the circus will affect Hetty's writing dreams?